"If thou gaze long into an abyss, the abyss will also gaze into thee."
—*Nietzsche*

"Abyss: The primeval chaos. The bottomless pit; hell. An unfathomable or immeasurable depth or void."
—*The American Heritage Dictionary*

ABYSS

You're holding in your hands one of the first in a new line of books of dark fiction, called Abyss. Abyss is horror unlike anything you've ever read before. It's not about haunted houses or evil children or ancient Indian burial grounds. We've all read those books, and we all know their plots by heart.

Abyss is for the seeker of truth, no matter how disturbing or twisted it may be. It's about people, and the darkness we all carry within us. Abyss is the new horror from the dark frontier. And in that place, where we come face-to-face with terror, what we find is ourselves. The darkness illuminates us, revealing our flaws, our secret fears, our desires and ambitions longing to break free. And we never see ourselves or our world in the same way again.

QUANTITY SALES

Most Dell books are available at special quantity discounts when purchased in bulk by corporations, organizations, or groups. Special imprints, messages, and excerpts can be produced to meet your needs. For more information, write to: Dell Publishing, 666 Fifth Avenue, New York, NY 10103. Attention: Director, Diversified Sales.

Please specify how you intend to use the books (e.g., promotion, resale, etc.).

INDIVIDUAL SALES

Are there any Dell books you want but cannot find in your local stores? If so, you can order them directly from us. You can get any Dell book currently in print. For a complete up-to-date listing of our books and information on how to order, write to: Dell Readers Service, Box DR, 666 Fifth Avenue, New York, NY 10103.

Obsessed

RICK R. REED

A DELL BOOK

Published by
Dell Publishing
a division of
Bantam Doubleday Dell Publishing Group, Inc.
666 Fifth Avenue
New York, New York 10103

ISBN: 0-440-20855-6

Printed in the United States of America

Published simultaneously in Canada

July 1991

10 9 8 7 6 5 4 3 2 1

RAD

For Milton White

1

Joe MacAree had just murdered a woman, and all the things he felt when he killed the other four he was feeling right now. How would he describe it? In his journal, he might call his feelings an "elevation of the senses" or "an ethereal quality bringing the world into sharp focus."

After each killing the reaction was the same. There was a moment of sharp pain right behind his left eye, an instant where the pain was so intense as to block out the act he had just committed, the blood and the ripped flesh . . . then a moment where brilliant flecks of silver light swam before him, and he could not keep his eyes from rolling, trying to follow the patterns the stars made.

And then the clarity.

As he guided his light blue Honda Accord along Harlem Avenue just south of Chicago, everything seemed more alive, as if to contrast the death he had just brought about. He noticed things he never noticed: the shifting red, amber, and turquoise of the reflections the stoplights made on the rain-slicked pavement. He noticed how the color spread, muted, over the slick black roadway. Even his radio, usually sounding tinny tuned to WLS, seemed more vibrant. He heard the different instruments in "Hungry Like the Wolf" as if Duran Duran were in the car with him, playing. Although it was February and his windows were rolled shut, he listened to the sounds of the other cars, the hiss of their tires on the pavement, the bass of their engines. He felt each perforation on the cover of the steering wheel. He thought he could even sense the mechanical smell of his own and the other cars as they all made their way northeast, to the Eisenhower Expressway and the city.

And in his mouth, he savored a slight metallic taste.

Randy Mazursky had lived in Berwyn all his life. The suburb just west of Chicago had been where his father grew up and where his grandfather had set up his home when he came over from Poland to work in the meat yards of Chicago.

Randy liked Berwyn. It was familiar: The streets, gridlike, had always made it easy to get around and easy to give new people directions to his house on Oak Park Avenue. And best of all it was close to where he worked, the North Riverside Mall, where he managed an ice cream parlor called Whipped Dream.

Tonight he had spent a little longer at the restaurant than usual, since one of his waitresses had come down with the flu that everyone (his wife, Maggie, included) seemed to be getting just as it looked like winter was about to come to a close. She had left midway through her shift, leaving a busy Friday night crowd of screaming kids, hassled parents, and birthday party victims.

Randy had donned the blue and white striped waiter's cap he had worn when he started at Whipped Dream three years ago and, like the trooper he thought himself, had gone out and served up Tin Roof sundaes, blown whistles, banged drums, and sung "Happy Birthday" with the rest of the crew. He knew it wouldn't hurt the "kids" to let a pro show them how it was done.

Randy had enjoyed the change. But it had been a long time since he had waited tables and he barely had the strength to hold the steering wheel properly. It was only ten minutes to his home and Maggie, but the eagerness to get there made the ride longer.

He knew he didn't have to worry. Maggie would have a great dinner waiting for him. Ever since Maggie had quit her job as a proofreader of Sears catalogs, she had become a virtuoso cook, even taking classes in Chicago. Randy had gained fifteen pounds.

He and Maggie had been married for only seven months and already she was pregnant. The baby was unplanned; they had wanted to wait until they had a chance to buy a house before they had children. Right now they rented the second floor of a two-flat.

But when Maggie had whispered "we're going to have a baby" in his ear right before he fell asleep one night, he felt nothing but delight. That delight and anticipation had not worn off in the two weeks he had been aware of his imminent fatherhood.

Now as he backed the car into a space in front of their yellow brick home, he felt a sudden urge to run up the stairs and hug Maggie. He knew she didn't like him working late and wished he had thought to bring her something.

Well, he could make it up to her in other ways. As he closed the door of his car he smiled: There was no trace of the exhaustion he had felt just moments before.

Quickly he unlocked the two locks on the outer door and took the steps two at a time. As quietly as he could, he slid the key into the door of their apartment, hoping he could surprise Maggie in the kitchen.

He opened the door and closed it behind him, trying to stifle the click of the door as it closed. Randy crept through the living room, not wondering why the apartment was so still, why their stereo, Maggie's constant companion, wasn't on. He noticed only the yellow block of light that was the entrance to the kitchen as he made his way toward it on tiptoe.

As he stood in the archway, he began laughing. And the laughter did not stop until almost an hour later when paramedics put him under sedation.

Maggie, her dark hair a bizarre contrast to the pasty white of her usually dark Italian skin, lay dead in the middle of the kitchen floor, her throat and wrists cut. Her hair fanned out on the beige linoleum and her arms were out, almost as if she had been crucified.

The cat, Scruggums, sat beside her, licking his paws.

From the *Chicago Tribune,*
February 18, 1989,
page seven:

Murder has come to west suburban Berwyn once again. Margaret Mazursky, 23, was discovered early last night by her husband Randolph in their second-story home at 2511 S. Oak Park Avenue.

The victim's death was attributed to massive loss of blood from stab wounds in the wrists and throat, Cook County coroner Michael Senn told officials.

Little blood was found at the scene of the crime, a Berwyn police official commented. Trace elements were found in cracks in the linoleum floor of the kitchen, where Mazursky's husband discovered her body. Otherwise, according to officials, as much as a quart of blood was removed by her attacker.

Joe MacAree placed the newspaper on the oak desk in his home office and looked down at it lying on the green blotter. He was grinning. Page seven. Surely, he thought, if they had known about the others, the story might have been front-page news.

He leaned back in his leather desk chair, listening to its squeak, and placed his hands on the back of his head. The others. He remembered the first.

You always remember your first. First kiss. First fuck. First murder and taste of blood. The other firsts never had the kick of the last.

He had never known her name. He remembered the night, deep in the middle of August when Chicago sweltered amid ninety percent humidity and daily temperatures as high as ninety-eight degrees.

Two years ago. He had left his wife sitting in front of a fan in their Sheridan Road apartment, a sweating glass of iced tea in her long, delicate hand.

Everything, in minute detail, was clear about that night. Anne sat in front of rotating fan blades, wearing a pair of faded cutoffs, her long black hair pulled to the nape of her neck.

He explained he had to go out . . . get some air. His clothes stuck to him all over and he felt like he couldn't breathe. Maybe near the lake there would be a little breeze, at least some air. Anne had been too wilted by the heat and humidity to protest. She asked him to turn up the Vivaldi on his way out. He closed the door quickly behind him, the volume of the music making his temples throb.

He had made his way down Sheridan, not noticing the heavy traffic. The air was still, not a leaf stirred. No one was out.

There was a large beach at Ardmore Street, and it was here that Joe ended up. He walked slowly along the low concrete wall that bordered the beach, looking for a place dark and cool to sit.

He reached a turn in the wall and seated himself on a bench overlooking Lake Michigan. A maple hung over the bench and the leaves whispered in the darkness. Joe listened to the rhythmic pound of the lake against the beach, observed the full orange moon above, its brightness obscured by a mist that hung over it like a caul. He remembered his grandmother telling him when the moon looked like that it was going to rain soon. Joe hoped so.

Joe was just beginning to realize his walk wasn't going to offer him much consolation when she walked by.

He knew she didn't see him sitting in the darkness. Without yet knowing why, he stood and moved under the tree, standing rigid, his back pressed against the bark.

She was young. Straight blond hair, blunt cut at the shoulders, tall, perhaps a little too tall for most men, but Joe was a big man, six four.

She approached. She was wearing a white bikini bathing suit top and white linen shorts. Even in the darkness Joe could see the contrast of her tan skin against the white.

Joe felt his penis begin to stiffen. And he was filled with a strange longing . . . not yet knowing what he wanted.

Suddenly she veered to the left and began padding through the sand, making her way to the water's edge.

He observed silently, saw her look around, making sure no one was watching. It seemed for an instant that she was staring right at him, but then her gaze moved on. Even from his distance Joe was certain she hadn't seen him.

She undid the halter tie at the back of her bathing suit top and threw it on the sand. She slid out of the shorts and stood naked on the beach. The moonlight gave her body an opalescence, a silvery shimmering. Joe traced the outlines of her bikini on her nude figure.

She ran into the waves. Waist deep, she put her arms above her head and dove. When she surfaced moments later she shook the water from her hair and began a slow side stroke deeper into the water.

Joe felt as if someone else was taking over. A part of him was screaming to go back even as he began striding across the sand. He dreaded and desired the woman . . . not even sure what he wanted. At the water's edge, he shucked off his pants and pulled his green T-shirt over his head. Here, the air felt cold against his naked body, drying his perspiration. He made a few strides into the water, letting it come up slowly around him. The water was surprisingly warm; even in August Lake Michigan was so cold it numbed.

He looked out at the girl. She was out far, treading water, her head turned from him.

Joe slid silently under the water and began swimming toward her. Every few seconds he would let his face emerge, gulp a few breaths, then slip back under, hoping she hadn't noticed.

Finally he saw her legs: perfectly shaped, long, moving back and forth. As he drew closer he made out the dark V of her pubic hair, the soft protrusion of her belly.

Joe needed air. This time there would be no way she wouldn't notice him. When he emerged from the water he saw her turn and gasp. Her eyes shimmered with fear.

Joe grinned.

She began to dog-paddle quickly away from him. Easily, he followed her movements.

"What do you want?" She stopped for a moment, and through her fear (Joe remembered this part best; it was his favorite) she gave this brave little smile.

It was then Joe made his move.

He dove and went straight for her legs. Wrapping his arms around her thighs, he pulled her under. She kicked and squirmed, but Joe, whose arms were roped with good muscles from years of working out, found it easy to pull her under. Once he had her all the way under, he grabbed her hair and held her down while he rose to the surface. Gasping for air now, Joe held her down. She struggled for what seemed like five, ten minutes. Rationally, Joe knew it wasn't nearly that long.

Her struggling didn't ebb away by degrees. She stopped all at once. And Joe knew she was dead. He felt nothing, thought nothing. Only a crazy desire filled him as he began swimming back toward shore, pulling her with him.

The beach was deserted. He heard the drone of traffic on Lake Shore Drive, but that didn't worry him. He left her lying half in, half out of the water as he dried himself with her shorts and top. He amazed himself with his calm as he pulled his pants back on, slid the T-shirt down over his chest.

This was the best part: He dragged the girl into a copse of trees and there, with a brick, bashed her head in.

As he saw the dark blood his desire became clear. He bent to the wound and sucked up some of her sluggish blood.

His first . . . he drank only a little, although he wanted more. But a bicyclist had been coming along the concrete wall, and Joe crouched behind a bush until he was long past.

He bent once more, drinking. The blood was beginning to clot. He slid his fingers around his lips and face and then sucked the blood off his finger.

He felt his penis begin to throb and took it out, watching as his come arced out onto the grass.

Up until that point, he had never felt more alive. The night was filled with sound—night insects, horns, the lapping of the dark water at the shore—and with smells and sights.

His dark communion had given him the life he had stolen. He felt no guilt as he stood and began his walk back up Sheridan Road to Anne, whom he knew would be concerned.

2

Randy Mazursky could have been posing. He sat in the Berwyn police station, and even the most casual observer would have known at a glance that he was in agony, that he was the victim of a tragedy. In a gray room Randy sat on a worn oak chair, his head in his hands. His ash-blond hair looked dirty and tumbled over his forehead. The khaki slacks he wore looked almost as rumpled as his oversize tweed sport coat.

Randy's sobbing was soft, but had continuity.

Near Randy sat his parents. His father, a thin man dressed in denim coveralls and a blue shirt, studied his son with a dull expression, betraying no emotion. His hands were long, the fingers bone-thin, the palms flat. His hands trembled.

Randy's mother sat on the other side of her son. She had tied a purple nylon scarf over her gray hair and worn a deep-purple cardigan sweater over a yellow cotton shift. She held a balled-up Kleenex, wet with tears and mucus. Her eyes were rimmed in red. She seemed to be trying to abate her sorrow, to comfort her son.

"Oh, baby . . ." she whimpered, placing her hand on his arm. Randy raised his head. "We don't understand now. Maybe it's never for us to understand why Maggie was taken from us. But you gotta believe it's what the good Lord planned and one day . . ."

The woman's voice droned on; there was no indication on her son's face that he heard any of what she said. His eyes were vacant.

Randy Mazursky's mind was uncluttered. There was only one thought and that one thought repeated: a litany. *Maggie is dead. . . . Maggie is dead.* In spite of the repetition he was unable to make himself believe it. Surely Maggie would come into this barren room any second now explaining how it was all a mistake and wouldn't he come home now? Or she, along with his parents and the detectives he had spoken to, would all join in and laugh at the macabre joke they had played on him. She couldn't be dead. They were going to have a baby.

He scanned the room, seeing it for the first time. His parents stared at him, their eyes begging. What did they want from him?

"Son." His mother's voice was raspy. "Listen to me, we'll go see Father Frank. He'll still be up; let him talk to you." His mother stood and Randy noticed her knees were knocking. He started to laugh.

The pain was apparent on his mother's face.

"Please son. C'mon." She tugged at Randy's arm. He let her lift it and when she let go, the arm slumped back down to the arm of the chair, as if he were asleep.

His mother turned to his father. Her voice was tinged with bitterness. "Why don't you do something for the boy, Papa? Why do you sit there like that? Our boy needs help. For God's sake, help him."

The old man stared at his wife as if she were a stranger. After a time his mother slumped back into her seat and began weeping.

Randy's mind wandered back to his evening's work at the ice cream parlor. Maybe if he went back there and started over again, the evening would have a different outcome. He would go upstairs to the apartment and the radio would be on. The corridor would be filled with the smell of supper cooking. Maggie's footsteps on the kitchen linoleum. The small slap of the refrigerator door closing. He would place his key in the lock and all the muted sounds and smells would increase and he would know he was home. Maggie, wearing old jeans and a hooded red sweatshirt, would hurry in from the kitchen. Maybe he could go back.

Jarring: *Maggie is dead.* They were supposed to play volleyball the following night.

Randy stood and stretched. "I need to be by myself. I'm going to walk. Tell the detectives I'll be home in a couple hours."

His father nodded. His mother, panic already spreading over her features, said, "No, Randy. I don't think that's a good idea. You gotta stick around, in case they find out anything. You don't wanna be alone, huh? At a time like this . . . Let me take you to see Father Frank."

His father's voice cut into the room. "Let the boy alone, Theresa, please. If he wants to be alone, for Christ's sake, let him be."

Randy glanced at the family tableau as he left the room. His worn mother standing above his father, staring. Her mouth was open. His father once more bowed his head. And his hands . . . Randy noticed the trembling.

Pat Young had lived across from the two-flat at 2511 S. Oak Park Avenue for five years. She had watched the Mazurskys move in from the same window she watched from right now. She had been drawn to Randy's wiry good looks and made certain to position herself at the window when he went to and came home from work.

Pat had plenty of time to do her watching. An employee of U.S. Steel in Joliet, she had been injured when she had fallen from an overhead crane.

Everyone had told her how lucky she was. She didn't think a broken back and being confined to a wheelchair for the rest of her life was any kind of luck. But, she supposed, she *was* alive. And as long as she lived she would collect her disability checks from the mill. It was easy to get around her first-story studio, and when the soaps got too boring there was always her window.

Pat had been a studier of the neighbors' comings and goings for over a year now. And the

Mazurskys were by far the most interesting of her neighbors. They were so insufferably happy.

Pat took a certain glee in watching them. She wondered how two people could spend so much time together and remain happy. She decided it was all a facade; Pat watched with anticipation for the day when she would see some trouble. She wanted to see them as she knew they really were.

Today had held a special reward for all of Pat's efforts. She had just finished her lunch of a sandwich and an hour of *All My Children* when she glanced out the window and saw a not at all unattractive young man following Maggie Mazursky up the stairs. Pat knew, because it was early afternoon, Randy would not be home from work for hours. She had had only a glimpse of the man, but she was certain he was a real looker. She had managed to notice the broad shoulders and the powerful physique, the curly brown hair, and even the handsome mustached face in the few seconds she had seen him.

Pat giggled as she thought about what must have been going on in the Mazurskys' upstairs apartment. And she was determined to have another look at the man when he came out. Being crippled prevented a lot of things, but it didn't stop her from fiercely admiring the opposite sex. Her small apartment was crowded with issues of *Playgirl* and *Cosmopolitan*.

She had made sure to keep glancing toward the window as she watched *General Hospital*. In less than an hour the man emerged, and his behavior confirmed Pat's suspicions. There was a great energy to the way he walked; he practically glowed. She grabbed her binoculars from the table alongside the window and focused them. She had the man in a much closer perspective now. She was not disappointed; he was much better-looking than she had hoped . . . and he was smiling.

Pat sat back, a smirk of satisfaction on her pale face. So the Mazurskys, the "happy couple" on the block, were not as happy as they seemed. Perhaps Maggie was even happier. Why shouldn't she be? Pat would be, too, if she had two men who looked so good servicing her.

Bitterly, Pat thought perhaps she could have had the man who'd just left Maggie Mazursky. Could have had . . . once. Before the accident Pat had been twenty-three and the object of considerable lust among her coworkers. She had not minded the leers, the whispering when she walked by.

She no longer cared. Pat rarely left her apartment and her skin had taken on a whitish pallor; there was a dullness to her eyes, eyes that had once been green and vibrant. Her red hair, once long and wavy, was now cut by Pat herself. She snipped away in front of a mirror until all but a couple of inches clung close to her skull.

Who cared about looks anyway? There wasn't much a man could do with a cripple, right?

Later that evening Pat's glee turned to morbid fascination. Randy hadn't returned home from work at his usual time, and Pat laughed aloud at the thought that maybe he had something going as well.

She had forgotten the Mazurskys when she

heard the sirens. She clicked off the television and the table lamp by the window and wheeled herself close; her knees touched the wall. She watched, shrouded in darkness. Two heavyset men emerged from the building, carrying a stretcher. On the stretcher was a form covered by a white sheet. Pat swallowed hard as she saw Randy Mazursky, close to the stretcher, his tall body stooped. He was crying.

The red whirling light reflected off the pale brick of the Mazurskys' building. Pat watched as Randy climbed into the back of the ambulance with what must have been Maggie.

Pat felt a mixture of emotions, fear and curiosity the most prominent.

Pat wheeled herself away from the scene. It was time for *Jeopardy!*

Halfway into the show Pat heard a knock at her door. She was tempted not to answer, but the volume of the television was too loud and her lights too bright to ignore any visitor.

Wheeling herself to the door, Pat wondered who could be calling on her. As she opened the door she saw the familiar blue uniform of a Berwyn police officer. She took the young man in with a grin; he was good-looking: tall, broad-chested, slim-waisted, with brown eyes and black hair.

Pat took on an innocent expression. "Can I help you, officer? Is anything wrong?"

"I'm afraid so, ma'am. There's been a murder in the apartment building across the street. Margaret Mazursky. Did you know her? Know who she was?"

Pat smiled up at him. "I'm sorry . . . no . . . I don't get around much." She gestured at her legs.

The officer looked sympathetic. "Well, we're trying to get around to the neighborhood people, trying to see if they remember anything suspicious. Do you think you saw anyone leave the Mazurskys' apartment today? Did you maybe see someone in the neighborhood you haven't seen before?"

Pat shook her head. "No on both counts, officer. I saw nothing."

"Are you sure, now? Sometimes we see things and don't think anything of them. Maybe in a different light you'd remember."

"No, officer, I don't think so. You see, I haven't been feeling well lately. I was asleep most of the day. And I've pretty much been watching TV the rest of the time. I'm sorry . . . I didn't see a thing."

The policeman scribbled something in a notebook. "Could I have your name, please?"

"Pat Young."

"Thanks a lot, Ms. Young."

He turned to leave. Pat called after him, "Officer, is it going to be safe around here?"

"Well, we'll be having a lot more patrol cars in the area for a while. Try not to worry. We'll be watching. And keep your doors locked."

Pat closed the door. The TV volume seemed louder than she'd left it. She shut it off, annoyed with the electronic voices. "Shut up," she whispered to the TV. "I have my own reasons for doing what I do."

She conjured up an image: the handsome man stepping lightly from Maggie's apartment building. He glowed.

She must find out who he was. Then Pat would see who was glowing. The disability checks from the mill seemed to get smaller and smaller with inflation eating into them. A nice little supplement could help out a lot.

After all, he was dressed perfectly. Clothes like that didn't come from K mart.

Pat wondered about his relationship to Maggie. Had she known him? Why had she let him in?

She didn't know how, but Pat Young was determined to find out the handsome stranger's identity.

And when she did, well, good-bye Berwyn.

After hours of walking Berwyn's orderly streets, Randy found himself in front of the building he and Maggie lived in. There were still police vehicles parked in front, and as he looked up, he saw lights and silhouetted forms moving in front of the windows. Every so often he saw a flash from a camera. Evidence technicians. Would they find anything? Randy wondered how there could be any clues; Maggie had no enemies.

He no longer felt that the building was home—it could never be that without Maggie. He glanced up at the February sky: black, stars glittering, a three quarter moon shining, lighting the winter-dull street with silvery light. Somehow Randy felt the earth should look different, in deference to his loss. But the wind overhead, the bare branches stretching into the night, the sound of cars whizzing by en route to more orderly and untouched lives surrounded him. Didn't anyone care?

He glanced up at the windows once more. With the lights still burning, the apartment had the nerve to look warm, almost inviting. Randy rubbed his arms through the wool of his sport coat and realized he was cold. Even his own body betrayed his loss. He walked on, trying to get his blood to move once more, trying to ignore the cold.

When he came back an hour later the apartment was dark and the official vehicles were gone. The street looked normal once more, as if nothing had happened.

Randy felt in his pockets for the front door key. Inside, it would be warm. If he couldn't stand being in the apartment his mother would love it if he came home to her. Barring that, Chicago was filled with hotels, YMCAs.

Randy swallowed, took a breath, and made his way up the walk to the door. Barring all thought, he put one foot in front of the other going up the creaking, dark-stained wooden staircase.

Across their door was a sign that something had gone awry. A large yellow banner hung across it. CRIME SCENE—ONGOING INVESTIGATION. DO NOT ENTER. Randy thought the officers wouldn't mind if he went inside, and he slid his key into the lock.

As he opened the door Scruggums pounced for

his feet. Randy picked the cat up and sat down on the couch. The cat clawed at his tight embrace, but Randy needed something to hold on to.

The sobbing began. Dry and painful at first, Randy's mouth opened in silent anguish, his eyes wide, his shoulders shaking with the force of his grief. When the tears began, the cat jumped from his lap. She gave him one curious look before she disappeared under a ladder-back chair in the dining room.

Randy stood and made his way around the empty apartment, turning on every light. The apartment filled with light, hummed with electricity. Randy stood in the kitchen, taking large quivering breaths as he sought to end his tears. As much as he tried to take in the plain surroundings of the kitchen, all he could see was Maggie, lying sprawled on the floor, her dark hair fanned out behind her as if arranged, the slight protrusion of her stomach, the white tinge of her skin. Every detail stayed with him in vivid color; he would never forget.

He glanced around the room, trying to force himself to see it for what it was: a room. It held nothing. As he glanced around he saw a glimmer near the refrigerator. At first his eyes swept by, seeing only the chrome of the refrigerator's bottom. Quickly he realized there was more. He stepped to the refrigerator and knelt.

A silver lighter lay near the refrigerator. Randy grimaced as he picked it up, noticing that a dark brown blotch covered the lower portion of the lighter. The blotch had to be Maggie's blood.

Randy scraped some of it away and revealed the initials *J.D.M.* engraved in script.

Randy filled with anger and his tears returned. He fell forward on the floor, clutching the lighter tightly in his hand. "I swear by God," he whispered, "I'll get you, J.D.M. I'll get you if I have to die doing it."

Randy curled into a ball, holding the lighter close. Near him rested the chalk outline of his wife's body.

Randy knew he could not stay in the apartment. He dialed his parents and they offered to pick him up. He said he would rather walk, and they let him.

The lighter was in his pocket as he locked the door behind him.

3

Anne MacAree took off the black sable coat and handed it to the photographer's assistant. She glanced back at Louise, the photographer, who called after her, "Thanks so much, Anne. These are going to be terrific."

Anne had just finished shooting several ads for Evans Furs. They were having an end-of-winter sale, and the ads would be appearing in the *Tribune* toward the end of March.

The weariness overcame her as she sat in the cramped studio dressing room. As she tissued off her makeup she noticed how tired she looked, not a good sign for a professional. There were dark rings around her eyes that the makeup had buried. Her shoulder-length blunt-cut black hair didn't have the oriental sheen it usually did. Her eyes lacked something—vivacity.

She ran a brush through her hair and put all of

her things into a worn leather satchel, slung it over her shoulder, and left the studio. Outside she hailed a taxi and took it to Harry's on Rush Street. Maybe an afternoon Tanqueray would be just the thing to help her sleep. She had gone without the past two nights.

The bar was filling up with the afternoon happy-hour crowd. She got a small table to herself near the wall. Giving her drink order, she stared at the business-suited men and women, feeling only slightly out of place in her jeans, boots, and white cotton sweater.

The drink came and Anne, in her exhaustion, toned down the voices, filtered out the smoke, and sipped her drink, trying to quell the thoughts in her head.

For three months Anne had considered leaving Joe. It was not because she was being unfaithful, or wanted to, not because he was (as far as she knew), and not because he was neglectful or she was bored. Her reasons were more insubstantial. Things would have been much easier if there *were* another woman or man.

But the Joe MacAree she had married was not the Joe MacAree she lived with today. The change had been gradual; Anne could never pinpoint a time when the change had occurred.

Anne knew, though, that the change in her husband had gone beyond a tolerable point. And she could pinpoint when he had passed the point of tolerability. Last night Joe had come home seeming filled with an inexplicable joy, so happy he was just about quivering with it. But when Anne, smiling, pressed him for an explanation, so she "could be happy too," he could do no better than reply he was just feeling good, "no special reason, Annie, darling." She had not known where he had spent the afternoon, since the desk in his office was clean and their answering service had given her a whole list of calls to be returned. When she asked him about this, he replied he had spent the entire day at the Lincoln Park Zoo. Anne had to laugh at that, but it was not a comfortable laugh.

Later, things turned dark. Joe's passion that night was unmatched by anything in their five years together. At first Anne had been flattered by his lust. But soon things shifted out of her control, away from anything she would have desired. He took her roughly again and again, until she cried out in pain. But her fists beating on his back and her cries went unheard or unacknowledged. Anne had been used the entire night.

She had decided the next morning she would leave him. He had gone for the day, this time on *real* business . . . seeing several of the clients he wrote ads for. Anne had seated herself in his office to write him a letter, not a good-bye letter but just one to let him know she was leaving for a while and she would be getting in touch soon.

As she looked through his desk for paper she found the shoebox. On top was a clipping from that morning's *Tribune.* It described the murder of a Berwyn woman. Anne was puzzled.

Below that were other clippings, all about murders of women in different areas in and around Chicago. A chill swept over her then: Who was this man she was living with?

Anne stuffed the clippings back in a drawer. She tried to ebb her fear: *It's nothing. Your husband, like the men who read those detective magazines, has a rather unusual preoccupation with murder. It's nothing. Even if it is unpleasant, it's probably completely normal. Primitive aggression in the urban male, something like that.*

She turned off the light in Joe's office and left quickly. She would ask him about the clippings later. Maybe she shouldn't leave him just yet. He might need her help. Maybe last night was an isolated incident. Surely every marriage has at least one episode like that.

Surely.

And where was he all day yesterday?

Anne drained the drink. She had spent the last night unable to sleep, unable to keep the clippings out of her mind. Joe slept soundly beside her, his presence an unwelcome warmth.

She had read until dawn.

Anne put a dollar down on the table and left the bar. Outside, a wet gray snow had begun to fall. Joe said he would have dinner waiting.

Joe had gone all day without missing the lighter. He had spent the morning with the Nature Snack people—owners of a chain of health food stores who would have worn gas masks if Joe had lit up a cigarette.

Now at home, Joe put his portfolio and briefcase away in the closet of his office. He switched on the green and brass desk lamp and sat back in his leather desk chair, allowing himself a few minutes to relax before starting to plan the newspaper ads that Nature Snack wanted him to do. He reached into his pocket for the box of Marlboros that had been burning against his chest all morning, shook one out of the pack, and dug deep in his sport coat pocket for the silver lighter Anne had just given him the previous Christmas. With a mildly bothered expression Joe pulled his hand from his right pocket and reached into his left. No lighter. Joe checked his pants pockets. Both of them. Empty.

Beginning to feel a slight panic he would not acknowledge, Joe rose and went to the office closet where his Burberry overcoat hung. All pockets were empty. Faster now, Joe began going through each desk drawer with empty-handed results.

Joe sat for a moment. His breathing was fast; his blood pounded in his ears. Even though the office was a sunroom conversion and even though all that glass kept the room especially cool throughout the winter, Joe felt beads of perspiration breaking out on his forehead. Calm down, he told himself, you could have lost the lighter anywhere, anywhere at all. It could have fallen out of your coat pocket when you were at the Nature Snack offices. You might have dropped it somewhere right here in the apartment. . . .

Joe was on his knees, scanning every nap of their champagne-colored carpeting, praying for a glint of silver. He checked the nightstand next to their bed. Nothing. He opened and closed every drawer and cupboard in their high-tech black, red, and chrome kitchen. Nothing. Anne's pockets, purses. Nothing. In the bathroom. Nothing.

Joe returned to his office and sat down, trying to calm his pounding heart. He told himself it fell out on the street; the lighter lay at this very moment underneath the coatrack in the Nature Snack offices.

In spite of all his assurances he knew where the lighter was. It was in Berwyn, in the apartment of Maggie Mazursky, the late Maggie Mazursky. His lighter . . . with his initials. Damn! He slammed his fist down on the green blotter. He had always been so careful never to leave a clue to his identity. And now the police would find a one-hundred-fifty-dollar sterling silver lighter that could easily be traced to the Michigan Avenue store where Anne had purchased it two months before and had made sure to have his initials plainly engraved on the face.

Joe went to the window and stared out at the traffic on Lake Shore Drive. Beyond the orderly lines of cars lay the lake. Today its waters were gray and churning, pounding against the beach with fury. Anguished and uselessly eroding, the waves rose higher against the pearl gray sky. Joe forced himself to concentrate on the water. Forced himself to trace the rise of a wave from far out on the dark water and follow its progress to the shore.

The mental calming would not work. Joe looked down at his sweat-slicked palms, his shaking hands. What would Anne think when she came home? How could he explain such anxiety?

Joe crossed to the tiny bathroom he had off his

office. Inside the medicine cabinet Joe found an old bottle of Valium, prescribed to Anne years ago when she had lost their first and only child to labor complications. He gulped down the small yellow pill without water or thought and returned to his office. Sitting down at his desk, Joe forced himself to close his eyes and wait for the drug to take effect.

After a while the sweating stopped and Joe regained control over his shaking hands. He walked once more to the window, stared out.

"I've got to get that lighter back . . . and soon."

Joe had just put the fettucine in the boiling water when he heard Anne's key in the lock. He decided he had better work on the cream sauce for the Alfredo rather than run to greet her at the door. Things had not gone well with them since he had let himself get out of hand in bed the previous night. Joe thought he would have to keep the sustenance he got from his victims in check or Anne would grow suspicious.

"Something smells good," Anne said without much enthusiasm.

Joe turned from the stove and smiled at her. She did not meet his eyes. Sitting down at the small red lacquered table, she began leafing through the stack of mail that had come that day, all the while wondering how she would confront him with her questions on the clippings she had found in his drawer. Maybe now isn't the right time, she thought, maybe never. It would only embarrass him. Perhaps it's nothing.

"How'd it go today?"

She finally looked up and met his eyes. He was smiling, with an eager-to-please expression. His brown eyes seemed so alert, his smile so genuine that Anne was unable to believe there was anything wrong between them.

Her first impulse had been to reply that things could have gone better had she had a little sleep the past two nights. But why chafe against him? Surely things weren't going to get better if she resisted his efforts at friendliness.

"Things went . . . very well. They always do with Louise. She makes me feel more comfortable, less afraid to experiment."

Joe waved his hand. "Ah . . . with your looks it really doesn't matter who's behind the camera."

"*Please.*" Anne laughed and got up from the table. "How soon till dinner? I'd like to take a quick shower. Do I have time?"

"Go ahead." Joe went over to the red sink, straining the noodles, his face obscured by clouds of steam.

As Anne walked by Joe's office she noticed the door ajar. Glancing in, she was stunned to see the usually orderly room looking as if it had been ransacked. The desk drawers were pulled open, Joe's overcoat was in a heap on the floor, and his sport coat was flung across his leather chair.

Anne's fragile sense of well-being disappeared as quickly as it had come. What was he up to?

As she headed toward the shower she heard him in the kitchen, humming. Things weren't fitting together. How many people was she living with?

She knew she should find out, just come out and ask him. Wasn't that what they were always saying, "keep the lines of communication open"?

As the hot water hit her Anne thought, let's wait. There can be no harm in giving things a little time. A little time to restore equilibrium. No, there could be no harm in that at all.

Anne hoped.

The fettucine Alfredo was wonderful. And Joe prepared the veal simply, cooked in butter with a light flour coating. Joe even went out before dinner and bought a bottle of Liebfraumilch, Anne's favorite wine.

Shoveling the last forkful of fettucine into her mouth, Anne thought to herself, boy, the way to my heart is no secret. She sat back in her chair, the glass of wine in her hand, and looked across the table at Joe.

In the light from the burning-down candles his face had a radiance, a glow of innocence. The candle's flame brought out a tinge of color in his cheeks, and his eyes reflected the light. Anne wondered how she could have ever imagined leaving this beautiful man.

The two did not speak. The corners of Joe's mouth turned up in a smile as he raised his wineglass to her, and she returned the gesture. Anne thought one thing that was comfortable about their marriage was the silence.

Anne finished her glass of wine. After a time of sitting and looking at each other, Joe rose and blew out the candles. Now the room was lit only by the bright moon outside their floor-to-ceiling windows. The room was silvery. Joe crossed to Anne and, taking her hand, led her to the windows. He faced her toward the glass and draped his arm over her shoulders. Both stared out at the shimmering waters of Lake Michigan below them.

Slowly, Joe slid to his knees and encircled Anne's legs with his arms. He unfastened the buttons of her jeans and worked them down over her hips and further. She did not move except to lift her legs to get out of the jeans. Joe began kissing her ankles and worked upward until he was slowly licking the insides of her thighs.

Anne murmured and reached down to bury her fingers in his curly hair. His tongue went to the outside of her panties and he pressed his lips against the outline of her vulva. Soon her panties (pale blue) were wet enough from herself and Joe's actions that he could see the outline of her pubic hair through the satin. With one finger he pulled her panties aside and thrust his tongue deep inside her as she moaned, unsure of her ability to stand much longer. She hurried to get out of the panties to allow him to move more freely. Joe's tongue moved up and down her vulva with alternating soft and hard strokes, stopping every so often to press and swirl against her clitoris. Joe forced his tongue deep inside, tasting her.

When she came, she practically winced, one hand against the cold glass of the window, the other pulling at his curls.

"Please," she whispered, reaching down and placing her hands under his arms to pull him up. Once she saw that he was standing Anne pulled the white sweater over her head. Joe's hands immediately covered her breasts. Gently, she took them away, saying, "Wait; it's your turn."

She unbuttoned his shirt, kissing him after each button. When the shirt was off she removed his pants and underwear. She giggled, "Take off your socks." Then she slid down him, her body never losing contact.

In one swift movement she swallowed him and he cried out, his hands holding her head while he thrust into her mouth. She swirled her tongue around his cock, trying to meet his thrusts with her lips, her tongue.

All too soon, she could tell by the rapidness of his breathing, he was ready to come. She pulled quickly away from him, squeezing tight on his penis. "Not yet," she whispered and lay back on the carpeting.

He knelt between her raised knees, positioning himself. Then, supporting his weight with his arms, he entered her swiftly, burying his cock deep, then pulling out almost to the point where he was out of her, then plunging back in again.

It was over in minutes. They came together, each crying out into the silver darkness of the room, Anne digging her nails into his ass, contracted to shoot his come deep inside.

He lay on top of her for only a few moments, then he lifted her and carried her into the bedroom. Once under the maroon comforter they rested in each other's arms for no more than twenty minutes, then she climbed on top of him and they took their time.

After, nestled in the crook between his arm and chest, feeling the easy rise and fall of his breathing, Anne whispered, "What about the clippings?"

Because she was so near, she felt him tense, his breathing suspended for a moment. No, she thought, please, I didn't want to ruin this moment.

"What clippings?" he asked in a voice that showed his anxiety more clearly than if he hadn't tried to be casual.

Anne tried to laugh, make it seem as if they meant nothing to her as well, but already she was worried. "The ones in your desk. All those murders. Planning on writing a book?"

His breathing became easy once more. He laughed. "How did you know? That gory stuff fascinates me no end. I'm kind of embarrassed, but I think it would make great best-seller material. Don't you?"

And because she was a much better actor than he, she was able to look at him, smile and say, "Yes."

Soon she felt the regular breathing of his sleep. Her anger ebbed. Perhaps he was just using the murders as source material for a novel. Why else have the clippings?

Because she wanted to believe so much, she did.

* * *

When Joe was certain Anne was asleep he got up from the bed and went to his office. As soundlessly as possible, he closed the door behind him. He went to his chair, placed his face in his hands, and wept.

Why? he asked himself over and over. Why would he kill all those women? How could he and feel nothing? Now he was faced with Anne's knowing and he could not, would not, lose her love.

Nothing meant more to him.

After the sobbing subsided and he had blown his nose, Joe went to his desk and removed the shoe box he had put the clippings in. Stupid, he thought, stupid to leave these lying around. And as he began shredding them into his wastebasket, he swore to himself he would never be so stupid again.

Staring out the window, he swore he would never kill again. He could never replace the lives he had taken, but he would take no more. *And he would not be caught.* His mind flashed on the lighter. Stupid to have lost it, but he must get it back. How he would get it back was still open to a plan, but when was clear: tomorrow at the latest. He could not risk discovery. He would get his lighter back and that would be the end of it, never again.

He pulled the calendar on his desk over and circled the date he had killed Maggie Mazursky in red. The red would serve as a reminder. A hot touch to his pain . . . he must never forget. The pain would keep him away from the sickness and he would keep Anne. But the pain, yes, the pain, must always be kept fresh in his memory.

This last one was pregnant.

Tomorrow Joe would pay his second visit to Berwyn. He prayed he would think of a clever way to retrieve what was his. A clever way to save himself from the loss of all he held dear.

4

When Joe awakened the next morning the first thing he noticed was how bright the light filtering through their Levolor blinds was. He rose and walked to the window. Pulling the cord to glance outside, Joe was confronted with a world of blinding white. The sun sparkled down from a cloudless blue sky on at least four inches of snow. Normally Joe wouldn't have minded the sight, but thoughts of breaking and entering and retrieving a lost lighter sprang into his mind. He thought of icy roads and unexplainable car accidents in Berwyn. "What on earth were you doing in *Berwyn* of all places?" he could hear Anne asking. He thought of looking particularly conspicuous against a backdrop of white snow and brilliant sunlight. "Hey, mister, you wanna tell me what you think yer doin' nosin' around here?" he could hear a policeman asking. He thought of schools being out of ses-

sion, canceled due to the weather, the surround-
ing yards filled with children building snowmen
and having snowball battles. "Hey, there's some
guy standing outside the house where that lady
got killed! You think we should tell somebody?"
he could hear a snot-nosed boy asking.

He heard the rattle of a pan in the kitchen and
tensed. Anne was supposed to have an early
morning shoot; the modeling session had been
marked on her calendar: 8:30 A.M. He looked at
the digital clock on the nightstand next to their
bed; it was nine forty-five. Could someone have
broken in? Cautiously, Joe reached for his robe.
Then he heard Anne's voice clear and high on
"Take the A Train." What was she still doing
here? He had counted on her absence, counted
on not having to make up a story. The problem
with their closeness was that Anne knew his
schedule very well; she could have easily rattled
off the meetings he would have to attend for that
week. He knew she would be curious and he
hated lying to her. Somehow, breaching the hon-
esty they shared was unthinkable to him. Absurd,
he knew, in light of some of the acts he had committed during their marriage.

Joe slid into his robe and wandered out to the
kitchen. Smells of a country morning greeted
him: bacon frying, coffee percolating. The sound
of eggs sizzling in butter and the sight of the table, set with a crystal pitcher of orange juice and
a matching crystal bud vase with a white rose,
caused him for a moment to forget his mission.

Anne turned from the refrigerator, a bowl of
orange wedges in her hands. When she saw him

she smiled, lifting the bowl of oranges to him in greeting. "Guess what? The shoot for Marshall Fields has been postponed until next week. You're in luck . . . your free day doesn't have to be spent all by your lonesome."

Joe smiled at her. Think fast, he told himself; there was no time for hesitation.

"Everything looks great. But, honey—"

The disappointment on her face was swift. Joe felt a sickness in his stomach; he dreaded lying to her, felt certain the falsehood would show through on his face. "What is it? I checked your calendar. Joe, I had the whole day planned."

"Sorry, honey. Yesterday the Nature Snack people asked if I couldn't come in for a little while this morning. One of their buyers is going to be in from New York just for today. I couldn't say no." He added, "I just didn't have a chance to put it on my calendar."

He went to her and put his arms around her. "But it shouldn't take the whole day. And I still have time to do you the honor of eating this great breakfast."

"Thanks a lot," Anne said, disappointment plain. She smiled anyway.

Joe sat down at the table, and even though the feeling that there was a plate of worms before him persisted, he ate with obvious hunger. It was his best performance yet.

Anne finished her breakfast quietly, staring at the brilliant blue sky outside their kitchen window.

Joe took his plate, rinsed it, and put it in the dishwasher. He leaned down close to Anne and whispered, "Really, it won't take that long. I'll be back before you know it."

Anne said nothing, but crossed to the window and looked down at the drifting mounds of white that had fallen during the night. "We could have made angels."

Joe showered and dressed in jeans, a Ragg wool sweater, and hiking boots.

The plan came to him while he was in the shower. On his way to Berwyn he would make a quick stop at Sears and buy a khaki-green work shirt and matching pants. With his hiking boots and workman's outfit, Joe thought, he wouldn't make a half-bad meter reader. At least, he prayed, no one would question his entering the building. He decided he should buy a clipboard for good measure.

After parking his car in a high-rise parking garage downtown, Joe proceeded to Sears, and after a long look around on several floors (why did Anne's shoot have to be canceled? he lamented. I feel like I'm in some kind of loony *Beat the Clock*), he found the men's work clothes and bought his sizes without taking the time to try them on first. He hurried to the stationery department, got a clipboard, and hurried from the store, his parcels tucked under his arm.

Joe got into the back seat of his car and prayed no one would come by while he changed. Fortunately for him, he had parked on a high floor where there were cars all around, their owners otherwise occupied working in the Loop.

Joe managed to change, and even though the

pants were baggier than he would have liked, a quick look down at himself convinced him he made a fair meter reader.

Joe didn't want his car to be spotted in the Berwyn neighborhood once more, so he left it in the parking garage and headed for the subway. A combination of the Congress line, a bus, and his legs would carry him inconspicuously to Maggie Mazursky's home, which Joe prayed would be empty.

Pat Young had risen at 7:00 A.M., and even though the clock read only eleven-thirty the day stretched endlessly before her. Nothing was happening on the soaps, and the snow had canceled the local schools. She had heard the disgusting squeals of the little monsters outside, already more than she could bear.

She looked out the window. Oak Park Avenue looked the same as it always did. Boring. Row after row of brick two-flats. Unchanging.

Pat almost wished for another murder. At least it livened things up a little.

She groped for the remote control and upped the volume to drown out the voices of the children outside.

They were building snowmen, making angels.

"Attention, passengers. This delayed southbound train will make Austin the next stop. Austin will be the next stop. Other trains are following immediately behind."

Joe grimaced and looked down at his watch. Noon already. And he hadn't even gotten near

Berwyn yet. He grabbed onto the stainless steel pole in front of him and got off the train, along with a few grumbling passengers. He watched the subway train as it pulled away. It was now almost empty. Good work, CTA, he thought.

He looked around the station and saw he was at Clinton Street. At least the announcer on the train had said there were other trains immediately following.

Joe peered down the empty subway tunnel and wondered what "immediately" meant. He went over and took a seat.

Five minutes passed. Ten. No train.

After fifteen minutes Joe got up to look into the darkness of the subway tunnel. A cold wind blew, bringing up a scent of mildew. Otherwise, there was silence. The platform was getting crowded with people. Joe felt many of them were staring at him, staring at his clothes.

Paranoid.

Twenty minutes later a train arrived. Joe shut his eyes when he saw the passengers crammed against the doors. The train stopped. No one got off. Joe ran from car to car, trying to find an inch of room near the doors where he could squeeze on.

Maybe if he pushed a little. Joe tried to get his foot in the subway car. There was a chorus of groans, cries of "C'mon, man!" and "There'll be another train."

Reluctantly he stepped back. He looked behind the train and could see the headlights of another, waiting. Well, thank God for *that*.

The next train whizzed through the station, horn blaring, not stopping.

"Fu-uck," Joe whispered, and returned to his seat. The bench was full. Five minutes passed before another train came through. Joe saw right away it, too, was jammed, but like it or not they were going to make room for him.

The doors of the train opened right in front of where Joe was standing. Three teenage girls got out, giggling and looking him up and down. Later, girls, Joe thought, and hurried onto the train.

After a stop of University of Illinois–Chicago Circle, this train ran express to Cicero, which couldn't have suited Joe's needs more perfectly. He got off the train and made his way down the decaying, weed-covered Cicero Avenue to Roosevelt Road, noticing the abandoned warehouse of a place called Muldeen's. The whole area looked abandoned.

At the corner Joe caught a westbound bus he hoped would go as far as Oak Park Avenue.

The bus's run didn't extend that far. "Naturally," Joe whispered, and got off. The walk wouldn't be that long, he thought. Already it was one in the afternoon.

As he made his way south on Oak Park Avenue, Joe began to feel an aching nausea growing. This was crazy, he told himself, was this really worth the risk?

But it wasn't the worry of being caught that overcame him when he saw the yellow-brick two-flat in front of him. A memory of what had gone on upstairs flashed before him with all the clarity and definition of a movie, and Joe's erection was swift. Swift, too, was the revulsion that rose up in him. He covered his mouth with his hand, trying to stop the vomit that was forthcoming.

Joe ran between two of the closely spaced buildings and retched up the breakfast Anne had so carefully prepared for him.

He sat down for a moment on the cold concrete. He had never before returned to the scene of one of his crimes and was certain he couldn't bring himself to actually enter the Mazurskys' apartment and search, not with the vivid memory of that pregnant girl before him.

Another scenario: *"Chicago Police Department, ma'am. Is your husband in? We'd like to speak with him."* Joe peeks out from the living room and sees two middle-aged men wearing overcoats and hats.

"What is it?" Anne asks.

Joe sees a flash of silver. The lighter.

"Does this look familiar, ma'am?"

"Yes, I gave that to my husband for Christmas." Anne's voice is questioning. *"Why? What are you doing with it? Was it stolen or something?"*

"Really, Mrs. MacAree, hadn't we better talk to your husband? That's what we're here for. Please, ma'am, step aside."

Anne steps back from the doorway. Zoom into her face: the mixture of pain and confusion evident there.

Joe stands frozen as the detectives come closer. One holds a pair of handcuffs.

The dizziness ebbed and Joe stood, holding on to the brick wall for support. He had to get the lighter.

Suddenly he noticed the voices of children. They were all around. Snowball battles. Joe ducked as a snowball whizzed by him. He saw a laughing boy of about ten, his cheeks red from the cold, staring at him.

"Sorry, mister, I wasn't aimin' at you."

"That's okay," Joe said, and started down the street toward the Mazurskys' side door.

If it hadn't been for the damned snowball hitting her window and cracking the glass, Pat Young might never have seen him.

"Goddamn kids!" Pat shrieked. She switched off the TV and wheeled herself to the window, ready to throw it open and already practicing a few choice words for their innocent ears.

Hands on the windowsill, Pat stopped abruptly. She grew calm, her eyes narrowed. The man walking down the street (looking around him every few seconds) certainly looked familiar. Very.

A smile spread across her face. "Oh, baby," she said to herself, "what they say is true: They always return to the scene of the crime."

Pat laughed out loud. Laughed in spite of the cold air blowing in through her cracked window. Even laughed in spite of the pile of snow already rising on her windowsill.

She spoke to the handsome man. "Go ahead and take care of business, sweetheart. I can wait.

And then you and I, we'll take care of a little business of our own."

All these kids, Joe thought, I can't get in the house with all these kids around. Joe looked at them one more time. He had slowed down in front of the Mazurskys' place, but didn't dare stop. He kept walking, finally turning the corner at a cross street. He thought perhaps if he went in through the alley behind the house, he wouldn't be detected.

It took him a few moments to make sure he had the right building, and he hurried to the back entrance. He tried the door.

Of course. He cursed himself. Of course it's locked. He pulled hard on the door.

The woman's face jarred him. She was standing right next to him, smiling. Joe noticed the bright teal of her down coat.

"Meter reader," Joe blurted out, his face hot.

"Door used to be open."

"Huh?"

"The door," she said. "It used to be open before the murder."

Joe stiffened, his face seemed to be burning hotter with each passing moment. "What murder?" he asked in a voice much too soft.

"Maggie Mazursky, upstairs. It was in all the papers. Didn't you see it?" The woman eyed him.

"No, I must have missed that. Big news?"

"Well, around here it was."

Joe stared at the woman for a few minutes more, hoping she'd go away. When she didn't, Joe turned from her, saying, "I guess I'll have to come back another day." He started walking away.

"Hey!" the woman called, "ain't you gonna leave one of them tags?"

"What?" Joe stopped, hating the woman. What did it matter to her anyway?

"You know, one of them tags they put on the door when you ain't in."

"All out," Joe said, and kept walking. He could have kicked himself: The woman had had a good, long look at him. She would be able to identify him easily if it ever came to that.

Joe turned out of the alley and continued south on Oak Park Avenue.

Pat couldn't imagine what he was up to. She had seen him disappear into the alley, could even see him between the houses, talking to that busy-body Margaret Harris. But now he was leaving, and Pat was certain he had never gone inside.

What was the point then? What was the point?

Pat headed toward the closet to get her coat.

Joe walked three blocks and turned around. This time he would move quickly and without hesitation. He couldn't afford to arouse any more suspicions. It was already two o'clock and it would take him at least an hour to get home.

Anne would be disappointed. Perhaps she had even called the Nature Snack people.

Joe quickened his pace.

He stood at the back of the Mazurskys' apartment building. Looking around only once, he hurried to the back door and put his gloved fist through the glass. There was a moment when it seemed that all activity ceased, listening. But of course that was his imagination. Everything was quiet, but probably because the children had gotten too tired and too cold and had gone inside to watch the TV shows they missed while they were in school.

No one emerged to see what had been broken.

Joe reached inside and turned the door handle. He made his way up the back stairs. Surprisingly (and in spite of the crime-scene banner across the door), someone had not done his job. The door was not locked. Joe could even see the marks in the wood where he assumed the police had installed an additional lock. This was too easy, Joe thought, turning the knob and letting himself in.

The kitchen looked normal; that was what was so surprising to Joe. He didn't know how he expected it to look, but felt it should be changed. He remembered Maggie Mazursky, remembered the warmth of her body, the rich, hot, metallic taste of her blood.

"May I help you?" Her face seemed small, reddening from the chill wind.

"I'm with the Fuller Brush Company, ma'am. Before you say anything, let me say that I am positive that I have something here in my sample case that will make your life easier." He smiled and her face softened a little.

"I'm sorry, but I really don't need anything right now." She started to close the door.

He held out his palm to block the door. "Just a

*minute, please. It won't take ten minutes. I'll be in
and out."*

*The line of her mouth became more set. "I re-
ally think you'd be wasting your time. Bye."*

*He put on his most desperate face. "Please,
ma'am. I have a family. I need the money. Just
look." Pleading: "Okay?"*

*She hesitated, but said, "I really only have a
minute."*

*"Understood." Smiling, he followed her up the
stairs.*

All at once Joe was dizzy and he sat down on
the floor. For a time he could think of nothing
but her flesh and the taste of her hot blood as it
pumped slowly into his mouth. As much as logic
fought it, Joe found a furious desire welling up in
him. He wanted to do it again, and soon.

He must be more careful next time. No more
coming into women's homes. Get someone safe.
No one would miss a hooker, a runaway. Maybe
tomorrow; he was sure Anne was working.

But now he needed relief. He looked down at
the way the baggy work pants had tented out.

He heard the sound as he was unzipping his
pants.

Joe tensed. The sound of a key in a lock below
him was clear. He stood and moved quietly into
the living room, where he peered out from behind a sheer curtain at Oak Park Avenue. He rec-
ognized at once (and with horror) the brown
Chevette he knew belonged to Randy Mazursky.
(He remembered Maggie's look of embarrass-
ment when she explained their only car was a
brown Chevette.)

There was the sound of a footstep on a stair. Followed by another. And another.

Joe looked frantically around the room. Good God, what was he going to do? The man could be staying at home the rest of the day.

Give yourself up, he thought, have it over once and for all. An image of Anne, naked, flashed before his eyes. No.

Joe hurried into the bedroom and, with a total lack of imagination, slid under the bed. He felt safe there anyway, in the dark, among the dust balls. Maggie might have done a lot of things well, but she didn't clean thoroughly, Joe thought, and then chastised himself.

He heard the front door open. Randy Mazursky was now inside, and Joe could tell by the solitary footsteps he was alone. He seemed to be making a tour of the apartment.

Then Randy was in the room with him. Joe saw the worn leather of his cowboy boots. He was wearing jeans. A drawer opened. Joe watched as Randy slid a suitcase out from a closet and started throwing in sweaters, jeans, and underwear.

There was a pause. All Joe heard was the sound of his own breathing. Then something dropped to the floor. Joe positioned himself so he could see what it was. A teddy bear.

The bed creaked as Randy threw himself on it. And then Joe heard him weeping.

Never again, Joe thought. Please God, allow me to get away this one time and it will never happen again. The nausea Joe felt returned as he listened to Randy's sobs. The sob a man would let out only when he thought he was totally alone.

The crying went on, uncontrolled, for what must have been a half hour. Joe wondered if this was the first time Randy had really let himself go. By degrees the sobs quieted, ebbing away with small sighs.

The bed creaked again and Randy opened another drawer. A few more articles of clothing went into the bag. Joe watched the boots move in the direction of the bathroom off the Mazurskys' bedroom (Joe had washed up in there). Randy returned to the bedroom. A can of Noxema shaving cream, a razor, a tube of Colgate, Right Guard, and a toothbrush went into the bag.

Finally Randy bent to zipper the bag shut. Joe slid further back into the shadows and watched as Randy's hands outlined the suitcase with the zipper.

Joe held his breath until he heard the door close. He counted each footstep as Randy descended the stairs.

Cautiously, Joe slid out from beneath the bed. He walked into the living room and watched as Randy threw the suitcase into the hatch of the Chevette, watched until he drove away.

Now, dammit, fast. Find the lighter.

Joe began in the living room. On his hands and knees, he made his way through every room, searching both with his eyes and his hands.

He went over the entire apartment twice, three times. It was growing dark outside and he didn't dare turn any lights on.

Quickly he walked through the apartment, giving it a final once-over. He turned up nothing. Someone had found it. Randy? How long would it be before the police knocked on his door? Joe closed his eyes. "Please, please let me have left it somewhere else," he whispered aloud to any God who was listening.

He knew, though, with a certainty as sure as his love for Anne, the lighter had been left here.

Joe looked out all the windows once more. No one was about. He went to the back and went down the stairs. He peered into the alley and saw no one. Quietly he closed the door behind him.

He began walking quickly, thinking how he at least had to make it home before Anne started dinner and hoping she hadn't called Nature Snack and they hadn't called him. Something had to go right for him.

As he turned out of the alley onto Oak Park Avenue, he detected a quick movement of something small behind him. A kid?

Joe turned. Behind him sat a hawk-faced woman in a wheelchair. What was she doing out in this snow?

"At last we meet," the woman said. "I'm Pat Young." She smiled. "I understand you were good friends with Maggie Mazursky."

5

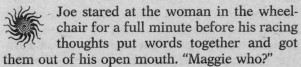 Joe stared at the woman in the wheel-
chair for a full minute before his racing
thoughts put words together and got
them out of his open mouth. "Maggie who?"

The woman frowned, pulling the blue blanket
she had draped over her shoulders closer around
her. "Mazursky. Come, come now. We're beyond
pretending, aren't we?"

"I don't know what you're talking about. I was
just here to read the meter. Now that you mention it, Mazursky was the name on the doorbell."
Joe smiled weakly, feeling very sick. He felt his
lower lip begin to tremble and tried constricting
his face muscles to stop it.

The woman's hawklike features took on a determined stare. "Look, I saw you enter and leave
Maggie Mazursky's apartment the day she was
killed. Cut the shit with me. I don't want it. I
don't need it."

Joe stared at the woman. His mind was a blank; there were no excuses for these accusations. Perhaps he should just turn and run. She wouldn't be able to catch him. But what if she knew his name?

Joe spoke. "So? That doesn't prove anything."

"I live across the street." Pat gestured at her building. "No one else was in that place that day. I know; I was watching." Pat snickered. "Call me a busybody."

"I suppose you can see through the building as well . . . to the back."

"Look. We both know you killed her. Now, I don't know why and I don't know how." She smiled again. In the dying light of the day there was something grisly, something predatory in her upturned lips. "But I really don't care about any of those things. I don't want to turn you in . . . handsome."

Joe shifted his weight from one foot to the other. "Then what do you want?"

She shivered. "Look, it's awful cold out here. Why don't you step around behind me and grab hold of the chair and push me across the street? We can talk in my apartment; it'll be a lot more comfortable."

Not thinking he had any other choice, Joe grabbed the handles of the chair.

Joe's feeling of entrapment crystallized once he was inside Pat Young's apartment. The room seemed even more closed in by the dark brown carpeting and the deep beige of the walls. The room had more the look of a junk store than an apartment.

Pat Young smiled up at him once more. "Please, let me take your coat."

Numbly, Joe removed his sheepskin jacket. He handed it to her, the nausea growing. He feared throwing up.

Pat disappeared into the small entranceway that curved off the main room. She was gone longer than he would have imagined it would take. Finally Joe shrugged and decided it took a crippled person longer to hang something. Why not?

When Pat returned, she was still grinning.

Joe could stand it no longer. "Please," his voice came out an octave higher, agonized, "what do you want from me?"

Pat took a breath. "Why, I only want justice for that poor girl's life you took."

Get it over with, Joe. "Are you going to turn me in? It's a mistake, all a big mistake. But if you want to turn me in, why not just do it and get it over with?" Joe crossed the room and picked up the telephone, holding it out to her.

She waved him away. "Put that down. I told you, I don't want to report you. What good would that do? The crazy legal system would have you out on the streets again in no time. You'd probably write a best seller on your experiences in prison to boot. No, all I want is a little insurance that sweet girls like me aren't following in Maggie Mazursky's footsteps."

"What kind of insurance?" Joe felt himself calming. He was beginning to think of ways to cope with the situation.

Pat rubbed her fingers together in the classic gesture for money.

Joe laughed.

Pat's calm expression turned to one of wariness. And Joe's nervous expression turned to a big smile.

"What?" Pat blurted, suddenly afraid.

"You dumb bitch." Joe took three steps to the wheelchair and tipped her out of it. She hit the floor with a thud, barely having time to break her fall with outstretched arms.

Before she even heard the slam of the apartment door, she knew he was gone.

Pat groped her way back to the chair and hoisted herself into it.

She was smiling.

As he ran down the street Joe wriggled into his jacket. Five o'clock and darkness was complete. How in God's name would he ever explain his absence to Anne? He was certain by now she would have called his clients at Nature Snack, would have called The Everleigh Club, the bar he liked to go to occasionally, would have called his old friend Ted Mateer, who used to work with him at Ogilvy and Mather.

His trip had been a disaster. A total failure all around. As Joe hurried north to Roosevelt Road he wondered if perhaps just this once he had slipped too far, if perhaps just this once he would be caught.

Anne had never looked more beautiful. She wore a jade green satin dress with a small grape-leaf pattern and mandarin collar. Her black hair lay in striking contrast to the green of her dress.

She stood, leaning against a mirrored art deco breakfront in the dining room.

Before her, spread on a Venetian lace tablecloth, was the dinner. It included two Cornish game hens, their orange glaze gone dull and cold in the candlelight, a Caesar salad on warm plates that had once been chilled, and an uncorked bottle of Moët et Chandon, gone flat in a sterling silver bucket now filled with tepid water.

Anne had tried to remain composed when Joe finally showed up at half past eight, wanting her anger to be cool-edged, hard: an ice-cold razor. But even before she had gotten out "where have you been all day?" the tears had begun.

Joe had been unable to reply. He had hurried into the powder room, slamming the door behind him. So now Anne stood, frozen, tears ruining a makeup job that had taken her well over an hour.

Dejected, she seated herself at the perfectly laid table and waited for the ferret to come out of its hole. Dimly, she heard rushing water, the creak of the powder room door as Joe opened it.

She looked up at him. His face was still ruddy with cold, his mustache a little wet from the frost melting. She bit her lower lip, certain he had been unfaithful. Certain that what she had feared through all the years of her marriage had finally come true; dim recollections of her mother's warning when it looked as if she and Joe were getting serious: "Find someone else, honey; with looks like his he'll never be yours alone. Ones like that, even if they do have will power, break down eventually because someone's always after them. Take my advice, honey, marry someone rich." She had laughed then and her mother laughed with her, but she knew her mother well enough to know she wasn't kidding.

"Well, where?" she looked up at him, eyes appealing, screaming, *Lie to me*.

Joe started to speak, but Anne cut him off. "And don't tell me you were with Nature Snack. I already talked to Arnie Brickman. He told me you hadn't been in and weren't due to see him until Friday. So forget that excuse."

She watched Joe mentally shift gears. The pain cut into her; she wanted to vomit.

Joe sat down at the table with her. He took one of her sweat-stained palms in his. Looking deep in her blue eyes, he began: "Honey, I didn't want to have to admit this to you."

Anne sighed. The churning in her stomach increased. She didn't want to hear what she was sure was coming.

"I guess the best way to tell you is just come right out and say it." Joe took a breath. "I lost the lighter you gave me for Christmas."

Anne laughed. She laughed on and on, clutching the Venetian lace tablecloth in a ball. She doubled over in her seat, tears streaming.

Joe had a worried smile on his face. "What? What's so funny?"

Anne reined in her laughter. "Nothing, Joe. I'm sorry."

Anne smiled, on the edge of hysteria as Joe explained how he *had* been at the Nature Snack offices, but had talked only to Priscilla, the receptionist. She hadn't seen his lighter, and a further check through their offices had turned up nothing.

Anne's tension began to dissolve.

"And then the car got towed . . ."

Joe's voice became a drone. Tell me anything, sweet baby, Anne thought, anything at all. Just don't tell me you were sleeping with somebody else. There's nothing worse you could ever do.

To stop his talking, she covered his mouth with hers, exploring it with her tongue.

Joe awakened, sweating. The image of small eyes and a long, sharp nose swam before him: Pat Young. She had been with two policemen. Anne was crying. The dream had been vivid.

Joe got out of bed. Beside him Anne slept soundly, as she always did after they made love. He slipped his robe on and went into his office.

Outside the window the sky was beginning to lighten, a band of opalescent white over Lake Michigan.

The dream had brought on a decision. Joe would have to return once more to Berwyn. He would have to kill one more time. This one, he promised himself, would be his last.

Pat Young also stared out of a window, waiting for the sun to rise, the parade of soap operas and game shows to commence.

How long? she asked herself, how long till he returns? Pat smiled. She knew he would be back. And wouldn't that be sweet? Because now she knew his name, his address, driver's license number, social security number, height, weight, and the color of his eyes. Although she didn't need the driver's license in her hand to tell her the color of those brown eyes; she had taken them in right away. They had been the sexiest eyes she had ever seen.

She glanced down at the driver's license she had stolen from his wallet when she hung up his coat. It had been too easy. Even his telephone number was listed right in her Chicago directory.

The ruse of a letter with a friend to be opened in the event of her death was cliché, she knew. Even beneath her modest standards. But she knew it would work.

The stakes were too high for Joe MacAree to call her bluff.

6

 The neon black and green of the video terminal hurt Milo Schwartz's eyes. Ever since they had started making him use a word processor here at the Chicago *Sun Times*, Milo had hated the damned things. The screen hurt his eyes and he felt a lack of connection with the machine; somehow, he just didn't feel like he was a real reporter unless he was banging out a story on a battered manual.

Using the word processor was cheating.

Milo was sixty-one years old, and had been in the newspaper business since he graduated from St. George High School. Things were different then. Chicago was different. Oh, sure, over the years it had known its share of crime and corruption, maybe even more than some of the other big towns, but Chicago always seemed to deal with its own. Nobody got away with anything. At least not for long.

Not like now. Milo began to punch the story into the word processor. It would appear in that day's final edition.

Randy Mazursky waited at the newsstand while the truck delivered the final edition of the *Sun Times*. He was aware of how he was following his life's routines without much thought. Like buying a paper: Since Maggie was killed, Randy didn't really care much about what went on in the world. But since he had always bought a paper after he finished his shift at Whipped Dream, he bought one now, even though he knew his parents would have the *Sun Times* there when he got home. Forces of habit: It was the small things that kept him from collapsing, the small things leading each minute into the next until the day was done.

"Hey, Bill, how's the news business?" Randy smiled for the old guy who ran the newsstand. From the first day Randy stopped there, Bill always had a joke for him. What made Randy like Bill even more was that the jokes hadn't stopped after Maggie's death. How much easier things would be if people weren't always reminding him by tiptoing around, hushing their voices whenever he came near.

"Same as usual. Say, Randy, know how proctologists examine their patients?"

Randy rolled his eyes. "I'm not sure I wanna know."

"With rearview mirrors." His deadpan delivery made Randy laugh in spite of himself.

Randy shook his finger at the man. "Someday you're gonna get in trouble."

"Sure, sure." Bill turned to hand a woman a *Cosmopolitan*.

Randy unfolded the paper as he headed toward the car. On page three, a headline midway down the page caught his eye. Randy unlocked the door to his Chevette and sat down inside the car to read the story.

The case had been sensational. The press had given it prominent coverage because of the appeal it had to people like Randy's mother, who would shake her head, cluck her tongue, and observe, "He should burn in hell for what he done to that baby." Now as Randy read the story he, too, shook his head. Adrienne Murphy, a Chicago trial lawyer, had charged her live-in lover with first-degree murder in the death of her son, Matthew. The boy had been beaten, the fatal blow administered by his head being slammed into a toilet bowl. Child abuse cases often didn't merit such attention, but the lawyer's prominence had forced the case into Chicago's news-hungry eyes.

Now Randy stared down at the photo of the couple, Adrienne and Caleb Rice, leaving the courtroom, hand in hand, smiling. Mr. Rice had been acquitted when Adrienne Murphy had reconsidered, saying that "in her grief Murphy had misinterpreted Rice's actions." The story went on to tell how she had dropped all charges against her lover, finally coming to the understanding that the boy's death had been an accident.

An accident? Scores of bruises and lacerations an accident? A little boy fell with such force against a toilet as to split his head open? Randy closed his eyes. How could the legal system let such a monster get away?

It happens all the time, Randy thought. Technicalities. People are always getting off on technicalities.

And what of Maggie's killer? There were no witnesses, as far as Randy knew, no fingerprints. If and when they apprehended her killer, would he, too, walk the streets free because of "insufficient evidence," because he hadn't been properly advised of his rights?

Randy started the car. He remembered the photo of the bruises the little boy had suffered before he died. Horrible things. He had thought then that some people didn't deserve children. And he had thought then of his own child, now buried, dead inside its mother.

As he steered the car off toward Berwyn he remembered the brief call he had made to the police station that morning. He had wanted to talk to Tom Grimes, the detective handling his case.

The voice on the phone had been sleepy, male. "Yeah?"

Randy was sure he had the wrong number and had gotten some poor guy out of bed. He asked anyway: "Uh . . . this isn't the police department, is it?"

"Yeah." There was an edge of annoyance to the voice.

Randy waited for the man to say something else. The line was silent. With elaborate effort the man finally asked, "Can I help you with something?"

"Well, I'd like to talk to Detective Grimes . . . please."

"He ain't in."

Randy waited for the man to ask if he could take a message. No request was forthcoming. Finally Randy said, "You wouldn't know when he'd be in?"

"No."

"Would you happen to be able to put me in touch with someone who knows something about the Mazursky case?"

"Who?"

Randy felt his anger growing. He thought he'd shame the guy. "Maggie Mazursky, the woman who was murdered a few days ago." Randy paused for effect. "This is her husband."

"Hold on." Randy was thrust into the white-noise world of hold. At least, he thought, maybe now I'll get some satisfaction.

After waiting for almost five minutes Randy heard the man come back on the line.

"Hello?"

"Yes, this is Randy Mazursky."

"Yeah?"

"I thought you were seeing if you could get someone to help me. My wife was murdered, don't you understand?" Be calm, he told himself, be calm.

"Oh." There was a pause. "I don't think there's anyone here right now knows anything about that."

"Well," Randy sighed loudly, "could you give Detective Grimes a message for me?"

"I guess."

"Tell him I think I might have something useful to the case." Randy glanced down at the silver lighter in his hand. "So could you have him call me just as soon as you can?"

"Sure." The line went dead.

Randy pulled into a parking space in front of his parents' house. He could see his mother peeking out from behind one of the living room curtains. Randy was afraid she'd never let him leave home again.

Inside, his mother took his coat from him almost before he had slid out of it and hung it in the closet. She kissed his cheek. Randy smelled cabbage cooking. His father read the evening paper in a green La-Z-Boy recliner in the living room.

Mrs. Mazursky reached into her apron pocket. "Before you do anything I want you to call Mr. Grimes, the detective. He called for you today. Do you think there's any news?"

"No, Ma, he's just returning my call." Randy took the note from her and headed upstairs, where he had his own phone.

Once away from the smell of cooking cabbage and his mother's intense stare, Randy relaxed on the bed. He looked at his mother's penciled scrawl of the detective's name and number and wondered if he should bother calling back. Downstairs, his father was probably reading about how that Rice guy got off scot-free after killing a baby. He remembered how he had been treated when he called the station that very morning.

Opening the nightstand drawer, Randy removed the lighter. He stared at it for a moment, then picked up the phone and dialed the police station's number.

A woman answered this time. "Berwyn police."

"Detective Grimes, please."

There was a click as he was transferred. He heard a phone ringing somewhere else. Randy pictured a scarred desk, disordered papers, a harsh light illuminating glass ashtrays filled to overflowing, paper cups with days-old coffee.

"Grimes."

"Mr. Grimes, this is Randy Mazursky."

"Right. They said you had some information."

"I feel ridiculous. I was just calling to see if you'd made any headway. I was afraid you wouldn't call back if I just said that."

"Mr. Mazursky, you shouldn't do things like that. It makes matters very confusing, not to mention frustrating. We are working on the case and you will be apprised of the facts as they make themselves available."

Randy's thank you was cut off by the click of the detective's phone.

"I don't know how, but I'll get you, you son of a bitch."

Randy replaced the lighter in a drawer, covering it with Kleenex.

7

Joe watched Anne as she came out of the shower the next morning. She was wrapped in a pale blue towel and her wet black hair against her face looked provocative. Even from his position in bed, her skin looked soft, dewy from the shower's steam. She was always the most beautiful, Joe thought, when she thought no one was noticing.

Joe watched his wife out of slit eyes. He didn't want her to know he was awake, waiting for her to leave. Anne had been chosen by Takimi, a Japanese designer of huge formless shirts and dresses, all in blacks and grays, made of jersey and leather. Joe thought the clothes unattractive, but Anne, with her dark hair and pale skin, brought an elegance to them. The stark black-and-white test shots Anne had brought home approached art. Joe was proud of Anne. Her photographs would appear in a *Chicago* magazine article exploring Chicago's growing place in high fashion.

Anne sat down at her vanity table. She applied a small amount of moisturizer and pulled her wet hair into a chignon. She rose and pulled jeans, an emerald green sweater, and her black cowboy boots out of the closet. Anne never dressed up for modeling assignments; she didn't need to.

Joe was relieved when he heard the front door close. He rolled over and stared toward the window. The sky outside looked gray. No sun. Just milky white covering the entire expanse of the sky. Joe hoped it wouldn't snow.

Joe showered and dressed in the same outfit he had worn the other day: Ragg wool sweater, jeans, and hiking boots. Not bothering with breakfast (murder was better on an empty stomach), Joe put his jacket on and left the apartment quickly.

He had a razor-sharp switchblade in his jacket pocket.

Joe didn't take the precautions of public transportation this time. Just missing rush-hour traffic, Joe made his way swiftly down Lake Shore Drive, then to the Eisenhower. He parked his car on Roosevelt Road and walked to Pat Young's on Oak Park Avenue.

Pat had been waiting for a week for the knock at her door. She had even seen Joe MacAree coming down the street. She looked around her. She was ready this time: She had spent all of yesterday cleaning the place up. It looked better than it had when she first moved in and everything was in place. She had bought fresh flowers and put them in jelly jars around the room; she had lemon-oiled all the wood-veneer furniture she owned, polishing the wood until there was a high gloss on every surface.

In short, it looked like a good room for blackmail. Pat laughed.

She pressed a button on her wheelchair, directing herself toward the door.

Joe leaned against Pat's doorway in a deliberately casual pose. A spark seemed to light in her eyes as she drank his tall figure in.

"Mr. MacAree," Pat said, and Joe's heart skipped a beat. "So pleased to see you. You will come in?"

The wheelchair made a soft whirring noise as Pat moved to admit him. Joe quickly looked around the room; he didn't notice Pat's work.

"Why don't you sit down, Mr. MacAree?" Pat motioned to a chair.

Joe took the chair, mainly because he was uncertain how much longer he could stand. He had counted on Pat's not knowing who he really was, counted on her bluffing. Now she knew his name. How had she found out?

"Can I get you something?"

Joe closed his eyes for a moment. This was all too unreal. He felt the cool hardness of the switchblade pressing into his thigh through his pocket. "Look . . . why don't we just cut this out?"

Pat smiled at him. There was something rodentlike in her face when she smiled, something predatory in her eyes. Joe was afraid of her. "Cut what out, Mr. MacAree? You're the one who came to see me. Something on your mind, Mr. *MacAree?*" She laughed.

Joe leaned forward in his chair. "How do you know my name?"

Pat dared not tell him the simple truth. She didn't know why, but she feared his knowing would make it too easy for him to slip away from her. "Oh, I know lots about you, Joseph. Or do you prefer Joe? How do you like living on the Gold Coast? Must be nice. Do you have a view of the lake?"

"What?" Joe felt the perspiration breaking out on his upper lip, felt the dampness under his arms. Absurdly, he considered informing her he was too far north for the Gold Coast. "I'll ask you again: How do you know who I am?"

"I know where you live, who you are . . . I know you murdered Maggie Mazursky. Why did you do it?"

With such fury and suddenness it stunned even him, Joe felt his rage rise up and overpower him. He leaped from his chair and lifted Pat Young half out of her wheelchair, his hand clutching a fold of her pink polyester blouse. "Listen, you skinny little bitch," he whispered, spitting his words out, "tell me how you know who I am."

Pat placed her hand over his. "Or what? I don't reveal my sources."

Fear stabbed into Joe's mind. Sources? Were there others who knew? Oh, God, did this mean the end? Gently, he let go of her, lowering her back into her seat. "You mean, other people know?" The anger had ebbed completely from his voice, replaced by a hoarse fear.

His question gave Pat inspiration. She wouldn't have to use the silly ploy about a letter having to be opened in the event of her death. Thank you, Joseph MacAree, for providing my insurance. Pretending to be annoyed, she snapped, "Of course there are others who know! You don't think I'd just let you in here to kill me if other people didn't know?" She noticed the look of his face when she mentioned killing her. Another point for Pat. "Yes, I know you came here to kill me. But just try it and the police will be on your tail before you can make it back to your Gold Coast."

"Okay, so what do you want from me?"

"Money."

Joe lowered his head and stared at the floor. For the past three years he and Anne had managed to keep up an affluent front for their friends. But that was all it was—a front. Both of them made substantial amounts of money from their respective careers, but the money came in spurts, often leaving them the victims of collection agencies and lawyers. They had no money once the bills were paid—and barely enough to cover those. More than once their phone had been "temporarily disconnected." More than once Anne found herself finding a buyer for a designer dress, coat, or jacket. More than once Joe had asked for advances on freelance writing projects. They lived well, Anne and Joe, well beyond their means. Even if Joe could manage to get some money to Pat Young, Anne's and his funds were so jointly held that even the smallest withdrawal from their accounts would be noticed by Anne. And then would come the questions. Questions from a woman Joe was certain was getting more than a little suspicious.

Joe stared at the floor like a shamed boy and murmured, "I have no money."

Pat's mocking laughter was sudden, so high-pitched Joe winced. "What do you mean? I may not be able to get around as well as the next guy, but I am in no way impaired up here." She tapped her forehead. "So, please, spare me the lines. Now, I'll be needing a modest thousand dollars a month. That's not unreasonable, is it? A mere thousand? Why that's"—Pat paused to think —"only about thirty dollars a day. You probably spend that on lunch."

Joe looked at her. Her small, close-set eyes were trained on him. The eyes seemed to have no color; bland and dark, they managed to inspire in him a fear and nausea greater than any he had ever known. How could he ever make this woman believe him? He spoke louder this time, but the words were the same: "I have no money."

"I told you already: I'm not buying."

"I can't help it. I don't have that kind of money to give you. I live beyond my means, you might say. I don't have a spare dollar to give you."

Her eyes narrowed to slits. She took a breath and then said, "Well, I guess I'll just have to turn you in." Joe closed his eyes and listened to the soft "whirr" of her wheelchair. He knew she headed in the direction of the telephone. Without opening his eyes he listened as she lifted the receiver out of its cradle. He thought he even heard the dial tone; he was certain he heard the tones as she punched the number in.

Her voice was confident. "Berwyn police? Yes, I have some information about the Maggie Mazursky case." A pause. "Well, I'd rather go into that with a detective. Yes, I'll hold."

Joe's breath began coming more quickly. He felt dizzy, cold sweat running down his face, under his arms. He groped for a chair and sat down.

The next thing he heard was the receiver being replaced in its cradle. He finally opened his eyes to see Pat smiling at him. She moved close.

"You really don't have any money, do you?"

Joe shook his head and ran from the room. In the bathroom, he vomited. The attack was violent and Joe found it hard trying to quell the endless dry heaves that followed. When he finally stopped, he rinsed his face, stood straight, and looked at himself in the mirror. He was shocked his emotions could cause such a physical transformation: his eyes were wild; they seemed larger. His skin had taken on an ashen hue. An ironic comparison came to him then: His skin far too closely resembled the flesh of his victims.

When he returned to the main room of the apartment, Pat waited for him, a smile on her face. For someone who smiled so much, she had no problem conveying menace.

With mock sympathy Pat asked, "All better now?"

Joe ignored her. He edged close to the front

door without even realizing he was doing it. Quickly Pat blocked his path. "Not going so soon?"

Joe looked confused for a moment, "No . . . I . . ." Joe went toward the chair he previously occupied and sat down.

For a long time neither of them said anything. Joe placed his head in his hands, trying to recover some composure, and Pat, like a beast of prey, watched and waited.

Finally Joe lifted his head and looked at her. There was pleading in his eyes. "What do you want from me now?"

Pat had known, from the day she had seen him outside Maggie Mazursky's apartment, what she wanted. Poring through years of *Playgirl* had never satisfied her, and even though she felt nothing from the waist down, she wanted Joe. Perhaps the cruelest thing about her accident was that it stole from her her ability to consummate what had always been a very strong sex drive. In the years since the fall her desires had not diminished, even though her ability to act on those desires was gone forever.

She wheeled herself toward him. Unable to speak but certain she had him so in a corner she could do anything she wanted with him, she placed her hand on his thigh. Tentatively, she slid her hand up until it covered the bulge in his jeans.

"I want you," she whispered.

Joe couldn't believe what was happening. For an instant he was sure she was playing some kind of joke. A smile flickered across his face.

But the want evident in her eyes was too desperate for her to be anything but serious.

"How?"

For once she lost her composure. Staring at the floor and perhaps her withered legs, she whispered, "I could watch you."

Joe heard and understood. His stomach turned at the thought. He had to escape this woman. She was insane. Hoping he could embarrass her out of the idea, he asked her to repeat herself.

This time she lifted her head and looked at him. "I want to watch you. I'd like to see you get off." There were tears in her eyes and as he stared at her, they brimmed over and ran down her face. "Is that clear enough for you?" she screamed. "Now get undressed or I'll call the police."

Joe saw the fear, hunger, and confusion all mixed together on her face. He continued staring at her, making no move to undress.

Pat closed her eyes, wiped the tears away. When she opened her eyes once more, the tough veneer was back. "Stand up and take off your clothes or I'm reporting you."

Hesitantly, Joe stood and took off his sweater, then began slowly unbuttoning the shirt beneath it.

"Faster!" she screamed.

Joe undid the remaining buttons and let the shirt fall to the floor. He didn't look at Pat but heard her breath quicken as she stared at his chest. He stooped to untie and remove his boots, then his socks. Finally unzipping his jeans, he stepped out of them. He stood before her in a pair of pale blue bikini briefs Anne had given him.

"All of it." Pat's voice was hoarse.

Joe hooked his thumbs into the elastic waistband and pulled the briefs down over his hips and off. Pat moved closer. He felt her breath near his navel. Joe looked down at her; she was staring at his penis.

"Get hard," she whispered. She looked up at him. "Do it." Pat rolled back from him and waited.

Joe began caressing himself, closing his eyes and trying to put himself someplace else . . . with Anne. It wasn't working. The more he thought of how much depended on his performance, the less willing his cock seemed to be to harden. He handled himself more roughly, let his fantasies grow more desperate, more perverse. Anne lay prone before him on the bathroom floor, her body covered with baby oil, motioning for him to come to her, pulling her labia apart.

It still wasn't working.

"You disgust me," Pat said. She wheeled next to him, and with a swift gulp took him in her mouth. The warm sensation of her mouth was startling, and for an instant he began to get hard. But as soon as he told himself where he was and what was happening, he went limp once more.

And then, almost unbidden, came thoughts of Maggie Mazursky. He remembered the look of fear on her face when he removed the razor from his coat, the quick, vertical slashes he made down her forearms, the sudden rush of blood.

She was too surprised to scream. Joe covered her mouth and forced her to the floor. Taking her hand as a love-struck suitor would to propose marriage, he brought her wrist up to his mouth and began to suck. The warmth, the metallic taste, so odd and yet so comforting, filled his mouth. The blood came so quickly now he almost choked and was swallowing it in fast gulps. He looked up to see that Maggie had gone faint. He removed his hand from her mouth and began to suck from the other wrist. When the blood in her arms had gone from a wild pump to a barely sluggish movement, Joe made a slit in her throat and drank from this well until it, too, was dry. And then he pulled the clothes from her limp body and fucked her.

Pat stared up at him. "God, you're beautiful."

Joe looked down with wonder at his hard cock. With a minimal touch, almost like a wet dream, he began spurting his semen. The first few drops fell to Pat's brown carpeting, the rest she caught in her palm.

Joe watched as she waited until he was finished, cupping her palm as it filled with his come. When he was through, she pulled on his cock, milking it for the last few drops.

With nausea he listened to her moans as she spread the semen over her face, licking some of it from her fingers. Her eyes were closed; she was lost to her own passion.

Suddenly her moans stopped. She turned her wheelchair and wheeled quickly into the bathroom. She slammed the door behind her. In a moment he heard her voice, broken by sobs, "Get out of here."

Joe picked up his clothes and dressed. He ran from the apartment.

Even over the sound of running water he could hear Pat crying.

He ran blindly north on Oak Park Avenue. Not wanting to think because his thoughts were telling him he understood Pat Young better than she would ever know.

8

"All right. What did you lose *this* time?" Joe had burst into the living room to find Anne, sitting in their bentwood rocker, waiting for him. Although there was a calmness (a deadness of tone, actually) in her voice and her features betrayed not even the slightest emotion, Joe could tell at a glance her cool was a facade. She was a pot about to boil over.

He stared at her for a full minute without saying anything. Her modeling assignments often took her into the late evening hours. Joe had assumed, since this assignment was one of her biggest, he would not be seeing Anne until after dinner at the very earliest. Yet here it was not even two thirty in the afternoon and she was home.

He shouldn't have asked (because it said much about his guilt), but he did: "I thought you were modeling for a spread in *Chicago;* what are you doing home so early?"

Anne stood and walked rapidly toward the window. She stared out at heavy gray clouds, hanging low, foretelling heavy rain or snow. "I should've known you'd ask. The shoot was canceled for today—postponed, I should say—because Ching, the photographer, has come down with this bug that's been going around. You know, everyone's been getting it. I noticed a lot of people home in the building today; I think they're all sick. Probably with the same bug. Anyway, the shoot should be tomorrow or the next day. Some time real soon anyway. There are deadlines, you know. If Ching can't do it someone else will. So it should be tomorrow . . . or the next day. At the very latest." Almost automatically, her shoulders went over and she began to cry. She wept silently and then said, "So you'll be free to do whatever it is you do when I'm not around." She laughed, but there was not a trace of humor in it. "You can go to the zoo, I guess."

Joe came over to her, tried to embrace her. She shrugged his arms away and turned to face him.

Joe was stunned by her face: angry red, framing eyes liquid and bloodshot. Her lip quivered as she stared at him.

"Don't touch me!" She ran over and sat down on the couch. Grabbing a pillow, she clutched it to her stomach, trying to wrap her body around it. She began to rock slowly. "You must be seeing someone, Joe. That's the only explanation. I don't believe you were at the zoo that day a few weeks ago; you hate the zoo. What a lame excuse! And I believed it. Maybe you did lose the lighter I gave you, maybe so. I hate to admit it, but I called Priscilla and asked her if you were at Nature Snack the day you said you were."

Joe looked surprised.

"So we both don't have to pretend on that one anymore. Maybe you lost the lighter at *her* place, whoever *she* is. Or maybe it's a he?" Anne laughed. "What's the story for today? You told me last night you would be here today. Said you'd get the bathroom floor washed. Anyway, what's the story?"

Joe had had too much in one day. "I was only out for a few minutes," he said weakly. "Just getting a little air."

Anne closed her eyes, trying to will out the pain. "I have been here since ten o'clock, Joe. It's a quarter till three. You're going to have to do better than that. I deserve a better story. And surely a creative mind like yours . . . Wanna try again?"

"Anne, it's the truth."

"Oh, don't bother." Anne looked at him, her eyes brimming with tears. Then she turned and rushed into the bedroom.

Joe stood for a while, his stomach churning, knowing it was too late to make up an excuse. He went into the bedroom.

Anne had already flung her closet door open and begun throwing clothes on the bed. Joe began to cry.

He tried to grab her hand; she snatched it away. "Please," he said, "don't go. It's not what you think."

She looked at him. "For so long I've been telling myself lies. I've wanted to believe them more
than you hoped I would. No more." The veneer
of tough assurance broke. Her features softened.
"Maybe this doesn't have to mean forever, Joe. I
just need some time by myself, to think. I'll be
staying with my mother."

Joe tried to speak. She put her finger to his lips.
"No. Don't say anything. We're both too upset to
be rational, and I don't want to say the things my
mind is telling me to say. And I know you don't
want to hear them. So just leave me alone. Let
me get my things together."

He stared at her, unable to halt the tears.

"Please." Anne bit her lip.

"All right," he whispered, and hurried from the
room.

For a while he listened to her finish packing.
There was the hard click of her boots on the
bathroom floor as she emptied her makeup into
the Louis Vuitton bag he had bought her at
Christmas, never thinking she would use it for
this purpose.

All too soon Anne emerged from her bedroom,
laden with two suitcases and the satchel. "I called
a cab from the bedroom. It should be downstairs
by now." She regarded him for a while. Although
he didn't say a word it was obvious from his eyes,
his expression, he was pleading with her to stay.

She went to the door, set one of the suitcases
down, and opened the door. He stared at her,
numb. She picked up the suitcase and walked
out. After a moment she closed the door behind
her.

Joe hurried to the window just in time to see the Checker cab pull up in the circular drive. Before long he saw the driver get out and help Anne with her bags.

"She's gone," he told himself again, his voice weak with crying. "She's gone. She's gone. She's gone." The words were a litany as Joe walked in small circles, around and around the kitchen. He took a big butcher's knife from the block on the counter and went into the bedroom with it. He sat on the bed and pointed the knife toward his stomach. "She's gone and I can't live without her."

Darkness found Joe sitting with the knife still poised at his abdomen. His eyes stung. His throat was raw.

Joe put the knife down on the floor and walked over to the bedroom window.

The sky had cleared. A big moon had risen over the lake. There was a look of autumn to the moon, its brilliant orange reflecting off the dark and churning waters.

Undressing, Joe made his way to the shower. There was no thought to his actions; they were rote. Joe was an automaton.

After showering, Joe dressed in dark clothes: black Levi's jeans, a dark-gray sweatshirt, black boots. He knew there was a black leather jacket of his somewhere.

Where had Anne put it?

The door was framed in warm yellow light.

Joe sat in the darkness of the living room willing himself not to open it. He was seated in the bentwood rocker Anne had been in not three hours ago when he returned from Pat Young's.

This always happens when my defenses are down, Joe thought. But I can't . . . I'm going to lose Anne for sure if I go out and do it again. Another time could be the time I get caught. And his mind shot back: Now is the perfect time to do it. Anne had gone to her mother's for an indeterminate period of time; she would have absolutely no suspicions. Make one last kill; make it everything you ever wanted it to be. Pull out all the stops. Throw caution to the wind. Make it your farewell. Satisfy yourself so thoroughly you'll never want to do it again. Then you'll be able to return to Anne a healed man. You can start a new life. Maybe move to New York where you and Anne can find even more work . . . and leave behind all the mementos that keep drawing you back.

Joe stared at the door. Pat Young already knows who you are and where you live; she claims there are others who know. Doing it once more could mean the end of everything for you. You could be caught; you could leave even more clues behind than you've already left. And if that happened, would you really expect Anne to hang around, visit you in prison?

But Anne won't know. How could she? And you won't get caught. You're far too clever for that, Joe. You haven't been caught yet . . . not really. And you get more clever with each kill. Besides, you need it. You know how good it's going to make you feel.

A slight smile played about the corners of Joe's mouth.

That's right . . . it's so good. Remember Maggie? Remember the others? Remember how everything felt? Nothing, not even Anne, can compare. Remember how alive you were afterward? Think about it: Think about the young flesh of those girls, their warm blood. The feel of it pumping into your mouth . . .

Joe's cock began to thrust itself jerkily upward in his pants.

He stood.

Walked to the door and opened it.

Yes, yes, this is so right.

The elevator, its doors yawning, waited for him at the end of the corridor.

Tammy Stone was cold. Three weeks a runaway, she was now questioning her motives. Sure, her stepfather had tried to put the moves on her, but at least at home she had a warm place to sleep at night. At least at home she had three meals a day and all the snacks she wanted. At least back in Lafayette, Indiana, she could talk to Shelley Perkins when things were really getting to her.

Tammy curled into a tighter ball on the park bench. She supposed, since she had passed a sign for the Lincoln Park Zoo a while back, that she was in Lincoln Park. The wool coat she was wearing was inadequate for the Chicago winds now blowing. Tammy thought she should get up and move around; she would stay warmer that way. But she was just too tired.

An entirely different scenario was what Tammy had envisioned when she ran away late one night, long after she heard her mother and stepfather go to bed. She had expected to come to Chicago and find work immediately as a model. Even though she was only fourteen everyone told her she looked older. Everyone told her she looked a lot like Brooke Shields. The only problem Tammy thought she might have in Chicago was deciding which agency to go with.

But after she found her way around the Loop and the near north side, the agencies she called on wouldn't even look at her unless she had some samples. Tammy had not even brought snapshots. She was turned away by sympathetic yet firm receptionists at every agency she called on.

When she had exhausted all the listings in the yellow pages, Tammy gave up. Visions of her stepfather leaning over her bed at night were enough to keep her from hurrying back to Indiana, but it was hard to steal enough food to quiet the pangs in her stomach, which sometimes got so bad she would eat anything—even people's garbage at McDonald's.

She had lost fifteen pounds since she had purchased her one-way bus ticket to Chicago, bringing her down from a thin 113 pounds to an almost starved 98 pounds. Tammy knew she could find no work as a model in Chicago, or anywhere. She remembered once seeing a number on TV that runaways could call for help. She wished she had the number.

"What's a pretty lady like yourself doing out on a night like this?"

Tammy was startled by the male voice behind her. She sat up straight and turned to look. The man standing behind her looked to be about thirty. Even in her starved condition Tammy noticed how good-looking he was, powerfully built, with dark curly hair and a mustache.

"Nothin'," Tammy said, and turned her back to him.

He walked over and sat down beside her. She noticed he smelled good, clean, like Dial soap. His smile seemed warm. Maybe she shouldn't ignore him.

He spoke again. "I hope you're not afraid of me. I'm not going to hurt you."

Tammy smiled at him. "Oh, I didn't think you were. I just wanted a little time alone." She thought for a moment, then lied. "Boyfriend trouble."

The man smiled at her. "Oh . . . well, that can be upsetting. Would you like to talk about it?"

"Anything but." Tammy laughed. Maybe she could get this guy to buy her something to eat.

The man held out his hands. "No problem. What's your name?"

"Alexis." She noticed he had moved closer and put his hand on her leg. The moves seemed so casual she thought nothing of them. The man didn't seem to even realize he was doing it. Besides, Tammy was trying to think of a way to turn the conversation to food.

"Chilly out here tonight, isn't it?" He slid his arm around her.

"It sure is. And you know what? I've been

pretty stupid staying out here all evening." She looked at him. "I've missed my supper."

The man smiled. "Well, why didn't you say so? Come on." He stood up. "Let's go grab a bite to eat and then I'll see you get home safely."

He held out his hand and she took it. He seemed like an awfully nice man. It wasn't long before they came to a copse of trees around a little pond.

"This is the lagoon. It's really very beautiful," the man said. Tammy's mind was so set on dinner she didn't notice the intensity that had come into the man's voice. "There are little silver neon fish that swim in the water. They glow at night and you can see them swimming. It's really something. Wanna take a peek?"

"Sure." Tammy followed him down the little incline closer to the water. She thought she better go along with him; she didn't want to jeopardize a meal.

When she got close, all she saw was dark water with two Pepsi cans floating in it. No fish. She looked at him, starting to say, "There aren't any—" when she noticed the odd look in his eyes, the way he was smiling at her.

"Keep quiet," he whispered, "this won't take long."

The next thing she knew he had locked his leg into the space behind her knee and she was falling over backward. His weight was on her suddenly and his calloused hand broke open the buttons on her coat, then ripped at the blue flannel shirt she was wearing.

She screamed as long as she could. He slapped

her so hard that silver flecks of light danced before her eyes. He began to struggle, tugging at her jeans.

She felt more than heard the zipper ripping away from the denim. One of his fingernails cut her as he ripped down her panties. The air's coldness rushed in; the feel of the frozen grass beneath her was painful. "Please, don't," she pleaded.

Another blow, more forceful than the first, caught her other cheek, causing her head to swivel into the frozen earth. She bit down on her tongue with the force of the slap and tasted blood. She thought, "I can get this at home."

He paused for a moment, one hand pinning her to the ground while the other fumbled to unzip his jacket and open his pants. Please God, she prayed, let it be over quickly.

Just as he was about to enter her he tensed, and Tammy dared not hope for salvation.

"What's going on over there?" The man's voice rang out over the lagoon. Tammy managed a grunt before he covered her mouth. "Just shut your fuckin' mouth and keep it shut," he whispered.

There was a rustling. Someone was searching the area around the lagoon. Tammy squirmed. The man tightened his hold on her. "Move again," he whispered hoarsely, "and I'll kill you."

The rustling noise stopped. He waited, poised above her, for subsequent noises. After a while there was no further sound. Tammy clamped her legs together as the man tried to enter her. His hands were strong as they pried her legs apart.

She felt the head of his cock pushing to enter her dry opening. "Damn," he breathed. "What's wrong with you? I only want you to be nice to me. Just for a couple minutes." He was smiling above her. Next she felt his finger enter her. She knew she was going to be sick and tried to hold back, but threw up anyway.

"Jesus Christ!" He withdrew his finger and Tammy thought for a moment she had saved herself. But he quickly pushed the head of his cock in her slightly lubricated vagina. "Gettin' better," he grunted, and pushed savagely at her.

She couldn't help it; the pain sent streams of heat through her as he entered.

She screamed.

His punch, landing squarely on her upper lip and the bottom of her nose, was swift. "I told you to shut up!"

Tammy was just as surprised as her assailant when two strong hands grabbed the man at his shoulders and pulled him back off her. Tammy heard a loud cracking sound and then a splash as the man was thrown into the water.

Tammy looked up into the face of her hero, dazed.

"C'mon," the man with the dark clothes said, "we better get out of here before he manages to climb out."

He helped her up as the other man swore and flailed about in the freezing water, trying to get out of the lagoon. Together they dressed her as well as they could and then ran.

Tammy was too happy at being saved to feel the pain of the blows she had received. She looked over at the man beside her and could not believe her good fortune.

He smiled at her. "My name's Joe. Joe MacAree."

The Chicago Center Inn sat at a busy intersection on Peterson Avenue. Its large sign, with a big pink neon circle, spelled warmth and comfort to Tammy. The sign spelled anonymity to Joe. There would be no need for the girl to leave the car while he registered under the name of Chester Worth, and no questions when he left the room.

Tammy had bought his story about his being an out-of-town salesman here for a few days. Had agreed with his suggestion that she come to his room and clean up before continuing on to the hospital. From there she could call her parents in Indiana. She had told him the whole story.

Joe returned to his car. He was smiling and holding a key on a plastic key ring. He opened the door and leaned in to whisper to her. "Sorry about the secrecy. They know I'm in town alone on business, and if they see me bringing you in they might get suspicious."

Tammy glanced over toward the office, expecting to see eyes peering out of a window. There was no one.

"I hate to do this to you, but could you wait till I go up and then after a few minutes follow me? It'll look better that way and I can get a hot shower running for you."

It didn't occur to Tammy to ask why he had to

go to the office for a key if he was already staying there. The only thoughts she was having right now were of getting home to her mother. Maybe if she told her everything that was going on, her mother would leave her stepfather and things would go back to normal; she could forget this whole episode. The fact Joe had rescued her from a rape elevated him in her eyes to a full-fledged hero. She would never have questioned any of his motives.

So she agreed to do as he asked, even promised to be extra discreet about leaving the car.

"Great, great," Joe said. "I'll have the shower running for you."

And indeed, upstairs, Joe did turn the shower on, regulating it just a fraction below being too hot to stand. The small tile bathroom filled with steam as Joe unwrapped a bar of soap, spread out a towel on the floor, and turned on the heat lamp.

As Joe heard the soft tap on the door, he thrust the X-Acto knife he had with him into a night-stand drawer.

"Shower's going," he said as he opened the door. "I know you're going to feel a whole lot better once you clean up." Joe was questioning his choice when he saw the girl in a better light. She probably was good-looking, but the beating had bruised and cut her face. Besides, she was filthy, her hair a mass of greasy strings.

She smelled bad.

The shower will take care of that, he cut himself off. There would be no turning back.

"Take your time," he said to her, using his most gentle tone.

"Thank you so much," she said, her words slurred by her swelling lips. She went into the bathroom, closing the door behind her.

With the door closed, Joe prepared the room. He dimmed the lights; all that was left was a desk lamp that he placed on the floor and covered with a pillowcase. There was a soft grayish light in the room that gave a quiet fuzziness to everything around it. The corners of the room were in shadows. He pulled back the sheets, although he would not let her stay in the bed once he cut her. That would have to be done in the bathroom, where the tile could be easily cleaned.

She turned off the shower sooner than he anticipated. When the girl emerged, wrapped in a towel, her hair in soft, wet curls, Joe felt he had made a good choice.

She looked with alarm at the darkness of the room and the turned down bed. For a moment, there was confusion on her face, then pain. "Not you," she said, on the verge of tears. "I thought I could trust you."

Making certain to stay right where he was, Joe said, "You *can* trust me, Tammy. I just thought you'd like to rest a little after being out so many nights in the cold." He smiled and could see the lines of tension in her face begin to dissolve. "Really. I don't have anything in for you. I'm a happily married man, got two kids." Joe smiled. "Why don't you lie down and get some sleep? I'll go out and get you something to eat. I know you've got to be hungry."

Tammy finally smiled. She hurried to the bed and sat down on it. "This is just too much! People like you just don't exist. Or, at least until tonight, I didn't think they did."

Joe looked bashfully at the floor. "C'mon, now, I just did what anyone would do. What would you like me to bring you?"

"Anything would be fine. At this point it doesn't really matter."

"Anything . . . coming right up." Joe grabbed his jacket from a chair, put it on, and hurried out the door, making certain to lock it behind him.

"I'll give her time to sleep," he thought. "It'll be much easier if she's asleep."

When Joe returned with a bag from McDonald's in his hand, he could see, even from the outside, that the room was brilliantly lit. He took the stairs two at a time and unlocked the door.

Inside, all the lights had been turned on, the bed was slightly mussed and . . . empty.

It was then he heard splashing in the bathroom. Tammy's humming voice, high and girlish, came through the bathroom door. Joe was disappointed she wasn't in bed and asleep. Things would have been so much easier if she was a little groggy.

But, he consoled himself, she had placed herself right where he would have put her.

Deciding not to carry the charade any further (because his desire would not let him), he tossed the Big Mac, fries, and chocolate shake into the wastebasket and removed the X-Acto knife from the drawer.

He paused for a few seconds outside the bathroom door.

From Joe MacAree's journal, February 23, 1991:

She was stunned when I flung open the bathroom door. I don't think she was aware even that I was back in the motel room. My sudden appearance in the doorway and the loud "bang" of the door slamming against the tile wall caused her mouth to drop open. She stayed that way for a few moments, giving me a full view of her naked body in the tub. Feebly then, she covered her breasts and crossed her legs beneath the water.

In all the women I've killed, I don't think I've seen one as terrified as Tammy. And for a split second I questioned why I was doing it; there was a tinge of remorse. Maybe that's something I can be proud of, maybe that means I'm coming to the point where I won't be driven by these . . . needs . . . compulsions? . . . anymore.

I know she said something to me. I know she screamed. But the funny thing was: I couldn't hear any of it. That's when the humming started. A low drone, like white noise, started up and it was like I was deaf. There were those sparks again, little flecks of silver light that my eyes wanted to follow. All the while this was going on I was moving rapidly to the tub. She stood for a moment then slid in the water. I laughed when she went down because she struck her head against the rim. There was a look of confusion on her face for the briefest of moments and then she was out. I knew then this was preordained; I knew for sure she was part of the plan; this turn in the scheme of things made things too easy for me, too convenient. It was meant to be.

I lifted her out of the water and lay her on the cold white tile. Her skin didn't offer much of a contrast. Her flesh was so young, damp and warm from the bath. I licked her all over, then bit down hard on her breast. That brought her back to consciousness. She groaned as my teeth sank deep into her and I had my first taste of blood.

I still couldn't hear anything. Or if I could it was as if it was at a distance.

Then she started to fight me. I felt her fist come down hard on my neck. I didn't want to take my mouth away from her bleeding breast, but she was squirming and hitting me, harder each time. My movements seemed automatic. I looked up at her like an angry dog being disturbed while it was eating. I can picture myself clearly at this time, as if I was outside myself, watching. There was something funny in the predatory look on my face, the ring of bright red blood around my lips.

I lashed out at her face with the X-Acto. She screamed, and it was as if someone had lifted the volume for just a second. The shriek was painful to my ears. I grabbed her head and slammed it against the bathtub.

And I couldn't stop myself. I slammed her head again and again into the hard porcelain. I did it until long after she was dead.

But it was beautiful! There was blood flowing from the cuts on her face, blood oozing out of the back of her head, running through her light brown hair, puddling on the floor. I began sucking

*it up as fast as I could, fearing it would congeal.
The blood was hot . . . coppery. The blood was
everything. I cut into the arteries in her arms with
the X-Acto and let the hot blood pump into my
mouth. I could barely swallow fast enough, and I
felt some of it sluicing over my chin and wetting
the front of my shirt.*

I came two times in my pants.

Joe put down his pen and lay his head on the
green blotter at his desk. The onslaught of tears
was sudden and furious. The guilt overwhelmed
him. He remembered the girl, that beautiful
young girl. The eyes he had seen alive and shining, staring up at him with admiration and hope.
The eyes that had shown gratitude for saving her.
Those eyes in the darkness looked glazed, focused in on a final nightmare.

He wept bitterly. He had felt alive in the park,
as he had all the other times in the past. He could
smell the damp wood of the trees, the humus of
the earth beneath him.

He could smell spring coming. He felt its revi-
talizing power; he felt seventeen again.

But now none of it seemed worth it.

He closed the leather book he had written in
and returned it to its hiding place under a false
bottom in one of his desk drawers.

Outside, dawn was filling the city with gray
light. A few cars moved quickly along Lake
Shore Drive. Joe wondered about the girl's family, where they were and if they missed her.

He fell to his knees and begged God to forgive
him this one last time. He promised God it would

never happen again. He promised himself he would never, ever let it happen again.

He begged God to return Anne to him, to give him the strength to avoid the desire that drove him to kill, to lust for the taste of blood, so foreign yet so basic.

"Just give me strength," he sobbed. "I'll never let it happen again."

And if a God did look down, He would have thought: "I've seen this scene six times now."

9

The test shots were nowhere to be found. Last week when Anne had done the spread for Evans Furs, she had asked her photographer, Louise Sullivan, if she could borrow the initial test shots to study them. Anne used the shots from each assignment to learn something new about her look.

A search of every room in her mother's Lake Forest home revealed nothing. She had even searched through drawers where she was certain the photos couldn't be; that was better than the alternative of calling, or going back to, Joe.

Sitting in her girlhood bedroom with its lace and canopy bed, she lowered her head to cry at her frustration. The past two days hadn't been happy ones. She had lifted the phone so many times to call him.

Too many times. Last night she had called and decided to let the call go through before hanging up. With relief, she listened to the ringing of the phone a dozen times. She wouldn't have to try to make small talk, since she really had nothing to say. She longed for the sound of his voice, even if she didn't want to admit it to herself or to Joe. But her relief turned to anger as she called sporadically throughout the evening. The calls got more frequent as the evening wore on. As the hour grew later, Anne grew more and more angry. *He seemed so upset when I left,* she thought, *was it really just an act?*

Or was there something wrong?

A sharp gust of wind outside sent a pine tree's branch crashing into her window just as the bedroom was filling with dawn's black-and-white unreality. Anne awoke, and Joe was the first thing that came into her mind. She lifted the white receiver and punched in the buttons of her phone number.

Anne wasn't sure she had the right number when he answered. His voice was caught somewhere between a sob and hoarseness. Anne, feeling a mixture of sorrow and longing, hung up the phone without a word.

And now, at midmorning, Anne found herself trying to stop her sobs as she heard her mother knocking on her door.

"Anne?" Phyllis Hobson's raspy, cigarette-scarred voice came through the door. "Is everything all right?"

Anne took a breath, tried to muster up a normal voice. "Mother, I'm fine."

Her mother rattled the locked door. Anne

heard her sigh. "Well, I'm running into North-brook for a few things. Is there anything you need?"

Anne wiped her eyes and got up. She opened the door. Her mother, a barrel-shaped woman with silver hair and hard features, faced her. She wore pince-nez glasses on a gold chain and a brown Ultrasuede pantsuit. Anne's looks had come from her father: a tall man with Irish features, black hair, blue eyes, and the kind of face that made women stop to look at him. Her father had died in a plane crash when Anne was five years old. Her mother never missed an opportunity to tell others how unfortunate the accident was: "He was on business and wasn't supposed to leave until three hours later, but the meeting he had to stay for was canceled and he decided to hop an earlier flight. You see, it was Annie's birthday." Actually, it was two months before Anne's birthday . . . and Anne never understood her mother's need for melodrama. But her father had left his wife and young daughter well provided for. His knowledge and hunches on the stock market were always right on target, and his investments in Chicago real estate left his survivors enough money to insure their never working.

Her mother's expression turned to one of concern. She touched Anne's cheek. "Honey, you've been crying."

Anne smiled to show her everything was all right. "It's okay, Mother. Listen, have you seen a big manila envelope around here? There are some test shots I'd like to see."

Her mother shook her head. "No, nothing like that. Listen," Phyllis said, dismissing the envelope, "why don't you throw some clothes on and we can both go over together?" She smiled. "I'll treat you to lunch."

"Oh, I don't think I'm really in the mood. I wanted to look over those test shots. I must have left them at home."

Phyllis frowned when she called the apartment *home*. "Well, dear, they're not here, so why don't you come with me?"

"No, I really should get dressed and go down and get them."

Phyllis closed her eyes in a subtle gesture of disgust. She had never trusted Joe and through a thin veneer of concern had made her happiness at Anne's return obvious. "Do you really think that's such a good idea? He might have one of his little girlfriends there with him."

Anne shook her head. She wished she hadn't spilled all her suspicions to her mother. "If he's there, Mother, I'm sure we can behave as adults. I'm not worried about it and you shouldn't be either."

"Suit yourself. Can I get you anything from Northbrook?"

An hour later Anne steered Phyllis's Saab down Lake Shore Drive. Part of her prayed Joe wouldn't be in the apartment when she got there, and another part told her that if she didn't really want to see him she wouldn't be going there in the first place.

She pulled into the visitor's section of their un-

derground parking garage and took a quick walk
back to see if Joe's car was there. It wasn't.

The apartment hadn't changed, which really
wasn't so odd; she had only been gone two days.
Anne supposed the turmoil of those days had led
her to think things should look different.

But all was in place, including the envelope of
test shots Louise Sullivan had let her have. Anne
picked it up from the dresser in the bedroom and
turned to use the bathroom before she headed
back to Lake Forest.

The X-Acto knife caught her eye as soon as she
walked into the bathroom. It lay on the sink that
she had stood at so many mornings. Anne recog-
nized the dark residue at once as blood.

It shook her. Had Joe tried to kill himself?

She heard a key being fitted into the front door
lock. The knife in her hand, Anne froze.

Anne looked wildly about the room, as if she'd
been caught burglarizing her own apartment.
She threw the knife in the wastebasket.

In the living room, she had just managed to put
her jacket on when Joe opened the door. He
came in, his coat folded over one arm, and stared
at her for a minute, almost as if he didn't recognize her. Then he smiled.

"Anne . . . have you . . . have you come
back?"

For a moment Anne considered saying yes
when she saw the hope in his eyes. As much as
there was wrong with their marriage, she still
loved him and hated to extinguish that hope.

"Joe." She smiled. "I . . . uh . . . wasn't really expecting to see you. I just came to pick these up." She held the envelope up.

"Stay for breakfast?"

Anne laughed. "Joe, it's afternoon."

"Lunch then?"

"No, I really have to be getting back." She wanted to ask him where he was all last night, wanted to ask why the X-Acto knife was bloody. But she didn't want to risk complications, wasn't sure she could really take what the answers might be if she heard them. So she said, "Joe, I really, as I said, need some time. It would be better if I just get on my way. Okay?"

She could see the pain on his face and his effort to circumvent it while he was with her. "Okay. Be on your way then." He opened the door.

"Thanks, Joe." She glanced down at his bare wrists.

There were no marks.

The Saab wouldn't start. Anne looked around the dark parking garage as if an answer was hiding in its shadows. Once more she turned the key in the ignition, now furiously jamming her foot into the gas pedal. "C'mon," she cried, her voice heavy with impatience. After a few sputters the Saab was silent once more. Anne slumped back against the leather upholstery. She closed her eyes and pressed her hands to her temples, where a headache was beginning. "Oh, please . . ." she whispered.

She glanced around her and saw Joe walking toward the car. She could see the mixture of pain and hope apparent on his face. "Shit," she said to herself and looked away, hoping he didn't notice her looking at him. His face was so innocent and vulnerable; she could always read everything there. How could he be lying to her? There was no way that face could conceal a falsehood. So why all the unexplained hours?

He was tapping on the passenger window. She turned and looked at him, and he made a motion for her to roll down the window. Why was he making everything so hard?

"Yes, Joe?"

"Having some trouble?"

"Yes, as a matter of fact, I am." Joe didn't even know how to change a flat tire. Anne knew it would be useless to have him take a look at it. "I'm sure I'll get it going here in a minute. It's just being temperamental; you know how these little foreign cars can be." Weakly, she smiled at him. "Is anything wrong?"

Joe laughed, but there was no humor in it. "Funny you should ask. My wife just left me."

Anne closed her eyes and placed her head on the steering wheel. This I don't need, she thought. Taking a breath, she looked back at his face, examined the pain there. "What I meant was, why are you down here?"

"Um . . . I thought maybe you could reconsider about lunch. I could make a real Caesar salad for us." She saw the animation go out of his face when she shook her head. "The truth is I don't know why I'm down here. I had hoped there'd be some way I could stop you. Not likely, huh?"

"Not likely," she said so softly she barely heard herself.

She saw tears brimming in his eyes. *Shit.* Turning the key in the ignition, she tried the Saab once more, the only result a futile sputtering.

Joe leaned into the window. "It's just that I don't know what I'd do if I ever lost you. I don't think I could go on."

"Don't do this to me!" She hadn't meant to scream, and she caught her mouth with her hand. "Please stop with the melodrama. This isn't as easy for me as you think."

Holding back her own tears now, Anne got out of the Saab, slamming the door behind her. "Would you mind reaching in and locking that door?"

She started walking away from him. There was a phone in the lobby; she could call a cab from there. These Lake Forest cab rides were getting expensive.

"Anne, wait up." Joe ran after her and she paused, not looking back at him. "What are you going to do?"

Anne was beginning to think Joe sounded like a child; and the whining was starting to inspire more pity than love. "I was going to the lobby to call a taxi."

Finally even with her, he matched her paces to the lobby. "To Lake Forest? Annie, that's getting pretty posh. Don't be crazy; I can at least drive you."

"That won't be necessary. I'm sure Mother won't mind paying for the cab."

"Don't talk crazy, Anne. I'll drive you back to Lake Forest and that's it."

Suddenly, Anne was too tired to argue. "All right, Joe."

He said he had to grab a coat upstairs and wouldn't she come up with him. Wordlessly, she followed him. Back in the apartment she told him she had to use the bathroom and went in, closing the door behind her and locking it.

Her eyes went first to the wastebasket, where she had tossed the X-Acto knife. She wanted to make sure she wasn't mistaken about the blood.

But the knife wasn't there.

"Anne, are you sure you won't stay for lunch? I have some great pastrami I just bought."

What was going on?

"No, Joe, I really have to be getting back." She opened the bathroom door. She looked at him, standing there beside the bed they had shared and thought, why not just come right out and ask him?

"What was with the X-Acto knife in the bathroom?"

The way his face contorted and the involuntary jerk of his arm told her all she needed to know. Something very strange was going on.

"What knife?" He laughed.

"The X-Acto that was on the bathroom sink a little while ago. It looked like there was blood on it."

Joe smiled, but all the color had drained out of his face. "My, getting gruesome!" He didn't say anything else, but she could see by his face, his eyes, he was frantically looking for an explanation to give her.

"Well?"

"I cut myself," he said, and all of his features softened. "I was doing a little pasteup work this morning. I cut myself and went into the bathroom to wash it off. Why the third degree?"

"No third degree. I was just curious if you had hurt yourself."

"It was nothing."

They said nothing for a short while. Then Anne said, "Well, shouldn't we be getting on our way?"

"Sure." Joe slid his leather jacket on (I haven't seen that in a while, Anne thought) and held out his arm to her. "Let's go."

Anne didn't have the courage to ask him if she could see where he had cut himself. She didn't know what she was more afraid of: seeing a wound or not seeing one.

"Joe, how good it is to see you." Phyllis Hobson's face and greeting couldn't have been more of a contradiction.

"Good to see you too, Phyllis." He stopped to kiss her cheek. "How's everything?"

"Good, thank you." She stepped back away from the door. "Come in, Joe. I was just getting ready to fix a little lunch. Maybe you could stay?"

Or maybe not, Joe thought, completing the question. "Oh, no, I just brought Anne here back. Seems your little Saab conked out on her. I'll call a repairman to have a look at it."

Phyllis gave Anne a troubled look that said, If you had just come with me . . . "Oh no, Joe, our mechanic is the only one that knows the Saab. It'll be much easier all around if I just give him a call."

"Suit yourself. I better be getting back. Got a late afternoon meeting."

"Sure you can't stay?"

"Positive." He gave Anne a quick kiss on the mouth and hurried back to his car. Joe honked the horn and waved as he backed down the drive.

In her clutches, he was thinking, I'll never get Anne back.

10

 From Joe MacAree's journal, February 26, 1991:

This is how I picture fat Phyllis: She is lying in the middle of her designer living room in Lake Forest, her rolls of naked fat covering the parquet floor. There are several open wounds on her, inflicted with a butcher knife. The blood pumps out of her. She is gasping, trying to reach out for the little pince-nez glasses on the floor beside her.

A dark heel enters the frame and stomps down on the glasses. There is the sound of glass crunching. The wooden floor is scarred and Phyllis's eyes widen in terror as she looks up at the face above her.

All we can see are the dark, black boots of the stranger. One of the feet lifts and comes down on her fingers, the heel connecting with the flesh that connects them to the hand.

Her knuckles are crushed.

Phyllis does not cry out. Her eyes close tightly and her head lolls to one side. She gurgles. Her throat has been slashed.

All around her there is a mist, kind of like they use in TV dream sequences. The mist closes in, obscuring the black heel of the stranger. Zoom into a close-up of Phyllis. Her face is in agony. Tears stream from reddened eyes.

The black boot comes in fast and kicks her teeth. Blood spurts from her lip. The warm red squirts out at least four inches and her teeth are broken.

The mist closes in, obscuring everything.

The next scene is in sharp focus. The elegant Tudor edifice of the Hobson home is in plain view. The double oak doors open and Anne runs out, her face contorted by terror. She is screaming, but there is no sound.

Anne wears a white dressing gown and stops for a moment, catching her breath.

She looks around her, searching wildly for help. Her face softens and she smiles. A white car pulls up in front of her, the door opens and I step out. Anne collapses in my arms.

And I comfort her.

Joe looked down at what he had written, pen poised to cross it all out.

He got up, lit a cigarette, and looked out the window. It was another overcast and gray day; Lake Michigan looked still and murky. He glanced in the mirror. The same Joe looked back at him. He assured himself there was nothing wrong with him. He knew his mother-in-law was poisoning his wife against him, knew that with Anne in Lake Forest he didn't stand a chance of getting her back. She would convince Anne he was wrong for her.

He made a decision. Sitting back down at his desk, he picked up the phone and dialed. Anne picked it up on the second ring.

"Hi."

"Joe?"

"Yes, babe, it's me. I called with a proposition."

Anne sighed and Joe thought for a moment he was doing the wrong thing.

"What is it?" she whispered, her voice ragged, as if she had been crying.

"Come back."

There was annoyance in her voice as she cut him off. "Please, Joe, we've been through all this already. I need some time to think."

"I know you do. That's why I'm asking you to come back—"

"Joe, I don't under—"

"I know. Shh. Just let me explain. I was going to say that you shouldn't be all the way up there, away from your work and everything that means anything to you. It must give you a distorted perception of things, not to mention just being plain inconvenient."

"I don't think you understand, Joe."

"I do, Anne. That's why I'm offering to leave and you can have the apartment." He heard the catch of her breath, soft, but he knew he had her.

"Think about things here. I'll find a nice place to hole up in while you think."

"Why?"

"All right, I am being a little selfish. I wanted you to be someplace where you'd be reminded of me. But I promise, I'll leave you alone."

There was a long pause and Joe began to fear she would turn down his offer. He needed to get her back here, in their home and away from her mother, who had disliked him from the start. But he didn't want to beg; that was the most certain thing to make her turn and run. She had to believe it was her decision. Finally, to break the silence, he said, "All right, Anne. I guess I can understand. We have a nice apartment, but I suppose Lake Forest is a lot better for this sort of thing." He tried to make certain there was no sneer in his voice. "It's a lot quieter and I'm sure your mother likes the company."

"Now, I didn't say that. Give me some time to think about it, Joe." She paused and then asked, "Where would you go?"

Even Joe didn't know the answer to that question. "Oh, I'll find someplace in a second. Don't let that worry you. I promise, Anne, I'll give you all the time and space you need."

"I might, Joe, I might. No promises, though. I'll let you know."

The line went dead before he had a chance to say anything further. In a way he was grateful. He would have begged; he knew he would have been unable to stop himself from doing so. There was a lot, he thought, he was unable to stop himself from doing.

The *Chicago Tribune* for that day was outside the apartment front door. Joe picked it up and brought it in with him.

It hit him like ice water.

He expected to see a story about the girl buried somewhere in the back pages. He did not expect the front-page story: SLAIN GIRL FOUND IN LIN-COLN PARK, INVESTIGATION CONTINUES. Joe sat down for a moment and closed his eyes. His hands were shaking, making the newspaper in them flutter. He took a long breath that ended in a quaking sigh and made himself stop trembling.

He scanned the story; certain words and phrases seemed to jump out at him: *runaway; evidence of sexual molestation; the victim was found nude; severe blow to the head; several lacerations to the skin with a very sharp, but unknown, instrument, possibly a razor; victim was almost entirely drained of blood*. And a final, almost editorial note: ". . . one of the most brutal crimes in recent history, prompting law enforcement officials to redouble their efforts to apprehend the perpetrator of this bizarre slaying. Unconfirmed reports speculate the crime may be tied with several other unsolved local crimes over the past year."

Joe let the paper drop to the floor. If Anne saw that, he thought, remembering her asking about the X-Acto knife in the bathroom, she could put two and two together and . . . no, she'd never believe he was capable.

Anne put the test shots back in the manila envelope. It was twilight outside, and Anne stared

out her bedroom window at the deep blue of the
sky and the trees that stood out in black contrast
against it. She followed the pale blue up to where
the sky was darker, deepening into purple. She
thought of Joe.

She had always considered the future with
him. And now she began to wonder if she really
knew him. She thought back to when they were
first a couple and had talked so much. But he had
evaded her questions about his family, and after
the first few times she had stopped asking, thinking he would tell her about them when he was
ready. And yet that time had never come. When
they were married she pleaded with him to invite
some of his family, but he told her they were out
of the country . . . he wasn't sure where. Without the least attempt to conceal his lie he told her
he had lost touch with all of his family and
hadn't seen them since high school. She had
caught the pain in his eyes, the look of a trapped
animal, and had not pressed further.

Anne lay back down on the bed, her head
pounding. She was certain she didn't know Joe
now, but wondered if she ever had.

"Anne?" Phyllis's voice filtered up the back
stairs from the kitchen. Anne got up and opened
her bedroom door.

"Yes, Mother. Is dinner ready?"

"You guessed it. Why don't you come down."

"I'll be right there."

"I was wondering if you had plans for the
weekend." Phyllis passed Anne the bowl of peas
and smiled.

"I'm not really sure. Why?"

"Well, you remember Mrs. Carlisle?"

"Of course, Mother. The two of you have been pals since high school. I've certainly seen enough of her." Anne lifted a bite of lamb chop to her mouth.

Phyllis laughed. "Well, it turns out she has tickets to this play downtown at the Feldstone called *Inappropriate Laughter.* Have you heard of it?"

"Yes, Mother. I hear it's supposed to be pretty good. Funny, anyway. Are you thinking of going with her?"

"I was thinking we could both go. That is, if you're not busy."

Anne thought of how much time she had been spending in her room lately, brooding about Joe. "Sure, I'd love to go."

Phyllis smiled at her daughter as she cut into her second lamb chop. "Pass the mint jelly? Listen, there is one little catch."

Anne pretended to be unconcerned, but knew what was coming and shifted into an excuse mode to try and get out of the evening.

"Mrs. Carlisle would like to bring her son, Philip, along. He just completed his Ph.D. at Marquette, and he's home for a few weeks before he starts teaching in the summer at USC. They've given him an associate professorship there. He's really an intellectual, Anne, good to talk to."

Phyllis and Mrs. Carlisle had been trying to get Anne and Philip together since high school, when they both went to Lake Forest High. Philip was very bright and good-looking in a porcelain sort of way: pale skin, dramatic cheekbones, dark hair, and pale blue eyes. Tall and much too thin, he did complement Anne's looks in a very similar way; he could have been her brother. He had many qualities that appealed to Phyllis: He came from money, he was polite and deferential and a brilliant student. What Phyllis didn't know and what Anne had known since high school was that Philip was gay.

The fact of Philip's homosexuality had eluded their mothers. Even though he had never dated a woman in his life, Philip was still expected by his parents to find the right woman. "He's just far too busy with his studies," Etta Carlisle reasoned, "to while away his time with women. Once he's established, then he'll be fine. You really must admire his tenacity."

Anne could think of nothing more pathetic than a separated woman and a gay man being fixed up and accompanied by their mothers on a date. Anne was tempted to tell her mother the truth and have the ridiculous matchmaking come to an end.

"On second thought, Mother, maybe I'd better not. I just remembered I promised Louise I would go out with her early on Sunday for some test shots near the lake. I really don't want to be out late."

"Oh, heavens! We won't be out late at all! We'll have dinner somewhere nice, then we'll go to the play. It'll be over by ten and we can come right home. I'm sure Philip's looking forward to it."

"I'm sorry, Mother, but I'd really rather not go. But please don't let me stop you. I'm sure the three of you will have a wonderful time."

"A wonderful time? A nice-looking man like Philip is going to have a 'wonderful time' with two old bags like us? I'm sure he'd love to be out with a beautiful young woman like you."

Anne had to laugh. "Two old bags? Come on, Mother. Besides, I don't really think I should be dating. Not yet, anyway. No, I think I'll just stay at home." Anne stared down at her plate, pretending to be absorbed in cutting her lamb.

If she had been looking up at her mother, Anne would have seen her face take on a look of determination, edged with anger. "I've already told Mrs. Carlisle you'd be coming. We made dinner reservations and have already bought the tickets." Phyllis's voice was obviously under a strain, trying to stay level.

Anne put her fork down. "Well, you can just unmake the plans for me. You should never have gone ahead and done those things without asking me first."

"You always were ungrateful."

Anne sighed. "It's not that I'm not grateful, Mother. I really just don't want to g—"

"Five minutes ago you said you'd love to go. What's wrong with you?"

"I don't owe you any excuses." Anne felt her voice rising, in spite of her efforts to keep the conversation on an even keel. "It was insulting to hear you made all those plans without having the courtesy to ask."

"I would have asked, but you weren't here. I just assumed you'd enjoy an evening out, a chance to take your mind off your troubles. Excuse me for trying to do something nice for you."

Anne would not let her mother make her feel guilty. "I appreciate the effort, I really do. Please, let's not argue."

"Who's arguing? Would you please just say you'll come? What will Philip think?"

"I don't care what Philip thinks! My marriage is falling apart, I don't know who my husband is anymore, and I'm supposed to sit here and worry about hurting some acquaintance's feelings?"

"Anne, you've always been hard-headed, but never inconsiderate. I don't know what living with that man has done to you, but I'm glad to see you're getting away from him before it's too late."

The words stung. Phyllis had never liked Joe, but she had never so blatantly condemned him.

"Joe has nothing to do with this."

"The case is closed, then?"

"The case is closed."

"Fine. I'll just stay home on Saturday night. I suppose I can watch *The Golden Girls*. It's what I do every Saturday anyway."

"Enjoy it." Anne picked up her plate and took it into the kitchen. Numbly, she switched the water on and rinsed her plate, glass, and silverware. There was no sound in the dining room. She knew from past experience that if she went back in, Phyllis would be sitting and staring off into space, not outrightly weeping but with silent tears pouring down her face. The tactic had been used many times, with varying degrees of success. Anne was certain she'd have to put her arms around her, say some comforting words, listen as her mother described how hard it had been to raise her daughter alone, how lonely. Anne would placate her with more words, the most comforting of which would be "I'll go with you on Saturday; please don't feel bad." Her mother would turn and ask if she was sure, that she felt like she had railroaded her into it. And Anne would say nothing could be further from the truth, that she should stop moping so much and get out more.

No, she was not going to live like this. Anne knew that if she stayed she would be berated every weekend. Undoubtedly her mother would try to fix her up on other occasions with Philip, since he would be at home throughout the spring.

Anne turned and hurried up the back stairs. There was a light feeling in her stomach. She wasn't positive she was doing the right thing. Joe would be overjoyed, even if he wouldn't be staying with her. But she couldn't tolerate living with her mother, couldn't stand her glee if Anne decided to make leaving Joe permanent. And there were practical reasons for going back. Her agent had called early that morning with an armload of assignments. Starting next week she would be very busy, and living in Lake Forest did not make things convenient.

She flicked on the light in her bedroom and went to the phone.

Margo kneels on his back, her knees digging brutally into his young shoulder blades. Near his ears, the sharp red nails hold his face down into the green carpeting, the nails digging into the tender flesh behind his ears. All he can smell is the dustiness of the rug. "Daddy's coming," she whispers. "Now you're going to get what I had all these years. Now it's your turn, brat."

And the footsteps grow louder.

Joe awakened from the dream, sweating. The phone was ringing, and for a few seconds he didn't know where he was, how old he was, and it scared him. The terror remained with him as he stood on weak legs to answer the telephone.

"Yes," he breathed into the phone, desperately trying to regain control. He gulped lungfuls of air.

"Joe, are you okay?"

Anne's voice, through the phone, comforted him.

"Yeah, I fell asleep. I must have dozed off."

"Oh, Joe, I'm sorry. I didn't mean to wake you up. Listen, hang up and go back to sleep."

"No! I mean, I'm fine. It's too early for bed. What is it? Eight o'clock?"

"A little after. Sure you're okay?"

"I'm fine, really. What's up?"

"Well, I think I'd like to take you up on your offer. I'd like to come back."

"Great! I can't believe it . . ."

"Now, Joe," she felt guilty. "I mean the whole offer. I still need some time to be by myself, some time to think. So I hope you were serious about giving me that."

"Of course I was." Joe fingered the phone cord, twisting it around his forefinger again and again. He had hoped she'd be coming back to him. But he'd change her mind. He had to.

"Good. I don't know how much time I'll need, but I do need it."

"I understand."

"I'm glad. Do you know yet where you'll stay?"

"Um, I'll probably just get a cheap motel room somewhere. Maybe I could stay at the Y."

"Can we afford that?"

"Sure. C'mon, the fucking Y?"

Anne laughed. "All right."

"When do you think you'll be back?"

"Well, Mother's not going to like it. Give me a couple days. I don't really have any work in the city until Monday. Maybe Saturday?"

"Anything you want. I'll make dinner for us."

"Joe, I'd really rather you didn't . . . Oh, what the hell. Okay, I'll see you on Saturday."

"Anne, I love you." He whispered the last part into the phone right before the line went dead. He wasn't sure she heard.

11

The session had been a real bitch. She hoped the effort was worth it. She had never worked with the photographer before. Ching was a perfectionist, already amassing a following in the galleries, his fashion photographs coming out in the fall in a tabletop book.

She had been at his studio at eight o'clock that morning. Now, at midnight, she was just pressing her key into the lock of their apartment. As she inserted the key she pressed her forehead against the door and let her body sort of fall into the apartment.

People who thought models had it easy were crazy. Trying to look perfect for eighteen hours was no easy task, and she hoped she had survived, hoped the film didn't show any of the weariness she was feeling toward the end as Ching urged her, "Lift you chin . . . *Higher!* Give me that look."

Anne closed her eyes. The photographs would appear in *Chicago* magazine this summer. She hoped they'd find their way into one of Ching's shows, or better, one of his books.

The apartment was cold. She had turned down the heat the night before and had forgotten to turn it back up before she left in the morning. Anne shivered, wanting nothing more than to slip into a hot shower and then sleep for hours.

Anne had been alone in the apartment for a week now. She hadn't really had time to think about Joe and their marriage. They had been in touch over the phone a couple of times. They had played games: he, trying to find ways to come back to the apartment, and she, trying to find out where he was staying. She could not understand why he was being so evasive.

Unless he was staying with someone she shouldn't know about . . . But then why was he so eager to get back together again? Anne shrugged, heading for the shower. Maybe he's in love with us both.

Struggling out of her clothes and turning on the water full blast, Anne decided she was too tired to think. Too tired for anything but this hot water.

The sheets felt cool after the shower. Anne stared up at the cream-colored plaster ceiling, at the delicate pattern of swirls. She remembered the first apartment she and Joe had shared. Rogers Park. A little studio the developers had chopped into a "one bedroom." Joe had painted the ceiling navy blue and studded it with glitter, meaning to imitate the night sky.

Anne rolled over, pulling the comforter close around her. He had wanted to make love right after the ceiling was painted. "It'll be like being outside," he had said. In order to see the stars, though, some lights had to be left on, and Anne never really felt like she was outdoors. But Joe's gesture had been romantic, and she wondered where the romance had gone.

Flicking off the lights, Anne closed her eyes and tried to sleep. In spite of her weariness there was no sleep for her. She was wired from the photo session. And she couldn't help wondering if there *was* another woman. Had Joe been channeling all of his romantic impulses into that relationship?

She found herself wondering where Joe was right now . . . and what he was doing. Was he with someone else? Had she driven him into the arms of another? What were they doing? Was she telling him how she really loved him and that his wife would be with him now if *she* loved him?

Outside, a wind blew up, rattling the glass in the window.

Anne sat up, restless. Tomorrow was another shoot, for Carson, Pirie, Scott. She knew the assignment was not a challenging one, modeling spring hats. A lot of facial close-ups. Anne knew if she appeared with bags under her eyes she wouldn't be used by Carson's again. That was the frustrating thing about her job—the competition.

She needed something to calm her. Joe kept

some Seconal in the medicine chest, but Anne had never liked to take it. But as she glanced at the clock on the nightstand and saw that it was one twenty, she knew she had to take some out-of-the-ordinary measures to get some sleep. She was supposed to be at the studio at eight.

Anne got out of bed and slipped into her robe. In the bathroom she discovered Joe had taken the Seconal with him. She sat down on the edge of the tub feeling frustrated and weary.

After a moment or two she rose and went into Joe's office. She knew there was some pot in there. She remembered him buying it for a party they had had on New Year's Eve. It was a little old now, but it would do the trick. He had kept it behind his files in the lower right-hand drawer. Stooping, Anne pulled the drawer open and found the Baggie under some papers in the back.

She pulled out the bag and the E-Z Wider papers that were nearby. Laughing to herself, she whispered, "Let me see if I can remember how to do this." Anne made several attempts at rolling a joint, and on the fourth try she managed.

"Now all I need are some matches." She took the joint back to her room and checked her purse. None there. "Shit." She headed back into Joe's office and rifled through his top desk drawer. There among the pens and paper clips (she avoided the X-Acto knife) was a book of matches.

Anne picked them up and noticed they had hardly been used. She sat down as she noticed they were from the Chicago Center Inn motel.

This was supposedly Joe's first week away from home. What was he doing with these? Anne tried thinking of some logical explanation, but could think of none.

She put the joint down on the desk blotter. Rapidly massaging her temples, she wondered what was happening. Was there more? Anne began going through his desk drawer like the wife she never thought she'd be, searching for clues of her husband's infidelity.

It was not long before she was rewarded. At the bottom of one drawer, under Joe's directory of advertising agencies, was a file full of magazines. Slowly, Anne took them out.

She was sickened by what she saw. They were all graphically pornographic. Each depicted women being beaten, women in chains, women with painful-looking clamps on their nipples, labia, women being tortured by faceless men. Come shots on blood, come shots on bruises. Anne paused, her stomach churning at a centerfold of a nude woman. She had deep gashes in her abdomen, her breasts, her body covered with blood. Were these real? The woman looked to be in genuine agony, her face covered with purple welts.

Anne placed the magazine on the desk before her. Trying to hold back the bile rising up in her, she covered her eyes. Too stunned to even think, Anne fought hard to control her breathing, the overpowering nausea. Who was this man she had married, lived with for years? Joe's handsome face came to her in memory, in a thousand different guises: smiling and boyish over a mechanical dog in F.A.O. Schwarz, clouded with concern over her doing something (like water skiing) that made him fear for her, his lids at half-mast, lust for her on his face . . .

She closed the magazine with a slam, lifted the stack, and threw them in the trash. What else, she thought, what else?

No longer thinking, she began going through his drawers, throwing the paper and supplies in each one wildly over her shoulder as she looked for more evidence.

After the room was a total wreck, looking as if a vandal had broken in and ransacked the place, Anne sat down on the floor, her breathing heavy. She had found nothing more.

She stood up, in control of her breathing now, and went into their bedroom. Methodically she removed each drawer from his dresser and emptied it on the floor. She watched as the heap grew: expensive woolen sweaters she had bought him over the years, belts, cuff links, underwear, socks, tie clasps, T-shirts, sweatshirts, sweat pants, shorts, a plaid flannel shirt. Anne stopped. There was something odd; something strange had passed her field of vision, but she didn't know what. She glanced back at the blue flannel shirt and thought, I've never seen that before. So? she asked herself, Joe probably has quite a few things you've never seen or noticed.

But it was so small. She picked the shirt up, knowing it wasn't Joe's. And it wasn't just the size. The shirt belonged to a woman. The buttons were the real giveaway. They buttoned on the wrong side.

Anne crumpled into a small ball on the bedroom floor. Her worst fears had to be true. She began to weep.

12

The ringing of the buzzer awakened her. Anne opened her eyes to a gray room, focusing in on the bedroom window. The shade was lowered and framed in brilliant light. She glanced at the bedside clock. It was one thirty in the afternoon.

The buzzing continued, more insistent. She got up and slid into her robe.

"Wait. Wait just a minute!" Anne hurried to the intercom. "Who is it?"

"Anne, it's Joe."

Anne slumped against the wall. She couldn't face him, not after what she had seen last night. Not yet.

She pressed the button again. "Joe, you promised. This isn't giving me any time. Please . . . just go away." Damn it. She didn't want to cry.

Anne walked away from the intercom. It buzzed.

Reluctantly, Anne pressed the button once more. She said nothing. His voice, mechanical, came through the box. "I just need to get some things out of my office. Please, Anne. I don't have my keys with me. It will just take a few minutes. We don't even have to look at each other."

Anne thought about his ransacked den. What would he say? She wasn't ready for a confrontation. "No," she said into the intercom, betraying no emotion.

Once more she started away from the intercom. It began buzzing once more: short, furious blasts punctuated by longer ones. Anne forced herself to walk slowly to the bathroom, where she dropped her robe, switched on the radio, and started a shower for herself. Once under the hot jets she no longer heard the buzzing. And once she emerged, her body revitalized by the water, the apartment was silent.

Joe stood outside, staring at their windows. What had happened? Why? he thought. His hands were trembling. Has she found something out?

He turned and looked out at the traffic whizzing by on Lake Shore Drive. All those people, he thought, going off to lead normal lives; why wasn't I made like them?

He looked back up at the windows, hoping maybe she would pass one of them. He wondered if she had found his journals, hidden under a fake bottom in one of his desk drawers. Those journals contained everything that could ruin his life. Detailed descriptions of each killing.

Joe bowed his head as a few tears escaped. The journals were also an attempt to exorcise his past. No one, even vicariously, should have to re-live that past.

Joe placed his hands in his pockets and walked away.

Watching from behind miniblind slats, Anne stared as her husband walked away from the building.

She turned and went back to the bedroom, where the yellow pages lay open on her bed.

Anne thought, as she sat down on the bed, she had no idea how to look for a private detective. She also thought she should be doing her own searching, trying to unmask what Joe was hiding from her. But that idea frightened her, forcing her to confront an unknown she wasn't at all certain she was ready to face. And the idea of a detective appealed to her; it seemed romantic, making her feel like the put-upon heroine of some 1940s B movie. More realistically, though, a private detective could be a witness for her in court if it ever came to that.

She stood up and let her damp hair fall from the towel. Pulling a comb through it, she stared at her face in the mirror. Perhaps it was better, she thought, that I missed the shoot for Carson's. Her eyes were ringed in darkness, underneath were puffy ridges, bloated and red. She walked to the window and stared outside at the snow, hardened and crusted over with soot.

"Enough," she whispered to herself. "Get to work." She sat down on the bed, flipping through a few pages until she came to the section marked "Private Detectives." She giggled for a moment, stepping outside herself and observing. Did people really do this?

She ran her finger down the list, stopping at words like *licensed, bonded, insured, surveillance, confidential, civil, criminal, matrimonial* . . . Which one to choose? She noticed a display ad for an agency called Women United. The ad promised "strict confidentiality" and that the agency was staffed by "women who understand the problems of women." Anne drew a red circle around that ad. Finally she circled one other listing, for a detective named Nick MontPierre in Evanston, because she liked the name.

She picked up the phone and dialed the number of Women United. While she listened to the ringing she imagined the agency being staffed by a group of butch feminists determined to brainwash her into leaving her husband and joining them, as a sort of female James Bond. Anne laughed at the idea. After four rings someone on the other end picked up.

"Women United Agency. Can I help you?"

Anne thought the voice sounded pleasant, and not in the least masculine. Still, fear burrowed into her stomach.

"Yes . . . I'd like to speak to one of your agents about some . . . surveillance work. Is there someone there I could speak with?"

"Well, hon, I'm the only one here and there's only one other agent working for me. I'm Joan Blake."

There was a pause as the woman waited for

Anne to give her name. Anne thought she would be waiting a long time.

After the silence became awkward, Joan asked, "What kind of surveillance? Industrial, matrimonial?"

"Um . . . matrimonial, I guess."

"Husband cheating on you?"

"Well, I don't know for sure. That's why I'm calling you."

"Hon, you wouldn't be calling me if you didn't already know. Every woman calls here's lookin' for the same thing: verification of something she already knows. Just doesn't want to face it. Makes it a little easier with us tellin' them the truth about dear hubby. What's the symptoms? Don't answer: Let me tell you. He's been gone for hours at a time with no good explanation for his whereabouts; he's been getting caught in lies, seems a little distant. Maybe you found a little material evidence, a phone number, an earring, maybe an article of clothing. Men. They're all alike. It doesn't take much to figure them out. Of course, I could be wrong about yours. Wanna come in and talk about it? There's no charge to talk."

Anne felt dizzy. The woman hit too many sensitive spots. Anne didn't like her tone. She seemed so down on men, so confident she already had the answers.

"Well?"

"Oh, I'm going to have to think about it."

"Okay, you do that. But I'm telling you. Men are all alike. Take it from one who knows." The woman snorted and hung up.

Anne flopped back on the bed. She glanced down at the next name, Nick MontPierre. Maybe a man would be better suited for her. Besides, his name sounded romantic.

After dressing and making herself some tea, Anne sat down at the desk in the living room with Nick MontPierre's number before her.

After one ring, a man picked up the phone. "MontPierre."

Anne heard a deep voice, slightly coarse, as if he had a sore throat.

"Yes, I was interested in talking to you about doing some surveillance work." Anne spoke with more confidence now that she had a little practice.

"What kind?"

"Matrimonial. I think my husband is—"

"I charge twenty-five dollars an hour, plus expenses. It's reasonable."

"That would be okay. As I was saying, I have reason to believe—"

"Wait. I don't like doing business over the phone. I'm free this afternoon. Can you come to my office?"

"Yes. What time?"

"Be here all day. Bye."

Anne stared at the dead receiver in her hand, wondering if she had made the right choice.

Nick MontPierre's office was on the third floor of one of Evanston's oldest office buildings, near Northwestern University on Sherman Avenue. The small office building had tile corridors, wooden doors with frosted glass panels.

His door was open. Anne went into his office, surprised to see such a young man sitting behind the desk. He couldn't have been more than twenty-six. He stood up as she entered and Anne noticed a tuna fish sandwich spread out on his blotter, with waxed paper underneath. There was a carton of chocolate milk and an apple.

He extended his hand. "Nick MontPierre."

Anne heard the same gravelly voice and hurried to shake his hand.

"Sit down, sit down." He motioned to one of two green vinyl chairs across from his desk. He took a sip of milk and Anne noticed a scar on his cheek. His face had a lot of character. His light brown hair was curly and clipped very short on the sides. He was clean shaven, with wide-set gray eyes and lashes so long they were almost feminine. But any feminine characteristics ended there. His face had a toughness to it: thin lips and a large straight nose. He was handsome in a way not everyone would notice.

"So what can I do for you?"

"I called earlier, about the possibility of you doing some surveillance work for me."

"Yeah. I remember."

Anne waited for him to say more. When he didn't, she continued. "My husband and I have recently separated, but I want our marriage to work. I guess I'm worried there's someone else in the picture and I'd like you to find out if I'm right. If there isn't, something strange is going on."

"Why?"

"Lots of reasons. Recently I caught him a couple times missing for hours, and then he comes in with no really plausible excuse for where he's been. I found a woman's blouse in his drawer. I have called our apartment while we've been separated and once he was gone all night." Anne stopped, realized how ridiculous she must sound. So what if he was gone all night, she imagined Nick MontPierre thinking, you said you were separated. She was afraid she'd start crying. She lowered her head and made herself take several deep breaths. She looked up and managed a smile. "Guess you don't hear much of this. I mean, I must sound pretty petty."

"Not at all. Unfortunately this kind of work takes up a lot of my time. So, yes, I do hear a lot of this, and no, you don't sound petty. People's marriages are important. When would you like me to start?"

"Right away, I suppose. It won't be easy. He won't even tell me where he's staying."

"Well, that's for me to figure out. I guess what I need to know from you is everything you can tell me about your husband, including the things you left out just now."

"How do you know I left anything out?"

"People always do. And you'll waste my time and your money if you don't tell me everything."

Anne looked out the window at a tan parking garage behind him and began.

Nick scribbled notes while she spoke, looking up every so often, as if checking her expression, making sure she wasn't making things up. Anne wondered if what he was hearing was everyday to him or if it was bizarre.

When she finished, he had scribbled several pages in a notebook in purple ink. Outside, it had begun to rain. The cold sleet tapped on the window; everything was dark.

The fluorescent light overhead hummed. Anne lowered her head and cried. "I don't know what I did."

Nick was silent for a long time. He got up eventually and put his hand on Anne's shoulder and gave it a squeeze.

"Would it help if I told you a lot of the men I follow really do love their wives?"

"How could they?" she whispered.

"Because what they're doing may not have anything to do with love, or even lust."

She looked up into his gray eyes. She stood and touched his face quickly, drawing her hand back as if his face was hot.

"Maybe that scares me the most." She hurried from the office.

She heard Nick say, "I'll let you know as soon as I have something."

13

Randy climbed the porch stairs to his parents' house. The March day had given the area a cruel taste of what spring could be: sunshine and temperatures soaring into the mid-sixties. Now, as Randy felt icy sleet biting at the back of his neck as he searched in the darkness for his keys, he felt glad he didn't let the capricious weather lift his spirits.

Inside, his parents had the heat much too high and Randy smelled meat loaf made with onion-soup mix lingering in every corner. His parents sat in the living room, their eyes intent on the console color TV (Early American, maple finish). The canned laughter of an *I Love Lucy* repeat combined with the kitchen odors to make Randy feel nauseated. When Randy's mother heard the *swish* of his nylon jacket as he removed it, she took her eyes from the TV for a moment to look back at him. When she saw it was her son she jumped from the couch and started heading toward the kitchen.

"I'll get you some supper. Have to work late?" she shouted over her shoulder.

"Yeah, Ma. I worked late and grabbed a sandwich at work. It's okay. Why don't you sit back down and watch your program?"

Randy was tired of all the sympathy, all the attention. He just wanted to be left alone.

His mother paused in the kitchen archway. "A sandwich? What kind of supper is that? You want a sandwich for lunch, okay. But you eat something decent for supper. Come on in. Sit down."

Randy walked toward the kitchen. He stopped within a few feet of his mother. "Please, Ma. I had a sandwich, fries, some cole slaw. I'm really full. You don't want me to get sick, do you?"

"I guess not. But you look like you're losing weight." She yanked on the loose waistband of his pants to emphasize her point.

"Hey, we can all afford to lose a few pounds."

"Not you. You always been too skinny. Just like your father in there." The last part she said louder, so her husband would hear. They both turned to see his reaction. The old man turned his head toward them for a second, expressionless, then resumed staring at the TV screen.

Randy's mother shrugged at him. "You sure I can't fix you just a small plate? Maybe a little cake? I got Sara Lee—"

"No, Ma. Maybe later."

"Well, okay." He watched as his mother sat back down on the couch, settling herself in for an evening in front of the TV. Randy wondered what his parents had done before they had a television.

Randy lay in the darkness of his room much later that night, still dressed. In his hand he held the lighter, feeling over and over again the small scratches, the grooved indentations of the engraving, the dividing line where the lighter opened. He opened and flicked it, watched as the flame gave a glow to the room, wondered about the maniac who had used it.

He flung the lighter to the floor and the phone rang.

Randy picked it up quickly, not wanting it to wake his parents. He glanced over at the alarm clock on the nightstand. One forty-five.

"Hello."

"Randy?"

"Yes?" Randy tried to place the woman's voice.

"What are you doing? You weren't asleep, were you?"

"No."

"I didn't think you would be." The woman laughed softly, almost to herself.

Randy felt annoyed. "Who is this?"

"Never mind who I am. But you *can* consider me a friend. And I have some information that might make it a lot easier for you to sleep at night."

Randy felt cold all of a sudden. "What are you talking about?"

"Don't you know?" The woman laughed again.

Randy could barely get the words out. "No, I don't know. Now, what is this?"

"I know something. I know . . . who killed your wife." The last came out in a sing-song voice, childish and taunting.

Randy bolted up in bed. He felt his heart pounding. "What are you talking about?"

The woman's voice was calm. "Peace of mind doesn't come cheap."

"Who? Who do you think killed her?" Randy felt himself begin to cry.

"Peace of mind doesn't come cheap. Not here or anywhere. What's it worth to you?"

Randy slammed the phone down again and again, sobbing.

Pat Young hung up after the first click. She didn't expect much from her first contact with Randy Mazursky. Give him a little time, she thought, he'll come around. In a week he'll be waiting by the phone, praying you'll call him back.

Pat laughed. She thought about how much Randy would be willing to pay to find out who Maggie's killer was. Probably not much, because he didn't have much. But a few thousand . . . surely.

Pat picked up the telephone once more and dialed a different number.

Anne is in a bare warehouse loft. Behind her, frosted glass windows, crisscrossed with wire and smudged with layers of filth. Beneath her, dirty and scarred wooden floors, beyond any hope of repair. On either side of her, crumbling brick walls. One is spray-painted with a blood red heart. Inside: "Anne Loves Joe." A click. Bright lights. Someone is photographing her. She can't see; the lights shine in her face. A figure. Backlit. Dark. Indistinguishable.

Click.

The ringing of the telephone brought her out of her nightmare.

"Hello," she mumbled into the phone.

Click.

When Randy awakened the next morning, he felt as if he had been awake the entire night. He still wore the same clothes he had worn yesterday. The sun shining in the window showed it was late in the day. The alarm clock told him it was almost noon.

It was a good thing it was Thursday and he had the day off.

The house was quiet as he undressed and grabbed a towel for the shower. As he passed his parents' bedroom he remembered they had been gone for hours, working.

He remembered the phone call from last night.

A crank. It had to be a crank. Unless—and this was the part that chilled him—it was the killer who called. Randy turned the water on, hot, and stepped into the shower.

After the shower and a cup of coffee, Randy thumbed through the yellow pages until he came to private detectives. He had no idea there would be such an array. He chose one in Oak Park, because it was closest to him.

* * *

The detective wasn't what the TV shows made private detectives out to be. He was not debonair, handsome, rugged, witty . . . none of those things. He did not wear a raincoat, suck a lollipop, or work with his wife as a team. He had no gimmicks. His name was William Masterson and he had occupied the same office space for twenty years. He was short (five three), fifty pounds overweight, smoked too many cigars, and had gray hair and a big, black mustache. Large, pinkish lips and jowls gave him a bulldog look. His voice was gruff.

"What can I do for you, son?"

Randy sat on the opposite side of the metal desk, uncertain how to begin. "Maybe you could just start by telling me how much you charge."

He laughed. "They all want that up front. Not that I can blame them. Right off, I charge a five-thousand-dollar retainer. Then I usually ask for a fair hourly rate and expenses. Now, what's your problem? Wife trouble?"

Randy laughed in spite of himself at the macabre humor of the question.

"Well, I guess you could put it that way." Suddenly Randy's eyes were brimming with tears. He wiped them angrily away and took a deep breath. "Mr. Masterson, somebody killed my wife. I'm trying to find out who. Now, I have some evidence"—he took the lighter out and put it on the desk—"and I can give you all the information you might need to know. I also had a call last night from someone who claimed to know who the killer was. I . . ." Randy would have continued, but he noticed the detective shaking his head.

"Son, this is police business. I can't get involved. Now, my advice to you is to give that lighter to the police. You've already ruined what fingerprints might have been left on it, I'm sure. But it could help a lot. I don't think any private detective would get involved in something like this, not without at least working *with* the police. At least not a good one. Plenty will take your money. This isn't the movies."

"Just wait. I—"

The detective stood. "No. Son, I just can't help you."

Randy stood. "Okay. Have it your way."

"Take my advice and go to the police."

"Sure."

Randy closed the door.

14

Anne and Joe sat on a carved wooden bench, behind them the colors of autumn and part of a weathered barn. Joe alone, on some rocks near Lake Michigan, his face blurred in the mist from the waves. A close-up of Joe, his smile lighting up a face handsome enough to be Anne's masculine counterpart in modeling. An older photograph, black and white, perhaps college graduation: Joe with long hair, parted in the middle and pulled back into a ponytail, full beard and mustache. A recent color snapshot: Joe standing in a kitchen, leaning against a counter and raising a glass of champagne to the photographer. Another black-and-white: Joe on a living room couch, clean shaven, hair clipped short.

Nick spread the photographs out before him on his desk blotter. Morning light came in through his window, leaving a pale trail of light across the photographs. Anne had given him the photographs the night before, meeting him at a coffee shop on the corner of Sherman and Clark in Evanston. They had sat in a booth with orange vinyl seats and a plastic table. She had explained, "I tried to get a good sampling, in case he's changed his appearance." He had bought her coffee and himself pie and coffee. They had talked. She told him how she had been happy with Joe during the first years of their marriage, and how things had gradually disintegrated. He had isolated himself, she told him. Maybe it had started with his decision to leave the large advertising agency where he was next in line for a position as a creative director. Whatever it was, he had grown further and further away from her until the two found they had little to talk about when they were alone together—daily reports on their jobs, changes in the weather. The only thing that remained strong between them was sex. She stopped herself then, looking up at him with the faintest tinge of rose in her cheeks, embarrassed at the curious look Nick knew he had failed to hide. "Finally," she had said, sipping the last of her coffee, "it seemed he wasn't with me even when he was home. I could tell he was preoccupied with something else, looking ahead to some future moment I knew he wouldn't share with me." Nick watched as Anne lowered her head, staring at the table. He wondered how a man could cheat on such a beautiful wife. He reached over then and covered her hand with his. She didn't move away from him. She let him drive her home, under the pretense he was meeting someone in the city.

He had no one to meet.

Nick gathered up the photographs and put them in his jacket pocket. He straightened his tie and pulled on his gray overcoat. Anne had told him she had called every YMCA in the area and had found no Joe MacAree registered. Nick knew that meant nothing, although he couldn't understand why the guy felt he needed to hide.

Anne had also mentioned a small hotel in the Rogers Park area of Chicago. It was a boarding house, really, and Joe had lived there when he first graduated from Iowa and had moved to Chicago. He always had good memories of the place and liked to drive by, just to see if it was still in business. The hotel was called The Pratt, named for the street it was on.

Nick decided to start there.

The Pratt stood, a dirty white brick building, bunched close to other dirty white brick buildings, all of them exuding a faded elegance and an air of slowly going downhill. Parking was tight, the streets clogged with beat-up and rusting older cars and newer Japanese economy cars. Many of the apartment buildings had been turned into condominiums. There were FOR SALE signs everywhere.

Nick parked his car two blocks away from the hotel. He pulled his overcoat collar up and dug deep into his pockets as he walked into a winter wind blowing off the lake.

Inside the hotel he saw a woman behind a

desk. She had dyed red hair and a cigarette dangling from her lips. She wore a cotton housedress and had drawn her lips in larger than they really were with orange lipstick. When she saw Nick she stopped sorting mail, took the cigarette out of her mouth, and smiled.

"Lookin' for a room?" she asked as Nick drew near. He noticed she spoke much too loud, and then saw the hearing aid in her ear.

"Actually, no," Nick said, speaking up.

"Well, what is it you've come for?"

"I'm trying to find a friend of mine. I got a hunch he might be staying here. He always liked it here."

The woman smiled and nodded. She stooped down and brought out a blue binder from a shelf beneath the counter. She slid it toward him. "You're welcome to take a look at the register."

"Thanks," Nick opened the register and began looking at all the names registered from about a week ago, looking for some clue that might give Joe away even if he did use a false name and address.

But he found nothing.

"Sorry," he said to the woman, sliding the register back to her. "I don't see his name in here." Nick took out one of the recent photographs he had of Joe and placed it on the counter. "Doesn't look familiar to you, does he?"

"What?" she asked, picking up the photograph.

"Does he look familiar to you?"

"Oh, he's a handsome fella."

"But have you seen him before?"

"Why? Is he in some kind of trouble?"

"What makes you think that?"

"Well, you didn't see his name in the register . . ."

"Oh! No, he's not in any trouble. I'm just trying to locate him to give him back some money I owe him." Nick paused for a moment, thinking. "He's kind of eccentric. It would be just like him to register under another name." Nick smiled at her. "Just for the hell of it."

The woman stared at the picture. "He sure is good-lookin'. He could be a movie actor."

"So you'd remember if he'd been in here?" Nick was almost ready to give up.

"I might. But I see lots of people coming and going." She shrugged. "Nature of the business." She handed him back the photograph. "I'm getting older. Don't remember things as well as I used to."

Nick didn't like to use bribes, thinking it was a waste of his client's money, but he thought the woman was hinting. He took a ten-dollar bill out of his wallet and placed it on the counter. She snatched it up and Nick watched it disappear into one of the pockets of her aqua housedress.

"Memory's gettin' better," she said, and winked.

There was a pause. Nick slipped her another ten and watched it disappear.

"He was here," the old woman spoke slowly. "He stayed for a few days. Checked out this morning." She brought out the register and opened it. Pointing with an orange-frosted fingernail, she located the name Alex Waters. "Here's his registration."

Nick copied the name down in a pocket note-book. "Did he leave a forwarding address or any-thing like that?"

She shook her head. "No. People in here usu-ally don't. I don't ask anymore and they usually don't say."

"Really?" Nick asked, reaching for his wallet.

She caught his hand. "Really."

"While he was here, did you get to know him at all?"

"Not really. Like I say, I try to mind my own business. There's a lot to do, runnin' this place."

"I imagine."

"I mean, I'm friendly when they come to this desk, but beyond that I just don't have time to be bothered. This one, though, did impress me." She smiled bashfully at Nick. "I may be gettin' up in years, but I still notice a pretty face when I see one. And he was a looker." She laughed. "But he was a weird bird, that one. Got kinda worse-lookin' every day. Didn't shave, didn't seem like he even washed. When he checked out this morn-ing, I could smell the booze on his breath. And that was eight thirty! Said he was gonna find his wife."

"Well, Mrs. . . ."

"Mayo. And that's *Miss.*"

"Miss Mayo, you've given me a lot of help. Thanks a lot."

"Thank *you,*" she said, patting her pocket.

Nick found a small Greek restaurant near Loyola University and stopped there for lunch.

While he waited for his *avgolemono* and Greek salad to be served, he called Anne.

She answered on the first ring. She sounded breathless, as if she was waiting for someone to call.

"Yeah, this is Nick MontPierre."

"Oh, hello. I'm glad you called. Did you find anything out?"

"Your hunch was right. He had been staying at The Pratt."

She sighed, the relief obvious. "Then you've found him. Were you able to see him at all?"

"He wasn't there."

"So what will you do? Just watch the hotel until he comes back?"

"No, you don't understand. He checked out this morning. Left no forwarding address."

"Damn."

"But listen: There's hope. He told the woman at the desk he was going to look up his wife."

Anne was silent for a moment. "I don't know if I want to see him."

"You've got to, Anne. It's the only way I'll ever be able to put a tail on him and find out what's really going on."

"Surely he'll turn up. You can watch for him at some of his freelance contacts. I mean, he'll have to have some money sooner or later."

"Anne, this is the only way. Listen, I'll be at this place called The Greek Fisherman for the next hour or so. Copy down this number: 555-8762. If he contacts you I want you to set up a time to meet with him, and then I want you to call me so I can be there when he shows up."

"You'd only scare him away. I don't think this will work."

"Will you listen to me? I'm not going to let him know I'm there. It's just so I can follow him."

"I don't know."

"All right. It's your money." Nick hung up the phone.

He waited. A minute later it rang. "Yeah?"

Anne's voice came over the line, breathy and uncertain. "Okay. I'll see him."

"Call me when you have the time you're going to meet."

"Yes. What if he doesn't call while you're there?"

"After I'm done I'll come over to your place. If that's okay. We can wait for his call together."

"That would be fine."

"Well, let's keep the line clear."

"What if he doesn't call first? What if he just shows up here?"

"Make an excuse and call me. If I'm not here, I'm on my way. I'll be waiting in your lobby. If I buzz you and he's up there, pretend I'm a salesman. Got that?"

"Yes."

"I'll be waiting for him. Then maybe we can find out what the hell's going on."

He listened as she hung up the phone.

The phone rang. Once. Twice. Three times. Anne stood over it, her hand poised, listening to its ring. Finally, after seven rings, she picked it up. She didn't say anything.

"Babe? Anne? Honey, it's Joe."

He sounded so far away. She didn't know if the distance was in the connection or her mind.

"Yes?" she whispered.

"Honey, I need to see you. I know I said I wouldn't bother you. But I won't take long. I just need to talk with you for a little while. . . ."

"Where are you staying?"

"At some Y. That's not important. Can I come over for a little bit?"

"Joe, you promised you'd stay away."

"And I have. Please, Anne." She had never heard such desperation in his voice. He was acting like a child, whining and begging. She wondered why she'd ever loved him.

She didn't want to see him. Not yet. But she said, "You can come over, Joe, but you can't stay long. Just a half hour. Do you understand?"

"Yes." He hung up the phone. Anne felt chilled.

She sat down and dialed the number of the restaurant Nick had given her. He answered quickly. She explained Joe was on his way.

"I'll be right there."

Fifteen minutes later Anne heard a key being fitted into a lock. She was surprised. She had forgotten he had his own set of keys to the apartment. She went from the bedroom into the living room and waited for the door to open.

Joe was a different man. His clothes—jeans and a flannel shirt—were dirty and wrinkled. There was a large stain on one of the legs of his jeans. His overcoat looked rumpled, as if he had slept in it. He hadn't shaved for days and she smelled alcohol on his breath. Its scent filled the room, combining with the smell of his perspiration.

"What's happened to you?" Her words came out stunned. There was too much caring behind them.

"I've been so lonely without you. I don't care anymore." He started to cry and stepped toward her. She moved across the room, putting a table between them. "Why don't you sit down?" Anne gestured toward one of the chairs.

He clumsily seated himself on the couch, almost missing it. Once she would have laughed and teased him about it. Now she felt pity.

Anne sat down across from him. "Joe. You can't do this to yourself. Where have you been? What's been going on?"

He shook his head, dismissing what she was saying. "None of that matters. What matters is I need you to survive. I love you so much, Anne." His words came out between sobs. "I really do. You have to take me back. I'll be my old self again. You'll see. Please."

"Joe, I don't know."

"We'll take a nice vacation. Get it back. I won't do the bad things anymore. I can't help myself sometimes. But with you I know it'll be all right. If we can just get away together for a little while. It'll be just like it used to be. Remember?"

He got up and knelt in front of her, grabbing her hand and holding it tight. Anne felt nauseated by the smell of him. "Please," she said, pulling her hand away and standing.

"Annie, please." He was on all fours, begging. "Let me come home. I promise not to do the bad things anymore. I love you. I really love you. Don't you know that?"

"I don't know anything anymore!" she said, her own eyes filling with tears. "Please, Joe, please, go!" She hurried to the door and opened it. "If you really love me you'll leave now. Come back when you're straight."

The pain on his face reached somewhere deep inside her. She wanted to embrace him. She wanted to scream. "Please," she whispered, the tears flowing, "go."

She turned her head as he walked by her. "Annie, I'll be back. Remember, I love you."

She kept her face turned away from him, waiting until the heavy odors of alcohol and perspiration had cleared.

Then she closed the door.

Nick MontPierre started up his maroon Volvo when he saw Joe leave the building. He let it idle as he watched Joe go to a bus stop in front of their building and wait for a bus. After five minutes a southbound bus pulled up, Joe let three people go ahead of him and then got on. Several seconds later Nick watched Joe get back off the bus. He could see Joe screaming at the driver, but couldn't hear what he was saying. The doors squeezed shut and the bus went on its way.

Joe waited a moment, then stepped out into the road and hoisted his thumb up.

Nick pulled out into the traffic and stopped a few feet beyond where Joe was standing. He watched in the rearview mirror as Joe hurried to get in the car.

Once Joe was inside, Nick tried not to notice the smell, wondering how the handsome, meticulous man in the photographs had transformed himself into this greasy-haired, unshaven street person.

"How you doin'?" Nick asked him.

"You goin' downtown? Chicago Avenue?"

"Yeah, as a matter of fact that's right where I'm going. Have to pick up a couple things at Water Tower. Where can I let you off?"

"Know where the Lawson Y is?"

"Sure, you stayin' there?"

"Am now." Joe hunched down in the seat and stared out the window.

Nick eased out into the traffic on outer Lake Shore Drive. He tried to make conversation, to find out a little more about Joe. But Joe wouldn't answer and after a while Nick gave up.

Nick dropped Joe off at the Lawson Y on Chicago Avenue and drove around the block. He found a parking space and waited in his car for fifteen minutes.

Inside the Lawson YMCA, Nick asked to see the register, making up a story about needing to find a guy who had done some work for him, because he needed additional work done.

Joe used the same name. Alex Waters. He was in room 712.

Now Nick could find out just what the hell was going on.

15

Margo's nails are sharp, painted red. They dig into his wrist, forcing his hand down against the beige sheets of his parents' bed. Joe looks over, his eyes those of a trapped animal, to see her nails dig in deep enough to pierce the skin. There is a satisfied sigh from her when she sees the trickle of blood run down his arm. She takes the nylon cord and ties his arm to the bedpost. She has already tied the other arm down.

His father sits at the bottom of the bed, holding Joe's legs, one ankle in each hand. Joe looks down at his father, who is naked, his erection snaking up from between his legs. "No," Joe whispers, without emphasis. There is no mercy.

"You can go now," his father says to Margo.

"But I wanted to watch."

"Go on, get out of here."

Petulantly, Margo gets up from her side of the

bed and walks to the door. She looks over her shoulder at Joe and laughs. "Now you'll know," she says. "Now you'll have a taste of what I've had. Have fun!" She hurries from the room, laughing.

"Just relax, Joey. This ain't gonna be so bad if you take it easy."

Joe's fingers claw at the bed sheets as he watches a blob of spit drop from his father's mouth onto his penis. When his father looks up, it's as if Joe no longer exists. His father throws Joe's legs up, resting them on his shoulders. Joe closes his eyes, biting down hard on his lower lip as he feels the piercing pain, so bad he wants to scream. Fire boils through his veins.

He bites his lip so hard he tastes blood, and the warmth of it gives him sustenance. He keeps his eyes squeezed together, not wanting to see the specter of his father thrusting above him, the fat hairy belly above his own young thighs.

The pain lessens a little and Joe finds himself hearing the radio downstairs. WUSA. His mother is listening to the country-western station that is her constant kitchen companion. Loretta Lynn is singing "Coal Miner's Daughter." Joe smells bread baking and imagines his mother in her apron, bending over in front of the stove, sliding the stainless steel bread pans into the oven.

Why doesn't she help me?

Joe feels a warm wetness that begins with his father's groans. His father pulls out of him and lets his legs drop back down on the bed. He pats Joe's leg. "You're a good boy," he says.

At the door, his father pauses and calls Margo. His sister comes back into the bedroom.

"Clean up in there, willya?"

His father disappears and Joe hears the sound of the bathroom door closing. Margo comes in and looks at him. There is a smile on her face as she looks down at Joe, who wants to cry but for some reason can't.

"Yuck. What a mess," Margo says. She lifts her nose and sniffs. "And it stinks in here. Smells like shit." She giggles.

Joe looks down and sees the small round pool of blood beneath his buttocks on the beige sheets.

Why doesn't anyone help me?

Joe awakened from the dream, the pillow beneath his head pressed flat and smelling of his sweat. He lifted his head from the damp pillow and looked around the small room, seeing unidentifiable shapes in the darkness. He reassured himself, sitting up, that he was no longer in his parents' house, and he remembered checking into the Lawson YMCA that afternoon.

Joe got up and switched on the overhead light. He needed blood.

Outside, Nick MontPierre put down the *Sun Times* he was reading and perked up. He had managed to figure out which room was Joe's. Nick had been waiting through the afternoon and into the dusk for the light to come on, wondering if Joe had left by a fire escape, worried that he wouldn't be able to tail him, worried he would find out nothing for Anne.

He wanted to please her.

Joe stood and looked in the mirror. His face was grimy with sweat and a three-day-old beard. He didn't care. It didn't matter anymore.

He looked at his Burberry raincoat on the floor, splattered with mud courtesy of a Chicago cabdriver. The coat was wrinkled and filthy anyway; the extra mud didn't hurt its appearance that much.

My God, what have I done?

Joe picked up the coat and hugged it to him, as if hugging the old life back to him. It's gone now, he thought, what does it matter?

What I used to be is finally gone. I'm something else now.

He pulled the raincoat on, belting it tight.

He flicked off the light switch.

As soon as the light went out Nick started his engine. Even if Joe didn't come out, the car needed some warming up, and so did Nick. But it wasn't long before he saw Joe exiting the front of the Y. Nick placed his foot on the brake and put the car in drive, waiting. Joe started up Rush Street. Nick let two cars pass, then pulled out into traffic. Joe seemed so unaware of what was going on around him that Nick thought he could have walked alongside Joe and Joe wouldn't have noticed, but he didn't want to take any chances.

* * *

A hooker, Joe was thinking. A nice little whore nobody would miss. He walked up Rush, past the revelers out looking for a good time on Division, and on up north.

Two women stood in an apartment doorway, shivering in miniskirts and fake-fur jackets. Joe looked them over quickly. One was black, the other oriental. Both looked hardened and old: heavy eye makeup, lip gloss that stood out like a neon advertisement in the cold night. They would not do.

They turned away when Joe walked by. He supposed they were already too practiced in judging who could afford and who couldn't.

He needed someone not so jaded. Someone a little vulnerable.

He walked several blocks north, seeing the same women he had seen in the apartment house doorway a few blocks back in assorted colors and sizes, all with hardened expressions and knowing eyes that sized him up before he even got by. He began to tire, and these worn women began to look more and more fitting for his purpose.

He approached one.

Joe took out one of his last cigarettes, stuck it in the corner of his mouth, and walked over to a red-haired young woman who leaned against a black car.

"Hey . . . you got a light?"

"Beat it, man. You're gonna scare people away."

"What kind of people?" Joe asked, grinning.

The woman looked nervous. He noticed her

roots were dark and she had a black eye hidden under pancake makeup. "Never mind, just get away from me."

"Don't you want to make some money?"

"Yeah," the prostitute hissed, "that's exactly why I want you to get the fuck out of here." She lit a cigarette, brought the match close to Joe's cigarette, and let it drop to the ground.

Joe continued up the street.

Nick put his camera back down on the seat beside him. What would Anne think when she saw the pictures? What do I think? Why would this guy throw everything away? Why?

Joe was about to give up and look for an answer to his needs in some other way when he saw her. She looked so young, no older than fourteen. Her face was heavily made up and her blond hair was pulled back. She had three or four earrings in each ear and was smoking, but none of the affectations could hide the innocence in that face. This one probably still liked to play with dolls.

He walked up to her, pulling his dirty hair off his forehead, trying to comb it with his fingers.

"Hey," he said, "it's awfully cold out here. Wouldn't you like to go someplace warm?" He smiled at her, and watched as she looked him over. There was more than interest in her eyes, and Joe thought he'd have no problem with this one. Another missing runaway. Who gave a fuck? She must have stared at him for five minutes before she said anything. There was a little smile on her face.

"Fuck off," she finally said.

Nick snapped one more picture. He wanted to grab that little girl and take her home with him. She looked so young. And what did a creep like Joe MacAree want with her? Nick watched as Joe sat down on the street corner, lowering his head into his hands. His body shook. He seemed to be crying.

Nick looked down at his watch. It was after ten o'clock. It would be nice to pack it in. Get back to his warm apartment and develop tonight's photographs.

But Joe was standing up. He was heading south.

Joe needed someone. He had no money left. He needed to talk to someone. And other than Anne there was no one he could turn to, except the woman who had tried to blackmail him in Berwyn. In spite of her predatory ways Joe felt he knew her better than she realized, and that made him stop resenting her. He also knew that she longed for him and would probably welcome him back into the cramped apartment in which she lived.

He had enough change to pay for a subway ride and a transfer.

Nick whipped the maroon Volvo into the parking space in front of a fire hydrant and followed at a short distance. Joe descended into the subway. The weariness Nick had felt earlier began to dissipate. Maybe he would find out everything he needed to know about Joe MacAree in this one night. At least tailing him wasn't boring.

The subway train was just pulling out when Joe got into the station. He hurried to get on the next-to-last car. Nick sprinted to make the last car on the subway, forcing the door apart to get on. He sighed with relief as the train jerked into motion. Following someone on a separate subway car would be impossible, a test even he would fail. He walked up to the front and peered into the adjoining car. Joe sat on one of the orange plastic seats near the door. Here, at least, was one place Joe fit in, Nick thought. He didn't look a bit out of place.

Joe had walked all the way from Cicero Avenue and Roosevelt Road to Oak Park Avenue, looking behind him every few seconds to see if a bus was coming. He thought it must be too late and there weren't very many running. His ears were burning with cold and his fingers felt numb. Mucus in his nostrils crackled with every breath he took.

She'd better be there.

Nick had a difficult time following Joe. Was he getting suspicious? Was that why he kept peering back over his shoulder? Nick was forced to stop and jump into the shadows every time Joe made a motion to turn back.

* * *

Joe stood outside the apartment building and noticed the lights were out in her apartment. Damn, if she wasn't home . . .

But he knew, somehow, she would be. A woman like that just wouldn't get out much. He knew it. It had to be as true as the cold that was making his teeth chatter.

He went inside and rang the buzzer for her apartment. There was a long pause, and finally an answering buzz opened the door. Joe went inside.

Nick was able to stand outside and to the left of the little apartment house vestibule while Joe rang the buzzer. He snapped a picture of Joe standing in the vestibule. Since there were only five names on the mailboxes, it wasn't hard to see which one Joe pressed. As soon as Joe had disappeared into the hallway, Nick pulled the door open and went inside.

The vestibule was dim, lit by a low-watt bulb overhead. There was the smell of cooked cabbage. Nick took a notebook from his inside jacket pocket and wrote down Pat Young's name and address. More information to check on. Was this the woman Joe was sleeping with instead of his wife? Enough speculating, he thought, sort the facts when you have more information. Pat Young could be a man for all you know. And wouldn't that make things interesting? Pat Young could also be a friend, a client. Quit trying to make up a scenario without any of the facts. You'll never be a good detective like your father if you start relying on guessing and your imagination. Consider the facts.

Nick let himself get warm in the vestibule. He wished his car wasn't so far away.

"My, my. Isn't *this* a surprise?" Pat held the door open and stared up at Joe. "Well, why don't you come in?" Her words were mocking, but she moved the wheelchair back to admit him.

She was dressed in a white flannel nightgown with small flowers, and Joe thought she looked unusually vulnerable. There was a softness there Joe knew she would never admit to.

She slammed the door behind him and laughed. "What the *hell* happened to you?"

"I've had some bad times," Joe mumbled, wishing he hadn't come. There would be no comfort here. "My wife wanted us to separate. . . ."

Pat's laughter chilled him. "She had enough of a big boy like you? That woman must be crazy! Although if you looked like you do now when she threw you out, I can't say that I blame her."

Joe stared at the nap of the brown carpeting, his ears burning. "I came to you because of what happened last time. I thought I saw something in you that time, something maybe we have in common."

He watched as her face went expressionless, then as a faint blush rose to her cheeks. "What happened last time shows only that we have *nothing* in common. I'm not a murderer; I just happen to have a healthy interest in sex. Now, what did you really come here for?"

"I need some money. I don't have any." Suddenly, Joe felt like crying. Tomorrow he would get Anne back.

"If you want money," Pat said, "you have to earn it." She winked at him. Then with viciousness she said, "Only no help from me this time. You fly solo."

"All right," Joe whispered. He began to unbuckle his belt.

"Christ! Not like that! Get in there and take a bath first. Clean yourself up! Shave!" She sneered at him, pointing to the bathroom. "You're hardly very exciting in your current state."

Joe disappeared into the bathroom.

Nick, shivering and staring into the lobby Joe had entered, thought this stakeout would have to come to a close. Joe could be spending the night there. Nick would freeze to death waiting for him to reemerge. He would call a cab. Enough.

Pat licked his come from her hand. "What are you staring at?" She looked up at him. "Go on, get out of here!"

"I thought you were going to give me some money."

"Oh, sure, I'm just loaded. Beat it, asshole."

Joe bit his lip to keep from crying. He would not reduce himself to that in front of her. He picked up the grimy clothes, recoiling slightly as he put them on his newly clean self. After he was dressed he went to the door.

Opening it, he heard her call his name.

"Come here," she said. He walked over and stood in front of her wheelchair. "Kneel down; I want to look at your pretty face." Joe knelt and looked into her blue eyes.

"I've tried to get ahold of you a few times . . . seems I can only get wifey on the phone." When Joe looked panicked she said, "Don't worry; I hang up on her. I haven't told anyone about you . . . yet." Pat thought for a moment, then added, "Except, of course, for the people who already know, and they won't say anything without clearance from me first. You know, sometimes I just like to have you around. I like what you have between your legs." She giggled. Pat wheeled back and took her wallet out of a drawer. "If you'll tell me where you can be reached and promise me you'll come see me when I call, I'll give you a little money. Deal?"

"Yeah . . . it's a deal. I'm staying at the Lawson YMCA on Chicago Avenue in the city."

"You wouldn't lie to me, would you? I wouldn't like that."

With no emotion, Joe said, "I would have everything to lose if I lied to you."

"Right." She handed him a twenty-dollar bill. "Here. If you're a good little boy I might give you some more."

"Thanks," Joe said, and hurried out the door.

As she watched him leave, there was a mixture of agony and love on her face. What's happening to me? she thought.

Joe looked up at the night sky. It was black and starless. The pace of the night had slowed down. People were tucked away for the night. Normal husbands slept curled against normal wives, their normal little children asleep down the hall after a glass of water and being tucked in. Joe wished he were like them.

But he wasn't.

He needed the taste of hot blood pumping into his mouth. The feel of life ebbing out of someone and into him.

"Where the fuck you been until ten o'clock?"

Becky stared at the man she had married just three months ago. He was still handsome, even if he was furious with her, even if she could feel the slap that was coming. The slap that would jar her teeth and knock her into the Formica countertop in their kitchen. She'd been getting a few of those ever since they returned from their week-long honeymoon at Wisconsin Dells. The dark hair still gleamed, even if his face was red and angry; the eyes were as dark and sexy as they had been when she first fell in love with him in the back seat of his car on their first date. They had been seniors in high school then. Only a year ago. Why did it seem like such a long time ago?

"I asked you a fuckin' question."

"I was out . . . at Ma's. I told you that."

"I called your mom's. There was no answer."

"So? We were at the mall."

"Bullshit. You were with somebody else. You can't tell me any different. You think I don't know when my own wife is puttin' out for another guy?" He grabbed her by the front of her pink blouse, lifted her from the floor, and threw her against the cabinets.

It felt like something snapped in her sides. A rib?

Becky lifted herself from the floor. Ma was only four blocks away. The hell with him.

"Where are you goin'?"

"Ma's." She was sobbing.

He didn't say anything. When she opened the door she felt a bruising kick in her bottom. She fought to stay upright, but landed on her knees. Nothing hurt anymore. She heard him laughing before he slammed the door.

Joe was in a phone booth calling a cab when he saw her limping up Oak Park Avenue. No, he told himself, leave her alone. This is too close to the other one. You can't touch her. But as he was thinking, he was hanging up the phone and quietly opening the door to the telephone booth.

I can't do this, he thought. Somewhere inside, a voice said, "Just this one last time, Joe. Tomorrow you'll go back to Anne and start over."

No, no . . . please don't make me. . . .

He followed her for a couple of blocks, then she stopped and turned, looking back at him. She started to walk faster.

"Hey!" he said. "Don't be affaid. I'm not a mugger. Just an insomniac." Joe laughed. He caught up with her and she stopped, looking up at him, her eyes afraid.

"Please," he said, giving her one of his best smiles. "I'm not a creep. Really. I live right down the street, near eighteenth. I just couldn't sleep. Hell, I should be afraid of you. Is anything wrong? What are you doing out so late?"

She stared at him. She must have been debating whether she should talk to him. Finally she said, "I had a fight with my husband. I was going by my ma's."

"Oh, well, you know you shouldn't be out walking alone this late at night. A pretty lady like you. Listen, would you let me walk you to your mother's? I'd feel like I was doing my good deed for the day. I promise I wouldn't hurt you. I just don't like seeing someone as young and pretty as you out alone like this."

"I know you wouldn't hurt me." She looked like she was in thought for a moment. "Okay, I guess I'd probably be better off."

They walked along in silence for a while. Becky could see her mother's bungalow ahead. "Well, there it is. Thanks. I think I can make it the rest of the way by my—"

"Damn!" Joe shouted, grabbing his eye.

"What's the matter?" Becky turned to stare at him.

"My contact just popped out. Can you help me find it?"

Becky dropped to her knees and began groping on the dark sidewalk for something that wasn't there. She hardly felt Joe's joined hands come down hard on the back of her neck. And when her face slammed into the concrete, she was already unconscious.

Joe removed the X-Acto knife from his pocket.

16

Anne applied the last of the pale gray eyeshadow and looked at herself in the mirror. Years of modeling had taught her well how to hide distress, exhaustion, and abuse. Putting her makeup back in the top drawer of her vanity table, she told herself she was hiding her turmoil, and nothing more. No matter that her long black hair was brushed to a sheen, catching and reflecting the light, no matter that she had put on her finest pale blue silk blouse, no matter the jeans she wore showed off her legs better than any mini-skirt.

She thought of Nick MontPierre. He would be in her apartment in a half hour and Anne felt, in spite of herself, an excitement she hadn't experienced since her dating days back in college; she also felt a kind of dread. Nick had told her over the phone he had some information she would be anxious to hear. He also had photographs to back the information up. Nick hadn't told her anything of his findings, insisting he do it in person. Obviously the news wasn't good. Her mind went back to the photographs. . . . She pictured Nick on the fire escape of some tawdry hotel, taking pictures of Joe writhing on gray sheets with a woman, their bodies sweating and frantic with hours of coupling in the dark.

The buzzer sounded in the living room and Anne rose to answer it. Normally when she expected someone, she would just buzz them in without inquiring as to who was calling, but lately she was afraid of letting Joe in.

"Who's there?"

"Nick MontPierre."

She pressed the button to admit him and hurried around the living room, straightening things. She disappeared into the kitchen and put a pot for tea on the stove. There was a plate of Mrs. Field's chocolate chip cookies on the counter.

Nick looked solemn when she opened the door, his rugged face pulled down into a frown. He came in and sat down at the dining room table. Lighting a cigarette, he said, "Sit down."

Anne seated herself, thinking the line should have been hers. "You're not bringing good news, are you?"

"I don't know. I just give my clients what I've observed and try to let them decide whether the news is good or not."

"Okay," Anne said, certain such a preface could only mean bad news. "What have you found out?"

Nick took off his raincoat and pulled up the sleeves of his sweater. He folded his hands in front of him. "I've watched your husband the past couple days. For the most part he's been staying at a hotel in Rogers Park called The Pratt, the one you mentioned."

Anne nodded.

"Anyway, he moved out of there a couple days ago and checked into the Lawson YMCA on Chicago Avenue."

Anne thought of the Lawson Y, how seedy it always looked when she walked by. She couldn't imagine Joe, with his refined tastes, living in a place like that. She noticed Nick had removed a packet of photographs from his coat pocket. He placed it on the table in front of her.

"I wasn't able to get too many shots, but what I did get, I think, is significant. I watched your husband last night. He headed up Rush Street and approached several prostitutes who wouldn't have anything to do with him. Probably because he looked like a bum." He took out one photograph and Anne picked it up. Her hand shook as she held it out in front of her.

Anne saw Joe, in the harsh light of a street lamp, talking to a black hooker, the kind he would have made fun of in the past. Even through the graininess of the photograph, she saw the look of desperation on his face, more than need, more than lust . . . a frantic obsession. And that was what probably frightened the prostitutes away, more than his disheveled appearance. Nick put two more pictures in front of her.

"He seemed particularly anxious to please this one. He spent more time with her than with the others."

Anne picked up the photo and felt an electric jolt go through her. This couldn't be her husband. Joe would never try to seduce someone like this. She was just a little girl. The makeup and clothes could never hide her youth; she couldn't have been more than twelve. God, God, Anne thought, who was this man I married?

"He wasn't successful with any of them," Nick said. "Later I was able to follow him to Berwyn."

"Where's that?"

"It's a western suburb. Anyway, he went there to the apartment of a person named Pat Young." Nick threw another, the last, of the photos in front of her.

Anne saw Joe standing in a run-down vestibule, waiting to be admitted to the building.

"Does the name mean anything to you?"

"I've never heard it." Anne's voice was breathless, almost a squeak.

"He may or may not have spent the night there. I waited for quite a while outside for him, and I couldn't wait any longer. It was too damn cold. I had to follow him by subway, so I couldn't even sit in my car."

"I guess he's having an affair . . . affairs . . . something." Anne's voice was emotionless; she didn't want to break down in front of him. She took a breath and asked, "Were you able to find anything out about this Pat Young?"

Nick slid a typewritten report in front of her. "Near the bottom of the page." Nick indicated with his finger where the information about Pat Young started. "She's lived at the same address on Oak Park Avenue for the past few years. She's an invalid, paralyzed from the waist down. Fell from an overhead crane at the steel mill where she used to work down in Joliet. Lives on disability the mill pays. Doesn't really do much, that I could find."

"So Joe isn't having an affair with her? I mean, she's paralyzed."

"I don't know what the connection is."

Anne covered her face with her hands. None of this made any sense.

She felt Nick's hands on her shoulders, kneading. She put her hands down on the table. "I don't understand any of this. This isn't the husband I knew. If you didn't show me those pictures I'm not sure I would have believed you."

"I'll keep looking, Anne. I'll find out what's going on. Okay?"

Anne turned to look up at him. Stared into the dark eyes and thin lips. She felt a growing nausea. How could Joe do this to her? She thought of all the come-ons, all the offers she had had over the years, and how she had never once even been tempted. God, to be left for some cripple . . . How could he?

Nick's hands on her shoulders felt good. His grip was warm and strong. She reached behind her and covered his hands with hers. Calloused. Rough. He was a man who must do some real work. Joe's hands were always so soft, smooth. He rubbed lotion into them. Did the whores like his touch? she wondered. Did Pat Young?

Again, she turned to look up at Nick. He didn't realize she was looking and she saw in his handsome face a mixture: There was a calmness there, but it was tinged with confusion.

"You're fascinated by him, aren't you?" she whispered.

"What?" Nick stopped kneading her shoulders and drew his hands away. "What are you talking about?"

"Nothing. I thought I saw something in your eyes . . . when we were . . . um . . . looking at the photographs." Anne watched as Nick's face clouded, the thin lips turned down into a frown. His face was beautiful, Anne thought, so rugged. So unlike Joe, with his pretty-boy good looks. Did those black sluts like that face above them as he fucked? Did the little girl tramps see a handsome prince, a daddy, as he rammed his dick in them? Anne lowered her head. No, she thought, I will not cry. I will not.

Once more she felt Nick's hands at her shoulders.

"It's gonna be okay," he whispered. "Really."

And once more she reached up to take his hands in hers. She brought them down, letting them rest on her breasts. For a moment he cupped them through the soft material of her blouse, and for a moment Anne forgot about Joe's betrayal.

"Make love to me," she whispered, her voice barely audible even to herself.

Nick pulled his hands away and walked to the bank of windows. He lit a cigarette and stared out at the winter-gray day for a long time. "I'd like to do that. I really would. But if I did, what would it make me?" He looked over at her and she was stunned to see he was trembling. "I can't fuck my clients to make everything all right again. This has happened before, Anne. A little getting even. Although I can say it's never happened with someone so pretty." He tried to smile at her, to soften the rejection, but it wasn't very convincing.

Anne thought of Joe's smile, how it could light up a room. And how fake it was. How fucking fake. She stood and walked to Nick. She stared into his gray eyes, and as she walked toward him she unbuttoned the pale blue blouse, never losing eye contact, daring him to look down, down at the breasts she would soon be exposing. "This isn't what you think, Nick. I've wanted you since I met you." She dropped the blouse to the floor behind her and went to him—wondering if some whore had done the same with Joe—went to him and wrapped her arms around him. Kissed him, exploring the inside of his mouth with her tongue when his resistant lips finally went slack, tasting a bittersweet taste . . . cigarettes and Nick. She reached down to feel the effect she was having on him, sure of what she would find. "You want me, don't you?"

"That's not the point. This isn't right." There wasn't much, if any, conviction in his voice.

Anne unzipped her jeans. She wriggled out of them, pulling her panties down with them. She stepped back to stand naked before him. "I'm dripping, Nick. I want you so bad." Staring at him, she slid a finger inside herself and brought it back out. "Taste," she whispered. "Taste what you do to me."

He opened his mouth, sucked on the finger she offered.

And then he was grabbing her and pulling her hair as he ground his face into hers, kneading her breasts and finally lifting her and carrying her to the couch. He knelt between her thighs, struggling to get out of his clothes.

"Hurry," Anne whispered, closing her eyes and then opening them again quickly because all she saw was Joe.

Finally, his clothes were in a heap on the floor. Anne glanced down to see Nick's cock peeking out of its foreskin, dripping. She bit her lip and remembered Joe, remembered looking down the same way so many times in the past.

She grabbed his hips, pulling him toward her. "Please, oh, please . . ." she whispered, raising her hips off the couch to meet his thrust. He was in her and she bucked against him, grinding herself hard against him, writhing around and trying so hard *(oh, please),* trying to make it hurt. She grabbed his hands and put them on her breasts. "Pinch them, please," she gasped, "hard. Twist them. Bite me," she whimpered, the tears at last coming.

She clawed his back and bit his shoulder. "Hurt me, hurt me bad," she whispered, certain that through his own moans and grunts he hadn't heard.

And still she could not get the image of Joe out of her mind.

* * *

After, she lay with her head on the curly mat of hair on his chest. It didn't work, she thought, I wanted it to work so bad and it didn't. She stood and pulled her blouse on, sat on the floor, her back against the couch. She felt his hand on her shoulder. "What's the matter? Not good?"

"Oh, it was great." Anne said. She bit her lip. No tears. "You're a great lay, Nick," she laughed.

Nick closed his eyes, wishing she would stop. This wasn't what he hoped to hear. He had never found himself feeling this way about a woman before.

"Does that bother you?" she asked.

"Yeah, it does. I don't like to think of myself as a tranquilizer for mixed-up ladies." He sat up and reached for his pants.

"Wait," she said, grabbing his arm and pushing him back down on the couch. "Don't feel bad. It's not what you think"—*(oh, yes, it is)*— "I care a lot for you." She snuggled up to him on the couch. "Besides, we have things to talk about, right?" She took his chin, turned his face to hers, knowing that her eyes, her smile would put the hesitation out of his mind.

Anne picked up a plate of cookies in the kitchen and poured a mug of milk for the two of them to share. She returned to the living room and sat next to him.

"What's next?" she asked.

Nick sighed and looked at her. He shook his head for a moment, then began: "First we find out a little more about Joe. I was a little surprised you didn't know more. But I'll find out about his family, where he's from, things like that. Sometimes those things can help put people together. Who knows? Maybe Pat Young is Joe's sister, or his mother."

Anne felt a chill. She knew so little about Joe.

"I'll watch him some more. Maybe I'll find out what's going on that way."

"I just don't know. I want to know real bad what's going on, but part of me doesn't want to know in the worst way."

"Look, there's nothing to worry about. We don't know anything yet. Maybe it's all something very explainable. Maybe he's just in need of some psychiatric help."

"Well, I don't need a private detective to tell me that."

Nick laughed. "I'm just saying all the mystery might add up to something not all that awful."

"I hope you're right." Anne got up and went to the desk in the sun-room. She took out her checkbook and started writing. "Don't feel like a gigolo; I just want to give you your first check now . . . while I'm thinking about it." She finished writing the check and held it out to him.

He took it from her, folded it, and reached over to cram it in his pants pocket. "Let's make that the last one."

"As long as I put out, I don't have to pay?"

"That's not funny." He pulled her down beside him. "This is premature and against all my good judgment about women, but I think I'm falling in love with you."

Anne stared at him, surprised.

"Just try to forget it for now. I know you don't need a relationship right now. But I'm willing to wait and I'm willing to help you find out what's going on, because I care about you and not because it's my job. Please let me do that."

Anne looked at him and smiled. Anything you want, she was thinking. She felt a tightness in her stomach at the thought, which tumbled out with no concern for truth or even decency.

17

 Randy lay on his bed, staring out his window: gray, low-hanging clouds and naked branches of an oak tree in front of the house, reaching up to meet the sky.

"Randy! The paper came. You wanna see it?" his mother called up the stairs.

Randy hoisted himself up and went to the top of the stairs. His mother stared into the late afternoon shadows, holding the paper in front of her like a gift.

"Why don't you look at it, Ma? I don't need to be first."

"I gotta get supper on the table. Your father'll be home soon and you know he'll disappear into the bathroom with it. Come on, take it."

Randy went down the stairs and took the paper from his mother, knowing it would make her happy. He went into the living room and sat down with it.

Every Thursday the local Berwyn paper came out. It was mostly ads, listing of area movies, and articles on the city council's activities. Randy was about to skip over the front page and go right to the sports section when something made him turn back.

SECOND MURDER STRIKES BERWYN. The headline screamed out, and for a moment he couldn't focus. He felt dizzy, staring at the photograph of a young man in tears trying to turn away from the camera. The caption described the man as John Piccone and went on to say his wife, Rebecca, had been brutally killed late Sunday night when she was walking to her mother's home. The murder took place not four blocks from another killing, that of Margaret Mazursky last month. Story continued on page two.

Randy opened the paper and read, noticing the similarities, especially the cuts made with what seemed to be a razor blade, and the draining of blood. He read that the police thought there might be a connection between the two killings. Thought? Randy's contempt for the police force grew. The woman, Rebecca Piccone, had had her head bashed in on the sidewalk. At least he hadn't done that to Maggie.

"What's the matter? What are you crying about?"

Randy looked up to see his mother standing above him. He felt disoriented, as if he had left the house for a while and somehow been transported back. He held the paper out to his mother, and she took in the story at once. "Yeah, ain't that a shame?"

"Ma," he looked at his mother, pleading. "Don't you see? It's gotta be the same guy who killed Maggie."

His mother began shaking her head immediately. "No, Randy. That's not for you to figure. Just leave it to the police."

"What's wrong with you?" He screamed at his mother and then, ashamed, lowered his voice. Without the volume, though, his words had a more hateful intensity. "Why don't you face it? The police can't catch that bastard out there. They're too fucking stupid. He's going to keep killing innocent people until someone else puts that bastard out of his misery. If I knew who he was, I wouldn't hesitate to slit his throat and leave him bleeding on the sidewalk."

He looked at his mother, saw the tears in her eyes and didn't care. Not now. He hurried from the room. He heard his mother calling after him up the stairs, "Randy, you gotta let this go. You gotta get on with your life. Just let it go."

Never, Ma, never, he thought, closing the door behind him.

Pat Young let the Berwyn paper slip from her fingers, leaned back in her wheelchair, and closed her eyes. "Oh, Joe," she said aloud, "you naughty, naughty boy." She laughed and looked down at the grieving face of the husband and said, "Maybe I could get some money from you too." She wondered if she and Joe could go into business together: He would kill them and she could blackmail the loved ones.

In spite of her lack of sympathy over the tragedies, Pat found herself admitting that maybe she was a little bit afraid. She remembered the description of how the last woman had been killed, how she had been the victim of several hard blows to the back of the neck and how her head had been repeatedly beaten into the sidewalk. The worst part was that she had been cut in several places with a very sharp instrument and blood had been drained from her body. If Joe ever found out Pat was bluffing she could meet with the same fate, possibly worse, because of the pain she had caused him.

Maybe, she thought, maybe I should tell Randy Mazursky who Joe is. She had a feeling Randy would take care of things, if not by going to the police then by getting rid of Joe himself.

But then she thought of Joe's perfect body standing before her, naked, his hand stroking his long, thick cock. . . . He must feel something to be so excited by her. He must care.

She didn't know what she should do. She wheeled over to the TV and turned it on, thinking, I've got to get one of those remote control things.

It was time for *The People's Court*, Pat's favorite show.

Theresa Mazursky opened the can of green beans and dumped them into a pot. She sprinkled salt on them and threw in a couple of pats of butter, then turned the blue flame below them low. She sat down at the kitchen table and massaged her temples. Ever since Maggie had died, Theresa had had a headache. Sharp pain behind both of her eyes, like needles. She looked out at the sleet coming down in the purple dusk outside and remembered Randy as a little boy, winter days like this one, and how safe she felt in this kitchen. The cold wind outside just made the kitchen seem warmer, cozier with the smells of supper cooking.

She didn't feel safe anymore.

Upstairs, someone was in her son's room. He looked like her son, but he was a stranger. The physical resemblance ended with his eyes. Randy's eyes used to sparkle, almost with a life of their own. Always turned up with laughter or a smile.

Now those eyes were dead. The green in them had gone almost to a murky brown. Theresa crossed herself, whispering, "Father, Son, Holy Ghost."

Please, Lord . . . help me with my boy. Help him to get on with his life. Make him like he was before. He was always a good boy, you know that. Don't do this to him, no more. He's gonna ruin his life and he has so much to give.

Theresa stood up, the cold outside making her joints ache when she stood. She went to the stove, turned off the flame under the beans. She stirred them and took one out, ate but didn't taste. "We gotta make this right, Father. We gotta make this right," she whispered.

It was time to set the table.

Three-fifteen. Sleet pounded against Randy's bedroom windows, sounding like needles against the glass. He had pulled up the blinds his mother had lowered an hour or two ago, when she had crept into his room thinking he was asleep. He liked the silvery light that came into the room from the streetlight outside his window. The light and the sound of the sleet made him feel comfortable under the quilt his mother had thrown over him. He felt himself drifting off to sleep and looked over at the clock.

The phone rang. In the silence it sounded loud, jarring. He was sure his parents must be sitting up in bed now, their eyes wide and staring. He grabbed it before it had a chance to ring a second time. His heart was pounding.

"Hello," he breathed into the phone.

"Don't hang up on me," a woman's voice came through firmly. "I *am* your friend."

Randy lay back on the bed. Ever since he had read the story about Rebecca Piccone, he had been hoping this woman would call. "I won't hang up. Not this time." Randy felt chilled. The room seemed darker than it was a few minutes ago.

"Good. I'm glad to hear you're willing to cooperate. It's for your benefit."

"You said you know who killed my wife."

"That's right. I know."

"How do you know?"

"I told you, information like that doesn't come cheap."

"How am I supposed to know you're not just some nut trying to get a few bucks out of me? The world is full of people who want to exploit the desperate."

"Don't I know it. Listen: I have proof."

"I have some proof too. What do I need you for? Maybe I could just take this proof to the police station."

Pat sat back, thinking. He's bluffing; he has to be bluffing. "What do you mean?" she snapped.

Randy thought he had nothing to lose by telling her. "When my wife was killed, the murderer left a lighter in our kitchen. A very expensive lighter, and monogrammed."

Pat thought. It didn't take long for her to come up with her next idea. "I can tell you the initials on that lighter."

"Okay. So tell me."

"The telephone is such an impersonal instrument. Don't you agree?" Pat's voice went from cheerful to angry. "I tell nothing for free."

"When can we get together?"

"Can you meet me tomorrow morning, early?"

Randy thought that would be perfect. He could call into work and say he was having car trouble and would be late. He wouldn't say anything to his family, who would assume that when he left in the morning he was leaving for his job. "I can meet you then. How about eight thirty?"

"Make it nine." Pat wanted to keep in control. "I'd have you over to my place, but it's such a mess." Pat had thought about the meeting all evening, certain Randy was aware of the other, more recent killing. "I could meet you at a little restaurant I know of. It's called the Breakfast Barn in Cicero. You know it?"

"You mean the Breakfast Barn on Roosevelt? Isn't that kind of public?"

"It's safe. Besides, we'll whisper." Pat whispered the last part and hung up the phone. She smiled as she thought Randy wouldn't sleep much this night.

Randy put the phone back in the cradle and walked over to the window. He said, "Enjoy tonight, you motherfucker. There aren't going to be many more."

Outside Randy's room, Theresa Mazursky stared into the darkness. Her heart was pounding. She twisted and untwisted the crucifix at her throat.

Randy walked into the Breakfast Barn the next morning, worried. He had no idea how he'd recognize the woman who had called him. He looked over the small restaurant. Several women sat alone at the counter. One woman, with a wheelchair propped at the side of her booth, also sat alone. He thought her red hair and sharp nose looked familiar. He didn't think she could be the one and was about to turn to the women at the counter when she smiled at him and waved him over.

He walked to her table and stood above her. "Are you the one who called me last night?"

"Yes," she said, "I'm the one. Now, why don't you sit down."

Randy seated himself, thinking that the voice was right. He wondered where he had seen her before. Then it came to him. This woman lived across the street from them! Maggie used to feel sorry for her and she'd watch from their window, making sure the woman got out of her building all right and down to the sidewalk. He didn't know her name, but he was sure this was the same woman.

"I know you," he said.

"What?" she snapped at him, fear in her eyes.

"You live across the street from me."

"Get you a cup of coffee, sir?" A waitress with bleached hair appeared. Her uniform stretched tight across her hips. She placed a menu down in front of him.

"Coffee will be all," Randy said, handing back the menu.

"Don't be crazy," Pat said. "I live in the city."

"No, no, you don't. My wife used to watch you. She felt sorry for you."

Pat became angry, her thin lips becoming thinner as she set them in a line. "The bitch didn't need to. I can take care of myself."

"So you do live on Oak Park Avenue. The little building right across from us. That's how you know, isn't it? You must have seen."

Pat gripped the Formica top of the table hard enough to make her fingertips white. This was going out of control. He wasn't supposed to know anything about her. She was going to be anonymous. A mysterious stranger who, after being paid, would give him the information.

Pat stared hard at him. "You're right."

"Why didn't you go to the police if you knew?"

The waitress had come up to their table with Randy's coffee. She was looking at Pat with interest. She must have heard.

Pat waited until the woman had walked away.

"I didn't go to the police because they wouldn't pay, and I think you will."

The waitress had returned. She leaned over the table; Pat saw that she was interested in their conversation.

"What is it?" Pat hissed.

"Can I get you anything else?" The waitress was overly cheerful and falsely bright.

"No," Pat snapped. "Just our check."

When the waitress left, Pat leaned across the table to Randy and whispered, "Since you already know where I live it's kind of pointless continuing here with Marilyn Monroe over there hanging on our every word."

Randy nodded.

Pat took a sip of the coffee in front of her. "The coffee here stinks anyway. The damn cup wasn't even clean."

Randy glanced down at his mug. It was perfectly clean. "Okay, let's go to your place."

"I guess we will."

The waitress returned and put the check facedown on the table. "Thank you very much," she said, "and have a nice day."

She walked away. Pat slid the check to Randy. "Pay this. I'll meet you at the door."

Randy stood to help her get in her wheelchair. She waved him away. "Just pay the damn check!"

Everyone in the restaurant turned to look at them. Randy started toward the cashier. He heard the hum of Pat's wheelchair as she passed behind him.

* * *

Theresa Mazursky put down her menu. They hadn't seen her. But she had seen . . . and heard. And she remembered. She sipped the coffee gone cold in front of her. That crippled woman lived across the street from her son and daughter-in-law. She remembered when Maggie would point the woman out, struggling to get through her front door in her wheelchair. *I used to feel sorry for her.*

"Warm that up for you, hon?"

Theresa jumped when the waitress approached. "Huh? Uh, no, no. I gotta be goin'."

Randy felt closed in when Pat shut the door behind him. The little room was cluttered with enough furniture for three rooms. There were papers and magazines everywhere. A damp smell permeated the room.

Pat shoved a stack of *Playgirl*s off a chair and told him to sit down if he wanted to.

Randy took a seat.

"Before we get started with the information," Pat said, "let's talk finances."

"Wait a minute," Randy held up his hand. "You said you had some proof. I want to know for sure if you know anything before I agree to give you any money."

"So you will pay?"

"I didn't say that. I will pay if you convince me you really do know something."

Randy covered his face with his hands. He had been half-hoping she wouldn't know.

"I'm right, aren't I?" Pat asked. "If those aren't

the right initials, that lighter belonged to someone other than the killer."

Randy took a deep breath and looked at her.
"You're right."

"Good. Now we can get the money portion of
the conversation out of the way."

Randy thought he would pay anything he had
to get this guy. He quickly calculated how much
he was worth. In a savings account he had about
$3,500, along with another $285 in checking. If
he sold the car he could probably come up with
about $4,400. Maybe his parents could give him a
couple thousand, but he couldn't depend on them
for more. And he really didn't know if they'd give
him anything without knowing the reason. "How
much do you want?"

"I've given this a lot of thought," Pat said, folding her hands in her lap, "and I think fifteen
thousand dollars would do the trick. Yes, fifteen
thousand would do quite nicely."

"I don't have that much."

"Well, then, that concludes our business here,
doesn't it?"

"Please, you've got to help me. . . ."

"I don't *have* to do anything."

"Please . . ." Randy felt tears welling up in his
eyes. She had to tell him, she just had to. Didn't
she have a heart? "Listen, if you don't tell me
who it is, I'm going straight to the police with this
little scheme. This isn't legal, you know."

Pat laughed. "Go ahead! It's my word against
yours. And believe me, mister, I can be very convincing."

"Please . . ." Randy begged. "I can pay you installments. I promise. I'm living at home now. I'll sign my paycheck over to you every week."

"I have a sneaking suspicion that paycheck won't be around much after you find out who killed your wife. So I'm afraid the offer stands at fifteen thousand dollars cash, within the week. Monday it goes to twenty thousand."

Randy dropped to his knees and took her hand. "Please, you don't know how much this means to me. Please, I'm begging. I'll give you six thousand dollars. Please . . . in the name of decency . . . tell me."

Pat threw back her head and laughed. The laugh was shrill. "Get up! You're pathetic. You mean to tell me you really go out in the world and call yourself a man? Bad enough you can't protect your wife, so she ends up dead, but you can't even cough up a few bucks to find out who did the deed. Get the hell out of my sight until you have the money."

Randy didn't know what happened to him then. He grabbed the handles of the wheelchair and tipped Pat from it. Savagely, he kicked her in the stomach once, twice, three times. She groaned and coughed up blood. Then he picked her up from the floor and threw her into the glass front of a hutch near one wall. She fell to the floor, her face a maze of small cuts. Blood seeped onto the pale green blouse she wore. Randy sat on her chest and pounded into her face with his fists again and again until she was unconscious.

He stood.

"Oh, God," Randy said, "I've killed her." But

after a moment he realized that was impossible. His beating had been brutal (she deserved it and more, he thought), but not enough to kill her.

He went into the bathroom and filled a glass with cold water. He came back and threw it on her face. She didn't rouse. He went into the kitchenette and rummaged in her refrigerator. There was a two-liter bottle of grape soda on the top shelf. Randy felt the plastic. Cold. He untwisted the top and poured it on Pat's face. He saw a fluttering movement around her eyes.

He returned to the kitchen and looked in her cupboard until he found a bottle of vinegar. He pulled a paper towel off the roll.

She lay on the floor, staring up at him.

"Going to tell me?"

"No, you fucker! I wouldn't tell you for all the money in the world. The deal is off!"

Randy soaked the paper towel in vinegar. He pressed it to several bleeding cuts on her face. She screamed.

"Want more? How about a little salt? There's a nice deep one on your neck." He reached toward her face with the vinegar-soaked paper towel. She weakly held up a hand.

"No, please," she mumbled. "I'll tell you. His name is Joe MacAree. He lives in the city. His name is in the phone book. I swear it."

"You better be telling the truth, you miserable cunt, or I swear to God I'll come back here and kill you. And it won't be a swift death." He kicked her once more in the stomach. She gasped.

* * *

Randy sat in his Chevette for a long time, looking up at the windows of his old apartment, remembering the times he had shared there with Maggie. Then he looked at the blood on his hands.

He started the ignition.

He thought he had nothing left to lose.

"I'm going to kill you, Joe MacAree," he said. There was no emotion in his voice.

He pulled out onto the street.

18

Joe curled into a tight ball. The pounding on his door grew louder, more insistent. "Go away, Margo. Leave me alone, Daddy," he whispered, slipping his head below the threadbare blanket.

"You in there or not?" There was one last blow to the door, sounding more like a kick than a knock. Joe opened his eyes. The male voice outside his door was not his father's. He sat up in bed, looking around the YMCA room, seeing his trenchcoat thrown over the only chair, his pants and shirt in a ball on the floor. He rubbed the sleep out of his eyes and combed through his hair with his fingers.

"Yeah, I'm here," Joe said.

"Well, why the fuck didn't you answer?"

"I was sleeping."

"Great. You got a woman on the phone out here. You wanna talk to her or not?"

Joe's first thought was that it was Anne, calling to tell him to come home. His adrenaline level revved. He hurried to pull his pants and shirt on. "I'll be right out. Could you tell her I'll be right there?"

"You tell 'er. Phone's at the end of the hall."

Joe heard the man's receding footsteps. He examined himself in the mirror and then realized Anne wouldn't be able to see him through the telephone wires.

Hurrying down the hall, Joe began to imagine what she would say. "Joe, listen, I know I haven't been very understanding. And I know I haven't been very trusting, but, baby, I know I was wrong. I've been cleaning and cooking all morning and your home is ready for you. Please come back, Joe. I love you."

He picked up the phone. "Hello?"

"I hope I didn't get you out of bed. Lately you need your beauty rest." The woman chuckled.

Joe didn't recognize the voice, although he knew, with disappointment, that it wasn't Anne's. The voice *did* sound familiar. "Who is this?" Joe asked, not really caring since it wasn't Anne.

"Your sweetheart, honey." The woman laughed again.

Joe put his hand to his forehead. A headache was starting. "What do you want, Pat?"

"Don't take that tone with me, mister. You better be good to me if you know what's good for you."

"I'm sorry. Did you want me to come over?"

"That wouldn't be a bad idea. But I think under

the circumstances it might not be safe for you to come here so soon."

"What are you talking about?"

"I'm calling to save your ass."

Joe felt sweat breaking out on his forehead and upper lip. The phone suddenly seemed slippery. "I don't know what you mean."

"Maggie Mazursky's husband knows you killed his wife."

There was a thud in Joe's mind. For a moment he was afraid he would faint, and he grabbed on to the little ledge under the phone for support. "How could he know such a thing?" Joe's mind raced. "Unless you told him, you little bitch!"

"Wait a minute, buster! He found out mostly on his own. If you don't watch your step with me, have no fear: I'll go straight to the police. Understand?"

Joe felt humbled. She had all the bargaining power. "Yes, I understand. How did he find out . . . really?"

"You left your lighter with your initials in his apartment. Not the brightest thing in the world to do, but considering your state of mind at the time I would imagine it was completely understandable. Anyway he's been spending almost all his spare time lately making the rounds at jewelry stores, trying to trace it. Lucky for you, the lighter was a custom order, and once he found the right place there weren't too many more steps to find out who the original owner was."

Joe felt sick. He held down the bile he tasted. "So how did you find out?"

"He knew I was the invalid that lived across

the street. He thought I might have seen something that would help him."

"So I guess he's already gone to the police," Joe said, feeling more nauseated. He looked out the window across the hall and saw a police car in the line of traffic on Chicago Avenue. He wondered if they were on their way to pick him up.

"That's where you're lucky . . . or unlucky, depending on how you look at it. This guy is so filled with rage he wants to do the job on you himself. He's afraid he won't like the kind of justice the court would give you."

"Does he know where I am?"

"How could he? Who else knows where you are?"

No one, Joe thought. But I can't be safe here. I've got to hide. I've got to get away from here right away . . . and take Anne with me. "I don't think anybody but you."

"Then you're safe. Joe, I want you to know something I've been meaning to say. I wasn't quite sure how I should put it. . . . Joe, are you listening?"

Joe leaned against the wall, the sweat pouring down his face, certain he would throw up any minute. "What?"

Pat didn't say anything for a while. "I love you, Joe. And I want you to know that if I can help in any way, I'll do it. I don't care what you've done. Let me help, if I can."

"Okay," Joe whispered, without emotion, and hung up the phone.

* * *

Anne lay on the couch, her robe pulled tightly around her. She faced the back of the couch and tried not to think. Behind her, the Channel 5 news blared out of the television. Lately she had been keeping the television on almost all the time. It kept her company and kept her from thinking. She didn't want to think—not about her feelings for Nick MontPierre, not about her worries and feelings for Joe. Her mother had called several times, leaving messages on her answering machine. Anne had never returned her calls. The voice of Carolyn Dodd came out of the speaker at the side of the screen. It seemed the newscaster's message was especially for Anne to hear. She stiffened as she heard the report about the "continuing investigation into the brutal murder of a Berwyn woman. Rebecca Piccone, nineteen, was found with severe trauma to the head and several deep cuts made with what is believed to have been a razor or extremely sharp knife. The Berwyn police believe there may have been a connection between this murder and that of another Berwyn woman last month, Margaret Mazursky. Officials commented that the two killings exhibited similarities of more than just the proximities of the two women's apartment buildings." Anne hurried to the television and clicked it off, as if that would end the thoughts racing through her mind.

She sat down, her breath coming in quick gulps, almost hyperventilating. Hadn't she found a blood-stained X-Acto knife in the bathroom just a few weeks ago? Didn't Nick follow Joe to

Berwyn just last week? Berwyn, a place she was certain neither of them even knew about before?

She went into the kitchen and, with trembling hands, put some water on the stove for tea. She sat at one of the kitchen chairs and put her head in her hands. Joe could never kill anyone, she thought. That much you can be sure of. Right? There's some logical reason he went to Berwyn. And that reason has nothing to do with killing anyone. The whole idea is absurd. Lots of people went to Berwyn every day, she was sure, and that didn't make them suspects for murder.

She put a tea bag in a mug and poured boiling water over it. As she waited for it to steep, she couldn't get one image out of her mind.

She remembered the X-Acto knife on the white porcelain of the sink, the blade stained with brown, dried blood. Too much blood for a minor cut.

Joe dipped the razor in the water and took one more stroke along his neck. The beard looked great now that he had blocked it off and trimmed it. His hair, with a good shampoo and conditioning, had regained the luster it once held. His clothes, even though they were wrinkled, were clean from a washing in his sink early that morning. Even though he had lost a good bit of weight and the clothes hung on him, he thought he could truthfully look in the mirror and think he didn't look too bad. The fact that his clothes were rumpled and he was too thin might get a sympathy vote from Anne and make her even more willing to take him back. After all, he knew deep down she loved him. How could she resist? he wondered, winking at himself in the mirror.

He left his room and went down the hall to the pay phone. He hoped Anne would be home.

The phone rang three times before Anne's voice came over the line. "Hi, this is Anne. You've called at just the wrong time! But you can remedy your mistake by leaving your name, number, and message after the beep. I'll get right back to you."

Joe waited with disappointment for the beep. When he heard it he decided he would not sound whiny or pleading. "Hi, Anne, it's Joe. I'd like to get together for a short time, if we could. I'll call you soon."

When the phone rang Anne jumped, gripping the table. Probably Mother again, she thought. She went to the answering machine to listen. Joe's voice made her go cold. She was about to let him hang up when she grabbed the receiver before he had a chance.

Joe was about to hang up the phone when he heard a click. Anne's voice came over the line, sounding a little nervous and scared. "Joe?"

"Hi, Anne. Just get in?"

"What? Oh . . . oh, yes." She laughed. "I was just out getting a little air. Been feeling a little cooped up lately, what with the cold and everything."

"That's understandable. But you should be careful. It's late and you don't know who might be lurking outside. I wouldn't want anything to happen to you."

Anne wanted to laugh at his concerns, especially if her suspicions were true. But they couldn't be. Joe wasn't capable of hurting anyone, let alone killing them.

"Joe, I am careful. I just went down the block, turned around, came back."

"Well, try to get out in the day. Okay?"

"Okay."

The line went silent for a while. Finally Joe spoke. "Anne, I'd really like to see you."

"Joe, I don't know if that would be a good idea," Anne said, almost by rote. A part of her wanted to see him. That part wanted reassurance that the Joe she married really did exist.

"Maybe it's not a good idea. But it's important I talk to you. I've been patient. Please . . . I won't take too much of your time."

"Joe, I . . ." Anne couldn't think of anything. "Okay, tomorrow morning. Can you come then?"

"I can come anytime you say. I love you, Anne."

"I'll see you tomorrow." Anne hung up the phone.

Joe, smiling, hung up his end.

"Why?" Both of them were in tears. Anne sat on the couch, her feet curled under her, her wide eyes rimmed in red, a balled-up Kleenex in her hand. "I don't understand why this is so important to you."

Joe was on the floor, kneeling at her feet. There was snot in his mustache; his face was wet with tears. "The city is making me crazy. I think we can start over someplace else. Someplace where there's nature and we can be alone. Where we can get to know each other again."

Anne stood up to get away from him. She crossed the room and stared out the window at the traffic rushing by on Lake Shore Drive. She wished she were in one of those cars, on her way to a normal job in the city. What must it be like? she wondered.

"Please, Anne, if you really love me you'll do this."

She turned to him, frightened, and not at all sure she did love him anymore. Why was he so eager to leave the city all of a sudden? He had been the one who talked her into moving to Chicago when they graduated from Iowa. She had wanted to stay in Iowa City, where she was working as a legal assistant. For a moment she wondered if she would ever feel that carefree again. But Joe had insisted they move to the city, where they would both make lots of money and make all their dreams come true. He had been right, for a while. Up until everything began falling apart. But this desperation to leave so suddenly only fueled Anne's suspicion that Joe was involved with something very wrong. Not murder, surely, but something. She turned to him.

"Joe," she said, taking a deep breath and forcing herself not to cry, to sound firm, "I'm not going anywhere with you until you tell me why we have to leave so suddenly." He had been begging her for the last hour to pack her things and leave with him on a 6:00 A.M. flight to Wyoming.

"I told you," he sobbed, "because I think the city is killing us, killing our love for each other."

"Bullshit, Joe. I don't want to hear any more of this. We could leave in two months, when the lease is up on this apartment. That would give us time to find new jobs and a place to live somewhere else. What would be wrong with that?" She was baiting him, trying to call his bluff.

"That would be too long."

"Too long for what, Joe? You're not telling me something."

For a long time he didn't speak. He went up, put his arms around her, and began sobbing into her neck. "I love you so much."

Anne stiffened, her arms at her sides. After a while he noticed she wasn't returning his affection and let go. "You won't come away with me, will you?"

"Not until you tell me why it has to be so soon."

He stared for a long time at her, defeat in his tearing eyes. Then he walked away, went into the bedroom, and closed the door. She heard another door close.

Anne stared out the window for close to fifteen minutes. She didn't want to follow him. She just wanted him to leave.

The apartment was silent. Anne began to get scared. What was he doing? She wanted to go in the bedroom and see, but part of her was afraid of what she might find.

She waited awhile, hoping he'd come out and she could tell him to leave.

But he didn't come out.

Anne walked to the closed bedroom door and paused outside, her hand on the doorknob, listening.

The room was silent.

She opened the door. Joe was nowhere to be seen. She crossed the room and looked into the bathroom adjacent to the bedroom. Empty.

That left the closet. Why would he be in there? A feeling of dread began to rise up in her. Maybe she should call Nick. Maybe she shouldn't even think of opening that door.

Don't be ridiculous, she told herself, and crossed quickly to the closet door. Without thinking further, she threw the door open.

Joe was inside, curled into a little ball, sobbing. Oh, God, Anne thought, putting a hand to her forehead. "Joe, this isn't going to work."

He sniffed, uncurled, and looked up at her. "Please, Anne. I really do love you. Come away with me."

"Stand up. Get out of there. For Christ's sake, Joe." She waited for him to pass on his way out of the closet. She turned and walked into the living room, heard his steps behind her.

She sat down on a chair and he started to sit at her feet on the floor. Anne took a deep breath. She realized she didn't want him touching her, didn't want him near her. "Just go over and sit on the couch," she said. He did as he was told. He was breathing in small, quivering breaths, trying to stop crying.

She stared at him. His eyes were red. Looking away, Anne focused on a black-and-white picture of them hanging on the wall; Joe was smiling, handsome, boulders from Lake Michigan behind him. Where had that strength gone? Where had everything gone? Sucked out of him by some black whore? Anne looked down to see she had come close to breaking the skin on the back of her hands; she was clawing at them.

"Joe, I'm sorry." She bit her lip to keep the tears from flowing, or maybe to hold back the scream. She felt like a coil about to spring. "I don't want this anymore."

He started to get up. "I don't think I want to hear this."

Anne stood and pushed him back down on the couch. Her breathing was ragged. I just want this to be over, she thought. She stood above him, staring down, trying to concentrate on his whimpering. "You have to hear it. I don't know what's wrong with you, but I think you need some help."

"Stop. You're hurting me."

"Please, Joe. Don't make this worse than it has to be. I want you to get some help. Will you do that?"

"Will you take me back if I do?"

"I don't know, Joe." She felt a tear trickle down her cheek. "I don't know if I love you anymore. Joe, I don't think we should see each other for a long time." The crying was coming full force now, and Anne damned herself. "I want a divorce."

"There's somebody else."

"Oh, God. Whether there is or isn't has nothing to do with this." She wanted to scream at him— *And how many "somebody elses" have you had, you bastard? How many?*—but she also wanted to try and stay calm, hold the reins over this scene she felt was already about to spin out of control.

Joe stared at her. He stopped crying and Anne felt uncomfortable under the stare. Was the look in his eyes insanity? Or was she imagining things? He didn't say anything when she asked if he was all right.

To break the stare Anne got up and got his coat. "I think you should be going now," she said, handing him the coat.

Wordlessly, he took the coat and put it on, all the time staring at her. She tried to look away, but his gaze burned into her even when she wasn't looking.

She took his arm and led him to the door. Opening it, she said, "Joe, please try to understand."

He stared.

She was about to close the door on him when he grabbed her. He bent his head and kissed her. His tongue filled her mouth, probing, and she felt a line of his spittle running down her chin. She pushed him away.

He smiled at her. "I'll be seeing you," he said, smiling wider.

She slammed the door on him, afraid the smile would follow her into her nightmares.

Joe pulled his coat tighter around him against the cold air off the lake. "If I can't have her," he said to the doorman, "no one can."

He fingered the X-Acto knife in his pocket and felt an erection beginning.

19

Winter darkness filtered in through the living room windows. Anne sat on the couch, her feet drawn up underneath her, a cup of tea gone cold in her hand. The apartment was silent, so quiet she heard the hum of the refrigerator in the kitchen and the soft tick of the clock near the dining room table. She knew she had to accept there was something horribly wrong with Joe. Something so wrong, in fact, that he might be hurting others a lot more than he was hurting her. A part of her told her she should take him back, maybe he could be rehabilitated. What she considered a more selfish part of herself said no, it wasn't her purpose in life to rehabilitate him. She had a right to happiness.

She got up and crossed to the windows. Outside, the traffic moved sluggishly along the drive. Further east the lake looked angry, hurtling itself against the shoreline. At least, she thought, the lake eventually does make some impact, eroding the shoreline a little more each year.

From Joe MacAree's journal (undated):

Dawn light filters through winter silver. There. She waits. In her, I can see the blood boiling, same as I can see the fingers of the blood-sun boiling through the silver strata of the dawn sky. It's a brand new day, with brand new thirsts and hunger.

My friend made of cold steel (and sharp) lends its strength to me as I stroke it in my pocket. Up and down, up and down . . . as I walk toward her.

She sees me. Where do all these little homeless girls come from? And why do they end up in the park alone? Easy prey for a boy like me.

God! She sees me and smiles. Isn't she scared? I love the fear; I can smell it. It makes me hard.

She had called Nick earlier, begging him to come over.

"Montpierre." His voice was gravelly, rough. He had sounded tired.

"Hi, it's Anne. I'm in need of a little protection. Come over?" She had tried to keep her tone light, but wondered how much desperation came through in the timbre of her voice.

"I'd really like that, Anne. But I gotta do some work on my other cases sometime." He laughed to soften what he was saying. "I got an industrial case that I've really let slip. Lotta catch-up."

"Isn't there some work you could do here?"

"Nah. I really need to do it at the plant. See, they've got this guy who's been stealing and they need some proof. That's where I come in. Maybe I can come over a little later?"

"You know you can." Anne had replaced the phone in its cradle and looked around the empty apartment. It had been so long since she'd been alone. She almost wished for Phyllis to come down and take her shopping . . . Saks and I. Magnin. Anything. Anything so she didn't have to think. Nick, she knew, was not a man who would bend to her whims. Joe had always bent to her whims and realized if he had a choice he would probably like nothing more than to bend to her demands. But choice is seldom a reality, she thought. She would have chosen a life of happiness with Joe, like it was in the beginning. But that choice was ripped away from her. Just as it had been ripped away from Joe, she supposed.

She wanted to know more. She remembered the pornography in his office and how much it had upset her. But maybe if she looked again, she could find something out. Something that would let her help Joe and give her the freedom to start a new life.

She flicked on some lights, in the living room, the dining room, and the kitchen. She turned the stereo on and put a tape of Rickie Lee Jones in the cassette player. She didn't want to be alone.

The den felt cold because of the bank of windows on one side. Anne turned on the overhead light and the desk lamp and flipped on the little space heater Joe had put in the corner of the room. She ran her fingers over the polished oak of the desk, not really certain if she was ready to open it. She remembered when she and Joe had first seen the desk in an antique store on Halsted Street. They had been married for only a few months then and didn't have much money. She saw the glimmer in his writer's eyes as he slid the drawers open and closed, admired the brass handles. Christmas was coming up in a month or so, and Anne mentioned it to him. "Don't you even think of buying this for me," he had said to her. "We can't afford it."

But she had gone back and with the little money she had saved from before their marriage had bought him the desk.

Enough of this, she thought, pulling the center drawer open. It was filled with pens and pencils, a ruler, paper clips, some invoices he used to bill his clients, erasers, a packet of X-Acto knife blades—Anne picked these up and stared at them. She tossed them in the wastebasket. She reached in the back of the drawer to try and feel if there was anything else, but the drawer was empty. Just to make sure, she pulled the drawer all the way out of the desk.

She went on and searched each of the shallow drawers on either side of the center drawer, but found nothing. When she got to the bottom drawers, though, the deep ones used for filing, she noticed right away that the drawer on the left side of the desk was deeper than the one on the right. The bottom of the right drawer was also a different wood. The drawer must have a false bottom, she thought, groping around for an opening so she could pry the bottom up. Near the back she found a small niche she could just barely get the tip of her index finger in. She lifted and the false bottom of the drawer came away.

Inside were several composition notebooks with five-year periods marked neatly on the outside of each. They went back to 1963, when Joe was just a boy. Anne knelt and took the notebooks out. She thought, with some excitement, that she could finally find something out about Joe's family, about where he was from. She was also afraid to open the notebooks, frightened of what they might contain.

She set them in front of her, laid out in chronological order, and stared at them for a long time, afraid of opening them. Finally she picked up the one where she would have been mentioned for the first time. She remembered so well when she and Joe had first met. They had both been going to summer school and the campus was quiet. She had been running, taking a path that she thought only she was aware of.

She had always favored the woods, unlike those other runners who stayed with the roads, tracks, campus walks. Her roommates told her, "Annie, you're crazy going out there. Some creep'll grab you." But Anne had always felt safer in the woods.

Summer. The campus was quiet, but the woods were alive. Leaves whispering in the trees, bird songs, and a chorus of insects. And the sound of her own breath, rhythmic with the pound of her Asics on the packed earth.

A stream ran through the woods, and the

sounds of splashing contrasted, almost jarring, with the other summer sounds. Anne slowed, keeping her head down, and looked. A man. A beautiful man stood on the bank and then dove in. He was big and tanned. The muscles glistened in the sunlight as he jumped up, finally arcing in the air, to cut the cold, blue water with his dive. Anne watched breathless as he swam, the biceps bunching and relaxing, shining from the water and sunlight. Finally he emerged from the water and lay down on the bank. His penis stretched onto one thigh. The sun dried his skin. Skin she wanted to taste. She crept away, wishing she knew of a way to meet him.

Her wish came true not a week later when she saw him tending bar at one of the near-campus taverns she and her friends had never been to because, during the regular school year, it was a hangout for the fraternity and sorority crowd, something Anne wanted no part of. But in the summer, her friends convinced her, the bar was quiet, a nice place to relax. She had spotted Joe the moment she walked in the door, and it seemed to her that he noticed her right away too. She had gone back the next night, alone, hoping he'd be on duty. He was.

That was sometime in the summer of 1979. She began skimming through the pages, looking with interest at the story ideas, the descriptions of people he met in his summer job as a bartender, the women he had slept with, the classes he was taking. Then, on July 23, he made his first mention of her.

* * *

A beautiful woman came in the bar tonight. As a matter of fact, behind me I can hear the easy sound of her breathing as she sleeps. I wanted to get up and try to write about my feelings for her as soon as I could. I have slept with many women, all of them attractive in one way or another, and at times have even believed I have loved some of them. But I have never been in love. Because I didn't know what love was until tonight when Anne walked in. It's funny; I noticed her right away when she came in. I was surprised to see she was alone. But right away I felt she was alone because she was to be with me. When she came and sat down at the bar, I wanted to jump over and join her, take those long, pale white fingers in my hands and kiss each one. Her hair is blue-black, and when she undid it from the braid she was wearing it in and spread it over my pillow, I thought, I never want to be apart from this woman. Lust? I'm not a fool; I won't deny that lust plays a part in all of this. But I've had lust as a friend for years now, and I know what I feel for Anne is so much more. I never would have believed in love at first sight, but it's real. I know I love her.

Anne wiped a tear away. Where did it all go? She skimmed through, stopping to enjoy the parts where she was mentioned, reliving their first magic summer together, those times when neither of them could stand to be apart for more than a few hours. The times when they swam together in the stream in the woods and made love in the dying summer sun, the bank of the stream hot beneath her. For a while the memories came alive: She was there in Joe's little garden apartment, sitting naked with him on the floor, a candle between them, eating Chinese food. She was there when they would go sit beneath a fieldstone bridge they had found and he read to her . . . sometimes his own short stories or poetry, more often the works of writers he liked, writers that still filled their bookshelves: James Purdy, Eudora Welty, Raymond Carver.

She skimmed through the rest of that year: her senior year and his final year of completion of his Master of Fine Arts in Creative Writing. She wondered if she'd ever have a year as happy as that one again. Yes, there was a page, written in the winter of that year, when the pages were blurred with Joe's tears as he realized he had lost her. The breakup had lasted two days. She was amazed at the depth of loss he felt when she broke up with him because she thought things were getting too serious between them. They *had* been getting too serious, but Anne would give anything to have the old seriousness back. She wondered where the man who had written these pages had gone.

From Joe MacAree's journal (undated):

"'Lo, little lady. Pretty chilly morning to be out here, isn't it?"

The eyes! God, so brown, windows to nowhere. "You got any money?" *Her voice is soft, little-girl breathy.* "I mean, maybe you and me can work *somethin' out. I could do a chore or somethin' in exchange. You know?"*

This one's smart. Been picked up already? I look into those brown eyes, the sun rising in them. The day will begin soon and the park will get busy.

"Yeah. Maybe you and I could make an exchange of sorts." I giggle.

Near the day of their graduation, she noticed a weird entry. Joe had insisted he would not be going through with commencement, claiming it was meaningless to him. She had asked then about his family. He had always been vague with her before about them, but she pressed him, saying she didn't really want to go through with the ceremony herself but knew her mother wouldn't miss it for anything and Anne was doing it to please her. He said his family didn't care about things like graduations and asked her not to talk about them anymore.

But apparently some of his family had come for graduation.

What a pleasant fucking surprise! Bitch sister Margo arrived today on a Greyhound from Summitville. Said she wanted to see little brother finally get his sheepskin. She wanted to stay with me at my apartment. I'm surprised she didn't bring Daddy. Oh, yes, the two of them could give me a graduation present I'd never forget. I tried not to let her know where I lived, but that was easy enough for her to find out on her own. I gave her the keys and cleared my stuff out. Anne won't mind if I stay with her until we graduate, and

then the two of us can clear out for Chicago . . .
and please God, may I never see any of them
again.

Anne leaned back against the desk. The mystery of why he had moved in with her the last few days before graduation was explained. Explained, too, was the mystery of why he had been in such a hurry to leave for Chicago; he had been hired by Ogilvy and Mather but wasn't supposed to start until July. Originally they had planned to stay on and just celebrate getting their degrees. Instead, Joe had gone into hiding until graduation was over and they could load up his car and head to Chicago.

She read through (and relived) the early days of their marriage, the way each of their careers had taken off. There were long descriptions of weekends in Wisconsin—Lake Geneva in the fall, when there were fewer people.

Bitch Margo appeared again. I don't know how
she found me, but that's not important. She hurt
me . . . hurt me like Daddy never did. I run every night, along the lake and through the parks. It
was there she came to me. Margo had never
looked so hideous. She was laughing at me, said
she had something for me. I followed her into an
underpass, only because she said she knew all
about Anne and if I didn't do everything she told
me she would tell Anne about what Daddy did to
me.

In the tunnel the underpass made, Margo, smiling all the time, took out a knife from under the sweater she wore. Everything happened so fast I didn't have a chance to defend myself. I could see blood spurting and flowing out of me. I remember dropping to my knees, trying to catch the blood, trying to stop its flow. I felt sure that I would die. And I heard the cars whizzing by overhead and Margo laughing, that shrieking laugh she had, the way she laughed when Daddy fucked me. Louder and louder . . . drowning out the traffic sound.

I remember dreaming. I saw Daddy and Mother standing above me, their skin all peeled away, and you could see bones and muscle tissue; they looked raw. And Margo was pulling off what remained of their skin and eating it. She was laughing and would open her mouth to show me the chewed-up flesh. "Train wreck," she would say, "train wreck," and laugh. The dreams were in black and white.

When I woke up I was in a dirty storage room somewhere. Margo was with me; her eyes were luminous in the room's darkness. I felt sicker than I had ever felt and my skin felt itchy with dried blood. I turned away as Margo slit her arm with a razor, but something made me turn back. The blood ran down her arm, and I knew I wouldn't feel sick anymore if I could have some of that blood. She pulled my head to the open wound and I drank.

Later, she left me. The door closed and I stood, feeling better, more alive somehow, than I had ever felt. And I wondered what I had become.

This was all a dream. It had to be. I hope writing it down releases it. I don't ever want to remember this.

* * *

Anne closed the book and groped her way over to a chair. She sat down and leaned back, closing her eyes. What was going on? Had Joe died? Had she been living with a dead man, some sort of vampire for the last few years? Anne threw back her head and laughed. She laughed until her throat was raw, until the tears made red rings around her eyes and the snot made it hard to breathe.

The next day, Anne wasn't sure what she should do. Should she share what she learned with Nick? It was all insanity. It had to be. It just had to be. Sure, Joe had some problems, but he would never hurt anyone.

From Joe MacAree's journal (undated):

Bold. That's what I am. The hunter never hesitates going in for the kill. My prey backs up only for an instant when she sees the X-Acto. I hear her thoughts, just like I hear the blood thrumming through her veins. "He ain't gonna do nothin'. He ain't gonna hurt me, just make me blow him or somethin'." Little girl's so stupid.

Slash. Slash. Christ, look at it! Red and thick, spurting out of her like some kind of come. Oh, God, and just that gurgling, because the little bitch can't scream. She can't scream.

I attach myself to that hot white throat, feeling it flow into me.

Anne put water on for tea and sat down at the kitchen table. She didn't think she had slept at all the night before. She had forced herself to go over the early years of Joe's life, even though it upset her so much she had to stop reading to run, panting, into the bathroom and vomit. All the details were there: how he had been repeatedly raped through the years by his father, how his mother had looked the other way, never once trying to help, how his sister Margo had helped, even holding Joe down so his father could abuse him while she laughed. God, she thought, no wonder he's insane. Who wouldn't be?

The journals had ended shortly after Joe's entry about his sister, Margo, and Anne wondered if there were more. Joe had kept the journals religiously since he was a boy, never missing more than a week in all those years. Surely, there were more.

Anne had searched for the missing journals. Joe's den now looked like it had been vandalized. Anne had torn it completely apart to find the journals from recent years.

But what she was looking for was not in that office.

Anne poured the boiling water over the tea bag. She stared into the water, not thinking, just watching the tea darken the water. She didn't want to think about the missing journals.

My God, she wondered, what horrors would those journals contain?

20

The apartment was still filled with the smell of burnt Monterey Jack cheese. A pall of gray smoke hung near the ceiling in the kitchen. He'll understand, Anne thought, picking away some of the blackened cheese, Nick will understand why my mind wasn't on cooking after I tell him about the journals. She lifted the fluted white casserole dish and took it to the waste can. With a serving spoon she emptied the casserole into the trash. She had just put the dish in the sink when the buzzer sounded.

All through the day she had tried not to think about what she had read in Joe's journals. She had spent the day doing things: laundry, dusting, vacuuming, washing windows and mirrors. The casserole she had tried to make for dinner this evening was the most complicated recipe in her vegetarian cookbook. While the casserole was in the oven she had taken as much care with her hair, clothes, and makeup as she did with any professional assignment. The white knit dress and the way she pulled her hair back severely from her face served only to emphasize the beauty of that face.

But none of the routine worked. It was like telling a child to think about anything in the world but elephants. She kept reliving the scene with Joe and Margo over and over again, as if she had been there with them: in the underpass when Margo stabbed Joe and later in the storage room when Joe had awakened and taken the communion of blood Margo had offered him. The words Joe had written were no longer what she remembered. What they had described, though, had come alive as she went over it again and again, as if she had been a mute observer, undetected.

Nick was knocking at the door. Anne took a final look at herself in the mirror and opened the door.

She kissed him and led him inside. "Let me take that from you," Anne said, taking the bottle of wine he held. She left him to take off his coat while she put the white wine in the refrigerator.

"What are you making for dinner?" Nick asked when she returned. "Ashes?"

"Very funny," Anne said, picking up his coat from the chair he had left it on. "Let me hang this up for you." She left him once more to go to the hall closet.

He came up behind her as she was closing the closet door. He slipped his arms around her waist and pulled her close. He smelled clean.

"What's wrong?" he whispered into her hair. "It seems like you're avoiding me."

She turned to him and kissed him. Her kiss was hungry, full of a desire for all the comfort her fear and turmoil required. She stopped and looked up at him. "I'm not avoiding you," she said. "I'm trying to avoid thinking. It's not working very well."

"Why?"

"Could we just get out of here? I want you to take me out for dinner. Someplace noisy . . . someplace where there are lots of people, where it's brightly lit."

Nick looked at her for a while, expecting her to maybe break down and tell him everything. Everything that had been hidden in her voice since she had called him at his office that morning to invite him over for dinner. But she didn't return his gaze; instead, she reached into the closet and brought out his coat. She handed it to him and pulled hers out.

She squeezed his hand. "Let's go. The wine should chill for a few hours anyway. We can open it when we come back."

He followed her out the door. "Anyplace in particular you want to go?"

"Ever been to Dave's Italian Kitchen in Evanston? It fits the bill."

"Perfect," Nick said, even though he ate there at least three times a week.

The apartment was dark. Nick was glad. A winter moon shone in through the bedroom windows, giving a silvery-gray sheen to everything in the room.

Nick felt the silk of her hair as she placed her head on his chest. What was wrong with him? "I'm sorry," she whispered. "It wasn't your fault."

"Yeah," he said. Nick turned and grabbed a cigarette from the nightstand, lit it. He stared at the moon for a long time, wondering about himself, about this room he was in. The bedroom of some missing guy, he thought, and here I am fucking his lady. Well, not even that tonight.

Anne got up on one elbow. "Look, it really doesn't matter."

He knew it did.

"You're probably just keyed up."

Oh, no, why should I be keyed up? I'm in bed with the wife of some guy who's half off his rocker. Who's keyed up? He stubbed out the cigarette and turned to look at her. There was hunger in her eyes. He felt like she was staring right through him. He laughed, but there was no humor in it, only darkness. "Tongue still works," he whispered.

She smiled at him, but desperation came through. "Don't. That's not all I'm interested in, you know." But already she was kicking off the sheets, the silver-ivory thighs parting in the moonlight.

He could smell her. He kissed, starting at her ears and went downward. "Yes," she moaned when he reached her sex. What was it she said then? Take me away?

He felt like a machine. I should get away from all of this, he thought, get away before I'm too ensnared. But even then, he was grinding his tongue up inside her, taking her someplace else.

After, he told her he didn't feel as if she was really with him that evening. He asked if it was his fault.

"I think you know *who's* fault it is, but I'm sure you have no idea why, even though what you already know might make you think you know why." She burrowed her face into the hair on his chest. "I don't know how I can talk about this." Her voice was muffled. He felt the warm wetness of her tears. What's the matter? he wondered. Did she find out he's gay? A child molester? What?

He lifted her face and licked her tears away. "I'm going to get us some wine," he said. "Maybe that'll help."

She watched him walk naked through the bedroom, remembered seeing Joe do the same thing so many times before. Sitting up in bed, she drew her knees up to her chest and encircled them with her arms. Will my life ever be normal again? she wondered, staring out at the night sky.

Nick came back with two wineglasses and the bottle. He sat on the edge of the bed and poured each of them a glass. Anne gulped down her first glass and took the bottle from him and refilled. "Courage," she whispered, lifting the glass.

"Last night I found some of Joe's journals. What I found really scared me. I don't know what to think. Joe grew up horribly abused. . . ." Anne went on to tell him about the sexual abuse Joe received from his father and how his sister helped and his mother looked the other way. When she got to the last part she found it hard to continue.

"Anne, you've got to tell me everything," Nick said, "so I can help."

"He thinks he's some sort of . . . vampire." She got up from the bed and went to the dresser. She had kept the last journal there, in with her socks.

"Here," she said, returning, "read it for yourself."

Nick took the journal from her and switched on the bedside lamp. He looked more and more confused as he read. He had been face to face with a lot of odd situations in his work, but nothing compared with this. The guy had to be completely nuts, he thought. But then, who wouldn't be, with the kind of upbringing he had?

"Do you think there could be anything to what he's said?" Anne asked him when he finished reading.

"Yeah, I think there could be a lot. Not that he's some sort of vampire, but that he's really, really sick . . . and maybe he could hurt somebody."

Anne stiffened in bed beside him. She remembered the killings in Berwyn. "Nick, there's something else you should know. Over the winter there have been a couple of killings in Berwyn. In both cases a sharp instrument was used to slash the victims to death. Nick, Joe never, ever went to Berwyn for any reason before you saw him go there. Now, I don't know why he's suddenly decided to go there . . . and that's what worries me. What also worries me is that I found a bloody X-Acto knife in the bathroom a few weeks ago. I just don't know what to think anymore."

"Well, don't get too worried. The killings could just be a coincidence."

"Another thing: All the recent journals are gone. I'm sure he would have continued keeping journals. So he must be hiding something."

"Then why would he want you to see any of them?"

"I don't know. Who said he wanted me to?"

"Well, if he's hidden some of the journals, why not hide all of them?"

"I don't know." She thought for a long time. "Maybe he did want me to see them. Maybe it was a way of telling me, of letting me know how sick he's become. Oh, Nick, maybe what he wants is help."

"Well, he does need that."

"We have to find out more. Could you help, Nick?"

"I don't know how much more I can find out. He's not staying at the Y anymore. I've lost track of him."

"I mean, could you help by finding out a little bit about his past?"

"You mean by trying to find his family or something?"

"That's exactly what I mean. He was always evasive about his family, evasive to the point of obviously hiding something. Now, I can understand in light of what happened not wanting to have anything to do with them, but maybe they know something more. Something that could help us find him. I want to help him, Nick. And I want us to find him before he ruins what's left of his life."

"I don't know where to begin looking."

"I do. He mentioned the town in his journal. It's in Pennsylvania . . . a little steel town called Summitville, a little ways west of Pittsburgh. Please, Nick, could you go for just one day? I'll pay for the flight."

"I'm not worried about that. It's just that I don't know what good this will do."

Anne shook her head. "I don't know either. But we'll never know unless we try. You're a private investigator, you should know that. Sometimes you find things you aren't expecting. Please, Nick. Couldn't you do it for me?"

"Okay, but I can't spend longer than a day."

"When will you go?"

"I can't go until next week. But I promise to go early, Monday maybe. Tuesday at the latest."

Nick arrived at the Greater Pittsburgh International Airport Tuesday morning. He had never been to this part of the country and was amazed, as the plane descended, at the natural beauty of the area. There were big, tree-covered hills everywhere. The airport wasn't really near the city at all.

By the time he rented a car, the sunlight that had dappled the hills was gone. Outside the airport the sky was heavy with clouds and there was a fine mist in the air. He knew he'd have some fog to make his ride to Summitville a little more difficult.

Once outside the airport, he began heading west.

The Summitville Town Hall was brand new, a squat, red-brick, one-story structure in the middle of the downtown. After Nick had explained at the front desk that he was a private investigator, he was introduced to Eula Simmons, the woman in charge of taking care of the records housed in the basement of the building. Eula was an old woman who had probably, Nick supposed, worked in the records department since she was just out of high school. She was overweight and wore a bright pink dress and red shoes.

But Nick found that in spite of her appearance she was competent.

"Margo MacAree? The name doesn't sound real familiar, but then there's over sixteen-thousand people in Summitville; I guess I can't know 'em all. You're looking for a birth certificate?"

"Well, that'd be a start. I want to find out what I can."

"Sure you do! Listen, it would help if you knew what year she was born in."

"I can guess, in the late forties, early fifties."

Eula laughed. "I'll let you do the searching." She led him into the records room. "We aren't computerized, so I imagine you'll have to do some looking. Good luck."

She left Nick standing in the middle of a caged-in room. He located "1948" and decided to start there.

After four hours Nick came to the death certificate of Margo MacAree. She had been a suicide:

death attributed to massive loss of blood as the result of self-inflicted wrist wounds. Nick looked at the date, remembering Joe's entry in his journal. Joe's entry had been in 1981. The death certificate clearly stated that the approximate time of death had been 7:00 A.M., August 5, 1981. It couldn't have been long after she came to him in Chicago, if she really had come to him at all. *I suppose,* Nick thought, *I'd kill myself, too, if I'd stabbed my brother and then made him drink my blood.*

Christ, what have I gotten myself into?

Nick stood and stretched. What was going on? It was obvious: Joe MacAree had been crazy long before he even met Anne. Who knew what was true in those journals? Nick supposed it was all true for Joe. The poor guy.

He decided he should recommend to Anne that as soon as they find him they should have him committed. Nick reasoned he was probably harmless—Anne's fears about the killings were, most likely, paranoid. Nick copied down the address from Margo's death certificate to see if any of the MacArees were still living at the same address. Even if they weren't, he could probably track them down through the phone company.

His next stop was the Summitville Public Library. There he might be able to find a newspaper story about Margo MacAree's suicide. In a town as small as Summitville, it might be big news.

Big news it was. Nick sat in the basement of the fading old building, the smells of must and old men around him, and stared at the blue-tinged screen of the microfiche.

He shook his head. *This just gets weirder and weirder.*

Margo MacAree had killed herself in Pattison's Motel on the outskirts of town. She had exchanged the motel sheets for white satin ones and then, after slitting her wrists (deeply and vertically, with a razor), laid herself out, cruciform, on the bed.

Vivaldi's "La Primavera" was on the little portable record player she had brought with her.

Nick's time spent in the basement of the library had allowed the sky to darken into night. As he drove along the Ohio River to the outskirts of town, he noticed how dark the trees looked against the night sky and how steam rose off the river. Across the water, huge cooling towers rose into the sky, pouring steam into the air. The blinking lights of industry kept the river banks bright. Nick noticed the barges floating silently down the river.

He took a right turn and maneuvered the car down a bumpy road that led into a valley near the river. Nick thought that the people who lived down here must get flooded out a lot. He stopped wondering why they would live there when he saw the poverty of the area. Most of the houses were wood-frame, and most were in need of paint. Those that didn't need paint were covered with tar paper masquerading as brick. It was here, Nick thought, stopping and looking at the house, where Joe MacAree had grown up. Nick matched the address he had written down with the one near the mailbox. This was the right place.

The house was dark. But Nick thought he would try anyway. He was supposed to fly back to Chicago late that evening, and if he didn't get the chance to find the MacArees tonight, he never would.

When he got out of the car he noticed how quiet it was, except for the river rushing by. There was a fishy smell in the air, mixed with the steel-mill smell of sulfur. Rotten eggs and fish. What a wonderful place to live.

There were no sidewalks in this neighborhood, and Nick's feet sank down into mud as he walked to the front porch of the house. As soon as he put his foot on the front step, it creaked. The creaking aroused a dog in the backyard who started barking. Nick heard the metallic sound of the dog straining to free itself from the chain that must have confined it. A porch light went on, and before Nick had a chance to knock he saw a man coming down the steps in the house. The man switched on a few lights inside before he came to the door.

Without opening the door the man shouted, "Who's there?"

Nick couldn't see his face very well because he was looking through sheer curtains that hung in the front door.

"My name is Nick MontPierre. I'm trying to locate the MacAree family. Are you Mr. MacAree?"

The man opened the door, and Nick stared at a balding old man holding a can of Black Label beer in one hand, a cigarette in the other. He wore a T-shirt and green work pants. "C'mon in," the man said, opening the storm door.

Nick stepped inside and looked around. The wallpaper was yellowed from what Nick guessed was years of heavy cigarette smoke. The whole house smelled of stale cigarettes, almost as if the windows had never been opened.

"Are you Mr. MacAree?" Nick repeated his question.

"Why?"

"I'm a friend of his son's; my name's Nick—"

"I heard you the first time." The man paused for a moment. "No, I ain't Mr. MacAree."

"Would you know where I could find him? The family used to live here, you know."

"I know. The MacArees is all dead, far as I know." The man spoke matter-of-factly, as if he didn't care about showing any sympathy.

"Do you know what happened?"

The man shook his head and stared at the floor. "Nah. I think the daughter mighta killed herself. I don't know about the boy. He disappeared. You say you know him."

"That's right." Nick lied. "We went to school together and I've worked with him since then."

"Where'd you say you was from?"

"Chicago."

"Oh."

"When did you move in here?"

"I don't know where that's any of your business, mister. I gotta be gettin' to bed. I gotta get up early."

"Well, thanks for your time."

The man closed the door in Nick's face.

The man turned around and peered into the darkness of the living room.

"Who was that?"

"Just some bum. He wanted to know about Joey, I guess. Or at least about his family. We're dead, accordin' to me." The man laughed.

"Yeah, as far as that boy's concerned, we are." His wife took the beer from his hand and drank.

21

Randy had waited several days to get up the courage to call Joe MacAree. If he was fortunate enough to speak with him, he had rehearsed what he would say. He knew he didn't want to scare him away, so he decided to pretend he was an auditor with the IRS. Randy had thought through several guises, among them a disc jockey announcing Joe had won a cash prize and would have to meet him to claim it, a long-lost relative who was in town on business, and dozens of other possibilities. Although most of the other pretenses seemed more pleasant, none would have the authority of an IRS auditor. Even a murderer couldn't refuse.

But on this Saturday morning Randy found it difficult to pick up the telephone; his palms were sweating. The muted floral pattern of the wallpaper in his bedroom closed in on him, making him feel trapped by his own impatience to see

Joe MacAree. His heart pounded because he had
never had such a desire to kill anyone before and
had never felt so eager to get a job done. He felt
nauseated each time he picked up the phone and
started to dial the number. He hung up just short
of hearing the ring each time.

He was in the process of dialing for about the
fifth time when his mother opened the door. She
stood looking at him, and Randy felt as if he had
been caught masturbating. His face flushed; he
could feel cold sweat on his forehead and upper
lip. When he spoke he heard himself speaking in
the voice of an adolescent: high and almost
quivering.

"What is it, Ma?"

"I thought you wanted some breakfast. I called.
How come you didn't answer?"

"I didn't hear you. I'm not hungry."

"C'mon, Randy, you gotta eat."

"I'll get something later."

"What? A piece of toast and a cup of coffee?
That's no breakfast for a man."

"Don't worry, Ma. I'll take care of myself."

She came over and sat on the bed beside him.
He noticed how lined her face had become, how
gray she was. When had she grown old?

She took his hand. "Randy, you gotta give this
up. It's hard, I know, but Maggie wouldn't have
wanted you acting like this."

He snatched his hand away from her. "How
the hell do you know what Maggie would have
wanted? Maggie wouldn't have wanted to die at
the hands of some psycho, but she didn't get any
choice in the matter." He was yelling and he saw

his mother recoil with hurt. She stood suddenly, tears glistening in her eyes.

"Okay," she whispered, "okay."

He watched her leave the room and felt even more nauseated. Later he would apologize. He was just nervous now and couldn't stand her doting. He picked up the phone once more, dialed the number he knew from memory. Resisting the impulse to slam the receiver back into the cradle, he listened to the ringing . . . once, twice, three times.

"Hello."

A woman's voice. Randy had never pictured Joe MacAree as having any kind of family. He thought that psychos were loners, people who holed up in filthy apartments and wrote weird things on walls, put blankets over their windows. If this was his wife or mother, what would she be like? Would she know?

"Hello?" The woman's voice became more insistent.

"Yes," Randy said, struggling to keep his voice even. "Could I speak to Joe MacAree, please?"

The woman sucked in some air, as if she was surprised. "Who is this?"

Randy didn't know what to say. The IRS scam went out of his mind completely. "This is just a friend of his. Is he there or isn't he?" The annoyance in his voice was apparent, he feared. Be calm, he told himself.

"No," the woman said, "he isn't here right now. Could I give him a message?"

Randy was tempted to tell her everything he knew. Maybe she didn't know, perhaps she was a completely innocent woman trapped in the middle of evil. Maybe, he thought, she's in some danger.

"Do you know where he is? Maybe I could call back later and catch him in."

"I really have no way of knowing."

"Who is this? His wife?"

"That's really none of your business. Who's this?"

Randy decided against telling her anything. Maybe she knew everything and telling her would just tip MacAree off to watch out for him. He couldn't afford to take that chance. Avenging Maggie's death meant everything to him now. He didn't even care if he was caught and had to spend the rest of his life in prison. It would be worth it. "I think I'll try him a little later."

"It's not likely—"

Randy hung up on the woman in midsentence.

He threw himself back on his bed and stared up at the ceiling, noticing the cobwebs in the corners and a long crack that ran from the light fixture to one corner of the room.

He decided he would have to find MacAree some other way. He didn't know what it would be yet, but there was no question: He would see that bastard die.

Anne put down the phone, confused. She had received many calls the past few weeks from Joe's clients, wanting to know when they could expect work they had commissioned, wondering why he hadn't kept in touch with them. Anne was tempted to say, "He's gone insane. At least that's what I think. It may be that he's not a human being at all, but some sort of living dead. Is that excuse enough?"

This last person, though, frightened her. He sounded insane too. Or frightened, Anne thought, picking up a cold cup of coffee from the kitchen table.

The buzzer sounded in the living room and Anne hurried to the intercom. "Who's there?"

The mechanical voice came through. "Anne, it's Nick."

She buzzed him in and ran to the bedroom to slip into jeans and an oversize red chamois shirt. She was pulling her hair back when she heard him knock. "Just a minute," she called, wrapping a rubber band around her hair.

Nick hugged her when she opened the door, holding her close to him for a long time. She breathed in his smell: Irish Spring soap and his leather jacket.

"Let's not stand here," she whispered, breaking away from him and leading him inside.

Once they sat down next to each other on the living room couch, Anne asked him, "Did you go? Did you find anything out?"

"Yes, I went," Nick said. Then he paused for a long time, thinking. "And I did find some things out. I just don't know if what I found will be any use to us." He got up and looked out the window at the traffic rushing by on Lake Shore Drive.

"That part of the country is really a mixture," he said after a while, staring out. "On one hand, it's really beautiful. I wasn't expecting the big hills. And the hills are covered with trees, almost a wilderness. It must be beautiful in the summer and fall. But then there's all this industry . . . steel mills, nuclear power plants with big cooling towers along the river . . . it's real industrial. A lot of the houses there are run-down; it looks kind of depressed."

"Nick, what are you talking about?"

"I don't know." He came back and sat down on the couch.

"What is it?"

"You remember how Joe wrote in his journal about his sister, Margo?"

"Yes."

"When did he see her last?"

"I don't remember exactly. Wasn't it around eighty-one? Before that," she added, "she showed up around graduation."

Nick took a breath. He lit a cigarette and looked around for an ashtray. "According to the records at Summitville City Hall, Margo committed suicide not long after seeing Joe for the last time—at least, according to his journal."

Anne stared at him.

"Anne, I looked up some stuff in the paper. She . . . um . . . she slit her wrists with a razor." Nick stared at her, trying to see what effect the coincidence would have on her. Anne's face showed nothing. "She spread herself out on a bed with white satin sheets. She was naked and in sort of a crucified position."

Nick could tell by Anne's expression she was trying to get this new information to register—without success.

"So you think maybe Margo might have something to do with Joe's behavior?"

"I can't say. I'm just an investigator, not Freud." Nick frowned at her. He felt himself wanting to get out, to go back to the industrial theft, the infidelity cases that made up his life before Anne walked into his office. "The point is I didn't really learn much that can help us find Joe now."

Anne stood and stared out the window. "We have to find him, Nick."

They hugged for a while. There was nothing left to talk about. Anne burrowed deep into Nick's chest, wanting to shut out everything she knew and more, everything she didn't know.

"We will," Nick whispered. He didn't want to admit it to Anne, but he was afraid too. He remembered the dark road along the river in Summitville, recalled how the mist rose off the dark waters and the black trees reached gnarled hands out over the silent rushing river. He thought, We have to find him because I sure as hell don't want him to find us first.

The morning sun coming in through the blinds woke Nick first. He looked over at Anne, her face looking calm against the pale blue pillowcase. The calmness was a rare sight lately. Even when they had made love the night before, she'd been distracted, and her obvious fear made him lose his erection. He had held her until she fell asleep.

Now, he was thinking, the real search has to start. The night before he'd thought the first person he should go to was Pat Young. She was the last person Nick knew Joe had seen. She must know something.

Trying not to wake Anne, he slid out of bed. As he was putting on his pants he saw her open her eyes.

"Where are you going?" she asked sleepily, forcing herself up on her elbows.

"I want to start looking for Joe."

"Are you sure?"

"I think we really have to find him as soon as we can."

Anne looked afraid, and he was sorry he had brought on that fear. She swung her legs over the side of the bed. "Maybe I should come with you."

"Really, Anne, I work better by myself."

"Don't start this macho stuff—"

"It's not macho. I just need to be by myself. I don't know exactly where I'll go. And maybe if I'm lucky enough to find him today, maybe it would be better if you weren't there."

"I think just the opposite." Anne got up and went into the bathroom. Nick heard water running. Then he heard her call, "Joe will come with us if I'm there. I know he will."

Nick went into the bathroom and watched her brushing her teeth. "Listen, Anne. What if he calls? Don't you think you should stay here in case he should try to call?"

She rinsed her mouth and looked at him. "Maybe you're right," she admitted. "But could you do me a favor?"

"Sure. Anything."

"Keep me posted on what you're doing. Give me a call a couple times today. Let me know how it's going. I'm not going to be able to think about anything else today."

He went to her and wrapped his arms around her. "I promise to check in with you, even if I don't know anything. Okay?"

"Okay."

"Now let me finish dressing. We're going to get this thing worked out."

She watched him disappear into the bedroom.

Pat Young looked at herself once more in the mirror. Her face was a puzzle of wounds, ranging from scratches to deep cuts. Both eyes were swollen into slits; large purple and yellow bruises surrounded them. Her upper lip was puffy.

She pushed herself away from the bathroom mirror. The TV was blaring Sunday morning gospel and she wheeled herself in front of it. She prayed that Joe would return to her. When he saw what that man had done to her, Joe would save her. Joe would punish him.

And if Joe didn't, she thought, she would make him. The police were just a phone call away.

The buzzing of the intercom startled her. She went to it and rang the person in, hoping it would be Joe. The knock on her door came seconds later. Pat peered through the peephole and saw Nick.

"Who are you?" she asked.

"My name is Nick MontPierre, ma'am. I'm a friend of Joe MacAree's."

Pat looked around the room. A messenger?

Maybe Joe had sent this man to get her and bring her to Joe?

"Who?"

"Joe MacAree. Please, could you open the door?"

Pat slid the bolt across and opened the door. She looked the man over, noticing how handsome he was. "You can come in, but you can't stay."

Nick looked at Pat Young, wondering if Joe had done this to her. He couldn't remember when he'd seen a person so badly beaten.

"What happened to you?" he asked.

"That's none of your damn business!" Pat snapped. "Now, what did you want?"

"I told you, I'm a friend of Joe MacAree's."

"So?" Pat decided she wasn't giving anything away. Joe would have told her if he was sending someone. Wouldn't he?

"I'm trying to find him."

"Why would I know anything?"

"You're a friend of his, aren't you?"

"Who told you that?"

"All right, Ms. Young. I'll lay my cards on the table." Nick took off his hat and sat down. "I'm a private investigator working for Joe's wife. We think Joe is very sick and want to help him. I followed him here one night."

Nick watched the anger come up in the battered face. The change happened in seconds. Pat spoke in a low voice, her teeth clenched. "How dare you associate me with anyone! I don't know any Joe MacAree."

"I saw him come to this building."

"I don't give a fuck what you saw. . . . He must have been coming to see someone else."

"I watched him ring your buzzer. I wrote it down."

"You bastard. You had no right. Anyway, it's common practice around here for people to ring just any buzzer to get into the building. We don't have any intercoms, so generally we just buzz in whoever's ringing. I don't get much company, so I think nothing of buzzing someone in and then not hearing a knock on my door. The plight of the sad cripple," Pat spat out.

"I think you know him."

"I told you, I don't care what you think."

"Would this help?" He took twenty dollars out of his wallet. Pat snatched it out of his hand.

"No, it wouldn't. Neither would anything else you have in your wallet." She tucked the bill into her bra. "Now get out of my house."

"Please, Ms. Young—"

"Get out or I'm calling the police."

"We don't want to hurt him. We just want to help him. He might be in some trouble."

"I really don't care. I told you. I don't know him."

Nick called Anne later from a phone booth in Berwyn. He told her that Pat Young knew something she wasn't telling and he would try to keep an eye on her.

"Sooner or later," Nick said, "he's going to show up at her place. I've got a gut feeling and I know I'm right."

22

From Joe MacAree's journal (undated):

His need for blood consumes. The world suddenly has turned crimson; everywhere he looks he sees the color, the shape of flowing blood. It spouts from the top of a lamp in a furniture store window, shooting high like some bloody ejaculate; a little boy in the zoo stops to drink from the water fountain and blood arcs out, and he envies the little boy who bends down and sucks up the blood hungrily. He watches it run down the boy's chin, staining his shirt. The animals in the Lincoln Park Zoo all sport open wounds. In some the blood oozes out; in others an artery has been hit and the blood spurts. The animals don't seem to mind, and he longs to vault the fence separating him from them. Everywhere he hears the sound of rushing blood, pounding in his ears like a siren's song.

He must drink blood.

The streets of the city shimmer in red. The snow falling is tinged with pink: bloodstained. Bricks of buildings are splattered with blood. Here, near the train station, the spaces between the bricks of the foundation ooze blood. He wonders if any of these commuters notice as they hurry by him, arms upraised to hail taxis, on their way home. He wonders if they even see him, hidden here in the warmth of the darkness, the shadows. He watches as they walk by, headed for the subway, waiting to see the one who will be right. The one who is ripe.

Then he sees her. Black. Huddled down into a fake gray-fur coat, the collar pulled up, obscuring all but a mountain of nappy hair that collects the falling snow. Miniskirt and high heels. Even from the shadows, he can see the legs are well formed as he traces the seam up the back of her stockings. The tightness in his pants tells him: This is the one. He has never tasted black blood and knows it will be warmer.

She walks alone, her hips swaying. He gives her some time to make her way into the darkness, toward the subway and away from the few stragglers who are still coming out of the train station. He tightens his grip on the ice steel of the X-Acto in his pocket. Slash, slash, he thinks, smiling to himself. She stops after a few moments and glances over her shoulder at him. He sees the fear in her eyes. In that instant he watches as the whites of her eyes turn red, filling with blood: She is ready. Increasing pace of footsteps, he hears her mind: "Damn these shoes."

The time has come. His effort to overtake her is almost too easy. She stops, facing him off. "Whatchoo want?" she asks, defiance and false bravery in each word. He doesn't answer because she knows, too, that she is ripe and he must save her. He gets behind her, grabs her around the throat, and covers her scream with his hand. Shadows await him, and he pulls her into the warm red darkness. Most people assume darkness is black, but he knows the truth: It is deep crimson, the color of clotted blood. Her struggling is nothing compared to his force. He takes out the X-Acto with the hand that was around her throat. He draws a pencil-thin smile across her throat with his blade, then probes inside with the pointed end. She gags, coughing up blood. He kisses her. She drops. He cuts.

The *Chicago Tribune,* in its late-afternoon edition, carried this headline: CHICAGO WOMAN MURDERED NEAR TRAIN STATION. The story described how Elizabeth Rawlings, twenty-six, of Cottage Grove Avenue, was on her way home from her job as a clerk in the Loop when she stopped in the train station to buy a pack of cigarettes before continuing on her way to the subway. The last person who remembered seeing her alive was Sam Jordan, a cashier at the magazine stand in the train station. The woman was slashed in a manner believed by Chicago police to be connected to other killings in the area this winter.

The *Chicago Sun Times* headline read: WOMAN BRUTALLY SLASHED; MADMAN SOUGHT. The paper also carried a photograph of the woman's body covered by a sheet in the gangway where she had been killed. The photographer snapped the picture just before the woman's body was loaded into the ambulance. There also was an inset of the woman's mother in tears.

By late that evening Chicago detectives were fairly certain that the two killings in Berwyn and this one were all the work of one person. Specialists had confirmed that the slash marks on all three victims were made by the same instrument, although they were unsure of what the instrument was. Most suspected a razor blade. Skin found under the fingernails of all three of the victims had been identified and matched: One person was responsible. Each had suffered a massive loss of blood, although very little blood was found at the scene of each crime. No one in the Chicago Police Department was sure of what became of the blood, and if the detectives assigned to the case were honest with each other and the press, they would have admitted they were afraid to speculate what had become of it.

During a midnight press conference, the mayor of Chicago announced that a task force was being formed within the Chicago Police Department and that the killer would be apprehended before he struck again. He sent out a plea that if anyone had any suspicions at all they should get in touch with the Chicago or Berwyn police department as soon as possible. A special hotline was being installed and the number would be available the following afternoon.

* * *

Elizabeth Rawlings's mother, Bella, stared at her daughter's two children: her two granddaughters. They had all shared this two-room apartment, supported by Elizabeth's small paycheck. Where would the children go now? Bella thought, I can't afford them. I'm too old to take care of them. Where is the man who took my baby away from me?

She slumped over in her chair, weeping. The children looked up from the floor where they were playing with plastic oleo bowls, building skyscrapers and houses for the little clothespin people Gram had made for them. Their dark eyes widened. They wondered why their mother never came home from work and if that had anything to do with why Gram was crying.

Bella got up from the kitchen chair she was sitting on and went into the other room. On top of the TV set was a photograph of all four of them, taken at Sears. Elizabeth had insisted on having the picture taken, Bella remembered, because she said, "Soon enough, my babies are gonna be women with babies of their own. I wanna remember."

"I wanna remember too, baby," Bella whispered, fingering the no-glare glass of the frame.

Anne gathered up the newspapers in the apartment and took them to the garbage chute at the end of the hall. She listened to the fluttering sound they made as they fell. She had read all the news stories, had copied down the hotline number. She had watched the news, listening as the newscaster recounted the murders over the winter by the unknown person now known as the "Chicago Slasher."

It was late, 3:00 A.M., and Anne had a photo shoot in the morning. She crawled into bed, wishing Nick were there with her to hold her and reassure her that Joe wasn't the Chicago Slasher. She pulled the comforter up to her ears and curled into a tight ball. Closing her eyes, she tried to force herself to think peaceful thoughts. But in moments her eyes snapped open, staring into the darkness of the bedroom.

This is useless, she thought, flinging the comforter off and getting up. She wandered into the kitchen, poured some milk into a pan, and set it on the stove to warm. While she waited she sat down at the kitchen table and tried to think of reasons why Joe couldn't be the slasher. He was too weak, she thought. He had never been the macho type; he was always sensitive. He used to feel sorry for the mice he had to trap in his college apartment. How could someone who felt guilty about killing mice take the lives of human beings? But, she told herself, Joe wasn't the man she fell in love with at school.

Pouring the milk into a mug, she noticed the pad on the counter where she had written the hotline number. The newspaper had said the number would be manned twenty-four hours a day. Could she actually pick up the phone and call? What would she say? She had no real evidence. "I found a bloody X-Acto knife in our bathroom. I think my husband is the killer. By the way, we're separated and I don't know where he is." She would be filed under disgruntled wives and given a low priority number. It wouldn't do any good, she lied to herself. I couldn't tell them about the journals.

Nick, she thought, oh, Nick, please find him soon.

The metallic shriek of the buzzer in the living room startled her. The mug of warm milk crashed to the tile floor. The mug shattered and Anne gasped as the hot milk splashed up on her leg.

The buzzer sounded again.

Anne ran to it, wondering. Nick had told her he had some industrial work to do tonight at a factory. He said he would be working all night. Maybe Nick got lucky, apprehended his suspect, and was coming home to Anne.

She picked up her pace as the buzzer sounded two more times. It almost sounded angry.

"Nick?" she asked, pressing the intercom button.

A singing voice came through the speaker: "I'll be seeing you." Anne cut off the weird laughter before it had a chance to fill the room.

"Who is this?" she asked after a moment.

Laughter. "I'll be seeing you," the voice sang again.

Anne screamed and gripped the wall for support. Joe. She gasped, taking in quick, panicky breaths.

When she pressed the intercom button again, dead air was all that answered her. She hurried to the window, looking down at the circular drive at the front of the building. Empty.

Oh, God, she thought, what am I going to do?

She hurried into the kitchen and picked up the phone, actually dialed the seven-four-four of the hotline number before hanging up. She leaned against the counter and listened to the pounding of her heart.

From Joe MacAree's journal (undated):

Paid Annie a visit. Don't know if she's ready for me yet or not. She has to be ready. That's part of the plan. When we get together again I'm sure it will be just like old times. Only this time, when I "take" her, it will be for keeps.

The bright lights of the bus station hurt his eyes. But it's warm here, Joe thought, slumping down on one of the chairs. And he realized he needed warmth and sleep.

But sleep wouldn't come. Even though just a day had passed since he last had blood, he could think of nothing else. The need pounded in his head, begging for satisfaction. Every time he closed his eyes he saw round red shapes rising up beneath the darkness of his eyelids. His imagination conjured up rivers of flowing blood, and the erection in his pants would not go away.

He stood and went into the men's room. Maybe if he masturbated, the urge would go away and he could sleep.

He sat down in a stall and closed the door. Next to him, a man's loafered foot moved over, closer to Joe's foot. Joe peered down at the foot, wondering. He leaned down to scan the floor below the partitions and saw that the rest room was empty. The foot on the other side moved over another few inches.

Joe moved his foot toward this other man's, not sure yet what he was going to do. The other man's foot nudged Joe's, and Joe returned the pressure.

Suddenly the man knelt, facing him. The partition covered him from the waist up. An erect penis pointed up at Joe's face.

Something inside him took over, and Joe knew what he must do. In almost one motion he removed the X-Acto from his pocket and slit the penis from its root up to its purplish head. He heard the man gasp, and Joe grabbed onto his legs and held him while he struggled. Joe lowered his head and sucked the blood that pumped wildly from the man's penis. Joe swallowed quickly, trying to take it all.

The man's scream came at last, resounding off the tile walls of the rest room. The shrillness of it hurt Joe's ears, and in his surprise he eased his grip on the man's bare legs enough to give the man a chance to get away.

Joe stood and pulled up his pants, hearing the slam of the stall door next to him and the footsteps of the man. Joe heard him say, "Please, God, somebody help me."

Opening the door, Joe was confronted with an almost funny scene. The man was fat, and he ran toward the door with his pants around his ankles. Blood ran down his white and hairless legs. This is almost too easy, Joe thought, coming up behind him and jabbing him in the neck with the X-Acto knife, cutting off his gibbering and causing him to lash out at Joe with his hands. The man dropped to the floor and Joe attached himself to his neck and tried to swallow the blood.

The door opened. "What the fuck!" There was terror in the question and Joe looked up into the face of an old black man. Joe brandished the bloody X-Acto.

"Keep quiet," he said, and shoved the old man to the floor.

As Joe ran through the bus station he heard the old man screaming for help, but couldn't hear anyone coming to his aid. Thank God for the cities, Joe thought, bursting out of the double glass doors of the bus station.

The night air was cold. Joe wiped the blood off his face with his coat sleeve. On the eastern horizon, the sky was turning pink.

23

Nick and Anne stared at each other across the scarred wooden table. The Fine Young Cannibals were blaring out of a jukebox in the corner of the room, singing "She Drives Me Crazy." The sound of a sizzling grill competed with the voices, and the smell of smoke and hamburgers filled the little bar.

Nick had insisted on bringing Anne here: a little Bridgeport neighborhood bar called Pilsen's. Since her last modeling assignment she had not left her apartment. Dark circles ringed her eyes, and there was something vague and tired about her features that aged her. Nick hated seeing her this way. He wanted to bring her someplace where the noise and bustle would cheer her, make her forget about the mess in her life.

He hadn't wanted to talk about Joe, and neither had she. But there was really no other subject for the two of them. News reports on television and the front pages of both newspapers caused them both to think of little else besides Joe MacAree and to wonder if they knew the identity of the Chicago Slasher and were keeping it secret.

Anne didn't want to hear why Nick thought Joe was probably the man responsible for the killings. Now, as she stared at him, she thought of how tired she was. How nothing seemed more attractive than going home and crawling in bed and sleeping until all of this was over. She didn't want to face this anymore. She wasn't responsible. Why did she have to be a part of it?

She had cut him off with her silence. He had tried to explain why they should go to the police, reminding her of what they knew. But Anne knew how to make her expression icy, knew how to look right at someone without giving them the dignity of seeing them.

He had stopped talking and the two of them now stared wordlessly at one another, each waiting. She was waiting for him to change the subject, take her home, order another beer. He was waiting for her to say something like "I'm sorry for cutting you off, please tell me what I have to hear."

"Anne, please listen. I'm just saying these things to help—" He stopped when he noticed her staring at the jukebox. He looked over at it, then back at her.

She waved her hand at some cigarette smoke that had gotten in front of her. "You know," she said, "I think Phil Collins should have stayed with Genesis."

"What?"

"I mean, he's a talented musician, but I just don't like him all that much alone. He"—she groped for words—"he's too slick. You know what I mean? In high school we used to call it bubble gum music. Like Barry Manilow. Only Phil Collins isn't quite like Barry Manilow. He's cooler." She laughed and glanced around her.

"Anne, what are you talking about? I'm trying to discuss something important here. I don't think I'm being melodramatic when I say it's a matter of life and death."

Anne rolled her eyes. "I've been trying to get it across to you that I don't want to talk about . . . him. Besides, I don't think Joe would ever hurt me." There was an added fierceness to her words that made them lack conviction. Anne massaged her temples, remembering Joe's voice coming through her intercom, singing "I'll be seeing you," at three o'clock in the morning.

Nick covered her hands with his. "Okay. Do you want to get out of here? We can hop in the car and be in Evanston in a jiffy. You hardly ever come to my place. It's not much to see—"

"I want to stay here. I like it. It reminds me of the bars I used to go to in college." Anne put on an overly bright smile.

"Okay," Nick said, leaning back and lighting a cigarette. "What should we talk about?"

"About this bar. How did you know about it?"

Nick glanced around the interior of the little bar, noticing once more the wooden spindle tables that had been carved over and over again, the fake-beamed ceiling, and the curving bar at the front of the place. There was a mirror behind the bar, reflecting in a greenish light all the bottles of booze lined up in front of it. "I've known about this place for a long time. I grew up in this neighborhood and my dad used to know the owner." At the mention of his father, Nick grew quiet for a moment. He knew Anne was staring at him, wondering why his face had grown troubled. He breathed in and forced himself to smile.

"Yeah?"

"Yeah . . . it was a different place when I was a kid. People used to come in here—families, people from the neighborhood. They served a mean Sunday dinner. The best Polish you ever ate. When my dad used to work late on Fridays, my mom used to send me over here for fish sandwiches for supper. I can still remember smelling the fish through the brown paper bag."

"Where are your parents now?"

"Dad got killed in the line of duty . . . a cop. Mom's living off his pension down in Florida."

"Where?"

"Near Tampa." Nick stared at her.

"So is that why you became a detective?"

"What?"

"Because your father was a cop. Is that why?"

"Yeah, I guess so." Nick seemed preoccupied. He scratched at the back of his neck, looked around the room, almost as if he was searching for a familiar face.

"What is it?" Anne asked.

Nick smiled, but it was nervous. He lit another cigarette. "Nothin'. Just keyed up."

"Is it something about your dad? Did you two not get along?"

"Oh, no, we got along great, just great." He took a drag off the cigarette and smiled at her. "Look, you want to come to my place?"

"No, Nick, I told you. I want to hear more about your family. So what precinct did your dad—"

"Will you shut up about my dad?"

Anne looked up, surprised.

"I'm sorry." Nick stared at the scarred surface of the table, tracing some of the carvings there with his finger. Finally he looked up at her. "I'm gonna tell you something. Something I never told anybody before. I'm gonna tell you once and then I don't want to hear any more about it."

Anne stared at him, looking for a clue in his face. "Okay."

"After my dad died, I had to go through some of his papers and, well, I found some letters."

Anne breathed out a sigh of relief. "He was having an affair, wasn't he?"

"Will you just be quiet and let me tell it?" Nick paused. "Yeah, he was having an affair, as a matter of fact. But the affair was . . ." Nick lowered his eyes once more to the table's surface. After a long while he looked back up at her. His face was red and shining with tears. Angrily, he wiped them away with the back of his hand and then almost spat the words, "But the affair was with a guy. A man, do you understand? My dad was a fag." Nick tried to meet Anne's eyes, but couldn't. He spoke to the table. "I guess it had gone on for years. A paramedic he met on the job. Dan Mc-

Kinney. God, he used to come to the house on holidays."

Anne covered his hands with hers. "Hey, that's not so bad."

Nick went on. "Funny thing is, you'd never in a million years guess about these guys. They were both big, burly guys, man's men. Hunting, fishing, liked to go to Bears' games."

"I'm sure your father was a good man."

"What do you know?" Nick smiled. "I'm sorry. He really was a good guy. But when I found this out, I felt like he had been an imposter. Here he was dead, and I felt like I never really knew him. I was sixteen then and I wanted to be nothin' like him. Look at me now."

They were quiet for a while, listening to music. "I guess I became a detective because of him. But not for the reason you think. He made me see something about people. About how there are always secrets, about how what's on the surface might not mean shit." Finally he met her eyes. "What are your secrets, Anne?"

Anne swallowed. "No secrets," she said, and thought how she wanted Nick to find Joe and how she wanted Nick to make her forget him. At least until she was better. At least until she could take care of herself again.

He didn't think she was aware of how she looked glancing around the room, looking from corner to corner as if she was afraid someone she didn't like would show up. He didn't know if she was aware of how she sounded when she spoke: just making fast noise to make sure there was no silence or the subject wouldn't change.

He covered her hands with his and squeezed. She met his eyes.

"Anne," he said softly, "we need to talk about Joe."

"Why?"

"Because we have to do something about him before he hurts somebody again."

"Oh, now, we don't know that he's hurt anyone." Anne smiled, but there was something sickly in her expression.

"I think I know, and I think you do too. I know it's hard to face, but we're just as guilty as he is if we don't face up to the very real possibility that Joe may be killing people."

"Joe couldn't kill anybody. He's much too sensitive."

"Will you listen to yourself? You don't even believe what you're saying."

"Of course I do." She stared at the table. When she looked back up at him, her eyes were glassy with tears. "Could I have another beer?" she asked.

Nick let out a sigh. "Sure," he said, "I could use one too. But when I get back, we have to talk about Joe. You've had my story."

"Okay."

Nick made his way through the bar, which was becoming crowded. A bluegrass band was setting up on a platform in one corner of the room, and Nick heard guitars being tuned and microphones being tested; every so often he heard a drum. At the bar he ordered two drafts.

When he got back to the table Anne was gone. I should have known this would happen, he thought, looking around the crowded room. "Damn!" He slammed the beers down on the table. A couple sitting at the next table over looked at him. The man smiled and whispered something to his date.

Nick slumped down in his chair and took a swig of beer. He was just about to put his coat on when he saw her weaving through the crowd toward him. He sighed. Looking at her, he wondered how he had been so fortunate to have such a beautiful woman with him. He wondered if she would be with him if circumstances were different.

"What's the matter?" she said when she got back to the table. She smiled. "Think I'd gone off and left you?"

Nick didn't answer. He shoved the beer toward her. She took a drink and said, "Okay. I don't know why you look so worried. I wouldn't leave you here." She laughed. "You're my ride." Glancing over at the band, which was getting ready to begin, she asked, "Are they any good? Have you heard them?"

"I don't know because I haven't heard them. Anne, please don't start this again."

"Start what?" Anne's face was a mask of feigned innocence.

"You said we could talk. We have to face—" Nick's voice was drowned out by the band, playing "Orange Blossom Special." They were very good, especially the girl on the fiddle. And they were loud. Nick pictured himself and Anne talking over the music about why Joe was the Chicago Slasher, shouting to be heard. The couple at the next table would love it.

"Drink up," he shouted. "We're going to my place."

"Can't we stay for a little while? They're fun." She nodded toward the stage.

"If I really believed you, I'd stay. C'mon, let's go." Nick drained his beer in one swallow and stood.

"Some date," Anne mouthed, putting down her beer and standing. Nick helped her put her coat on.

They were quiet on the ride to Evanston. Anne stared out the window, not wanting to talk, and Nick concentrated on his driving.

"This is nice, Nick," Anne said, touring his large studio. She seemed surprised to find it so neat and well decorated: rough-hewn pine and shades of navy and light blue made the room manly, but clean-looking, spare.

Nick switched on a lamp in the corner of the room.

"What? Think I've got no taste?" Nick smiled at her. "Sit down," he said, indicating the couch. "Can I get you something to drink? I think there's some Molson's in the fridge."

"That would be great," Anne said. *Anything to delay talking about Joe.* She leaned back against the cotton upholstery of the couch and closed her eyes, listening to Nick in the kitchen: the clink of glasses being taken from a cupboard, the refrigerator door opening and closing, the beer being poured.

She opened her eyes when he sat down beside her and handed her a glass.

They each took a sip. Nick leaned against her and kissed her, transferring some of the beer in his mouth to hers.

He set his glass on the table in front of them. "Okay, let's talk."

Anne shook her head. "I don't see why we have to."

"Yes, you do. Now, I know this isn't easy, but Joe—let's face it—he's insane. Everything in his journal points to it. It would be different if the journals were all like they were in his younger years. But you and I both read them. For years they were normal. The day-to-day thoughts and activities of a young man. True, what happened to him when he was growing up was awful, but even when he wrote about that it didn't seem like the ravings of a lunatic."

"He's not a lunatic."

"Anne, you can't deny that in the last few years those journals got crazier and crazier. A psychiatrist would have a field day with just a few of those pages."

"Maybe it's just creative writing. He is a writer, you know."

"Do you remember what he wrote about his sister?"

"Margo."

"Do you think that was just creative writing?" He didn't give her a chance to answer. "I know you don't. You said you didn't so don't deny it now."

She stared down at the floor. "Okay, so he's

written some crazy things. That's private. It's no reason to suspect him of murder. Maybe he just needs some help."

"What about the other night? When he was downstairs, singing to you through the inter-com?"

Anne hugged herself; she felt cold all of a sudden. She started to say something, then stopped.

"Weren't you afraid? Aren't you scared right now? Did his voice sound like the voice of a sane person?"

After a while she said, "You're right. But that still doesn't mean he's about to hurt me or anyone else."

"What about the knife in the bathroom? The one you said was covered with dried blood?"

"So? Maybe he cut himself. He said so himself."

"And you said so yourself: There was too much blood on that knife for a little finger cut." Nick thought for a moment. "And remember later, when you went back? The knife was gone from the wastebasket. He had taken it out of there and hid it in just the few seconds you were gone."

"*I don't know!*" Anne hadn't meant to shout; she covered her mouth with her hand. She spoke very softly. "Maybe he just saw it in the wastebasket and didn't want it thrown out."

"Then why hide it? Why not just put it back on the sink where it was?"

"You remember every little detail, don't you?"

"It's my business. And I also remember you telling me how nervous he was when you asked him about it."

Anne stared down at the hardwood floor.

"Don't you see, Anne? All the reports say that the victims of the slasher were killed with an extremely sharp instrument, like a razor. An X-Acto knife fits the bill perfectly."

"So does a razor blade. So does somebody else's X-Acto."

"You keep comforting yourself," Nick said. "I'll be right back."

She listened to the bathroom door close. She covered her face with her hands, trying to block out the uncomfortable thoughts that were trying to invade. She didn't want to listen to Nick, but she had to.

When he came back he smiled at her. "I'm not doing this to make it hard on you." He sat down next to her and put his arms around her, giving her shoulder a squeeze. "It's because I care about you."

"I know," she said, looking into his pale gray eyes. She picked up her glass. "Some more?"

When he had returned with new glasses for both of them, Nick said, "I think the fact that he's dropped off the face of the earth looks bad for him too. Why hide? He could have stayed at the Y."

"Maybe he ran out of money?"

"Don't you have a joint bank account? Couldn't he have taken some money out of there?"

"I guess so."

"Of course he could have. He's hiding. People hide for a reason. Usually because they're afraid of something."

"I suppose you're right. In a way, he was missing long before we split up," Anne said. "All those times I told you about . . . when he was gone without any explanation or at least a good explanation. And I know one of those times might correspond with one of the killings. I'm not sure."

"I think you're sure."

"Not enough to go to the police or anything."

Nick rolled his eyes. "What about his relationship with Pat Young? Would that make you more sure?"

"That *is* confusing."

"It's more than confusing. It's suspicious. That woman knows something, and she's not telling. I haven't been a private detective for six years not to have developed some pretty reliable instincts."

"Well, we need more than instincts to take to the police."

Nick shook his head. "Sometimes I don't believe you. We have a lot more than instincts to go on." He touched her face when he saw how hurt and confused she looked. "I'm sorry, babe."

They were quiet for a while, sipping beer and looking at each other. Nick finally spoke. "Anne, remember that Pat Young lives right across the street from Maggie Mazursky, one of the victims. She could have easily seen the killer come and go."

"Then why doesn't she come forward?"

"That I can't answer. I have a hunch she's protecting Joe. Why else deny knowing him when I spoke to her that one day? I know Joe went to her apartment. I saw it."

Anne stood up, placing her glass on the coffee table as she stood. Wandering over to the window, she parted the blinds and looked out. There was a full moon; the courtyard apartment building across the street looked silvery. The snow was melting. Spring was close.

"What are you thinking about?"

Anne laughed. "What do you think?" She let the blind fall back into place and turned to him. "I'm thinking that you're right. There is something wrong with Joe." She went over and sat down, arranging his arms around her. "There's a little part of me that's holding out for the theory that Joe is just sick and not a killer, but a larger part is telling me I'm stupid to go on denying it."

"Then I can go to the police with what we have?"

She sat up suddenly, stiffening. "No!" She started breathing more rapidly, looking at him like he had just suggested organizing a lynch mob for Joe. "We can't do that. I don't want him hunted down and shot. That's what they'll do. Have you read the papers? This whole city is against him. We have to find him ourselves. Convince him to turn himself in. It'll be safer that way and Joe will stand a better chance in the courts."

Nick was shaking his head. "Anne, we can't do that. For one, I'm afraid of what he might do to you. I know you don't want to face it, but Joe might hurt or even kill you."

"He'd never . . ."

"You don't know that! And don't argue with me about it. That just leaves me to look for him. If the police's task force know who they're looking for, we'll stand a much better chance of finding

him. I can't do it alone. Besides, we can't with-
hold this information."

"Please, Nick. I don't want the publicity.
They'll kill him."

Nick's mouth dropped open. *"They'll* kill *him?*
Anne, what's wrong with you? You've seen how
many people have died already. For the love of
Christ, you have to know this is going to happen
again and again and again." Nick searched her
eyes for some clue to what she was feeling.
"Think of the potential victims out there."

Anne lowered her head, letting her hair fall
down over her face. Nick could see she was trembling. My God, he thought, what a place for her
to be. He put his arms around her.

"No," she whispered, shrugging his arms away.
She continued to stare at the floor. When she
spoke, her voice carried no emotion. "You're just
like everyone else. You have no understanding. I
thought you were different, but you're not. You
want to see him hunted down like an animal."
She looked up at him, her face wet with tears.
"Don't you?"

He tried to reach out to brush away some of
the dark hair that had adhered to her face. She
slapped his hand away—hard. "I don't want you
to touch me."

They sat back against the couch then. Neither
of them spoke for a long time. Nick turned off
the light, thinking maybe the darkness would
help them speak. Finally he said, "What? What
can we do if we don't go to the police? Do you
want another murder on your conscience?"

She turned to him and, even in the darkness,

he felt her stare. "We don't know that Joe is anything more than disturbed. We don't know he's a killer."

I do, Nick thought, but knew that speaking those words would send her right out the door.

And out of his life. He imagined her walking out, the click of the door closing behind her. He reached down and took her hand, gripping, not letting go.

She whispered, "I have to talk to him."

He looked at her, saw the desperation in her face. Something inside him stirred. "Listen, Anne, I'll give it one more week. I'll try my best to find him. But if anything happens in that time, I go right to the police. And God help us . . . if he should hurt you I don't know what I'd do."

She put her arms around him. "One week," she whispered. "That's fair."

"I mean it, Anne, just seven days. I shouldn't even be doing this much for you."

Anne parked the car and got out. She stretched. The shoot, for Lord & Taylor, had been endless. Now, as she looked around the parking garage, she wished she had let Nick meet her, as he wanted to do. But she insisted he keep on in his search for Joe.

The lights seemed dimmer than usual, although she was sure her imagination was just working overtime. It often did when she was tired. She started to walk to the elevator when she heard footsteps behind her. When she stopped, the parking garage was silent. She listened for a long time; the sudden honk of a horn made her jump and scream. A car was coming up through the tiers.

She heard a sound like a person bumping into a car.

She turned and looked into the shadows, not seeing anything. Hurrying to the elevator, she caught it just before the doors closed.

Once inside her apartment Anne switched on all the lights, trying to dispel her fear. She put an Oscar Peterson tape on. Sitting down at the kitchen table, she told herself not to be afraid. She was safe in her own apartment now and there was probably no one in the garage.

Turning off the lights as she headed back toward her bedroom, she debated whether she should call Nick. If he was in she knew he would be glad to come and spend the night with her, as he had for the past three nights. But as she turned off the stereo she thought she was just tired enough tonight to have no trouble sleeping.

Once the music was gone, silence, like white noise, filled the apartment. Somewhere above her a toilet flushed. Anne was grateful for the sound and the footsteps above her.

"You gotta let me in, asshole. I know you've got a key."

The doorman, Alec Rooney, stared back at Joe, nonplussed. No way was he letting *that* bum in *this* building. Called himself Joe MacAree. No way. Joe MacAree was a nice-lookin' fella, polite.

"Look, Anne's up there, asleep. I just don't want to wake her up. I just had a little bad luck, that's why I look like this."

Rooney sighed. "You got some ID?"

Joe patted at his pocket. No wallet. "Come on, man. It's late. Just gimme the passkey."

"No can do. You can try to call Ms. MacAree on the phone right over there; she can buzz you in. Simple, huh?" Rooney turned away from Joe to stare at the bank of monitors behind him.

"Son of a bitch," Joe mouthed through clenched teeth. Without even looking around he brought out the X-Acto and slashed at the back of the man's neck. Rooney gasped in surprise. Joe grabbed his dark ponytail, pulling his head back. Quick and deep, he slashed Rooney's throat. Blood arced out and splattered a stack of reports on the desk in front of him.

And then Joe bent to cover the wound, sucking up the hot, coppery warmth as it pumped into his mouth, giving him sustenance and the strength to hold the struggling man down while he drank.

Rooney's struggling ebbed away. Joe looked around. There was no one. He knew there was a janitor's closet right behind the desk. He snatched up the blood-stained papers with one hand and with the other arm lifted Rooney from his seat. He dragged the doorman back to the closet and put him inside, throwing his night's work on top of him.

Joe rubbed his bloodstained hands on his pants. "There, you bastard," he said to the lifeless form. "That'll teach you a little deference, something a man in your position oughta have." Joe giggled.

* * *

Her eyes were closed and she felt herself drifting off to sleep when she heard the click.

She sat up in bed, instantly recognizing the sound and, at the same time, telling herself it had to be something else.

The sound of a key being fitted into a lock. Turning.

She felt sweat breaking out on her forehead, felt her heart pounding.

The door opened and closed. Softly. Silence.

A bang . . . the sound of a leg hitting a coffee table.

A whispered giggle.

Anne pulled at her nightgown, her palms sweating. There were some creaks in the floor as she heard him making his way to the back of the apartment.

Getting closer.

Anne looked about in the darkness, hardly able to breathe. Her instincts told her to curl into a little ball, offering some kind of animal protection that was no protection at all.

Almost without thinking, she slid from beneath the bedclothes and stood. She tiptoed to the closet and opened the door, praying it wouldn't creak. Inside, she stooped and closed the door behind her. In the back of the closet she curled up and pulled one of Joe's old ski parkas over her.

She listened and waited.

Finally she heard him in the bedroom. He was humming and laughing to himself.

"Annie . . . Annie," he said, "come out, come out wherever you are."

She heard him walk to the adjoining bathroom.

Then she heard him come back . . . toward the closet. He was giggling.

The giggling sounded so foreign to her that she questioned for a moment if this even was Joe. She wished she could make herself believe it was someone else. Even a random psychopath would be better than having the man you loved kill you.

The closet door swung open and Anne stopped breathing.

"Come to Papa, Annie. I have a surprise for you." More laughter.

He kicked over some boots, groping in the shadows of the closet.

The door closed and Anne bit her lower lip, tasting blood. She listened and heard a ripping sound, followed by others. Joe breathed heavily as he worked. Anne listened for what seemed like hours, wondering what the ripping noise was.

Finally she heard him say, "You bitch. I'll get you." His breathing was ragged, as if he had just sprinted a mile.

She heard his footsteps receding as he walked to the front of the apartment. He slammed the front door.

A trick? Anne didn't want to come out. She curled up even tighter, peering out from under the parka until the wan light of dawn came through the crack at the bottom of the closet.

When she emerged, all the bedclothes, the mattress, and four pillows had been shredded. Feathers were everywhere; all that remained were tattered strips of cloth.

Anne remembered the ripping noise and knew Joe must have added a bigger knife to his arsenal.

She picked up the phone and dialed Nick's number. "Please be home," she whispered.

" 'Lo?" He sounded sleepy.

Anne didn't care. "Nick, please come over right away. We have to contact the police."

24

From Joe MacAree's journal (undated):

A doorman's blood is different. Perhaps a little hotter, a little sweeter. One supposes that heat and sweetness come from the lack of use of the brain. He deserved to die. But I was sloppy, careless. I have to watch that. The story's plastered all over the Tribune *this morning.*

I should have taken Annie though. She was the one I came for. That poor, stupid son of a bitch just got in my way. Slowed me down, threw off my timing. But Annie, dear sweet Annie . . .

I'll get you next time.

Nick sat at his desk, hunched over the portable Underwood he'd had since graduating from Loyola Academy nine years ago. He concentrated on the outline he was preparing. He had an appointment to see Detective Pete McGrew at eleven and wanted to be sure the homicide detective had no doubts about placing this subject high on a priority list. Nick had grown up with Pete and knew he'd take the time to listen. It also didn't hurt that Pete McGrew was one of the leading members of the police department's task force on the Chicago Slasher.

As Nick tried to put facts to paper, though, he grew discouraged. Although it seemed clear the killer could be no one else but Joe when Nick was convincing Anne, the information he had was, at best, circumstantial. He took a sip of his coffee and glanced down at the erasable bond paper in his typewriter. One of the first things he had listed in his outline was the journals. True, no one would argue that Joe was a very sick man, but where was anything that pointed to his killing anyone? Anne suggested that the entries describing the killings were probably with Joe, wherever he was hiding. That didn't do him much good.

Nick glanced outside. His appointment was growing closer, and he was less and less confident that what he had was worth taking to the police. Ah, well, he thought, pushing the return of his typewriter, what he had was worth suspicion.

The next item he listed on his outline was the X-Acto knife. Great. More circumstantial evidence. It *did* fit, he tried to console himself, but his detective's mind wouldn't rest. Of course an X-Acto knife fit as the murder weapon, but why Joe's? There must be thousands of them floating around the city of Chicago, along with plenty of razor blades that could just as likely have been used as the weapon in the killings.

He sipped his coffee. Cold. As he started toward the Mr. Coffee in the corner of the room, the phone rang. He emptied his cup and refilled it with hot coffee before quieting the phone's ringing.

"MontPierre."

"Nick, it's Anne." There were traffic noises in the background. "I'm working right now, so I can't talk long, but I remembered something. I don't know if it's important or not."

"Don't worry about it," Nick said, hoping she'd give him something concrete, something that would make him feel he deserved his job as a private investigator.

"A couple of months ago I was going through Joe's things and I found a bunch of newspaper clippings . . . all about different murders in Chicago. I asked him at the time what he was doing with them, and he told me he was collecting material for a novel. In light of what's been going on I thought this might be useful."

Nick twisted the phone cord; this sounded good. "Anne? Can you get hold of the clippings? Where were they? In his desk?" If he could produce the clippings . . . well, it was still circumstantial, but it would help his case a lot more.

"They *were* in his desk," Anne said, and her emphasis on the past tense disappointed Nick. He knew what was coming. "But I think he got rid of them after I brought it up, which is another reason why I'm suspicious. If they were material for a novel why would he throw them away? But I've been over and over the things in his study so many times I'm sure they're not there."

"Well," Nick said, scribbling down what she told him on a Post-it notepad near the coffee machine, "thanks. I'll tell McGrew when I see him today." He heard someone in the background calling her name.

"I gotta go," she said. "See you tonight?"

"Sure." He replaced the phone in its cradle. He went back to his desk and looked at his outline; he added the information about Pat Young, detailing everything he knew about her and where she lived. He closed this item with a suggestion that she be rigorously questioned.

His next point was that Joe had been missing without an alibi for some of the murders (perhaps all, but they had no way of knowing for sure) and that he had been in Berwyn on the night Rebecca Piccone was murdered. McGrew ought to at least pay attention to that much. A voice in the back of his mind taunted, "But a lot of people were in Berwyn that night besides her hot-tempered husband."

Last he typed in what he thought was his ace in the hole: Joe's visit to Anne last night. The murder of the doorman, Alec Rooney, right in Anne's building, placed Joe at the scene of the crime. If McGrew saw this and didn't believe Joe was involved with the murders, then the man didn't deserve his detective title on the force. And then to come and terrorize Anne afterward . . . It almost seemed to clinch the case.

Almost. He didn't kill Anne, after all. And her

hiding in the closet wasn't the brightest thing she could have done. If MacAree had wanted to kill her Nick was certain he could have. So maybe McGrew would say the visit to Anne was merely the vengeful act of a wronged husband and the fact that the doorman was murdered around the same time was coincidence. Bullshit, there were too many coincidences. McGrew would believe him.

He had to.

Nick also thought the implied threat to Anne was obvious. Even if Joe hadn't been responsible for the other killings, he was responsible for threatening another person's life. Nick sat back and shuddered: My God, what would have happened if he had found her in that closet? Against his will his mind flashed on a scene of blood and terror. Anne lying prostrate in her own blood, her eyes focused on some distant horror: the horror of the last few minutes as her flesh was shredded with a razor. Her cream-colored bedroom walls were splattered with blood, and the air echoed with her screams.

Enough! Nick rubbed his eyes. Maybe his and Anne's suspicions weren't good enough to convict the guy in a courtroom, but Nick wasn't trying to convict him. He wanted only to call the task force's attention to Joe. Nick was confident Joe would take it from there.

He got up and looked in the mirror. Tightening his tie and running his fingers through his hair, he wished himself luck and prayed that all this would be over soon.

* * *

At twenty-five, Detective Pete McGrew was the youngest homicide detective on the force. This fact had not gone unnoticed by his peers, who credited his rapid move up the ladder with having a father who had held the position of captain of the Twenty-Seventh precinct for over twenty years. "McGrew's no better than we are," the talk went at Patsy's, a Loop bar near police headquarters where the rookies congregated, "he just has what it takes to get anywhere in this world—connections." Since most of them were still patrolmen, writing traffic tickets and quieting domestic disturbances, their jealousy of McGrew made them unfriendly to the young detective. Some of the older men on the force, who were comfortable in their positions, defended McGrew to the rookies, usually on quiet nights when their tours of duty kept them in their patrol cars.

The older men's defense was based on the Lyla Powers case. Lyla Powers was a shrewd businesswoman: she owned two massage parlors (not an easy thing to own in Chicago), a phone sex service, and occasionally pinch-hit for her own escort service when the client was worth it.

Lyla was found tied to a bed in the Ritz-Carlton after a tryst with a New York diamond importer. The red ribbon used to tie her up stood out in bright contrast to the paleness of her skin and her black hair. Like some macabre scarf, her fishnet stockings were wrapped around her neck and tied in a big bow. Covering her genitals (what was left of them) was a sign. Its message was simple: SEE YOU IN HELL, MOTHERFUCKERS!

The diamond importer was immediately located at his Long Island home and, in front of his wife, five children, and Irish setter, was arrested on suspicion of murder. He had no alibi; he was with her right up until the time she was killed. Two witnesses at the hotel corroborated this fact. A bellhop and a front-desk manager had seen them come and go, and were willing to testify in court as to the certainty of their vision. Lyla's private log disclosed their appointment and his name.

Even though the man insisted he had left her in perfect health, no one believed him.

All through the case, something bothered Pete McGrew. Lyla had a son who was about McGrew's age. His name was Bradley Powers, and as much as possible he had been sheltered from his mother's source of income. He seemed distraught when brought in for questioning. Most of the detectives felt sorry for him and believed his story. But McGrew had seen Powers waiting outside of interrogation, when he didn't think anyone was watching. The man was composed; not at all the victim of tragic death. That was why, to McGrew, the sobbing and blubbering he displayed in front of the detectives rang a false note.

On his own time, and against departmental regulations, McGrew began watching Powers. He watched as the New York diamond importer came closer and closer to life imprisonment. He watched as Powers began taking over all his mother's operations, losing many of the girls to pay cuts he imposed. Which was all right, because Powers just brought in new ones. To McGrew, Powers didn't seem so sheltered. To Mc-

Grew, Powers had a weak alibi (he was at home alone, watching *Dynasty*, the plot of which he described in detail) and a very strong motive. The oldest motive, in fact, in the world: greed.

McGrew worked hard, letting what social life he had slide. He made contacts with several of the girls in the escort agency, girls who had worked with Powers's mother and who were sticking it out with Powers. Most of them were bitter and didn't like Powers, which worked in McGrew's favor.

Just before the New York diamond importer was due to be sentenced, one of Powers's girls quit on him, not able to take the new pay cut Powers had imposed. Powers let something slip with her, and McGrew was there to catch it.

When Wendy Rodriguez was about to quit the agency, Powers threatened her, told her she could end up like his mother. Most importantly, he said, she could see her in hell.

The remark scrawled on the card left at the scene of the crime was never disclosed. Usually, homicide held back certain key details about a case, so that if someone confessed the detectives would have a way of verifying the confession. SEE YOU IN HELL, MOTHERFUCKERS! was one piece of information they held back.

It was a flimsy piece of information, but that, along with Powers's activities over the previous two months (not exactly in line with those of a distraught and overprotected son), was enough for detectives to look more carefully into the son's alibi.

A search warrant that produced a video-cassette of a crucial episode of *Dynasty* in the son's room (the one Powers was supposed to have seen while his mother was being murdered) and testimony from Lyla's second-in-command that Powers often went with his mother as a kind of bodyguard on her "dates" with clients were enough to lead detectives down the road to supplying the kind of information the district attorney needed to put Powers away.

All thanks to Pete McGrew.

Pete McGrew didn't have time to devote to wondering why success had come to him at such a young age. Ever since he was a kid he had wanted to be a cop and had never wavered from that dream. McGrew, if asked, probably would have credited his single-mindedness to his success. He might or might not have added that he was a little strange, as very successful people often are.

Pete McGrew was an observer of people. He never let his guard down; he was always questioning, watching, listening, and wondering about motivations, reactions. He rode the el as frequently as possible to watch people. Sometimes he would work through the car he was riding in, as if he were at a party, extending his hand and introducing himself to people on the train. He tried to draw them out, see how much of themselves they would give to a stranger. He wanted to see their reactions to someone being friendly on a public conveyance where eyes rarely met and conversations were limited. On elevators McGrew would turn his back to the doors and smile at people, trying to start a group conversation. In Laundromats, supermarkets, and bars, McGrew made himself known, usually as the weirdo who wouldn't go away.

But he found out a lot about people and he understood them better than many trained to understand people. He knew just the right chords to hit when questioning a suspect; he was almost flawless in interrogation.

Pete McGrew had gotten where he was because he was good.

Nick looked for a parking space outside the Chicago police headquarters, where the Chicago Slasher task force was housed and where McGrew had agreed to meet him. This part of South State Street was deserted, and Nick didn't have a hard time finding a spot. Just a few blocks north was the Loop, bustling and full of activity; Nick wondered what had happened to make the division so contrasting. He locked his car and thought he'd be on time for once. McGrew would be surprised.

Nick stopped walking when he saw Anne standing outside the pale building that housed police headquarters. She was wearing a white fur coat, and her black hair blew back away from her face.

When she saw him, the nervous look on her face softened into relief. She started toward him. "God, I'm so relieved to see you. I was afraid I'd missed you." She caught up to him and took his hand.

"What are you doing here?"

"I had a break in the shoot and I thought

maybe your case would be a little stronger if I was with you to back it up."

"Anne, I really don't think it's necessary. I can handle this by myself."

"Don't start this 'no women allowed' business with me. I'll bet your friend McGrew would want to hear my version of what happened anyway."

"You have a point there."

They stepped into the white-and-gray-marble foyer of the building. Anne was surprised that it was so quiet. "I was expecting *Hill Street Blues,*" she whispered to Nick. She looked around the neat foyer, took in the stainless steel elevators, the guard: a fat guy in a uniform who looked down his nose at Nick while Nick explained who they were here to see. She was reminded of the airport: They had one of those metal detectors you had to walk through. There was a TV monitor behind the guard. Anne felt observed.

After they were frisked Anne followed Nick onto the elevator. "I've never been here," she said.

"Well, it's no big deal." Nick bit his lower lip. "Don't be offended or anything, but I've spent the morning preparing how to tell him about this. So I hope you'll let me do the talking."

She rolled her eyes as they stepped off the elevator. "I wasn't planning on taking over. I just thought it would be a good idea if I was here."

"Sorry. It probably is. I'm just a little nervous."

Before Anne had a chance to ask why, McGrew was standing in front of them. He was a tall man with broad shoulders; he had black curly hair and blue eyes. Clean-shaven. Anne thought she could have imagined him: the perfect Irish cop. His nose was even a little red. She wondered if he was a drinker, then chided herself: That wasn't fair.

McGrew stared at the two of them. He shook his head, wondering how MontPierre had ever found himself such a looker. Nick had told him they might have some information on the slasher case. But why bring the woman along? To show off?

"Nick, how you doin'?" He shook Nick's hand. When he leaned forward, he noticed Anne looking at the gun and holster under his jacket.

"It's been too long," Nick said. He turned to Anne and introduced her. Pete shook her hand and appraised her.

"I know it's been a while, but we've really got to make this quick. I'm swamped."

"I understand," Nick said, following McGrew back to his office. They sat and McGrew asked if either of them wanted coffee. When they said no, McGrew was relieved. He had a shitload of work to do and wanted to get them out as quickly as possible. MontPierre's dad was a good cop, but Nick would never be anything more than a second-rate private dick. But he had to hear them out; who knows where that perfect lead might come from.

"Whatd'ya got?" he asked Nick, folding his hands in front of him on the desk. He was ready to listen.

Nick started with the journals and worked his way through the X-Acto knife, Joe's disappearance, his being in Berwyn when Rebecca Piccone was murdered, his relationship with Pat Young, the murder of the doorman in Anne's building, and finally his attack on Anne.

"Are you sure it was your husband, Mrs. MacAree?"

"There's no doubt."

McGrew met her eyes, looked into them for a while. She was certain, he could tell.

"Why do you think he came back?"

"I don't know."

"Really?" McGrew raised his eyebrows.

Anne looked at the gray metal desk. "I suppose he's angry with me for deserting him."

"I thought he left you."

"He did, but only after begging me to come with him." Anne explained about Joe's desperation to get her to come away with him and how it coincided with Rebecca Piccone's murder. "He acted like a baby."

"Well," McGrew said, "I suppose a lot of men, with a wife like you, might act like a baby if they were afraid of losing you." It wasn't a compliment.

"I know what you're thinking."

"What's that?" McGrew smiled.

"That Joe's behavior is that of a wronged husband."

"Well, I did spend some time working a beat when I joined the force. I saw a lot of ugly domestic scenes involving divorces and separations."

"You don't understand, Pete," Nick cut in. "This guy's really crazy." Nick told him about his surveillance of Joe, about the prostitutes and Pat Young.

"He didn't know anybody in Berwyn," Anne put in. "What was he doing there?"

"There could be a lot of reasons." McGrew smiled at them. "We never really know each other. We can't. We can suppose."

"Are you saying there's no validity in what we're saying?" Nick knew he had only circumstantial evidence, but it was damned good circumstantial evidence. He expected more from his friend.

Pete shook his head. "I'm not saying that at all. Come on." He stood. He led them down a corridor into a large room with several desks. Two women were on phones. Three detectives were working at a table. On every surface, computer printouts and sheets of paper were piled high.

"This is our task force headquarters," Pete announced, gesturing broadly around the room. "These papers are leads. Believe it or not, we get a few hundred calls a day. Granted, most of them are cranks, little old ladies who think their next-door neighbor is out too late, wives who want to get back at their husbands. But a lot of them are legitimate leads. The worst part of it is, almost all of them have to be checked out. Even if they sound crazy, most of these people have some basis for calling in. And if we skip one that sounds even barely legitimate, we might be skipping the one lead that could take us to the killer."

"What about our lead?" Anne asked.

"I'd say your lead was a pretty good one. We keep them organized by priority. Yours is priority one. If we can find your husband we'll want to watch him."

"Well, of course you'll find him."

"Mrs. MacAree, I've been working eighteen- and twenty-hour days lately. So has everyone on the task force. Patrolmen have taken a special interest in the case, worried about their wives or their sisters or their daughters. They've been putting in overtime. We are going to really try and find your husband, but I want you to understand what we're up against."

Nick nodded. "I guess being first priority is the best we can ask for."

Pete didn't answer; he led them back to his office. After they sat down he said, "Because you're a friend, Nick, and because Mrs. MacAree here is worried, I'm going to tell you something. I'm sure I can trust both of you, so I won't even ask you to keep this under your hats. I know you will."

Anne and Nick looked at him, their faces expectant. "You can trust us," Nick said.

"We got a lead in the other morning that makes us pretty sure the guy has been seen."

Both Nick and Anne leaned forward.

"There's a guy in Cook County Hospital right now with a mutilated penis and stab wounds to the neck. Sorry, Mrs. MacAree. He saw the guy who did it to him; he saw the weapon. It was an X-Acto knife."

Anne closed her eyes and gripped the arms of her chair.

"There was also a black guy who ran into the washroom where the attack took place and scared the guy off. But he got a good look at him. Our artists have made up a composite based on their descriptions."

Pete opened his desk and took out a photo-copied drawing. They stared down at the griz-zled, dirty face of a killer. Anne stared at the drawing for a long time. She traced the shape of the face with her finger.

"Anne? You okay?" Nick asked.

"This looks a lot like Joe," she whispered. She looked up at McGrew. "But there's something wrong with the nose. Joe's isn't that wide. I couldn't say for sure."

Pete smiled at her. "These sketches are usually off-base. Witnesses' descriptions always vary, and time plays tricks with what they remember. They could have seen your husband and this could be a pretty good likeness. On the other hand, what they remember could be way off and it's a coincidence that this looks like your hus-band. Hell, in the Son of Sam case, there was a police officer who was suspected because he looked like he sat for the police artist's sketch."

Nick stared at the drawing. "It does look like him though, Pete."

Pete nodded. "Right. And that's one more rea-son we're putting this guy in our number one pri-ority."

"You're not giving us the runaround, are you?"

Pete shook his head. "Nick, you're from the neighborhood. I hope you don't really want me to answer that."

"I guess not."

"What happens now?" Anne asked.

"You go home. I'll have a car pass by your place every once in a while. We'll put a tap on your line. If he calls keep him on as long as you can. But don't do anything stupid like inviting him over. If he really is the killer you may not live to testify."

Anne looked scared and Nick put his arm around her.

"Can I help?" Nick asked. There was hope in his voice; in his short career of investigating marital infidelity and office pilfering, he longed to get involved with something big like this.

"The best thing you can do, buddy, is see that this lady here is kept safe and stay out of our way. I know you're good, but just let us work. We don't want anything to fuck this up."

Nick tried to conceal his disappointment by smiling. "Sure. I got you." He stood. "Maybe you should be getting back to work, Anne. I'll drop you off."

She looked down at her watch. "You're right." She was deadpan.

Nick extended his hand to Pete. "Thanks for taking the time."

"Thank you," Pete said, shaking Nick's hand. "Keep us posted."

"We will."

Pete watched the two of them leave. Pretty lady, he thought to himself, how the hell did you get mixed up with a nut case like your husband?

Upstairs, Detective Pete McGrew wrote the name Joe MacAree on a card, jotting down the vital facts. He placed the card in a file and put it in a drawer marked PRIORITY ONE. There the file joined about a half-dozen others. Later the task force would go over any new leads they had gotten, and Pete would push for surveillance and possible arrest.

He hadn't wanted to frighten Anne, but this sounded like the guy.

25

Detective Al Schulty and criminal reporter for *The Chicago News* Beth Allison had a symbiotic relationship. Neither of them would have admitted it. Each would have claimed love, or at least lust, for the other. But deep down they both knew they didn't much like each other. Beth got good leads for stories, now and then an exclusive, and Al got good sex.

The motel room they were in was hot. They had just fucked, and Beth had a light sheen of sweat on her face and in the valley between her breasts. Al was panting, turned away from Beth and staring at the hunting scene depicted on one wall. Beth ran her hand down his thigh and caressed his half-hard penis, still wet from their activity. She leaned close to his ear and whispered, "I love fucking you."

Al turned to look at her, his dark eyes searching her blue ones, taking in the mane of light brown frosted hair curling around her face. Ten minutes ago, when they were in the act, he would have loved her comment; it would have turned him on even more. But now it seemed crude. He wished she hadn't said it.

She bit his lip and stuck her tongue in his ear. "Don't you just love fucking me?"

He smiled and laughed. "Yeah. But I wish you wouldn't talk that way."

She stroked the well-defined muscles in his chest, letting her hand roam down over his washboard stomach. "Don't talk . . . just do?"

"Right." He kissed her, hoping to end the conversation, ease gracefully out of bed, and begin getting ready to go back to work. He sat up and put his feet on the floor.

"Where you goin' so fast?" She tickled him and laughed.

"Bathroom." He got up quickly and went into the bathroom, closing the door behind him. He looked at his face in the mirror, how his black hair curled around his forehead from sweat. Shit, he thought, I don't even like her that much. He stood over the toilet and pissed. But she's the best fuck I ever had, probably ever will have. He thought of the tame couplings he had with his fiancée: the extra care she made him take, the constant instructions to do this, touch that, kiss there. She made him feel like a machine. But Beth was all action, ready to go even before he was, and able to go all night if he could keep up. She wrung him dry. He wondered if he'd be able to give her up once he married in the spring. Every time he saw her he planned to tell her how he felt, that this couldn't go on. She knew he was engaged and admitted it didn't bother her. He looked in the mirror once more, ran his fingers through his hair, and went back to the bedroom.

He slipped his white oxford-cloth shirt on and began buttoning it.

"That looks so sexy," Beth said, staring at him. "That big cock just peeking out at the bottom of that shirt. Come here."

"No, Beth. I really gotta get goin'. I'm supposed to meet with McGrew in about fifteen minutes."

She sat up, looking petulant. "Big break in the slasher case?"

He grinned. "You know I can't tell you about that."

She got up and came to him. She grabbed his cock and began rubbing it against her wet sex. "What can you talk about, big boy?" she whispered in his ear and then bit it.

In spite of himself, he was getting aroused again. He tried to break away, but she was strong. She held on tight, kissing his neck and working her way down his chest, then his stomach. She took his cock in her mouth and got him fully aroused. Then she broke away from him.

"I gotta go too!" she said brightly. "Gotta be getting down to that courthouse. Davidson's trial starts today," she said, referring to a rapist.

"You can't do this to me," he said, looking down at his penis, which was engorged and red, waiting. He felt like he did back in high school when all of his girlfriends were "saving it" for marriage.

"We both have work to do," she said, smiling at him. "I'm gonna hop in the shower."

Just as she was closing the door, he put out an arm to block it. "No, you don't," he whispered, his voice hoarse with wanting. He grabbed her arm and pulled her out of the bathroom. He lifted her, took her to the bed, and threw her down.

"You bastard," she said, but she was grinning. "This is going to cost, you know." She opened her legs and pulled her lips open. "This will cost plenty."

After it was over she said, "Now tell me about the break in the slasher case."

"What break?"

"Don't try to kid me. I've been around. I know something's up." She grabbed his face. "I can see it in your sexy face."

He smiled. "I shouldn't tell you. Protect your source."

"I always do."

"Well, it's not concrete, but something just happened to make one suspect look real good. . . ."

The late-afternoon edition of *The Chicago News* screamed the headline: SUSPECT BEING SOUGHT IN CONNECTION WITH SLASHER KILLINGS. There was a subhead that told readers, "Task Force Believes This is the One." The story, with a Beth Allison byline, went on to tell how several pieces of evidence had been amassed, all pointing a very strong finger to Joseph MacAree, who had recently left his Lake Shore address and disappeared. The story was an exclusive, and the

News saw its circulation jump that day from 158,000 to 380,000 readers.

Randy Mazursky was one of the 380,000 people who bought the *News* that day, over his usual *Sun Times*. When he saw the headline on the newsstand his hands began shaking; it was hard for him to get the change out of his pocket and hand it to the magazine-stand vendor.

He had been wandering around his old neighborhood (the one he had shared with Maggie) trying to plan his next move in finding Joe when he saw the headlines and the newspapers spread out over the usual pornographic magazines.

"Ain't that somethin'?" the guy behind the counter at the newsstand said, taking a puff on his cigarette. "They should string that fucker up by his balls."

"Right," Randy said, walking away. He sat down on the curb, not feeling the wet, dirty snow being sopped up by his jeans. He read the story three times, finding it hard to believe the police task force had come up with the same suspect Pat Young had given him weeks ago.

He looked up at the pearl gray sky; a warm breeze rustled his hair. Spring was coming.

And Randy didn't want the police to get hold of Joe MacAree. He didn't want to see the bastard get off on an insanity plea, like all the other pricks who killed without thinking. He didn't want to be a victim anymore.

Randy was due at work in fifteen minutes to work the later afternoon-evening shift. He had missed more days in the past two months than he had in his entire employment with the restaurant. His district manager was trying to be understanding, but Randy knew his patience was wearing thin. Randy also knew that once he found MacAree there would no longer be any need for a job.

He got in his car, forgetting about his job and heading for the Lake Shore Drive address where he hoped to find MacAree's wife.

Anne stepped out of the shower and wrapped herself in a gray towel. She wiped the steam away from the mirror with the palm of her hand. The circles under her eyes were dark; she had begged off of two modeling assignments because she didn't want anyone to see her looking the way she did. She picked up a comb.

The buzzer sounded in the living room. Anne pulled her robe from the back of the bathroom door and hurried to quiet it. It rang two more times before she spoke through the intercom.

"Who is it?"

"Randy Mazursky."

"I don't know anyone by that name."

"I know, Mrs. MacAree. But I need to talk to you." He paused. "It's about your husband."

Anne put a hand to her forehead, feeling a headache begin. She had seen the *News.* "Okay," she said, and pulled on a pair of jeans and navy blue turtleneck sweater. She pulled her hair back with a rubber band. By the time she was slipping into her Nikes, she heard a knock at the door.

"Coming," she shouted, wondering where she got the strength to speak. When would all this be over? She opened the door and looked at the man standing in the hallway. He was younger than she had expected, with sandy hair and a lanky frame. He was wearing cords and a beige sweater, boots. She was wondering what the connection could be between this young man and her husband.

"Can I come in?"

"I guess so." Anne stepped back to admit him, wondering if she was doing the right thing. Then it clicked: the name. Mazursky. One of the women who had been killed had been named Mazursky. Anne felt chilled. Had he come here to even up the score? A wife for a wife?

Why had she let him in?

"What do you want?" she asked, her voice growing trembly with fear.

He smiled at her, knowing she probably had nothing to do with her husband's problems. He wanted to reassure her. "Mrs. MacAree, please don't worry. I saw the look on your face when you realized who I was. Can I sit down?"

She gestured toward a chair, then sat down on the couch across from him.

He opened his hands in front of him. "Very simply, the reason I'm here is because I want to find your husband."

"So you can kill him?"

Randy smiled. "Of course not, Mrs. MacAree. Of course not. I just want to see him apprehended before he puts someone else through what I've gone through since I lost Maggie. I'm trying to assist the police. The Berwyn force knows I'm here. Do you have any idea where he might be?"

Anne shook her head, staring at the floor. "I'm sorry about your wife." She looked up at him, her eyes wet with tears.

"If you're really sorry," Randy said slowly, "you'll tell me how I can find him. You must have some idea where he might go. I know it's hard, but he has to be caught."

Anne looked at his face for a long time, wondering if there was any truth to what he was saying. What kind of police force would put a crime victim in charge of helping them find a suspect? She realized though, and the realization made her wonder about herself and her true feelings, she might help him if she could. "I'm sorry, but I've been searching for him myself. I've hired a private investigator. I have no idea where Joe might be. The last place he was staying was the Lawson YMCA on Chicago Avenue. But he hasn't been there for a long time. I think he's hiding."

"Surely you must know something."

"No."

Randy sighed and wrung his hands. "Listen, I know it's your husband, and I know he's probably very sick. You don't want to see anything bad happen to him. And you probably don't feel much for his victims. After all, they're impersonal to you, people you don't even know. Nameless."

Anne stared at him. "Don't you tell me what I feel. I was almost a victim myself! Don't you dare try to tell me how I feel!" She was sobbing.

"Hey . . . I'm sorry."

"Forget it. I think it's time for you to go."

"Listen, could you just hook me up with that

private investigator of yours?" Randy was already thinking ahead, picturing himself following the investigator, finding out where Joe was.

"No," Anne said, struggling to rein in her emotions. "I can't do that."

"Why not?"

"I just can't! Now, please, go away."

Randy could see she was too upset to reason with. He doubted she bought his story anyway.

"Okay, okay. I'm leaving. Could I just use your bathroom first?" Randy also doubted she'd let him.

She surprised him. "It's right in there, through the bedroom."

Randy followed her pointing finger and went into the bedroom. He looked quickly around the room. On the dresser was a round brass frame containing a picture of Mrs. MacAree and the man who could only be Joe. He picked it up quickly and stuck it under his sweater, then hurried into the bathroom.

When he came out he heard water running in the kitchen. He went in and saw her leaning over the sink, rinsing out a cup.

"I'm going now. I'm sorry I had to bother you."

"Are you planning on taking that photograph with you?"

Randy stopped, feeling a cold sweat break out on his forehead. "What?"

"The photo you took from the bedroom. I can see the frame's outline under your sweater."

Randy felt nauseated as he took the photograph out from under his sweater. "I'm sorry," he whispered. Anne's mouth was set in a line.

The two stared at one another for a long time. It seemed to Randy that Anne was trying to make a decision. She turned and glanced out the kitchen window, knuckles white on the countertop. Finally she turned back to him. She took a deep breath and said, "Listen, I think you should keep it. I want you to have it. To do . . . whatever you need to do with it." Randy saw tears standing in her eyes. She turned away.

"Are you sure? Look, you can have it back."

Anne didn't say anything. She didn't look at him.

Randy sat in the front seat of his car, sweating in spite of the cold. His stomach felt like a fist: doubled tight, white hot. He wondered how long it would be before the police and/or the press coaxed a photograph out of her to publish in the papers.

He looked down at the picture in its brass frame. This man, with his arm around a beautiful woman, looked normal. Randy expected a monster. He expected to see something in his eyes that would show how crazy he was. There should be some trace, Randy thought. How could this man have killed the only person that really mattered to Randy and look normal?

The traffic rushed by on Lake Shore Drive. Randy looked down once more at the picture in its brass frame. He noticed that his hands were shaking, and the glass in the frame reflected, off and on, the dull afternoon sunlight. With a shaking finger he forced himself to touch the likeness of Joe MacAree. He wondered what he would be like, how Maggie had felt when she'd opened the door to him. What had he said to her? Had she let him in? He remembered there had been no signs of forcible entry. His eyes brimming with tears, he asked Maggie, Why? Why did you let him in? But he remembered why he had loved her: She always believed in the good that existed in people. She left cars unlocked, gave bums change when they begged. She was the kind of person who would let a stranger in if he asked to use the telephone.

Was that what he had said? Had it been something as flimsy as that? Randy didn't want to think so; he preferred thinking MacAree had forced his way in once Maggie opened the door. That way she would have no responsibility for her death. Not that she did anyway.

For a moment, Randy felt as if he had left his car. The sound around him ceased. Then he looked down and noticed he had poked through the glass of the frame. Blood trickled across the photograph.

Once again his mother was crying.

"Randy, it ain't gonna do any good! You know nothing. You don't have an idea of where that monster might be." His mother stood in his bedroom, wringing a dish towel and staring at him, trying to make eye contact he refused to give. Randy was dressing to go out and hunt. He had put on black corduroys and a black sweatshirt. The only thing that wasn't black was the beige of his boots. He wanted to be inconspicuous.

"Ma, I have to look for him. He killed Maggie.

He ruined my life." Randy was beyond emotion; his words were empty, his voice that of a robot, no inflection or feeling.

His mother tried to take his shoulders and make him look at her. He shrugged her away. To his back she said, "Listen to me. I know what he did. He took Maggie away from me too. You don't think I loved her? She was like my own! But Randy, this should be handled by the police. They'll know what to do. You're just going to stir up more trouble, maybe get yourself killed."

For the first time Randy turned and met his mother's eyes. "You think I care?"

"Don't say that."

"The police will just let him out; there'll be some little technical hitch and the guy'll go free. That's what always happens."

"It is not, Randy, and you know it. Lots of criminals pay for what they do. Why do you think the prisons are overcrowded? At least—"

"I have to set things right myself."

"What are you talking about?"

Randy pulled on a pair of gloves and shrugged into his jacket. "Nothing, Ma. I just want to find him."

"Please, please don't do anything you're gonna live to regret. I've had enough pain. I don't want to see my boy in prison."

"Who says I'm going to prison?"

"Then what?"

"Then nothing."

Randy started toward the stairs, his mother behind him. "Randy, please . . . I'm begging you.

Don't go after that man. I'll call the police and
we'll all talk to the detectives."

"No, Ma." Randy descended the remaining
stairs and, without pausing, opened the door and
went into the evening.

He got in his car and started it. He let the engine warm and played with the radio dials, trying
to find a good station. Finally he turned the radio
off: no distractions.

The buzzing of the door seemed louder than
usual, and Randy hurried to get inside. The noise
hurt his ears. He took the three steps to the first
floor in two hops and stopped in front of Pat
Young's door.

The voice that answered the knock sounded
nervous and weak. "Who's there?" came out as a
whispered croak.

Randy paused, wondering whether he should
be truthful.

"Who the hell's there? I can't see through the
goddamn peephole!"

"Bob Kneffer."

"I don't know any Bob Kneffer. Get the hell
away from my door."

"I was sent by the super," Randy said, thinking
as he went along. "He wants to put new plumb-
ing in some of his buildings. I need to check
yours out."

"What? At night?"

"I do special jobs for the super when I'm not at
my regular job. This happens to be the most convenient time for me."

"Sure, sure. I'm going to have to call the super before I let you in."

"He's not home!" Randy shouted, thinking furiously. "Didn't he give you a note? He was supposed to send one to all the tenants. That damn guy. Listen, I have a copy of what he said he was going to send, with his signature and everything. Would that be enough?"

"I don't know. Maybe."

"All right, lady. Forget it. But I'm warning you, I don't know when I'll get back, if ever."

"All right, all right."

Randy listened as Pat slid the bolt across the door. When their eyes met, she gasped and tried to slam the door in his face.

But she wasn't quick enough. Randy slammed his arm into the door, flinging it open. He hurried inside, almost knocking Pat over in her wheelchair.

She started toward the telephone. "I'm calling the police. You have no right."

Randy got in front of her, picked the phone up, and ripped it out of the wall, making sure he pulled hard enough to yank the box away from the wall. She wouldn't be using her phone for a while.

"You prick!"

"Don't you call me a prick." He leaned down so his face was inches from hers. "You're protecting a killer and I want to know where he is."

"I don't know."

"Remember the beating I gave you last time? It's nothing compared to what you'll get this time if you don't tell me where he is."

"I told you; I don't know." Pat wheeled herself toward the little kitchenette, away from Randy.

"I think you do."

"Look, there's no way I can prove I don't know where he is," Pat said, finally reaching the kitchenette and backing into it. "I'd like to know where he is myself. But I don't."

Randy noticed her groping for something and walked closer.

She pulled her arm out from where it was hidden. She had a butcher knife in her hand. "Don't you come any closer to me, asshole! I'll cut you, I swear."

Randy smiled. "You're just like him, aren't you?"

"You don't know anything. Now get out of here."

Randy laughed and tried to grab the knife from her. He felt a coldness on his leg, like someone had placed ice there . . . and then wet. He looked down to see his pants hanging open on one thigh. Blood was soaking the material. "You bitch," he whispered. "I oughta kill you."

"Come on," said Pat, holding the knife up. "Come on, why don't you try?" She laughed.

Randy started limping toward the door, holding his hand over the cut in his leg. The blood trickled steadily between his fingers. "I'll be back," he said. "And you'll be sorry."

"Big man, big talk!" Pat shrieked, and laughed.

She watched as he opened the door and left. The door remained ajar. Pat wheeled over and closed it. She made sure both locks were in place.

"My God," she whispered, "where are you, Joe?

Where are you, my baby?" She thought to herself, hoping in some way, Joe would pick up on her thoughts: Don't you know you'd be safe with me? I'd do anything, *anything* to help you. Please come home, come home to me.

Randy drove west on the Eisenhower Expressway, back to Berwyn. His eyes burned, crying out for sleep. The wound in his leg had crusted over, black and caked. He hoped it wasn't infected. The expressway was quiet; Randy had only a few cars for company. The highway stretched before him, Berwyn a million miles away.

He had been to the Lawson YMCA, where they refused to help him, saying their registration records weren't open to the public. Randy hadn't wanted to tell the clerk whom he was looking for, not when everyone in the Chicago area was now familiar with the MacAree name. He had slipped the clerk twenty dollars and got a chance to look at their registrations for the last month. There was no Joe MacAree listed. Randy hadn't really expected to see one.

Dejected, he closed the book. He had completed his tour of solid leads.

From that point Randy had done nothing but lock the doors on his car and cruise Chicago's seediest neighborhoods, looking for the face in the photograph, certain he could recognize it even if it was disguised.

He had seen fights, he had seen prostitutes (all kinds, women, girls, and boys), he had seen a car broken into. He had not seen anyone who even resembled Joe MacAree.

Randy really hadn't expected to see him. But he had hoped. God, had he hoped.

Now, as he pulled up in front of his parents' home, he noticed the living room lights were still on. Annoyed, he wondered why his parents weren't in bed. He didn't think he could face his mother now. All he wanted to do was walk in the door, head up the stairs, and sleep . . . so he could begin searching again tomorrow. The hell with his job. It didn't matter anymore.

He headed up the front porch steps, fumbling in his pockets for his keys. He got them out, groping for the front door key. Before he could find it, his mother had peeked out from behind the curtain and then hurried to open the door.

"Randy," she said, stepping aside to let him in, "don't be mad. You father and I had to do what we thought was right."

Randy looked into the living room to see two men, dressed in suits. They sat stiffly on the living room furniture, holding cups of coffee. One stood when he saw Randy.

His father emerged from the living room. "Son, these are detectives from the Chicago Slasher task force." His father spoke with formality, almost announcing the men. Randy supposed it was his father's way of showing respect for their positions. "They'd like to talk to you."

"Did you call them?" Randy looked at his mother.

"I did what was best, Randy."

"Son, someday you'll realize this was the right thing to do."

"I don't have to talk to these men."

"I'm afraid you do," one of the detectives said.

The other detective put his coffee cup on the couch. He stood and extended his hand. "I'm Pete McGrew."

26

 "Look. I don't have anything for you," Randy said. "I'm tired. I'm going up to bed." Randy turned and headed toward the stairs.

"We can bring you in for questioning. We have that authority."

Randy turned and stared at the detective who had spoken. McGrew. He looked at the Irish face, the ice blue eyes, and the curly black hair. The guy was a kid. Can't be much older than I am, Randy thought. He's just trying to throw his weight around. Well, I don't have to listen to his shit. The cops didn't want my help when I was willing to give it to them.

"Randy, please," his father spoke up. He sounded tired. "You have to cooperate. Don't you want the killer to be caught? Do you want some other guy to lose his wife, or his daughter, or maybe his mother to this man?"

"I don't care about anyone else," Randy said. "He took that away from me."

"Who, Randy?" McGrew asked. "Who took that away from you?"

Randy shook his head. He smiled. "Whoever killed my wife."

"Stop this, Randy. Talk to these men. Before you get in trouble." His mother's eyebrows knitted together with concern.

The other detective spoke. He was older: bald pate, pot belly, suit going shiny in the elbows. He wore wire-frame glasses, aviator style. Randy supposed he thought they made him look younger. "Ma'am, why don't you and your husband go on up to bed. We can handle this. It might be easier with the room a little less crowded." He looked at both of Randy's parents. "Would you mind?"

"Not at all, officer. C'mon, Theresa." Randy's father led his wife out of the room. Randy didn't watch them but heard the stairs creaking.

"Mr. Mazursky, I don't want to be a tough guy with you," McGrew said, making eye contact with him and holding it. "It's late and all of us are tired. Sam and me have been working since seven o'clock this morning. Our wives and kids don't know what we look like anymore. If you force us to we'll drag you into the Chicago station for questioning. Tonight. Make it easy on yourself. Tell us what you know."

Randy sat down and stared at his hands, twirling the wedding band he still wore. He noticed the sculptured pattern of the olive green carpeting.

McGrew sat down next to him and squeezed his shoulder. "I know it must be hard. I know how I'd feel if I lost my wife. I'd wanna get the son of a bitch myself, make sure."

More than what the detective said, Randy responded to his touch. It was solid and caring. He felt something drain out of him. Not the desire for revenge, but maybe a little of the pain, a little of the loss.

"Listen, Randy. I can't give you license to do anything. As a matter of fact it's my duty to advise you to stay out of this and let the police do their jobs. But you gotta understand: If you have a lot of help, there's a much better chance of this guy getting caught and punished than there is with just you out there looking for him."

"Guys like him always get off. Technicalities. Insanity."

McGrew shook his head. "It won't be easy for this guy, Randy. The whole city's watching this case. They want blood. They aren't going to think much of us or the government if he gets off easy. There'll be sentencing . . . and it won't be light."

"How do you know?"

The other detective in the room spoke. "Will you listen to what he said? This case has generated so much goddamn publicity. The public isn't going to sit still for easy sentencing or insanity."

"Tell us what you know, Randy. It can't hurt." McGrew looked at him. "How can it hurt to have lots of trained professionals out there looking for this guy? Besides, we already have a lead on who he is, so even if you don't tell us anything here tonight, we're gonna crack this case any day now."

Randy looked at the other man. "Is that right?"

The other detective raised his hand, as if he were taking an oath. "It's true, Randy. We have witnesses and a lot of evidence. They're out there looking for someone right now."

Randy thought for a long time, a time in which McGrew thought the young guy wasn't going to tell them anything. Then he looked up at both of them and said, "Okay."

Sam, the other detective, sat down and took out a pad.

"Randy, do you know who killed your wife?"

"I'm almost positive. His name is Joe Mac-Aree."

The two detectives looked at each other, trying hard not to betray any emotion.

"What makes you think that?" Sam asked.

"It started when I went back to our old apartment to get some clothes about a day after Maggie was killed." Randy paused, took a deep breath. "I was just about to leave when I saw something shiny on the kitchen floor. It was a lighter. Turned out it was monogrammed 'J.D.M.' I tried to call the Berwyn cops at that time, but they kind of brushed me off." Randy ran his fingers through his hair and smiled at them. "I'm sorry, but it pissed me off."

The detectives nodded.

"I can get it for you, if you like."

"We'd like that, Randy."

"I'll be right back." Randy bolted up the stairs.

The detectives watched him. Sam said, "Do you fucking believe this?"

McGrew shook his head. "I didn't think we'd get this much. Shows you should listen to your hunches."

"Yeah. When the kid's mother called, I didn't know. Thought we were just gonna calm down some strung-out husband."

At the sound of Randy's footsteps on the stairs, McGrew said, "Be quiet. Here he comes."

Randy returned and held the lighter out for McGrew to take. McGrew turned it over, weighing it in his hand and looking at the initials. He handed it over to Sam, who, after giving it a once-over, put it in his pocket.

McGrew asked, "How did you connect this lighter with MacAree?"

"I got a phone call from this woman that lives across the street from me. She said she knew who killed my wife and would tell me . . . for a price." Randy's eyes became angry. "Can you imagine that? Calling up someone whose wife has just been murdered and trying to sell them information?" Randy shook his head. "I hung up at first. Then, when she called me again, I decided I would meet with her. Find out what she knew."

"What happened?" Sam asked.

"I met her at some coffee shop and, once she realized I knew who she was, she decided we should go back to her place." Randy then looked embarrassed. His face reddened and he rubbed at the back of his neck. The detectives thought maybe he was going to tell them he made it with her or something.

"I beat the shit out of her. She demanded thousands of dollars. I just couldn't control myself. I went a little crazy."

After Randy didn't say anything, McGrew urged him. "So did she tell you then?"

"Yeah. I guess I scared her pretty bad. She said his name was Joe MacAree. She claimed she didn't know any more. I went back to see her again tonight. She's still claiming she doesn't know anything, but I think she's hiding something."

"Why's that?"

"Just a hunch more than anything else. She seems like she's protecting him. I also think if I had given her the money she could have told me more. I don't know for sure."

Sam wrote in his pad. "You know this woman's name, Randy?"

"Yes. It's Pat Young. Just like it sounds."

"Where does she live?" Sam was still writing.

"Oak Park Avenue, right across the street from where I used to be. Her name's in the vestibule. You're gonna talk to her, aren't you?"

McGrew stood up. "You bet. I think we all need to get some rest." He took his coat from the back of the La-Z-Boy recliner, slid into it, and handed Sam his coat.

When Randy stood, McGrew noticed what he had kept hidden behind his hand. "What the hell happened to you?" he asked, pointing at Randy's thigh.

"Courtesy of Pat Young. Be careful."

"You should have someone look at that," Sam said. "Might get infected."

Randy walked with them to the door. "I hope you'll keep me posted."

McGrew shook his hand. "We will, Randy, we will. I promise. And for what good it'll do, consider yourself warned. Stay out of this. Okay?"

Randy said, "Sure," but there was no conviction.

"Good night, Randy," Sam said, shaking his hand. "We'll be in touch."

Pat Young was smiling. Someone had just won twenty-eight thousand dollars on *Jeopardy!* She didn't know she was smiling.

The buzzer sounded and Pat wondered: Could it be him? She wished she had an intercom. She tried to look out her window, but there was no seeing into the vestibule. Reluctantly, she pressed the buzzer to admit whoever was ringing.

In less than a minute she heard footsteps outside her door. She was tempted to call out, "Joe?" but thought it might be that Mazursky creep again and he would think she knew something.

"Who is it?" she asked, then wheeled back to shut the TV off.

"Detective Pete McGrew. Chicago police. Please open the door."

Pat's face flushed. She felt her heart pounding. My God, she thought, has Joe been arrested? Had Mazursky squealed on her? What could she say?

"What do you want?"

"I just need to ask you a few questions, ma'am. Would you please open the door?"

"Questions about what?"

"Ma'am. Open the door."

"How do I know you're a real police officer? Someone was murdered across the street, you know."

"I know. I'll hold my badge up to the peephole."

"I won't be able to see it."

"What?"

"I'm in a wheelchair."

The man outside sighed. "Do you have a chain lock?"

"Yes."

"Then put it on and open the door just a crack. I'll show you my badge."

Pat slid the chain on the lock and opened the door. She looked out at the man. He looked Irish. Kind of cute. He reached in his suitcoat pocket and took out a wallet. "Here's my badge and ID." He held it open for her to see.

"Let me see." She reached out and took it from him, examined it for a long time. She handed it back. "What does this involve, officer?"

"Could I come in?"

"I don't see why. I haven't done anything wrong."

"I think you have and if you don't stop this I'll see that you're arrested for obstruction of justice."

Pat laughed, but the laugh came out high-pitched and nervous. She couldn't stall forever. She slid the chain back and opened the door. "Won't you come in?" she asked, her voice dripping with sweetness.

McGrew came in and looked over the tiny apartment. When she saw his gaze wandering over her things, she said, "There's no place like home."

Neither of them said anything for a while. Finally Pat snapped, "Now, what is it you want?"

"I think you know something about the Chicago Slasher case."

"Whatever would make you think that? Because I live across the street? I already told an officer I didn't see anything."

"I have a witness who said you did."

"Who?"

"I'm not at liberty to give you that information."

"Don't I have a legal right to face my accusers?"

"You're not on trial, here, ma'am."

"Is it Randy Mazursky? Tell me."

The detective didn't say anything.

"Because if it is, you can just forget it. The guy's Looney Tunes. Thinks I saw something because I live across the street. I tried to tell him how sorry I was but I didn't know anything. I don't know why he won't believe me. Grief does funny things to people."

McGrew eyed her and realized Pat was an excellent liar. There was nothing in her composure to give her away.

"My witness has the name of a suspect he says he got from you. I don't know of any other way he'd get that information."

"Then you aren't much of a detective, are you?

I can think of one right off the bat: Maybe he knows the guy."

"He doesn't know the guy. Cut the crap."

"Why, officer, that's no way to talk to a lady—"

Pat stopped grinning when Pete lowered his face to hers, close enough that she could smell Dentyne. "Listen, lady, I mean it. I have enough on you to make an arrest. Obstructing justice. You wanna go to jail? Come on, I'll take you right now."

Pat stared at the handcuffs he brought out. She could hear her heart pounding, her palms getting slippery on the arms of her wheelchair. "All right. I might have seen something that night. It doesn't prove the person I saw was the killer. It only proves he was there."

"What was his name?"

"I don't know."

"Cut the crap, I said! Now, we both know you know his name. I need you to say it."

"Joe MacAree."

"That's better. How do you know him?"

"I saw him one day, returning to the scene of the crime, if you will. I went out and introduced myself."

"And?"

"I tried to blackmail him."

"Why would he tell you who he was?"

"I bluffed. I'm good at that. I got him in my apartment and stole his wallet. He didn't have to tell me who he was."

"Is he paying you?"

"I wish." Pat snorted. "No, seriously, he was furious with me." Pat lowered her head and stared at the floor for a long time, until the tears she was summoning began to run down her cheeks. "He said he would kill me too. That's why I was so scared when you came to the door."

"Why didn't you call the police?"

"I told you," Pat said, sobbing, "I was scared. I thought as long as I stayed locked up in here, I was safe. He said he'd be watching and if he saw anything suspicious, he'd come in here and kill me." Pat's face took on an expression of dread. "You didn't come here in a cop car, did you?" Without waiting for his reply, she hurried to the window and looked out at the street. She turned back to him. "Unmarked, right?"

"Right." McGrew looked around for a while, uncertain of what to say next. "Look. I want you to keep in touch with us. If he does anything, contacts you in any way, I want you to try and find out where he is and report back to us immediately. Do you understand?"

"Yes, sir."

"If you don't, I swear to God, I'll arrest you. And God help you when this town finds out you've withheld information about this killer."

McGrew didn't say any more. He left quickly, slamming the door.

The buzzer cut through the blackness of her room. Pat sat up in her bed and looked around, her gaze coming to rest on the silvery shapes of her furniture, the glow of the TV screen.

The buzzer sounded again.

She rolled out of bed and got into her wheelchair. She pressed the button on the wall to admit whoever was out there. This time, she knew, it had to be Joe. She prayed no one was watching her apartment.

The footsteps outside her door were slow, uneven. There was a soft knock.

"Who's there?" Pat whispered.

"It's Joe," the voice came back, barely audible through the wood.

She quickly unbolted the door and opened it. Joe hurried in, looking behind him.

"Don't turn on any lights," he said. "They're hunting for me. I have to hide."

Pat was afraid. She wanted to see him. She reached out and stroked his thigh. He stood still for her. She reached up, groping for his crotch, and he moved away. "No," he whispered. She heard the creak of her bed as he sat down on it.

"What do you want, Joe? Tell me."

"I want you, Pat. Someday, when this is over, I want you to go away with me."

Pat stared at his shape in the darkness, not believing what he said but every part of her crying out to take his words and get the solace she had been denied for so long. "Do you mean it?" Her voice was weak.

"Yes. But first I need your help."

"Joe, you know I'll do anything."

"I want you to help me play a little trick on my wife."

27

 Pat sat in front of the phone, staring at it. The damned thing almost seemed to be waiting for her.

"Just give her a call and tell her you're a friend of mine," Joe had giggled. "That oughta make her ears perk up." He had paced across the room, thinking. "All you need to do is tell her I want to turn myself in, but only to her. Don't you think that's a good idea?"

Pat had said nothing.

"Yeah. You can tell her I'm afraid the police will hurt me." He had giggled again then, and Pat felt chilled thinking about it even now.

"I can't tell her that," Pat whispered to herself, placing her hand on the phone. *Models aren't too bright, but she's not that stupid.* God, Pat thought, his idea sounds like something off a friggin' TV show. In fact, she thought she remembered an episode of *Hunter* where the killer had used the same ploy.

No, Joe's idea just would not do.

Pat picked up the phone and began to dial.

Anne let herself forget everything as the hot water rushed over her. Nick had just left, his clean smell still lingering on her sheets. Last night they had drunk too much wine, played Anne's REM tape much too loud, danced until they were breathless, and made love on the living room floor. Later, Nick lit candles and placed them all around the bedroom and made love to her, slowly, in bed. Neither of them had said a word about Joe. Each had made a promise to the other before the evening began. Anne didn't think it would be possible to forget about Joe, but she had. And now, as the cleansing rush of hot water poured over her head, she felt as if some of the tension had lifted. For the first time she was sure she no longer loved Joe, and that made the police department's closing in on him all the more appealing. It wouldn't be easy, but once he was apprehended she could start her life over again, with or without Nick. She wasn't sure just yet if she wanted another man in her life.

The jarring ring of the telephone caused the shampoo bottle to slip from her hands. The intercom's buzzer, the telephone—both instruments frightened her now, annoyed her, made her want to run and hide under the bed. Just a few months ago a small sense of anticipation filled her when the phone rang or the intercom buzzed. This was before Joe sang into the intercom, "I'll be seeing you." Before policemen and victim's husbands had called or shown up at her doorstep.

She stepped out of the shower, wrapped a towel around her head, and slipped into the robe that lay in a heap on the bathroom floor. The telephone rang on.

"Yes?"

"I'd like to speak to Anne MacAree, please."

"This is she." Anne listened for a while to silence. She did not recognize the woman's voice.

"Mrs. MacAree, I'm in love with your husband."

Anne was about to hang up. Nick had warned her the cranks would start calling and writing.

"And he's in love with me."

Anne stopped thinking about hanging up. Maybe this woman was for real. *Maybe she's part of the reason he's missing, part of all that's been happening.*

"Who is this, please?" Anne asked.

"Never mind, dear. Let's just say your husband and I have a real sweet arrangement. He trusts me, which is more than we can say for you."

"Are you calling for any reason at all?"

"Patience, sweetheart, patience." The woman on the other end breathed, letting Anne wait for her next word. The woman had all the power. "Your husband wanted me to get in touch with you. He had a message for you."

"Come on, please; you're wasting my time."

"Oh, aren't you the demanding little bitch. No wonder he left you."

"I'm hanging up. Good-bye."

"Wait!"

Anne heard the woman's shout as she put the receiver in its cradle.

Seconds later the phone rang again. Anne picked it up. "Listen, how do I know you're for real? How do I know you even know my husband? It's funny you should call only after his name is published in the paper."

"He told me to watch out for you, that you'd be skeptical. That's why he told me to ask you this: Remember making love under the stars on Sheridan Road?"

Anne wondered for only a moment what the woman was referring to. Her thoughts drifted back to when they were first married and Joe had painted stars on the ceiling. No one could know about that.

"Please, who are you?"

"That's not important. Think of me as just a messenger."

"What?"

"You know: a messenger. Someone who delivers messages, sweetie. Look it up in the dictionary. I can make other kinds of deliveries too."

"What are you talking about?"

"Joe needs money. He wants to get away. Has to get away . . . before it's too late."

"I don't know."

"Well, sweetheart, you better know this: You can meet me at the appointed time and place with a thousand bucks in hand or Joe can just drop by the old homestead and pick it up himself. Much as you and Joe have in common, I have a sneaking suspicion you might not like that. I shouldn't tell you this, but Joe doesn't even know I'm calling. I'm just trying to look out for you . . . honey."

Anne gripped the phone, feeling her face flush, her heart begin to pound. "I don't think I can do that."

"Do you want Joe strung up by some lynch mob? That's what'll happen, lady." Pat snickered. "This town wants blood."

"Of course not. But how do I know you're for real?"

"Honey, you know I'm for real. And I don't have time for these games. I'll tell Joe to go ahead and come by and pick the money up from you himself." Pat giggled. "I suppose he'll get his pound of flesh." She put a macabre emphasis on the last part, and Anne felt her stomach churn. "Good-bye, Anne. I'm sorry we couldn't do business together."

"Where?"

"What?"

"Where should I meet you?"

"There's an empty warehouse out on West Roosevelt Road, near Cicero Avenue. You can meet me there tonight. Okay?"

"No. Why can't we meet someplace public?"

"Because I don't trust you. This is not multiple choice. Just be in the general vicinity at the right time; I'll give you a sign so you know where to go. Okay?"

Anne paused for a long time, thinking about how she should handle this. The woman seemed to hold all the cards. Finally she said, "Okay."

The woman's voice dripped sweetness as she pronounced, "Good!"

"All right," Anne said, "I should be going now."

"Wait a minute! Remember: If you even breathe a word of this to anyone else, I'll make sure Joe knows. If there's any kind of trap he'll kill you." The woman paused. "I mean it, Mrs. MacAree."

"I know," Anne said. "I won't tell anyone."

"Joe's very sick. Can't you understand that?"

"Yes, I can." Anne asked, "What time should I be there?"

"Ten o'clock. And if you're late or don't show up I'll make sure Joe knows, and he won't hesitate to kill you."

Anne noticed the pleasure the woman took in threatening her. "I won't be late," Anne said, and hung up.

The shower was still running in the bathroom. Anne went in and shut it off.

Pat sat back, satisfied. Soon it would be all over and they could go away together, just like Joe had said. A thousand dollars wouldn't get them far, but used wisely it could get them far enough.

She looked out the window at the gray, heavy clouds. It would be hard for her to get to Muldeen's, the warehouse where Joe wanted to meet Anne, but she'd do it. Pat knew she had to get herself there, so she could see it for herself when Joe sunk that knife into his wife. There so she could lift the money from her cooling body and surprise Joe with it.

He would be so happy.

* * *

Anne turned around in a parking lot and headed back east on Roosevelt Road. She wished Nick was with her; she'd tried calling before she left, but he was gone. My God, why did he need to do other things besides protect her? She had gone back and forth between Cicero Avenue and Laramie now for the last twenty minutes. Maybe the woman's phone call was a prank: Maybe the stuff about making love under the stars was a wild, and very lucky, guess. As she passed what she thought might be the spot—an empty warehouse that used to belong to a company called Muldeen's—she heard a dull thud at the side of her car. A rock? Could that have been the hint?

Anne pulled over and looked at the dark and empty lot of the old warehouse. The metal link fence was rusting; holes where the wire had been pried apart stood out in the harsh light of the streetlamp. And there, near the building, was a dark shape. A woman? She stared, trying to force her eyes to focus in the darkness. She saw a part of the shape go up. An arm? Motioning for her to come?

Anne's breathing quickened. She put her hand on the door handle but couldn't open it. She felt sick; her stomach was churning. She no longer had the strength to open the car door. She looked over again, and the figure motioned more impatiently. The woman on the telephone's words echoed: "He'll kill you."

She took a deep breath and pushed the car door open. When she stood, her knees felt weak. Her throat felt dry and her heart was pounding so hard it was painful; she could barely breathe.

She reached back into the car for her purse, feeling inside once more. The feel of the cold steel of the blade gave her some fortitude, and she stood up straight and slammed the car door shut.

Making her way through the dirt and trash that littered the sidewalk, Anne thought about what she was doing. This is crazy, she told herself. You could die, right here. As she neared the chain-link fence she could make out the shape of someone raising an arm for her to follow and then watched as the shape disappeared inside a doorway. Once she got to the fence she had to grip a rusty post for support. "I can't do this," she whispered to herself. She felt bile rising up in her. She had never felt more afraid . . . or more alone. The occasional driver rushing by probably didn't even see her.

She felt something furry run over her foot and gasped, fighting down an urge to shriek and keep shrieking until someone came and helped her face this. Finding an opening in the fence, she squeezed through.

The barrier of the fence between the sidewalk and the warehouse parking lot made her isolation complete. She bit her lower lip and took a step forward. The wind blew and an aluminum pie pan danced across the parking lot, clanging.

As she neared the building she saw a peeling wooden door standing open. It was dark inside. So dark, Anne thought, the blackness looks palpable, as if I could touch it. Every nerve in her cried out, "I'm not going in there." But she forced herself to walk closer.

She stood at the entrance, peering into the

blackness. She began to cry, wanting to turn and run, but also wanting to believe that handing over the money would end everything right here and she could get on with her life.

She called into the darkness. "Is anyone in there?"

The wind blew. There was no answer.

"Please. I'm scared."

Still no answer.

Anne forced herself to take two more steps and cross the threshold into the darkness. It smelled damp inside, and Anne jumped at a scurrying noise. "Answer me!" She tried to make herself sound fierce, but fear made her voice tremble. She took a few more steps inside.

"Annie," the voice was whispering, her name coming out singsong. She heard low laughter, but could see nothing. Oh, God, Anne thought, her heart stopping, *it's him.*

Anne turned to run, the adrenaline finally finding its way through her veins and giving her strength to act. Just as she neared the gray entranceway, a shape came out of the darkness and the door slammed.

She stopped and screamed.

She heard a scraping sound and then saw Joe's face illuminated as he put a match to a candle. He stood in front of the door, blocking her exit. In the light of the candle she could hardly believe this was her husband. His face was covered with stubble, smeared with dirt, and his eyes had seemed to become lighter, the pupils dilated.

"Not thinking of going so soon, Annie?" He laughed again.

"I want to leave, Joe. Please . . ."

"Don't cry, Annie. We have things to talk about." He laughed again, and then the smile suddenly went away. He looked enraged. "Like why you stopped loving me, bitch." His voice was loud, deep, a voice Anne had never heard.

Anne sat down on the floor, her legs no longer strong enough to support her. His eyes . . . his eyes. She bit her lip once more and put her hand to her eyes to stop her tears.

"Whatsa matter? Your hubby not the handsome boy you married?" He laughed again, throwing back his head and laughing until he was gasping, until he gripped his stomach and fell to the floor. Anne noticed he hit the floor with a lot of impact. When he lifted his head she noticed, on one side of his face, the skin had ripped away and the jaw was swelling. He smiled at her.

"My cock's still the same, Annie. You always loved that." He flipped over on his back and unzipped his pants, pulled them down.

"No," Anne whispered, scooting away from him. "No, Joe, please. That woman who called me, she said you needed money. Why did you trick me?"

He laughed again. "My, I suppose my manners have slipped." He waited. "Getting you here under false pretenses."

He latched onto her ankle. She screamed.

"Don't scream, idiot. No one can hear you." He reached up further on her leg and used her leg to pull himself up and on top of her. "Now," he said, "now." His long nails scratched her as he reached under her skirt and ripped her panties off.

"No!" she said, and kicked him, bit his ear. She started to crawl away from him, but felt a crushing blow to her lower back. She collapsed, wincing in pain. He rolled her over and punched her face. "Such a pretty, pretty face . . ." he said, as his fist slammed into her face over and over again. She felt something give way in her nose, then felt a warm rush of blood above her lips. Joe bent down and sucked away the stream of blood coming out of her nose. He knelt above her, her blood ringing his lips, and laughed at her once more.

She was too numb to feel fear or anything else. He pried her legs apart and forced himself between them. "This will make you remember. Then everything will be all right again."

Anne turned her head as he thrust into her. His words were those of the old Joe. He sounded sad and pathetic. Crying out at the pain of his penis in her dry opening, she groped for the purse she knew was on the floor, somewhere in the shadows. She peered into the darkness and finally saw the purse, close enough for her left hand to reach. She caught her breath and grasped.

She had the handle in her hand.

She pulled the purse toward her, reached inside.

Above her, Joe stopped suddenly. He pulled his penis out of her. "What the fuck do you think you're doing?" His voice boomed, echoed through the empty warehouse. She gripped the wooden handle of the knife, but didn't bring it out. She watched as Joe groped in his trench-coat pocket. What was he doing? Then, even in candlelight, she saw him bring out his old X-Acto knife, and before she had a chance to think or become afraid, the razor was plunging toward her throat, Joe laughing.

She pulled the knife out and swung it at him. He dropped the X-Acto and reached up to grab the knife from her. The blade sliced his palm and left a sharp gash down his arm as they struggled. He tore the knife from her grasp and flung it into the shadows.

Joe looked at the blood on himself and his eyes grew wide. He blew out a breath of fetid air. "You little bitch. You hurt me." Before Anne knew what was happening, he had picked up the X-Acto again.

Joe swung the X-Acto in a wide arc, slashing Anne's face open. It didn't hurt; oh, God, Anne first thought, it didn't even hurt. At last she found her voice to scream as the pain and horror connected in one line of white-hot heat. The blood gushed from her face, rolling into her eyes and blinding her.

They both stiffened as they heard a cry from the shadows. "Yes! Yes!" The woman's voice was high, almost tittering with excitement.

As Joe turned to find the source of the voice in the darkness, Anne slid out from under him and ran. Please, she thought, please, let me get away from him. She ran blindly through the darkness, ignoring the scurrying feet of rats and the footsteps now coming heavily behind her. "Annie, wait!" Joe shouted, and she ran, her lungs aching, the blood flowing, thick, onto her face. *Good God, good God, let me out of here. Please . . .*

Anne gasped as she ran into the protruding metal edge of something that looked formless and black in the darkness. Ahead she could see a gray rectangle of light. The door. She sprinted, feeling his hands on her back, scratching, ripping at the fabric of her blouse. Pushing on the metal release, she swung the door out and the evening opened up to her. She turned just once, to put all her weight and strength into slamming the door on him. When she heard him grunt with pain, she turned to run. She would make it, she had to make it to her car.

At the slam of the door, Joe felt himself go over backward. He lay on the floor for a moment, dazed, feeling a tightness in the back of his head where he had struck the floor. *Next time, you bitch. Next time, I'll be sure.* He stiffened with fright as he heard a whirring, mechanical sound in the darkness. He looked over to see a wheelchair tire next to him. He turned to look up.

Pat's face, even in the darkness, was seething with rage. "Why didn't you finish the bitch off? Why didn't you? We could have been free, Joe. We could have been free."

Joe looked at her, getting to his knees. Her face, covered with tears yet hard with rage, looked through him.

"What are you talking about?"

"The dumb bitch brought money. We could have taken it if you hadn't bungled killing her, asshole. Could have taken it and gone somewhere." Pat lowered her head and sobbed, cursing herself for displaying these emotions in front of him.

"I didn't know," Joe whispered, feeling numb and confused.

"I just wanted to make you happy, Joe. I just wanted us to get away from here . . . together."

Joe wondered if he should get rid of her right now. He pictured sinking his X-Acto into that scrawny little throat, tickling her esophagus with it. How would her blood taste? Bitter. Besides, Anne still lived and Pat could help him. Pat could still help him in a lot of ways. He put his arms around her. "I'm sorry. Next time, I'll make sure."

He felt, then, Pat prying the X-Acto out of his hand. She held her own hand up in the gray shadows and, with a quickness that surprised Joe, made a cut across the back of her hand. She stared into his eyes, offering him her hand. "Take it, Joe. Take it."

He took her hand, bringing it to his mouth.

Pat leaned back in her wheelchair and closed her eyes. "This will bond us," she whispered, but Joe didn't stop sucking. He probably didn't even hear, she thought, but he knows.

28

Nick watched as Anne came into the waiting room of Sheridan Road Hospital. She looked better, but not much. They had cleaned away the dried blood that had caked her face. Nick looked for other good signs, but found none. The entire left side of Anne's face was swollen. Her upper lip had grown to twice the size of her lower lip, pulling up to expose her front teeth. The broken nose had left a dent in its ridge, and Nick wondered if the doctors had made any promises about how it would finally look and if Anne would ever be able to model again. Her right eye was a mass of black, yellow, blue, and purple bruised tissue, open just a slit. Nick thought the worst part was the deep razor gash that divided her face in two right below her nose. Nick shook his head and covered his face with his hands. He wanted more than anything to break down and cry. Instead, realizing that if he wasn't strong for her no one would be, he took a deep breath and pushed his anguish somewhere deep inside him. He stood and put his arms around her, giving her support. Her steps were so tentative and weak, Nick feared she would collapse.

"Are you feeling any better?" he asked as they stepped outside. Across the street, behind some high rises, was the lake. The sun was just coming up and its fire peeked between the buildings.

"They gave me a shot of Demerol." Her words were mushy from her swollen lip and she looked up at him, a silent plea on her face asking that he not make her speak.

"Okay," Nick said, guiding her to his car. "Don't worry about anything. What you need now is rest. I'm gonna take you home and put you to bed."

Anne looked up at him and nodded, her eyes welling with tears. He stopped just before the car and hugged her, feeling the fierceness of her grip at his back and the spasms going through her as she sobbed into the dark wool of his coat.

After a while she calmed herself and glanced at the sun coming up over the buildings. She turned and opened the car door. Nick helped her in.

"Just get a lot of sleep," he said, sliding into the driver's side, "and you'll feel a whole lot better." Nick started the ignition, looking over at Anne. She was staring out the window as if she were beyond feeling or thought.

She still hadn't told him what had happened. When they got to his apartment he led her to his bedroom. There he lifted her and placed her on the bed. She felt limp as he undressed her and put her torn clothing into his hamper. He tucked her in, then lay down beside her, stroking her hair and whispering that he loved her.

Later, when he thought she was asleep, Nick started to get up. She grabbed him, crying out, and pulled him, with strength he didn't know she had, back down beside her.

He lay beside her throughout the entire day, while she slept.

There was the mirror. Look at it, she told herself.

No.

Anne sat on the bathroom floor in Nick's apartment, the mirror from the medicine cabinet high above her. *Please, I can't look, not yet.*

You must.

Anne stood on wobbly legs, pulling herself up on the sink. She was trembling. Memories of the scene with Joe played and replayed in her mind endlessly; she had no control. She had closed her eyes, touching the bumps and scabs on her face, wincing at the pain.

Finally she opened her eyes.

Electricity rushed through her. She had never imagined it could be this bad. "God, God," she whimpered, staring at her ruined face, staring at her destroyed livelihood, at the mess her husband had wrought on her very perception of herself. She screamed. The scream started low, almost a growl, and raised itself up higher and higher, full of pain, loss, and anguish. Reaching up with one balled fist, she smashed the glass of the mirror, listening to its shatter and the music of the glass as it fell to the floor. She put her bleeding hand to her face, pushing hard against the bruises, making them hurt.

A pounding at the door. Nick. "Anne? Are you okay?"

"Go away! Just leave me alone," Anne shrieked. She dropped to the floor again, stretching prone on the broken glass. She sobbed. "Damn you, damn you to hell, you bastard."

For a long time Anne sobbed, muttering her rage into the broken pieces of herself that lay beneath her. After a while, though, she stopped, and her rage and loss grew cold. Anne sat up at last, drawing her legs up to her chest, encircling them with her arms. She leaned against the tile of the bathroom wall.

She sat that way, not thinking, not talking, not crying, for hours. She watched the top of the frosted glass window turn from yellow to navy, as the day wound down into dusk. Her breathing went from ragged to slow.

She stood. Her legs were no longer weak; the trembling had stopped. She felt nothing anymore. Turning, she stooped to pick up the broken glass littering the bathroom floor. Once finished, she turned to the sink and gently washed herself. She no longer felt: the washcloth on her cuts and bruises no longer hurt.

Nothing hurt.

She turned toward the window, whispering. "I'll find you. I'll kill you."

From Joe MacAree's journal (undated):

Our love is dead. I've killed her beauty now and wish I could be satisfied with that. But I can't. There was a time when the slightest thing, a paper cut, a bump on the head, could bring tears of sympathy from me. Now I long to see that paper cut deepen into a slick gash, severing an artery. And, oh, to see that geyser of blood. I want to see that bump on the head graduate into something fuller: a consciousness-stealing blow, full of sharp pain. She did this to herself. I accept no responsibility. She betrayed me.

And the punishment for betrayal is death.

I'm coming, Annie, I'm coming. And it'll be all over your corpse . . . soon.

Anne stared down at the hardwood floor. Nick was beside her, his breathing ragged, unable to speak. She had just told him what had happened to her the night before. She glanced up at him again, looking for a reaction. He was so enraged, he could not yet find words that would match his fury. Finally he stood and walked over to the window and stared outside for a long time.

When he turned to look back at her there were tears in his eyes, but his teeth were clenched in rage as he spoke. "Why? Anne, why would he do this to you? I'll never understand." Nick turned to look back out the window once more. Anne sensed he wasn't really seeing anything.

He whirled. "That son of a bitch! That motherfucking bastard!" He punched the wall and his hand went through the plaster.

Anne stood. "Nick, please don't. I can't stand it. Not now." She took his hand and looked down at his bleeding knuckles. "This isn't going to solve anything."

"How can you be so calm?" He stared at her and she felt chilled: It was almost as if he had never seen her before. It didn't matter; nothing mattered anymore.

He jerked his hand away from her and wrapped his handkerchief around the knuckles. "I'm going to kill him," Nick said, his breathing ragged and his eyes dark. "I'm going to kill him and stop this once and for all. He won't kill anybody else. I'm going to see to that."

Anne swallowed. She didn't want to encourage him, at least not so obviously.

"Why aren't you saying anything? You're not telling me you still care about this asshole, are you?"

"I hate him." Now it was Anne's turn to speak with intensity.

He looked up at her and realized he was venting his rage at her husband on her. He came over and put his arms around her. "I'm sorry, Anne. I'm not mad at you, it's just that I'm so furious at him for what he's done to you and those other people. . . ."

"I know. But we have to be careful. Cool-edged, sharp."

"What do you mean?"

Anne thought: If we're going to kill him, we have to keep calm, keep our wits about us. I want this done right. What she said was: "He's a dangerous man, Nick. He's shrewd and he'll kill us both if he gets half a chance. We have to be sure he doesn't even get half." She thought: We have to be sure he dies slowly, painfully.

"What the hell's that supposed to mean?"

"I think you know."

Nick shook his head. "I'm going to get him and make sure he doesn't hurt anybody again."

"Will you just calm down? The last thing we need here is some macho heroics."

"Sure." Nick picked up his coat and started toward the door. "I'll be back in a little while."

Anne stood. "Nick, what's wrong? Please don't leave me here alone."

But he went out the door without looking back at her. He had gotten to the vestibule of his building when he realized what an ass he was being. Anne was in his apartment, being strong and brave after being raped and brutally beaten by someone she once loved, and he, instead of giving her the support she needed and deserved, was about to leave her alone to go out and nurse a bruised ego. Pete McGrew *was* the person who should be handling this; if Nick was so jealous of McGrew he should see about getting into law enforcement. He turned and went back up the stairs.

Anne was sitting on the couch, curled into a little ball. She looked up at him when he came in, then went back to staring at her knees.

He sat down beside her. "Hey, I'm sorry. I guess I was just so upset about what happened to you I didn't know how to let it out. I'm really sorry."

She covered his hand with hers. "It's all right."

"Maybe I should try to call McGrew."

What she said surprised him. "No. McGrew wouldn't know how to handle this."

"What do you mean?"

"I mean we have to. I've got a plan."

"Anne, I don't think we should get involved."

"We're already involved. And I think we're the only people who can stop him."

"So what is it you want to do?"

"I think I should meet Joe one more time."

"Forget it." Nick got up from the couch.

"Nick, I think this would work."

"You have to be kidding. Come on, Anne, tell me you're kidding."

"I'm not kidding."

"Then you're out of your mind. Go look in the mirror."

"I know. But you'd be there to protect me."

"I'm sure he's going to meet the two of us."

"He wouldn't know you were with me. We could trap him. See, I would go to this woman Pat Young and tell her how afraid I am for Joe. That even though he beat me, I still don't hate him, because I understand how sick he is. And I would tell her I'm willing to see him again. I know he'd do it because he wants to kill me."

"It's too risky."

"It is. But somebody has to stop him and I think this is the best way."

"Absolutely not."

Anne leaned back and stared up at the ceiling in exasperation. While they were silent, the phone rang. Nick went into the kitchen to answer it. Anne listened as he spoke, his voice too low to distinguish any of the words he was saying.

When Nick came back into the room his face was white.

"What's wrong?" Anne stood and went over to him, searching his eyes for a clue.

"There's been another murder. Early this morning. Cicero. A fifteen-year-old girl was out walking her dog before school. The same method as the others. Fifteen years old."

For a long time neither of them spoke. They just stood, staring at each other.

Finally Nick said, "I'll try your plan. Something has to be done."

Pat Young did not recognize the woman coming up the walkway to her building, but she stared at her with interest. Her face had been beaten and her walk was halting, as if she was afraid. "What the hell happened to her?" Pat whispered to herself, and moved away from the window as the woman stopped and looked in her direction.

Pat soon heard her buzzer sounding and wondered why the woman would be coming to see her. Another cop? If this bitch was a cop she certainly couldn't handle herself very well. Out of curiosity, Pat admitted her.

When the knock on her door came, Pat thought she had nothing to fear and opened her door to the woman.

"Yes?" Pat asked.

The woman brushed some of her dark hair away from her face and took off her sunglasses.

Pat laughed and said, "I'd hate to see what the other guy looked like."

Anne didn't smile. "Could I come in?"

"Sure, if you want to go to the trouble of telling me who you are and why you're here."

"I'm Anne MacAree. Joe's wife." Anne paused, thinking she would see some expression on Pat's face, expecting Pat to hurry her inside.

"Beg your pardon?"

"I'm Mrs. Joe MacAree. I believe we spoke on the phone recently."

"No, I don't think so."

"Come on. Let's not play games."

"I don't know what you're talking about." Pat started to close the door, and Anne put up her hand to stop it. "Please," she whispered, desperate, "if you care at all about Joe, you'll let me talk to you."

Pat thought for a while, then let Anne in. She opened the door and wheeled away from the entrance. Once Anne had seated herself on the corner of a chair, Pat said, "Listen, I can't help you. Everyone seems to think I have some sort of connection with your husband, but I don't. I happened to see him leaving Maggie Mazursky's apartment on the day she was killed and I tried to blackmail him, but he didn't go for it. Beyond that, I really don't know anything about him."

Anne started to cry. She lowered her head and sobbed, but there were no real tears. "I still love him and I think you love him too, but of course you wouldn't admit that to me. I just want to help him. Can't you see that?"

"Ma'am, maybe you should go. I'm real sorry

about your predicament, but I really don't know more than I just told you."

"If I could see him just once more, I know I could convince him everything would be all right again. I just need to see him once more," Anne sobbed.

Pat thought about how much Joe wanted to kill Anne and wondered how she had managed to fight her way away from him. "Really. I can't help you. Please leave. I'm expecting company."

Anne stood. "I don't believe you. If you see him will you tell him? I'll meet him again, anywhere and anytime. And please tell him I still love him and understand how sick he is."

"I can't tell him anything because I don't know him."

Anne hurried from the apartment.

Pat wheeled herself over to the window, willing Joe to think of her and get in touch. With his bitch out of the picture once and for all, Joe would be all hers.

In Pat's dream, she was running. Even in the dream she knew she was dreaming, because her running days were long behind her. But that knowledge did nothing to decrease her terror. Joe MacAree was behind her, holding a huge knife in one hand, his erect and disembodied penis in the other. She was screaming, but no sound came from her lips. The only sound was a loud heartbeat that increased the faster she ran.

She awakened, sweating. Someone was pounding on her window. Pat looked over and saw Joe peering up into the window. She screamed. It took several moments for the terror from her dream to subside and for the familiar surroundings of her apartment to become comforting once more. She looked out into the darkness once more.

Joe was gone.

"No," Pat whispered to herself. "I need to see him." She pried up the window, not opened since last fall, and felt a rush of cold air. She pulled her robe tight around her and stuck her head out the window.

Joe was crouching below the window. "What are you doing down there?" she whispered. "Come in."

She reached down to help him climb through her window, looking all the while into the night to see if anyone was witnessing this strange visitation.

"Turn off that light," he said, once he was inside.

Pat hurried to the bathroom and flicked the light off. Joe lay down on her bed and whimpered, "I'm tired. I need to sleep."

She lay down beside him, holding on to him because the narrow bed really didn't allow for two people. He smelled bad, but Pat told herself she didn't mind. Her hand wandered down to his crotch and she stroked him. He gently moved her hand away.

"Your wife was here today."

Joe sat up. "What did she want?"

"She wants to see you again." Pat started to tell him what she said about still loving him, but decided he didn't need to know that part.

Joe stood. "Let's call her."

"What? Now? It's three o'clock in the morning."

"All the better. The sooner we get rid of her the sooner you and I can be together. Please, baby," he said, stooping down and kissing her, "do it for me."

Pat started dialing.

Anne was flipping through an old issue of *Vogue* when the phone rang. She glanced at the clock on the VCR: 3:10 A.M. She shivered and wondered if she should answer. She could face talking to Joe during the day, but not now. Not with the darkness outside and everything so quiet.

The phone continued to ring.

Nick was in the other room, she told herself. Nothing can happen over the phone. And how do you ever expect your plan to work if you don't even have the nerve to answer the phone?

She hurried to answer.

"Didn't get you out of bed, did I?" The woman, whom Anne was sure was Pat Young, laughed.

"No, as a matter of fact, I couldn't sleep. Have you spoken with my husband?"

"Maybe."

"Have you or haven't you?"

"Probably. There's only one way to find out for sure."

"What's that?"

"Ten o'clock tonight, same place. Come alone. No tricks."

"I will. Tell him I promise not to hurt him. Tell

him I love him." Anne realized she was speaking into a dead receiver.

Pat looked up at Joe. "Was that okay?"

"That was beautiful. You're my darling girl." He bent down and kissed her. "Soon," he said, after the long kiss, "we'll be able to take off together. Do you want that?"

"Yes," Pat whispered, "and I also want something else."

Joe laughed. "What could that be?"

She rubbed his crotch. "This," she said.

"Don't you know? It's yours." Joe unzipped his pants and took out his penis, which was already stiff.

"My, my," Pat said, "you're certainly in the mood. What were you thinking about?"

Joe's answer was a solitary moan as she touched him.

"We better do something about this." She lowered her head and surrounded his penis with her mouth. She made a humming noise as she swallowed him.

With one hand he pushed her head down further on his cock and with the other made a shallow slash at the nape of her neck with his X-Acto. Pat lifted her head and gave out a small cry, reaching back to feel the line of blood Joe had drawn. She looked at her finger, at the red drops adhering to the end of it, then raised that finger to Joe's lips. He raised his finger and worked it into the cut on her neck, using it to bring the blood to his lips, doing it repeatedly until the blood grew clotted. She lowered her head to his penis once more and continued to suck. The touch of his finger at her neck, the flowing blood, and the semen finally jetting out of him caused Pat to shudder.

29

Randy kept the apartment dark for two reasons. One, with the rooms filled with darkness the shadows obscured everything familiar . . . all the things that could remind him of his life with Maggie: the furniture they had chosen together, the snapshots on the wall, her decorations. That life now seemed like it had gone on such a long time ago, almost as if the things that had happened here happened to someone else. His previous life as a husband, prospective father, and manager of an ice cream parlor almost seemed like something he had read or dreamed about.

The other reason he kept the apartment dark was to make sure he didn't alert Pat Young to his presence. If she saw him, or knew he was watching her apartment, he could forget what he'd finally decided was his only way to get Joe MacAree.

He had left his parents' house two days ago over his mother's tearful objections and his father's silent reproach. He had told them he needed to get away, to have some time alone. His parents didn't disagree with this plan—in fact his mother saw it as a sign he was beginning to heal. But when he told them he didn't want anyone to know where he was going, they started to try to talk him out of it.

"What if those detectives need to talk to you?" his father had asked.

"Yeah, Randy, there might be a break in the case. Don't you want them to be able to get ahold of you?" his mother had asked.

Randy replied that it would probably be for just a day or two and he would check in with them for developments. Reluctantly, and because they could see by his determination that they had no choice, they let him leave.

And he had called his mother every evening after he was sure they had eaten dinner and talked to her about how good he was starting to feel, about how when he returned he could start looking for a new job. Make a fresh start. His mother sounded happy for the first time in a long time, and Randy wondered if he was being unnecessarily cruel. He knew when he hung up the phone and stared into the darkness of his former apartment that none of what he said was true.

Because he was going to kill Joe MacAree.

He had no other goal in his life and didn't think he ever would. His life had died when Joe had taken Maggie away from him. There was nothing left for him now but to make sure Maggie's death was avenged.

He tried to sleep during the day and watch Pat's apartment at night, because he figured that was when, if Joe was going to show up, he would appear to her.

Glancing down at the digital readout of his watch, he saw that it was two forty-five and wondered if this was going to be another wasted night. When he looked back up, he caught his breath and felt his stomach leap.

Someone was creeping alongside Pat's building, crouching to make sure he went under the dark windows. Could this be the man? Randy felt around him in the darkness until his hands rested on the binoculars Maggie had bought him just a year ago for Christmas.

In the darkness Randy was unable to tell for certain if this was the man he was waiting for. What he could make out was the face of a filthy bum, someone you'd see in the Loop panhandling. Could a few weeks of hiding do this to someone? Randy remembered the smiling face in the photograph he had stolen from the MacArees' apartment.

But then he saw something that made him think this was probably just whom he was waiting for. The man paused under Pat's window. His hand went up and rapped quickly on the window. Again. Finally the man raised himself up enough to look into the apartment. After a while a dim light went on in another room and Randy watched as Pat Young came to the window. She struggled to raise it and finally succeeded. As much as she could from her wheelchair, she helped the man climb into her apartment. Once he was inside Pat drew her curtains closed.

Randy leaned back against the wall and for the first time let himself breathe. This had to be the guy. Pat seemed like a recluse, and even if she did have visitors, why would they sneak into her apartment in the middle of the night?

Randy owed it to himself not to let Joe MacAree leave without his knowing it. He would follow Joe. If he missed his exit he might never have another chance. The police were closing in. And Randy knew what that meant: a cushy life in a mental institution because the "poor man" was "sick." Randy felt himself shaking with rage as he thought about it. Cool down, he told himself. This plan would never work if he acted on passion. Everything must be done with precision and care.

Theresa Mazursky sat shivering in the blue Buick Electra. *What's he doin' in there? What's goin' on across the street?* She wanted to sleep: Her eyes felt itchy and dry. It had been years since she had been up past ten o'clock.

She looked up at the dark window of Randy's apartment once more. I should just march right up there, she told herself, be a good mother and bring my boy home. That's what I should do. But her son had become a different man since his wife was . . . murdered. Theresa hated to even think of the word, think of it and all it had stolen from her.

She was habitually quiet, she knew, preoccupied with making dinner and cleaning up around the house, ironing. But she wasn't so dumb: She knew what her son was planning. And she knew how stupid it would be, even if he did rid the world of someone as evil as the man who took her daughter-in-law's life.

Across the street she had seen a man climb into a window. What kind of neighborhood was this becoming? Was he the killer? Theresa had thought she had seen movement at Randy's window when that happened. But she couldn't be sure.

Oh, but it was cold! Theresa pulled her coat tighter around her, pulling the crocheted muffler up over her nose and the stocking cap down more firmly over her ears.

Please let this be over soon, Lord. Let me stop my boy before he does somethin' stupid.

After about a half hour there was movement once more at the window. Randy watched, standing and struggling into his jacket, as the man climbed out the window. Randy ran to the door, flung it open, and bolted down the stairs.

Joe MacAree was walking up Oak Park Avenue as if he were a member of the neighborhood who was having trouble sleeping on this early spring night. There was no stealth in his pace, no nervous looking around. He seemed confident in his stride. Randy thought darkness and night must be the man's element.

Randy moved along behind him, keeping to the lawns of the two-flats and bungalows that lined the street. The grass under his feet kept his footsteps muffled, and the shadows provided by the dwellings kept him hidden.

Once they were on Roosevelt Road and heading east, keeping quiet was harder to do. There were no lawns to muffle his footsteps, and the brighter streetlights made it impossible to blend in with the background. Randy crossed the street and tried to put a block between Joe and himself. Even with that distance Randy was uncomfortable, fearing he'd lose this one opportunity if Joe saw him and fled back to wherever he was hiding.

After they had walked for well over an hour, Joe stopped in front of an empty warehouse that had once been a company called Muldeen's. Randy had an uncle who'd once worked for the company, a shoe manufacturer. The business had gone under years ago and the warehouse had stood empty ever since.

Joe waited until a car and a Mack truck passed by, then ducked into a tear in the link fencing. He looked behind him and then ran to a door at the side of the building. He opened it, and with a slam of the door was gone.

Roosevelt Road was silent once more.

Randy stared for a long time at the warehouse, wondering how long Joe had been there, hiding so close to Randy's parents' home. Wondering why the brilliant law enforcement agencies hadn't searched the spot, an ideal hiding place.

Suddenly Randy wasn't so certain he wanted to follow Joe inside. He had to admit: He was scared. The wind blew and seemed colder. Randy shivered and rubbed his arms. Something that felt like a lump of ice had filled his stomach, pressing. His mouth was dry. He looked up and down the street.

Randy crossed. He forced himself to stop thinking. From now on he would act as an animal of prey. He cut his hands sliding in through one of the tears in the rusty fencing. He put his hand to his mouth and tasted copper. The cut wasn't long, but it was deep.

Randy pulled his shirttail out of his pants and tore a strip off the bottom of the shirt. Wrapping the strip around his hand, he continued on to the door.

Outside the door Randy listened for movement inside, wondering if right now Joe was watching.

And waiting.

Randy pushed the door open about an inch. No creaking. With the next movement he pushed it open wide as quickly as he could to avoid squeaking. It worked. He closed the door and stepped into the warehouse.

It was so dark Randy almost felt he could touch the darkness. There was a small amount of gray light coming in through high windows up near the ceiling. Barely enough light, Randy thought, to even see my hand in front of my face. There were scuffling noises and Randy thought: rats. His deduction was confirmed by several high-pitched squeaks.

Randy stopped to let his eyes adjust as best they could to the low level of light. What would he do now? MacAree could be anywhere in this warehouse, and he could also have the advantage of knowing Randy was here.

Randy felt sick with disappointment. This might never work. He stood frozen in the darkness, wondering if he should turn around and wait for MacAree outside.

But then he heard a sound that was not a rat or the creak of rotting boards in the wind.

The sound was a footstep.

Randy froze, feeling all the anger, all the indignation and desire for revenge drain out of him. All were replaced by an awesome fear. Terror that made his spine constrict, made him feel cold, made him sweat. He gripped the gun in his hand tighter. His father didn't know Randy had borrowed his revolver: a Smith & Wesson he'd had for years.

There was a whispering touch at his back, and he felt his eyes widen in the darkness.

"No!" he shrieked. "No, you son of a bitch!" Randy whirled and pulled the trigger, jumping back at the gun's recoil.

It all happened so fast. The bright flash in the darkness, the smell of gunpowder.

Randy opened his eyes.

Opened his eyes and moaned into the darkness. The moan was one word, ripped from somewhere deep inside him, a place where pain knew no boundaries. "Nooooo!"

Randy fell to his knees and dropped the gun to the floor. He doubled over, holding himself. "Noooo!"

His mother lay before him, a dark hole in her forehead, her eyes staring upward.

"Randy, you gotta stop this." He heard her

whisper. Was it now? Was it before he fired the gun? Had she ever said anything?

Randy stayed doubled over for a long time, until the pain burrowed deep inside, masked by shock, hidden by cold rage. He finally stood and picked the gun up. "I've got nothing, nothing at all to lose now, you fucker." His eyes had adjusted to the darkness in the warehouse and he began to walk the aisles, searching.

He stopped when he heard a small sound issue forth from the darkness: a giggle. Randy whirled toward the direction from which the sound came and heard footsteps. Someone was running away from him. Randy clutched the gun tighter in his hand.

Randy started moving quickly after the footsteps. Soon he could make out the swinging motion of the man's raincoat. Randy cocked the revolver.

"MacAree?" Randy was startled at the force and confidence of his voice.

He watched as the man stopped and slowly turned. He was grinning at him. Before Randy had a chance to react, Joe had jumped on him. Randy felt himself going over backward, felt the sharp crack at the back of his head as it made impact with the concrete floor. And felt the worst feeling of all: the gun slipping from his fingers. He heard the scratch of metal as the gun slid across the floor, out of his reach.

MacAree was above him, laughing. Randy tried to shake his dizziness. He grabbed Joe's fist as it was about to slam into his face. He held fast to Joe's arm, veering it away.

Joe got to his feet. "Who the fuck are you?"

Randy climbed to his knees, then his feet, breathing heavily. "Randy Mazursky, though I don't suppose that name means anything to you, you bastard."

Joe laughed for a long time. Then he whispered, "She was the sweetest little cunt I've ever had."

Randy lunged at him, his hands poised to grab Joe's throat. The movement was just what Joe expected. His fingers were wrapped around the knife in his coat pocket. Just before Randy's body made impact with his, Joe removed the knife and held it erect in front of him.

Randy grunted as he felt the knife dig into his front, just above his stomach, like something hot. He looked at Joe in disbelief, then fell back. Joe looked blurry as he hurried away from him, snickering. Randy wasn't sure what he was saying, but it sounded like: "Hafta get ready for my date."

Randy lay back and tried to pull the knife from his stomach. The knife was slippery with blood.

30

Anne looked out the window, trying to force herself to think of something other than nine o'clock, when she and Nick would get in her car and, with Nick lying on the floor, proceed west on the Eisenhower Expressway to meet with Joe.

She heard the click of Nick's fork on his plate in the dining room. She had spent the day making spinach and prosciutto lasagna, homemade garlic bread, a Caesar salad. The work had taken her mind off the approaching evening. She tensed as she heard the chair sliding back from the table and the soft patter of his footsteps as his stockinged feet made their way across the hardwood floor.

Before she knew what happened, he was behind her and sliding his arms around her waist. She had no idea why his actions made her heart beat faster, made her throat constrict.

He whispered, "Scared?"

The question was so absurd it broke the tension. Anne threw back her head and laughed, struggled out of his grasp and laughed until the tears poured down her face, until her stomach felt tight and painful, until she was gasping. Half-heartedly, Nick laughed too.

"What?" he asked, a grin on his face. "What did I say?"

Anne at last reined in her laughter. "You asked if I was scared. Under the circumstances don't you think that's kind of a silly question?"

Nick laughed to show he got the joke. "I see."

"Of course I'm scared. I'm scared for both of us. I couldn't do this alone, but I'm scared of bringing you into it. We could both die."

Nick squeezed her tighter, burying his face in her hair and whispering, "That's just not gonna happen. We're the good guys. Remember?"

Anne thought about Joe, remembering him as he was when they met, as he was during the first years of their marriage. She tried to disassociate this man from the one they would be seeing tonight. She tried to think of the Joe she loved as dead . . . and felt a clutch in her throat as she realized she was already on a course that might see both Joes dead in truth before this evening was over.

She closed her eyes, trying to quell the nausea that rose within her when she thought about her husband. I've never felt this way, she thought, never, not about anyone. The hatred and anger was like a palpable thing within her, growing and filling her up. The fact that she did feel this way made her hate Joe all the more. How could she want someone dead? Especially someone she once loved? Someone she thought she'd be spending her life with, someone upon whom she had banked all her hopes. But how could he have done this to her?

Since her first look at her new face, she'd faced her reflection with only a hard anger. Nick had told her the bruises would fade and plastic surgery could remove the scar the razor had made, but she knew she would never be the same.

Nick thought about the plans they had made earlier in the day. He thought their plan was either beautifully simple or dangerously inept. Anne would drive to the warehouse where her meeting with Joe was to take place. Once they were on Roosevelt Road Nick would slide to the floor out of sight and would remain there until Anne had gone inside the warehouse. They both assumed that once Anne met with Joe he would no longer be watching the street and Nick could leave the car and follow her inside. But their assumptions were dangerous: They assumed Anne would be able to reason with Joe long enough for Nick to get inside the warehouse. Nick didn't know if he should depend on the reasonability of a psychotic killer.

"Take a shower with me."

"What?" Nick turned to look at Anne.

"I think a shower would make me feel better. Take one with me. Okay?"

"What? Now?"

Anne sighed. "Yes, now. I just think a really hot shower would make me feel better."

Nick realized how he could use the time alone. "No, I think it would make me feel worse. I've gotta get psyched up. Can you understand?"

"I suppose so. I won't be long."

Nick watched as Anne disappeared into the bedroom. He waited until he heard the rush of water before going into the kitchen. There he lifted the receiver from the phone and dialed the number Pete McGrew had given him in case anything significant came up. Nick prayed McGrew would be in his office.

The phone was picked up on the second ring. "McGrew."

"Pete," Nick breathed a sigh, "I'm glad I reached you. Something you should know about is going to go down tonight."

"Yeah?" McGrew sounded interested.

"Yeah. MacAree's wife is going to meet him tonight. She got contacted through a third party." Nick didn't think it would be wise to tell McGrew about his and Anne's plotting.

"Wait a minute. Are you telling me she's going to go through with this meeting?"

"Yeah. She thinks she might finally be able to put an end to this mess."

"Nick, buddy, you've got to stop her. This guy is very dangerous and I think he's completely, completely lost touch with reality. You have tried to stop her, haven't you?"

Nick was quiet for a moment. "Yeah, I did at first. And then she convinced me this might be the only way to catch this lunatic before he kills someone else."

"What are you saying?"

"I'm saying I'm going with her. I can handle myself . . . and I can make sure nothing happens to her."

"I'm not sure of any of that."

Nick laughed. "Well, maybe you're right. That's why I'm calling. I thought if you could supply some backups, we could do everything nice and safe and take this guy down. Deal?"

McGrew laughed. "Sure, Nick. We'll let you play crime-stopper."

Suddenly Nick wondered why he'd ever liked McGrew. "Look, I'm telling you this is it. Tonight. It could be all over. Just come on out to the location and send some uniforms in unmarked cars. We'll have this asshole behind bars before morning. City council will be thanking you for making Chicago safe again."

"Nick, this is the craziest thing I've ever heard. We can't let you do this."

"Well, we're gonna do it. With or without you, buddy."

"Just in case we decide to show up, where's this woman supposed to meet her husband?"

"Uh-uh," Nick said. "You play fair. Promise me the reinforcements *and* the cooperation and I'll tell you the location. Not until. I'm not going to be tricked so you can go bust in there and scare the guy. He's too shrewd for that. Strong-arm tactics aren't going to bring him down. That much I know."

McGrew sounded tense, insistent when he said, "Give me the goddamn address. We have a hell of a lot better chance than you'll ever have. Don't be stupid, Nick. Somebody's gonna get their ass killed tonight and it might be you."

"Listen, McGrew: I'm not going to tell you the location. Just forget it."

As soon as Nick hung up the phone it started ringing. Nick ripped it out of the wall. Then he took a deep breath, looked down at the phone in his hands, and laughed.

He heard Anne in the bathroom. "Nick? What are you doing out there?"

"Nothing." Nick was silent as he listened to her blow dryer. Finally he went into the bathroom, where Anne was bent over the sink, drying her hair. She was wearing a navy bathrobe. Nick wanted to cry: The scene was domestic. If someone could have peeked in a window and seen them, would they have believed what awaited them in less than two hours?

"You better hurry; we only have about twenty minutes."

"Don't remind me," Anne snapped. "I'll be ready."

Nick left her to sit on her bed, comforted by the dimness of her bedroom.

McGrew hurried out of the little cubbyhole he called an office, putting on his tweed jacket and lighting a cigarette as he went. "Come on, Sam," he said to his partner, who was sitting outside the office sorting a large pile of phone tips on the slasher. Sam's eyes were bloodshot and his face looked puffy and raw. He brightened when McGrew said, "Everything just might be all over . . . tonight. I'll tell you all about it in the car."

Fifteen minutes later McGrew pulled the battered Ford Fairmont up in front of a fire hydrant across the street from Anne MacAree's apartment building. He threw the gear shift into park and leaned back in his seat with his hands behind his head. Looking over at his partner, he noticed Sam's taut posture, as if he were a hunting dog ready to pounce. "Relax, asshole, we may not have much time."

McGrew laughed and stared up at the building.

There was the bag. Pat looked at her suitcase, lying open on the floor at the foot of her bed. She remembered back to when she was mobile, and how the bag had accompanied her on trips to Niagara Falls, Ft. Lauderdale, Lake of the Ozarks, and Dallas. Since the accident she had taken no trips, had had no use for the nylon floral-print bag.

Now it was full. Pat had gone shopping yesterday and bought an entire new wardrobe. She wanted to look good for Joe when they ran away. *Tonight, oh, baby, tonight.* She leaned back in her wheelchair, savoring the moment when that bitch of a wife would die. With her out of the way the two of them could go off together, start over. She's what caused all this craziness, Pat reasoned; she's what drove him to it.

Pat leaned down to look into the side panel of the suitcase. Crest, a toothbrush, a roll-on bottle of Secret, and a tube of K-Y Jelly. The fags use it, Pat thought, why can't we? *Oh, Joe, baby, I want to make you happy.* She picked up the K-Y, running her fingers over its smooth white surface, imagined applying it to Joe's hard cock, sliding her hand up and down.

Enough. She closed the suitcase, outlining its square shape with the zipper. She needed to get to the warehouse before tonight's little "date." She needed to be there, in the shadows, to make sure the job wasn't botched this time.

She would make certain of that. Pat Young patted the Saturday night special she had concealed in the waistband of her slacks.

It seemed like less than five minutes had passed when Nick came back into the bedroom. Anne was still sitting on the bed, in darkness.

"What are you doing? It's nine o'clock. We have to get a move on."

Amazed, Anne looked at the little blue digital numbers of the alarm clock on the nightstand: 9:01 P.M. Anne clutched her robe around her, feeling cold. "I'm not going."

Nick leaned against the door frame. He blew out a sigh, felt his stomach tighten.

"What?"

Anne stood and went to him. "I said I'm not going."

He looked down at her face in the darkness. "Anne, you have to. We've come this far. Hell, you convinced me." Suddenly Nick realized how important it was to him to make this meeting, to finally put an end to the insanity. And maybe, just maybe, begin a life with Anne. He placed his hands on her shoulders, the insides of his palms resting against the bare skin near her neck. Her skin was cold to his touch, damp. "Look," he whispered. "An end to this is out there. In two hours, maybe less, all of this will be over. Two hours, Anne. If we don't go tonight this could drag on and on and more people could be killed."

She looked up at him, her face masked by anguish, her eyes sullen, no longer able to cry. "Nick, don't do this to me. You can't hold me responsible."

He hugged her. "No one's holding you responsible. I just want to get this over with."

She stared into his eyes for a long time, tracing the small scar on his face with her finger. She kissed him. "I do too, but I'm not going."

Nick closed his eyes. If he didn't go through with this now he never would. "Then I'll go alone." He wrenched away from her and hurried back into the living room. He picked up his jacket and slid into it.

Anne smiled at him. Even with the bruises and broken nose, she knew a smile could get her "hero" to do just what she wanted.

The apartment was silent.

Anne lay back on the bed, letting go of a little of her tension. The door had just clicked closed, and she heard Nick's key in the lock.

When she closed her eyes, though, the tension rose back up, constricting her muscles. Joe's face appeared before her: his mouth ringed in blood, his eyes lit up with insane rage. A monster . . .

Anne sat up, feeling cold. What if Nick didn't succeed in killing Joe? What if Joe killed Nick? He would come then for her. He would slash her; he would make her his own.

* * *

Nick forced himself to shove the fear down deep inside, to not feel anything at all. Then he opened the door. He avoided the elevator and took the stairs, taking them so quickly that by the time he reached the bottom he was panting, thinking of little more than the sheen of sweat on his brow and the fire in his lungs.

Outside, the air was chill and Nick felt as if he were dreaming as he made his way to the car. There was a complete sense of the unreal in doing these things: placing his key in the car door, sliding into the car, starting it up.

He sat for a while in the car, staring at the concrete wall in front of him.

Anne pounded on the passenger-door window.

Nick looked over, surprised to see her. She seemed so certain upstairs that she couldn't go through with it that he hadn't even entertained the possibility she might change her mind. He reached over and lifted the lock.

She opened the door and slid in beside him. She squeezed his knee and he noticed her hand was trembling.

"You haven't changed your mind or anything?" he asked.

"I couldn't let you go by yourself." She paused for a moment, her breath quivering. "He'll kill you." The last part she said simply, with no emotion.

"Right." Nick put the car in gear and pulled out of the parking garage. Once they were on the inner drive he said, "Now, how do you think we should approach this. We—"

Anne cut him off. "Let's not talk. I can't. We've already been over everything. Please . . . just drive."

Nick didn't say anything. He watched the car's headlights consume the road in front of it. He didn't notice the headlights of the Ford Fairmont behind him.

Pat's wheelchair *whirred* through the darkness. She moved slowly in the warehouse, careful not to bump into industrial shelving or worse. She paused and listened to the squeaks and shuffling noises the rats made. This place must be full of them, she thought.

She whispered into the darkness, "Joe? Joe, you hear me?"

The darkness, heavy and palpable, gave no reply.

Pat found a spot where there was a gap in the shelving. The spot was near the door where Joe came in and out. She knew this was where Anne MacAree would come in.

"And never go out," Pat whispered, and patted the Saturday night special she had with her.

Pete McGrew looked over at his partner, Sam, who had once again assumed his bird-dog pose, and laughed. "We couldn't have timed it better if we tried, Sammy."

"It won't be long now," Sam said, not taking his eyes from the road.

Nick put the car in park and listened to the engine wind down. He was afraid to look over at

Anne. Afraid and ashamed, because his stomach was knotted with terror and his palms were all but dripping sweat. Finally he felt her touch on his arm.

"Look at me," she whispered. He looked over at her. Her face was pale, even in the darkness, and shiny with sweat. She could see the recognition in his face and managed to smile. "Yes, Nick. I'm scared too. Put your arms around me."

He hugged her quickly, too nervous for any touch at all to be comforting. "Look," he said. "He might be watching us. I've got to get down on the floor." He slid down and got over to the passenger side. "Slide over to my side," he said. "It's not going to look right if you get out the other side."

Anne did as she was told and looked down at Nick. She stroked his hair. "Thank you," she whispered into the darkness. "Thank you."

Nick felt he needed to say it . . . now. "I love you, Anne. And I hope that after all of this is over, we can start building something. Something that isn't based on fear—" His voice broke. "Ah shit." Nick put his hand over his eyes.

Anne pulled her hand away from him. "Please. I've got to do this . . . now."

She was out of the car before he had a chance to respond. He listened to the click of her boots on the pavement as she crossed the road. He climbed up on the seat, lifting himself just enough to watch her. He noticed how the streetlight caught the shine of her hair. He never felt lower: He was letting this woman he loved go

where she should never have to. He prayed he
would have the chance to make this up to her.

McGrew was two car lengths behind them on
Roosevelt Road and watching when Nick pulled
into a parking space.

"Let's just circle around the block so they don't
get suspicious," Sam said.

"Good idea." McGrew put on his turn signal
and started down a side street. Up ahead, an old
Pontiac with one taillight moved slowly. Pete
moved up on the car quickly, finally tailgating.
The car didn't move any faster.

"C'mon," McGrew whispered. "C'mon, goddamn you."

There was no room to get around the car.

Nick waited the time they had allotted: five
minutes. He turned himself around on the seat
so he was facing the passenger door. Opening it
quickly, he slid out of the car and slammed the
door, cursing the overhead light. He edged his
way along three parked cars, thinking that if Joe
was watching, Nick would look less suspicious if
he appeared nowhere near the car Anne had gotten out of. Finally, he stood.

He looked up and down the empty sidewalk,
taking a deep breath.

Then he stepped off the curb and started across
the street.

"Hold it right there."

The voice, coming suddenly out of the darkness, made Nick jump. He turned to look and
saw Pete McGrew behind him. The color drained

out of his face and his stomach twisted into a
lead knot. There was an overweight, balding guy
with Pete.

"How the hell did you . . . You followed us,
didn't you?"

"Bright boy," McGrew said. "Maybe you should
be some kind of investigator."

"You bastard."

"C'mon, Nick. Let's cooperate. I'm sorry." Mc-
Grew stretched his palms out in a gesture of appeal.

"Fuck you."

"Look, Nick," McGrew's tone grew harsh, angry. "We can't play games. Where's your girl-
friend?"

Nick looked wildly at the warehouse across the
street, noticing the dark, empty windows. Oh,
God, Anne was in there . . . alone. He bolted.
He was halfway across the street when he
stopped because of the blaring horn of a Ford
Bronco. He felt McGrew's grasp on his collar.

"Don't be an asshole!" McGrew pulled him
back to the other side. "Now, we're gonna take
care of this the right way." The reasoning in his
tone made Nick want to punch him, force his
nose back into his face.

"You don't understand!" Nick's voice was excited, almost high with terror and pain at what
the loss in time might mean for Anne. "Goddamn
it! You don't understand! You're gonna fuck this
up and she's gonna die in there!"

Anne stared at Joe's face, wondering where the
man she loved had gone. Nothing was left. His

eyes were reddened, wild. His skin was pasty and his lips stood out, too red, in the dim light. Dark stubble covered his face.

"Please, babe," she said to him for at least the fourth or fifth time, "I love you. You gotta understand that. Come with me now and we'll get everything back together."

Joe lowered his head and began to tremble. He was weeping. Anne thought she was beginning to break through, make contact. *"Lies! Lies!"* he shrieked, and his head came up suddenly, grinning and devoid of tears.

The X-Acto knife glinted in the moonlight. Anne was shocked that it didn't hurt as it sliced across her throat. It was the blood that made her knees go to rubber. The blood that spurted down and landed on the floor.

She collapsed. "Joey, Joey . . ." She reached up and felt her neck, warm and slippery with blood. Was she going to die right here? How stupid! She felt the cut and finally was thankful: She had pulled back when he slashed at her and the cut wasn't deep.

He knocked her backward. She bit her tongue as her head hit the floor. "Nick, where are you?" she wondered aloud, the room beginning to move, rocking like a boat. Joe knelt above her. In one quick motion his face was on her throat, sucking up the blood.

"No, please, God, no." Anne moaned into the darkness.

She looked up at Joe, looming above her, his grin ringed in blood. Suddenly his features contorted and he frantically clawed at the front of his pants. She watched as he pulled out his penis, watched, but could do nothing, as he shot his semen on her face. Listened as he groaned in the darkness. "Perfect, perfect," he mumbled.

Anne wondered for a moment why she felt nothing, not even her own breathing. Wondered why she couldn't scream, why every muscle in her body felt like liquid and there was no way to move.

Even as he groped in his pocket and brought out a hunting knife and raised it above her. "Now, you little bitch. Now." His breathing was ragged.

The flash of the gun jolted Anne back to reality, and its loud report brought her muscles back to life, released the screams in her throat. Screaming, she looked up at Joe, watched as his head, propelled by the bullet, whipped to one side. Wondered then where the other scream was rising from, rising up to join hers.

The knife clattered to the floor and Joe collapsed on her.

She screamed and screamed as she fought to get out from under him. Finally she managed to slide out from beneath his weight and get to her knees.

She vomited.

After she felt she could breathe again, she stared into the shadows, searching for something to connect with the gunshot. Was it Nick?

A young man walked into the light coming in through one of the high windows. Anne assumed the dark stain on his front was blood. He smiled at her and then fell to the floor. She heard the

metal of his gun as it hit the concrete and skit-
tered across the floor.

Then there were more gunshots. Two, in fact,
went off, their reports shocking, the flashes
bright, before Anne fell to the floor, groping her
way to the shelving. She crawled underneath and
lay cowering, like a small animal, as the gun continued to sound its report, filling the darkness
with the acrid smell of its smoke.

Her mind went blank.

The gunshots and the screams caused all three
men across the street to stiffen, their heads up
and listening.

"Damn you!" Nick screamed at McGrew. "If
anything's happened to her, I swear to God, I'll
kill you."

McGrew and Sam said nothing. They were already running across the street. Nick followed
and eventually passed them.

Nick was first in the door. He hadn't let himself think anything, not wanting to realize that
Anne might be dead. Once inside, he didn't see
her, didn't see her at all, just the body of some
young guy he had never seen before and Mac-
Aree. MacAree. Please God, don't let Anne have
paid for this. Don't let her pay.

Oh, God, where is she?

Nick glanced down at the two bodies on the
floor. "Who's the other guy?" he whispered to Mc-
Grew. Pete didn't answer.

Sam wasn't far behind. "What the hell?" Sam
shouted.

Nick watched as McGrew and Sam each knelt beside a body.

"Where's the wife?" Sam asked.

It was then that Anne crawled from beneath the shelving. She stood on rubbery legs, her eyes, vacant and staring, searching the darkness. Nick wondered what she was looking for, wondered if she even knew.

"Anne?" he whispered. "Anne? You okay?"

Nick was grateful when her eyes met his in the darkness. Just as he was going to her, a final shot cut through the darkness.

Anne dropped to the floor.

"What the fuck?" Sam shouted.

McGrew ran toward the direction from which the shot had come.

Nick knelt beside her. She looked up at him. "Am I gonna die?"

Nick felt and searched for the wound, finally stopping at Anne's left shoulder, where he felt a small hole, viscous liquid. He pressed on the hole. "No, I think you'll be okay. It's your shoulder."

There was a scream then in the darkness. A scream of disappointment and sorrow. Nick and Anne looked up to see McGrew yank a wheelchair out of the darkness.

Anne's eyes met Pat Young's. And she remembered. "My God," Anne whispered, "you tried to kill me. Why? Why?"

Pat ignored her and looked at McGrew. "The bitch. She's the one you should be going after," Pat shrieked. "She's the one caused all this shit. She caused it all. Joe was a good man." Pat wept freely now. "He was good. She made him do the things he did. Forced him to do all those killings. Arrest her, arrest that little bitch."

McGrew leaned down, close to Pat Young's face and said, "The only one around here who's getting arrested is you, lady." He stood up straight. "Read her her rights, Sam."

"Yeah, right away. But this one here, he's still got a pulse."

Anne and Nick looked down. "It's Joe," Anne said. "You mean he's still alive?"

Sam snorted, "Just barely. That's him, then? The slasher?"

Anne didn't respond. She began to tremble.

The only thing stiff about Pat Young was her face as the two uniformed officers loaded her into the back of the police car. She concentrated on her hate as she let her body go limp; she would be damned if she made this easy for them. Let them grunt and groan as they lifted her into the car, worried about dropping the cripple.

Outside, the night grew more and more alive, lit up by squad cars' flashing blue and red lights. Voices. Media people. Like flies to shit, Pat thought, and smirked.

There . . . there . . . that final image. Her Joey, his head flying back, the shock on his face (that beautiful face) as the bullet entered him. Pat couldn't get it out of her mind. Finally she lowered her head and, for the first time in years, wept.

After a moment she straightened, wiped the tears angrily away from her face. Anne would be coming out soon and Pat wanted to see her. Wanted to see her because if Joe couldn't have her blood, Pat would at least make sure that one day, no matter how long it took, Pat would have that bitch's blood.

McGrew put a hand on Nick and Anne's shoulders. Gently, he said, "C'mon, get out of here. We'll take care of this. Why don't you take her to the hospital?" He led Nick and Anne outside.

McGrew watched as Nick led Anne back to the car. There was something stiff in her stride. A tautness McGrew didn't know how to describe. Like something about to go off.

He heard her begin screaming when Nick put her in the car, and McGrew shook his head, staring down at the ground. "She'll be okay," he whispered.

He stared at the ground until he heard the sirens. When he looked up, at least fifteen minutes had passed. An ambulance and forensics were pulling up, along with about a dozen squad cars who didn't want to miss this. The media couldn't be far behind.

Sam was leading forensics and the crime lab in. He was excited, more excited than Pete had ever seen him, and he decided to let the old guy have his time in the limelight. McGrew followed them in.

One of the forensics guys went to the body and groped in a pocket. He pulled out a wallet. Flipping it open, he looked up at the men gathered around him. "Says 'Randy Mazursky' on the license. Is he the slasher?"

"No, it's the other one." McGrew stared at a dark puddle on the floor. Blood.

Epilogue

At Cook County Hospital, word had spread fast. As they wheeled Joe MacAree, the Chicago Slasher, into the emergency room, nurses, orderlies, aides, residents, and interns had all forced their way into the corridor, crowding around the entrance to get a look at this monster, this monster who had made all of them buy new locks and jump at every sound in the darkness.

He was already hooked up to an IV. Most of those who saw him thought he looked like a bag person, someone you'd see sleeping on a bench at Daly Plaza. One resident, Liz Sperry, turned to the nurse standing beside her and said, "He looks too weak to have killed anyone, doesn't he?"

The nurse just gripped herself tighter and stared down at Joe.

"What's the prognosis?" Liz shouted to the paramedics.

"Guy's in a coma," one shouted back, a stocky Irish guy with dark curly hair and a mustache.

His partner said, "If he lives he's not gonna be doin' anymore killing." She snickered, "Or even talking or walking."

"Serves him right," Liz Sperry whispered to herself, "serves him right."

The Irish man said, "If he ever does come out of it, they oughta string that fucker up by his balls, but he's in his own little world now."

Liz shivered; she wanted to be away from all of this. She started walking rapidly up the corridor, toward the elevator and pediatrics, where her current rotation was. She didn't want to think, but the paramedic's words continued to haunt her: "He's in his own little world now."

My God, what kind of world would that be?

Joe MacAree sat on the worn sofa, his hands shielding his face. The air was heavy with stale cigarette smoke, and the couch beneath him was worn almost to the frame. He rocked back and forth.

Margo came into the room, and he looked up at his sister. She smiled at him. "It'll heal, Joe. It'll heal. That's what's so wonderful about us. Things always heal." She sat down beside him and put her arms around him. She brushed his neck with her lips, ran a sharp nail down the inside of his arm. "I just wish it didn't take so long for you to realize where you belong."

Joe closed his eyes. The voice of his father made him tense and look up. "Welcome home, Joey." The old man grinned at him.

"Yes," Margo said. "You're finally home."

Joe slumped on the sofa and drew his legs up to his face.

He began to cry.